NICK ROCHE
Story & Art

CHRIS O'HALLORAN
Colors

Letters & Collection Design by
SHAWN LEE

Logo Design by
WAYNE DALY

Additional Children's Art by
MATILDA and
DANIEL ROCHE

Series Edits by
DAVID MARIOTTE

Collection Edits by
ALONZO SIMON
and **ZAC BOONE**

For my Co-Scarent, Whittle; and
for Matilda, Daniel and Hannah, who
terrify me every day. X

Scarenthood

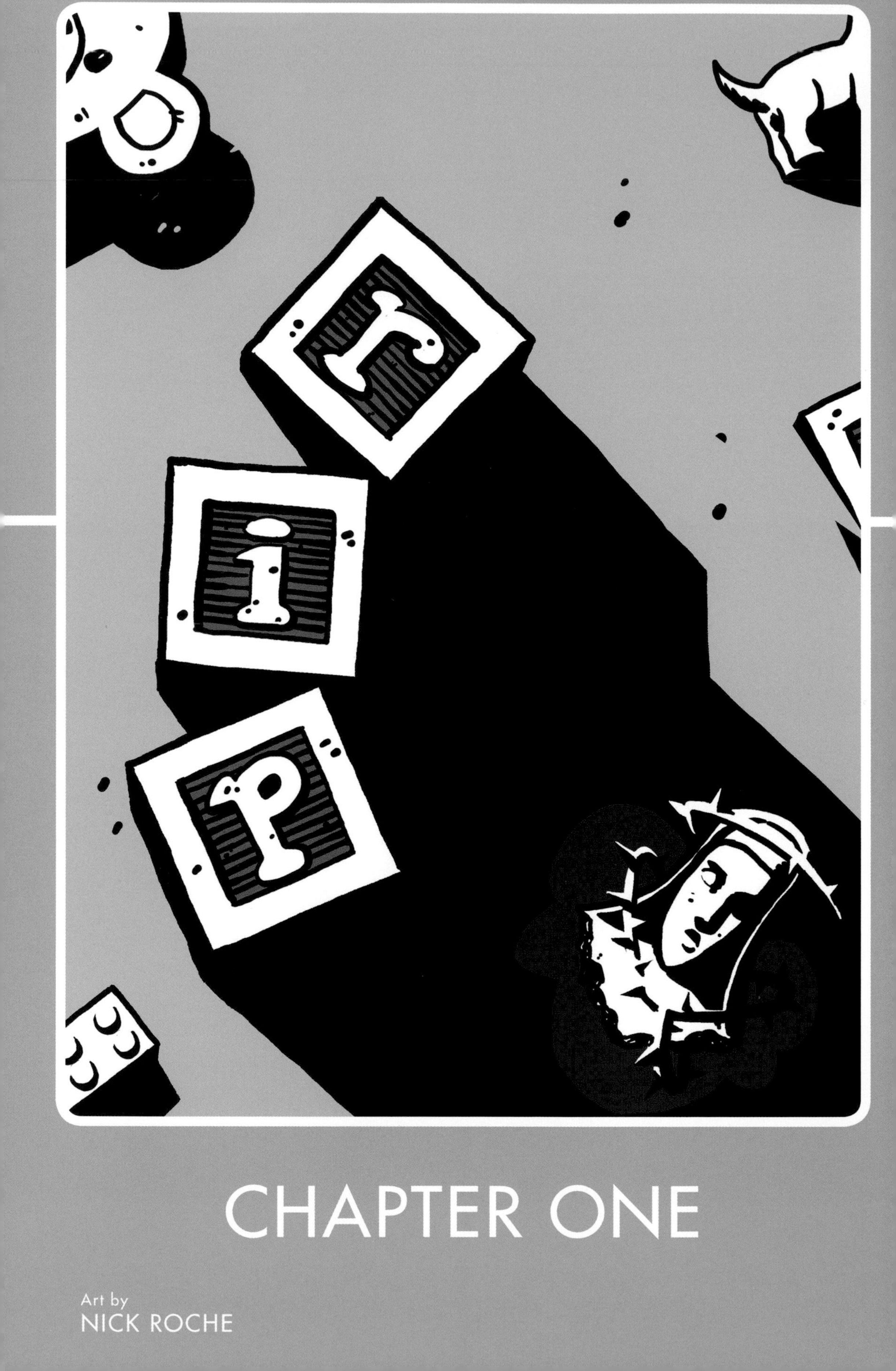
r
i
p

CHAPTER ONE

Art by
NICK ROCHE

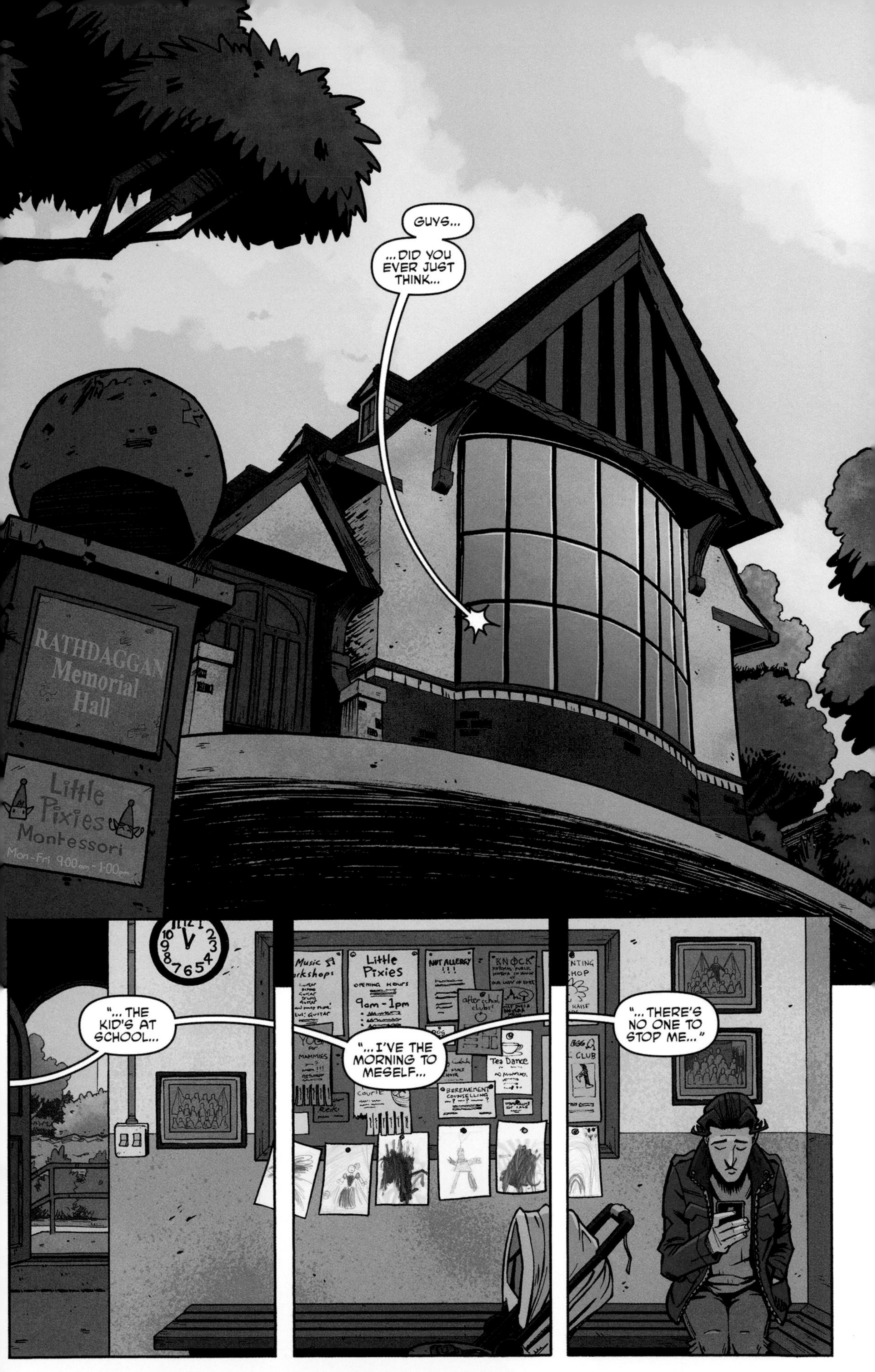
GUYS...
...DID YOU EVER JUST THINK...
RATHDAGGAN Memorial Hall
Little Pixies Montessori
Mon-Fri 9:00am - 1:00pm
"...THE KID'S AT SCHOOL...
"...I'VE THE MORNING TO MESELF...
"...THERE'S NO ONE TO STOP ME..."
Little Pixies
OPENING HOURS
9am - 1pm
NUT ALLERGY !!!
after school clubs!
Tea Dance
BEREAVEMENT COUNSELLING

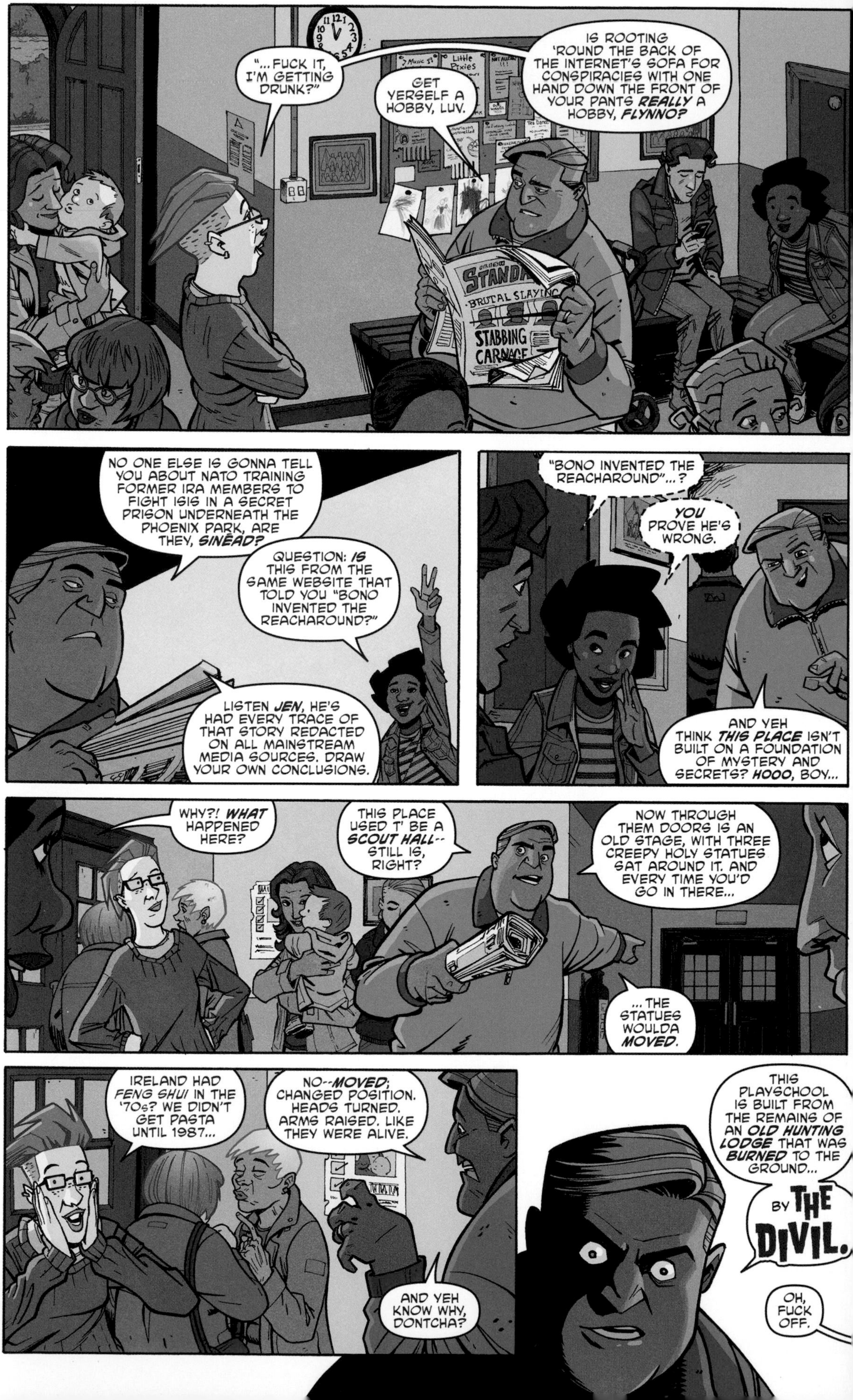
"...FUCK IT, I'M GETTING DRUNK?"
GET YOURSELF A HOBBY, LUV.
IS ROOTING 'ROUND THE BACK OF THE INTERNET'S SOFA FOR CONSPIRACIES WITH ONE HAND DOWN THE FRONT OF YOUR PANTS *REALLY* A HOBBY, *FLYNNO?*
BRUTAL SLAYING
STABBING CARNAGE
NO ONE ELSE IS GONNA TELL YOU ABOUT NATO TRAINING FORMER IRA MEMBERS TO FIGHT ISIS IN A SECRET PRISON UNDERNEATH THE PHOENIX PARK, ARE THEY, *SINÉAD?*
QUESTION: *IS* THIS FROM THE SAME WEBSITE THAT TOLD YOU "BONO INVENTED THE REACHAROUND?"
LISTEN *JEN*, HE'S HAD EVERY TRACE OF THAT STORY REDACTED ON ALL MAINSTREAM MEDIA SOURCES. DRAW YOUR OWN CONCLUSIONS.
"BONO INVENTED THE REACHAROUND"...?
YOU PROVE HE'S WRONG.
AND YEH THINK *THIS PLACE* ISN'T BUILT ON A FOUNDATION OF MYSTERY AND SECRETS? *HOOO*, BOY...
WHY?! *WHAT* HAPPENED HERE?
THIS PLACE USED T' BE A *SCOUT HALL*-- STILL IS, RIGHT?
NOW THROUGH THEM DOORS IS AN OLD STAGE, WITH THREE CREEPY HOLY STATUES SAT AROUND IT. AND EVERY TIME YOU'D GO IN THERE...
...THE STATUES WOULDA *MOVED*.
IRELAND HAD *FENG SHUI* IN THE '70s? WE DIDN'T GET PASTA UNTIL 1987...
NO--*MOVED*; CHANGED POSITION. HEADS TURNED. ARMS RAISED. LIKE THEY WERE ALIVE.
AND YEH KNOW WHY, DONTCHA?
THIS PLAYSCHOOL IS BUILT FROM THE REMAINS OF AN *OLD HUNTING LODGE* THAT WAS *BURNED* TO THE GROUND...
BY THE DIVIL.
OH, FUCK OFF.

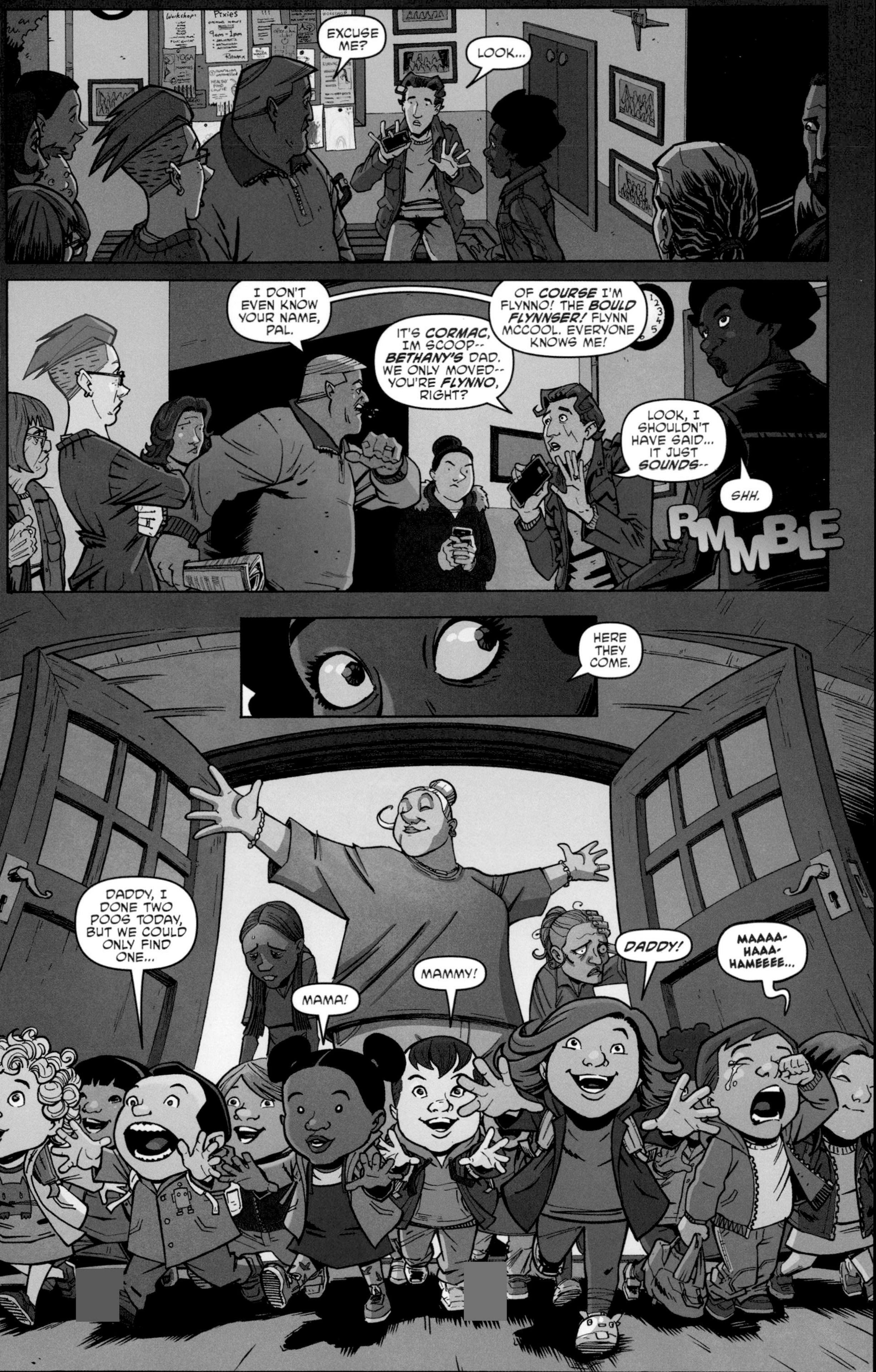
EXCUSE ME?
LOOK...
I DON'T EVEN KNOW YOUR NAME, PAL.
IT'S CORMAC, IM SCOOP-- BETHANY'S DAD. WE ONLY MOVED-- YOU'RE FLYNNO, RIGHT?
OF COURSE I'M FLYNNO! THE BOULD FLYNNSER! FLYNN MCCOOL. EVERYONE KNOWS ME!
LOOK, I SHOULDN'T HAVE SAID... IT JUST SOUNDS--
SHH.
RMMBLE
HERE THEY COME.
DADDY, I DONE TWO POOS TODAY, BUT WE COULD ONLY FIND ONE...
MAMA!
MAMMY!
DADDY!
MAAAA-HAAA-HAMEEEE...

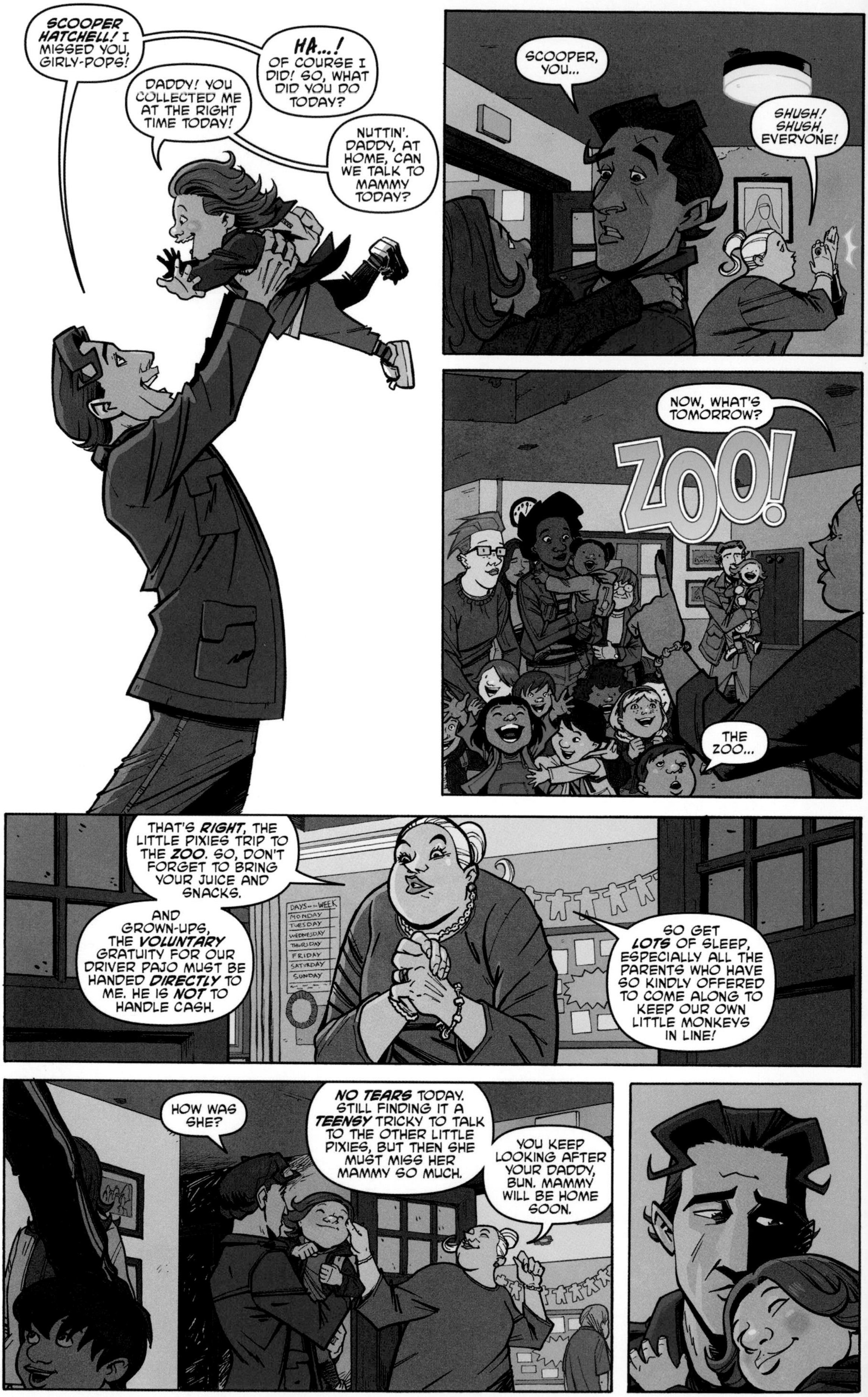
SCOOPER HATCHELL! I MISSED YOU, GIRLY-POPS!
DADDY! YOU COLLECTED ME AT THE RIGHT TIME TODAY!
HA...! OF COURSE I DID! SO, WHAT DID YOU DO TODAY?
NUTTIN'. DADDY, AT HOME, CAN WE TALK TO MAMMY TODAY?
SCOOPER, YOU...
SHUSH! SHUSH, EVERYONE!
NOW, WHAT'S TOMORROW?
ZOO!
THE ZOO...
THAT'S RIGHT, THE LITTLE PIXIES TRIP TO THE ZOO. SO, DON'T FORGET TO BRING YOUR JUICE AND SNACKS.
AND GROWN-UPS, THE VOLUNTARY GRATUITY FOR OUR DRIVER PAJO MUST BE HANDED DIRECTLY TO ME. HE IS NOT TO HANDLE CASH.
DAYS OF THE WEEK
MONDAY
TUESDAY
WEDNESDAY
THURSDAY
FRIDAY
SATURDAY
SUNDAY
SO GET LOTS OF SLEEP, ESPECIALLY ALL THE PARENTS WHO HAVE SO KINDLY OFFERED TO COME ALONG TO KEEP OUR OWN LITTLE MONKEYS IN LINE!
HOW WAS SHE?
NO TEARS TODAY. STILL FINDING IT A TEENSY TRICKY TO TALK TO THE OTHER LITTLE PIXIES, BUT THEN SHE MUST MISS HER MAMMY SO MUCH.
YOU KEEP LOOKING AFTER YOUR DADDY, BUN. MAMMY WILL BE HOME SOON.

I SWEAR IT'S LIKE BEING BACK AT SCHOOL SOMETIMES.

THAT BAD?

AH, FLYNNO...

HE JUST REMINDS ME OF THE SORTA LADS THAT I HATED WHEN I WAS A KID. OR HATED ME. BOTH, MAYBE.

IT'S WEIRD. YOU FORGET SOMETIMES HOW TO BE AROUND PEOPLE. GROWN-UPS.

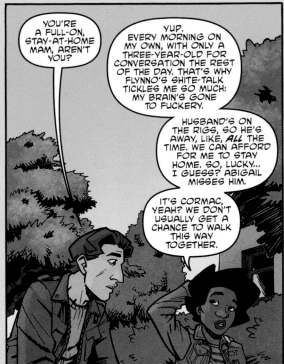

YOU'RE A FULL-ON, STAY-AT-HOME MAM, AREN'T YOU?

YUP. EVERY MORNING ON MY OWN, WITH ONLY A THREE-YEAR-OLD FOR CONVERSATION THE REST OF THE DAY. THAT'S WHY FLYNNO'S SHITE-TALK TICKLES ME SO MUCH: MY BRAIN'S GONE TO FUCKERY.

HUSBAND'S ON THE RIGS, SO HE'S AWAY, LIKE, ALL THE TIME. WE CAN AFFORD FOR ME TO STAY HOME. SO, LUCKY... I GUESS? ABIGAIL MISSES HIM.

IT'S CORMAC, YEAH? WE DON'T USUALLY GET A CHANCE TO WALK THIS WAY TOGETHER.

YEAH, I'M USUALLY... LATE. HAD TO WAIT FOR MY COMPUTER TO UPDATE. TYPICAL.

I WORK FROM HOME, SO I FIRE SCOOPE--I MEAN, BETHANY--INTO CRECHE AT 9, RUN HOME, WORK TILL 1, AND RUN TO COLLECT HER. THEN BACK TO IT AT NIGHT WHEN SHE'S ASLEEP.

JESUS. AND WHAT DOES YOUR WIFE DO--

DADDY! ABIGAIL SAID SHE DON'T LIKE MY SCHOOL BAG!

MAMMY, IT'S NOT GOOD AND BLUE. I ONLY LIKE BLUE SCHOOL BAGS.

GOD, THEY CAN BE SUCH...

YEP. COMPLETE AND UTTER ONES. I BLAME THE PARENTS.

C'MON SCOOPS!

AW, SCOOPER. WE'RE SO NEAR. WOULD YOU NOT THINK ABOUT WALKING?

I DON'T LIKE WALKING, DADDY.

DADDY?

YES, DUCK.

DADDY, WILL YOU PLAY WITH ME AND NOT DO ALL THE WORK TODAY?

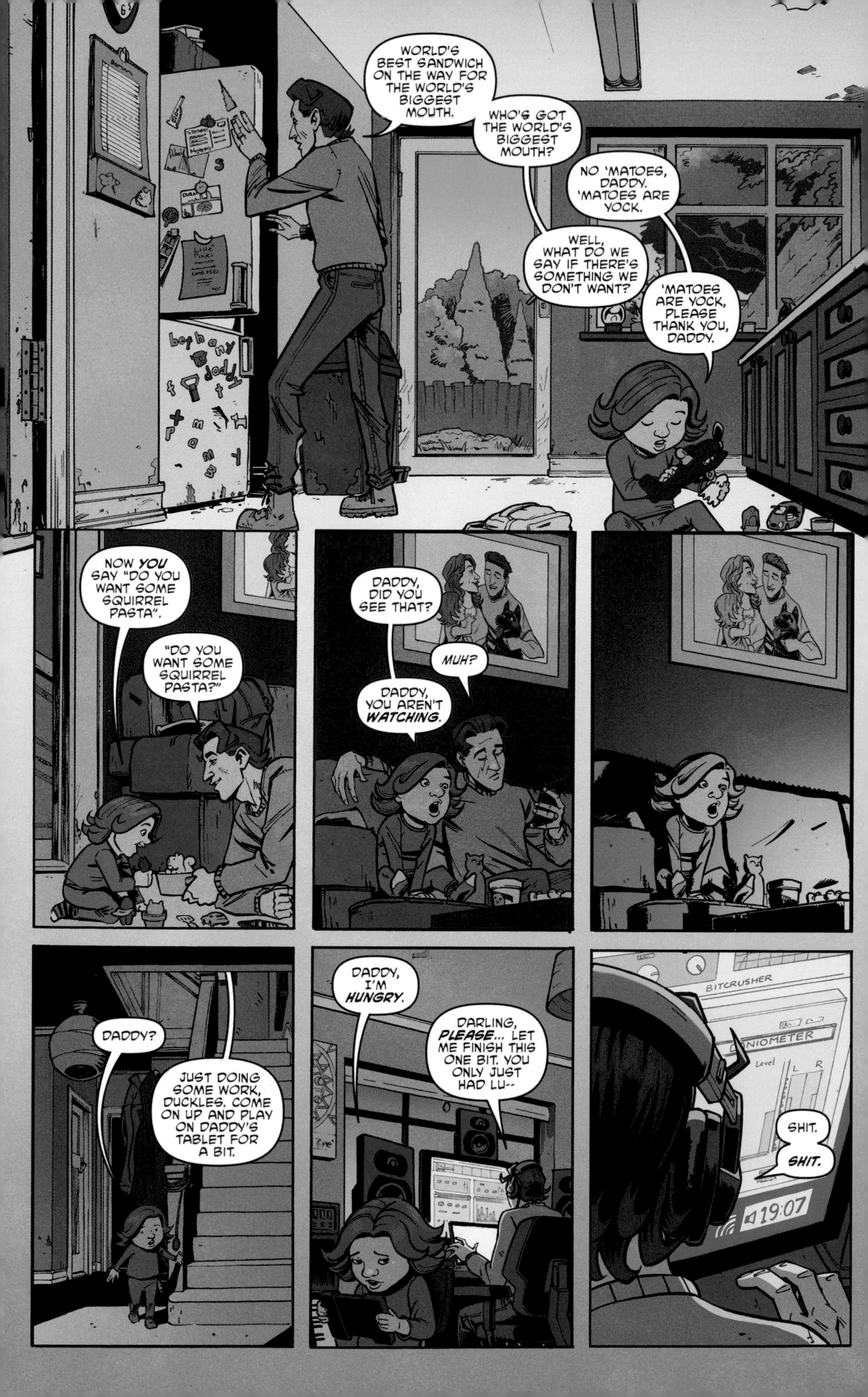
WORLD'S BEST SANDWICH ON THE WAY FOR THE WORLD'S BIGGEST MOUTH.
WHO'S GOT THE WORLD'S BIGGEST MOUTH?
NO 'MATOES, DADDY. 'MATOES ARE YOCK.
WELL, WHAT DO WE SAY IF THERE'S SOMETHING WE DON'T WANT?
'MATOES ARE YOCK, PLEASE THANK YOU, DADDY.
NOW *YOU* SAY "DO YOU WANT SOME SQUIRREL PASTA".
"DO YOU WANT SOME SQUIRREL PASTA?"
DADDY, DID YOU SEE THAT?
MUH?
DADDY, YOU AREN'T ***WATCHING***.
DADDY?
JUST DOING SOME WORK, DUCKLES. COME ON UP AND PLAY ON DADDY'S TABLET FOR A BIT.
DADDY, I'M ***HUNGRY***.
DARLING, ***PLEASE***... LET ME FINISH THIS ONE BIT. YOU ONLY JUST HAD LU--
BITCRUSHER
Level
L R
SHIT.
SHIT.
19:07

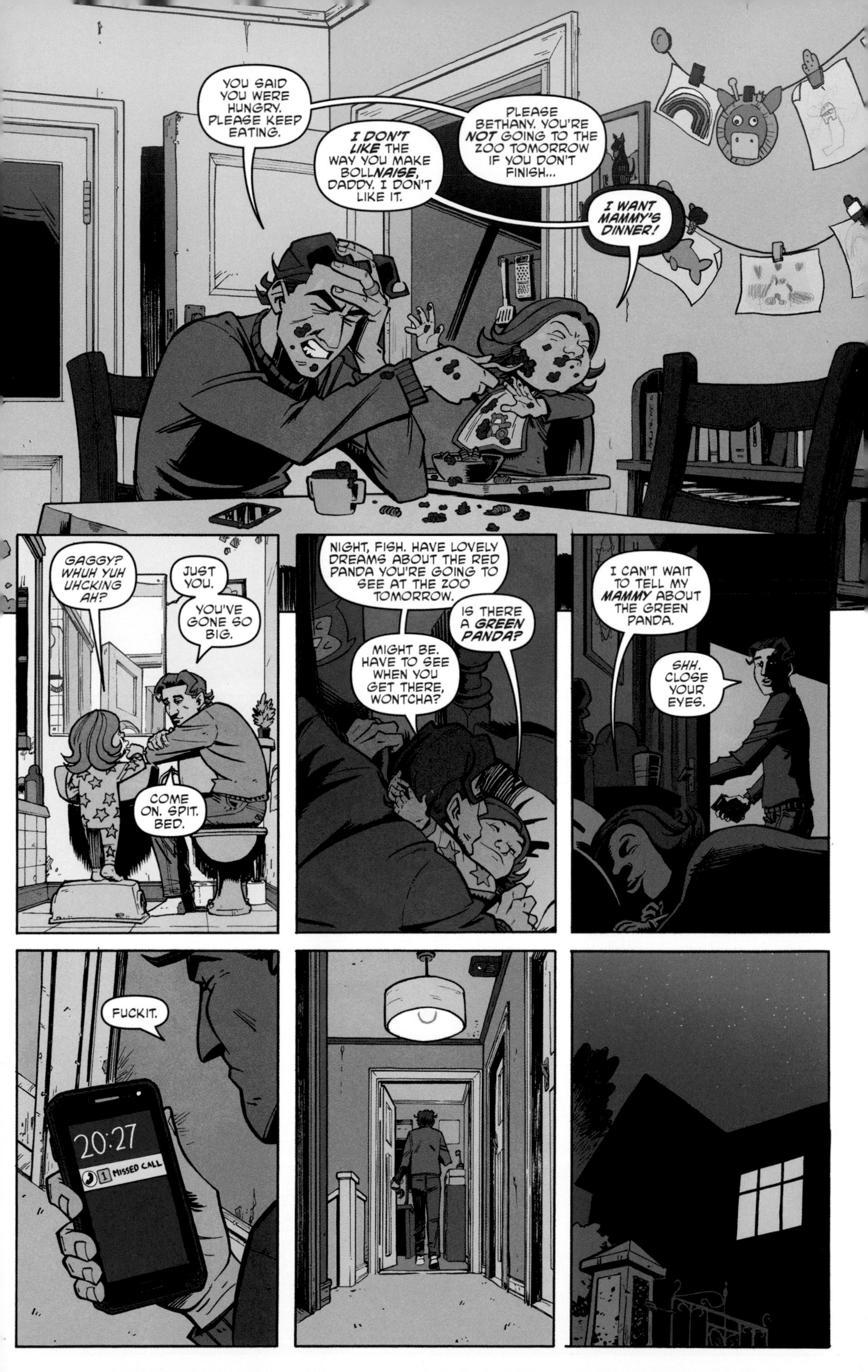
YOU SAID YOU WERE HUNGRY. PLEASE KEEP EATING.
I DON'T LIKE THE WAY YOU MAKE BOLLNAISE, DADDY. I DON'T LIKE IT.
PLEASE BETHANY. YOU'RE NOT GOING TO THE ZOO TOMORROW IF YOU DON'T FINISH...
I WANT MAMMY'S DINNER!
GAGGY? WHUH YUH UHCKING AH?
JUST YOU.
YOU'VE GONE SO BIG.
COME ON. SPIT. BED.
NIGHT, FISH. HAVE LOVELY DREAMS ABOUT THE RED PANDA YOU'RE GOING TO SEE AT THE ZOO TOMORROW.
IS THERE A GREEN PANDA?
MIGHT BE. HAVE TO SEE WHEN YOU GET THERE, WONTCHA?
I CAN'T WAIT TO TELL MY MAMMY ABOUT THE GREEN PANDA.
SHH. CLOSE YOUR EYES.
FUCKIT.
20:27
1 MISSED CALL

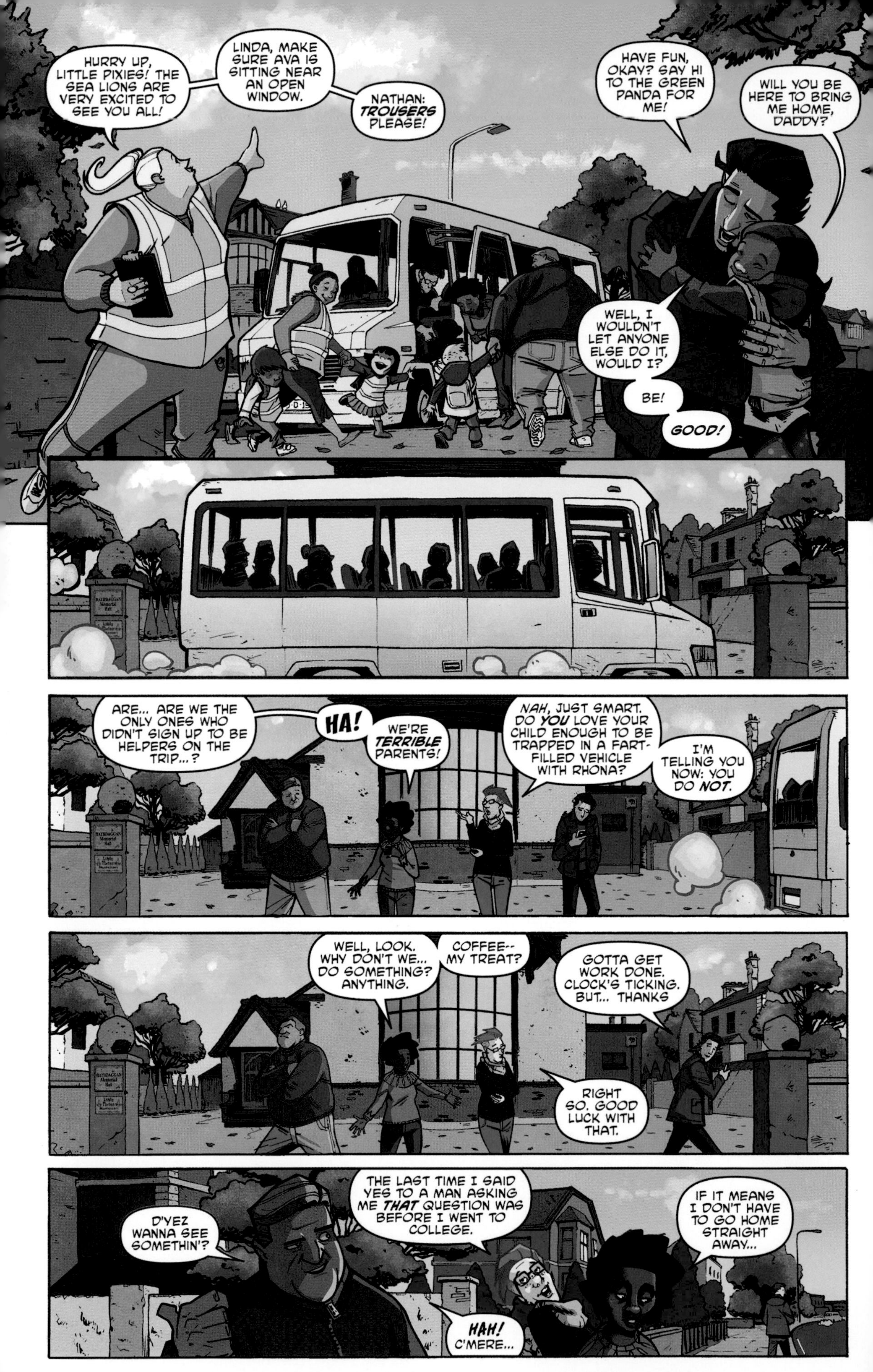
HURRY UP, LITTLE PIXIES! THE SEA LIONS ARE VERY EXCITED TO SEE YOU ALL!
LINDA, MAKE SURE AVA IS SITTING NEAR AN OPEN WINDOW.
NATHAN: TROUSERS PLEASE!
HAVE FUN, OKAY? SAY HI TO THE GREEN PANDA FOR ME!
WILL YOU BE HERE TO BRING ME HOME, DADDY?
WELL, I WOULDN'T LET ANYONE ELSE DO IT, WOULD I?
BE!
GOOD!
ARE... ARE WE THE ONLY ONES WHO DIDN'T SIGN UP TO BE HELPERS ON THE TRIP...?
HA!
WE'RE TERRIBLE PARENTS!
NAH, JUST SMART. DO YOU LOVE YOUR CHILD ENOUGH TO BE TRAPPED IN A FART-FILLED VEHICLE WITH RHONA?
I'M TELLING YOU NOW: YOU DO NOT.
WELL, LOOK. WHY DON'T WE... DO SOMETHING? ANYTHING.
COFFEE-- MY TREAT?
GOTTA GET WORK DONE. CLOCK'S TICKING. BUT... THANKS
RIGHT SO. GOOD LUCK WITH THAT.
D'YEZ WANNA SEE SOMETHIN'?
THE LAST TIME I SAID YES TO A MAN ASKING ME THAT QUESTION WAS BEFORE I WENT TO COLLEGE.
IF IT MEANS I DON'T HAVE TO GO HOME STRAIGHT AWAY...
HAH! C'MERE...

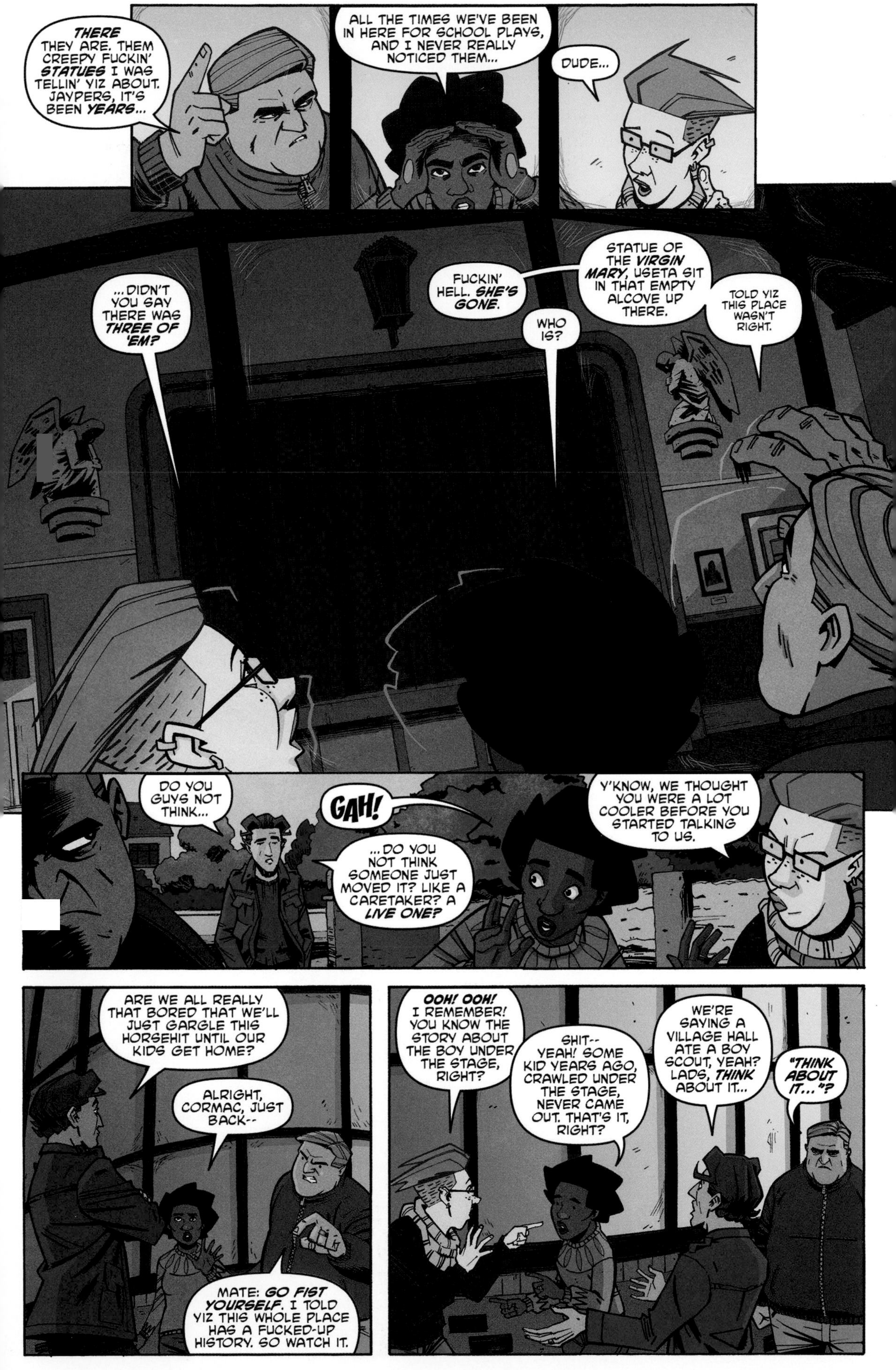
THERE THEY ARE. THEM CREEPY FUCKIN' STATUES I WAS TELLIN' YIZ ABOUT. JAYPERS, IT'S BEEN YEARS...
ALL THE TIMES WE'VE BEEN IN HERE FOR SCHOOL PLAYS, AND I NEVER REALLY NOTICED THEM...
DUDE...
...DIDN'T YOU SAY THERE WAS THREE OF 'EM?
FUCKIN' HELL. SHE'S GONE.
STATUE OF THE VIRGIN MARY, USETA SIT IN THAT EMPTY ALCOVE UP THERE.
WHO IS?
TOLD YIZ THIS PLACE WASN'T RIGHT.
DO YOU GUYS NOT THINK...
GAH!
...DO YOU NOT THINK SOMEONE JUST MOVED IT? LIKE A CARETAKER? A LIVE ONE?
Y'KNOW, WE THOUGHT YOU WERE A LOT COOLER BEFORE YOU STARTED TALKING TO US.
ARE WE ALL REALLY THAT BORED THAT WE'LL JUST GARGLE THIS HORSEHIT UNTIL OUR KIDS GET HOME?
ALRIGHT, CORMAC, JUST BACK--
MATE: GO FIST YOURSELF. I TOLD YIZ THIS WHOLE PLACE HAS A FUCKED-UP HISTORY. SO WATCH IT.
OOH! OOH! I REMEMBER! YOU KNOW THE STORY ABOUT THE BOY UNDER THE STAGE, RIGHT?
SHIT-- YEAH! SOME KID YEARS AGO, CRAWLED UNDER THE STAGE, NEVER CAME OUT. THAT'S IT, RIGHT?
WE'RE SAYING A VILLAGE HALL ATE A BOY SCOUT, YEAH? LADS, THINK ABOUT IT...
"THINK ABOUT IT..."?

I'VE THOUGHT ABOUT IT *EVERY* DAY FOR THE LAST *FORTY* YEARS.

THAT KID WAS ME *BRUDDER*.

MY OLDER *BRUDDER*, *BRIAN*, CAME HERE ON SOME SCOUT JAMBOUREE, AND HIM AND A FEW MATES DECIDED TO GO EXPLORING.

WHAT?

JESUS, FLYNNO...

HE'D HEARD ABOUT THE STATUES AND THE DIVIL, AND WANTED TO SEE FOR HIMSELF.

HE WOULDN'T HAVE BEEN SCARED OF ALL THAT, EVEN AT TEN YEARS OLD.

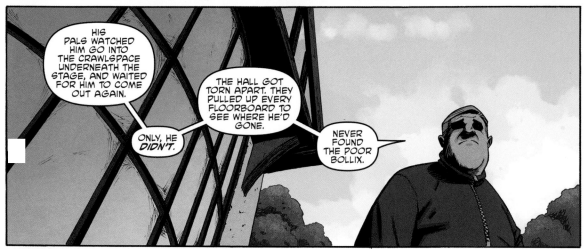

HIS PALS WATCHED HIM GO INTO THE CRAWLSPACE UNDERNEATH THE STAGE, AND WAITED FOR HIM TO COME OUT AGAIN.

ONLY, HE *DIDN'T*.

THE HALL GOT TORN APART. THEY PULLED UP EVERY FLOORBOARD TO SEE WHERE HE'D GONE.

NEVER FOUND THE POOR BOLLIX.

SO FLYNNO LOSES AN *ACTUAL* FAMILY MEMBER. ARE YA *DELIGHTED*? ARE YA?

FLYNNO. MAN. I'M SORRY. I DIDN'T MEAN TO UPSET YOU.

I GET IT. WHEN BAD SHIT HAPPENS, PEOPLE PUT UP SCAFFOLDING AROUND THEMSELVES TO STOP FROM FALLING DOWN. IT'S NATURAL. IT'S *SURVIVAL*.

BUT YOU CAN'T LET A CRUTCH DEFINE YOU.

I DON'T KNOW WHAT REALLY HAPPENED. BUT IT WASN'T THE BUILDING'S FAULT.

IF THERE WAS ANY WAY, I'D GO *INTO* THAT HALL RIGHT NOW, CLIMB *UNDER* THAT STAGE AND SHOW YOU THAT ROOM... IS *JUST* A ROOM.

YEAH?

LET'S HAVE YOU, THEN.

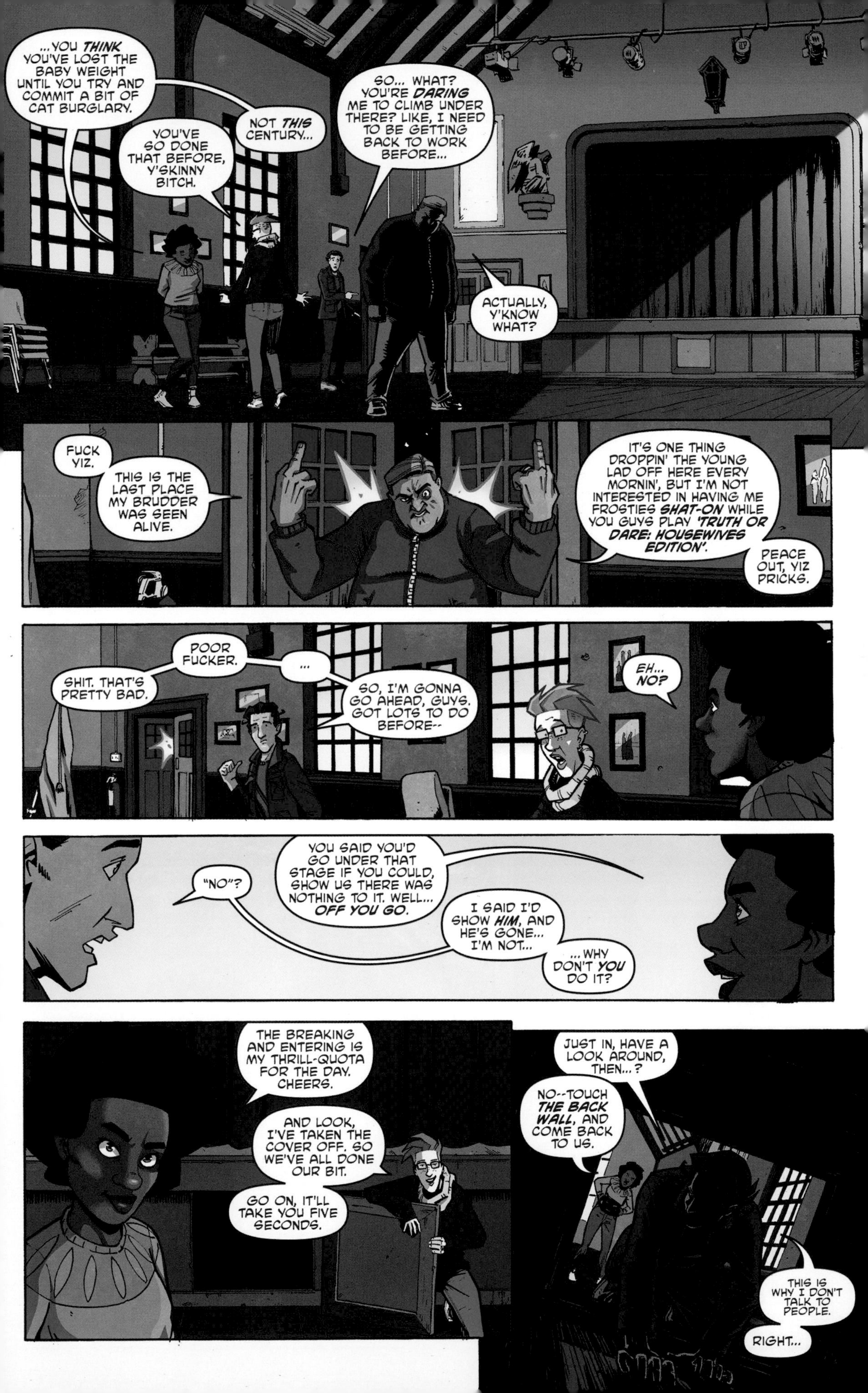
...YOU THINK YOU'VE LOST THE BABY WEIGHT UNTIL YOU TRY AND COMMIT A BIT OF CAT BURGLARY.
YOU'VE SO DONE THAT BEFORE, Y'SKINNY BITCH.
NOT THIS CENTURY...
SO... WHAT? YOU'RE DARING ME TO CLIMB UNDER THERE? LIKE, I NEED TO BE GETTING BACK TO WORK BEFORE...
ACTUALLY, Y'KNOW WHAT?
FUCK YIZ.
THIS IS THE LAST PLACE MY BRUDDER WAS SEEN ALIVE.
IT'S ONE THING DROPPIN' THE YOUNG LAD OFF HERE EVERY MORNIN', BUT I'M NOT INTERESTED IN HAVING ME FROSTIES SHAT-ON WHILE YOU GUYS PLAY 'TRUTH OR DARE: HOUSEWIVES EDITION'.
PEACE OUT, YIZ PRICKS.
SHIT. THAT'S PRETTY BAD.
POOR FUCKER.
...
SO, I'M GONNA GO AHEAD, GUYS. GOT LOTS TO DO BEFORE--
EH... NO?
"NO"?
YOU SAID YOU'D GO UNDER THAT STAGE IF YOU COULD, SHOW US THERE WAS NOTHING TO IT. WELL... OFF YOU GO.
I SAID I'D SHOW HIM, AND HE'S GONE... I'M NOT...
...WHY DON'T YOU DO IT?
THE BREAKING AND ENTERING IS MY THRILL-QUOTA FOR THE DAY. CHEERS.
AND LOOK, I'VE TAKEN THE COVER OFF. SO WE'VE ALL DONE OUR BIT.
GO ON, IT'LL TAKE YOU FIVE SECONDS.
JUST IN, HAVE A LOOK AROUND, THEN...?
NO--TOUCH THE BACK WALL, AND COME BACK TO US.
THIS IS WHY I DON'T TALK TO PEOPLE.
RIGHT...

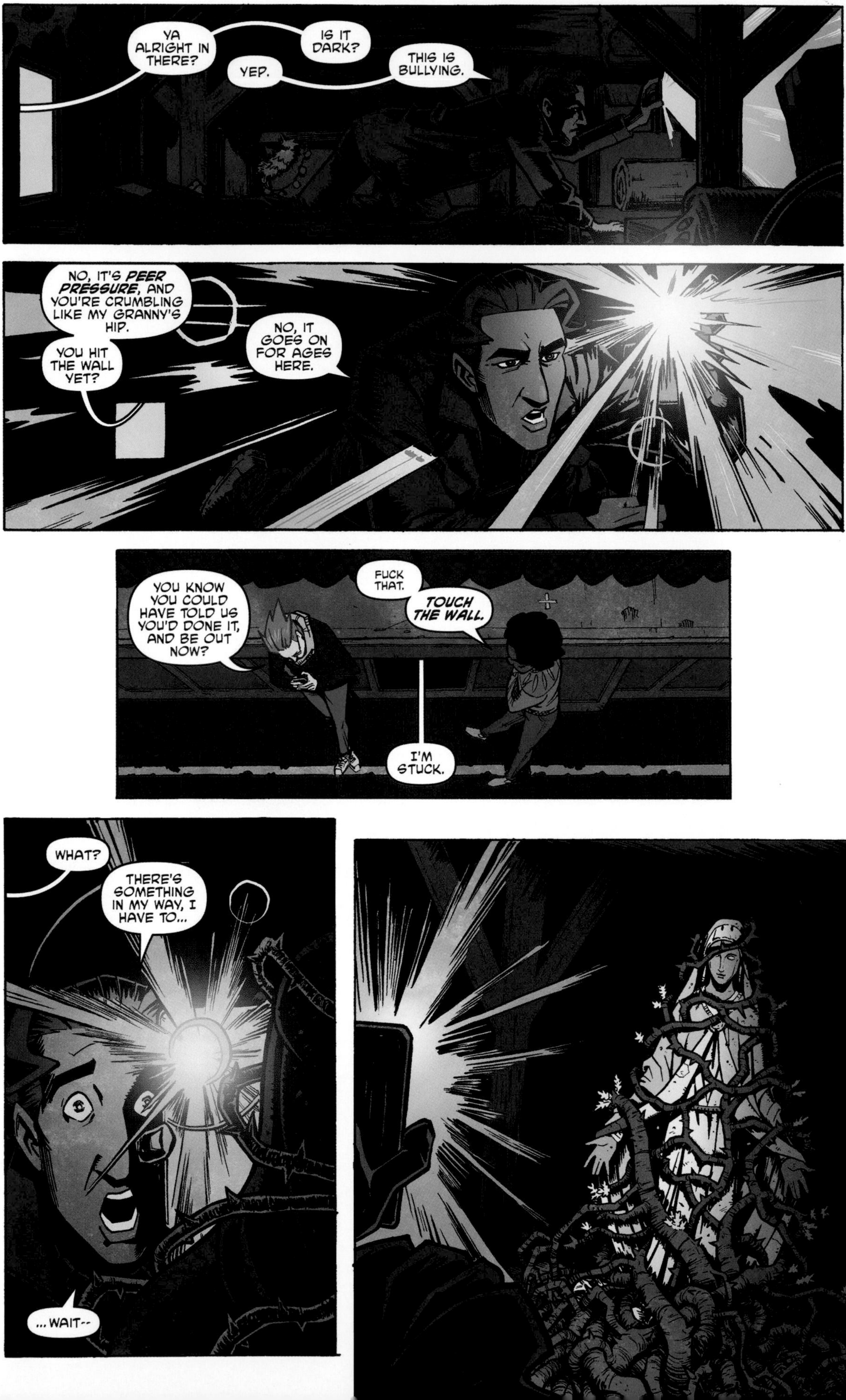

YA ALRIGHT IN THERE?
IS IT DARK?
YEP.
THIS IS BULLYING.
NO, IT'S PEER PRESSURE, AND YOU'RE CRUMBLING LIKE MY GRANNY'S HIP.
YOU HIT THE WALL YET?
NO, IT GOES ON FOR AGES HERE.
YOU KNOW YOU COULD HAVE TOLD US YOU'D DONE IT, AND BE OUT NOW?
FUCK THAT.
TOUCH THE WALL.
I'M STUCK.
WHAT?
THERE'S SOMETHING IN MY WAY, I HAVE TO...
...WAIT--

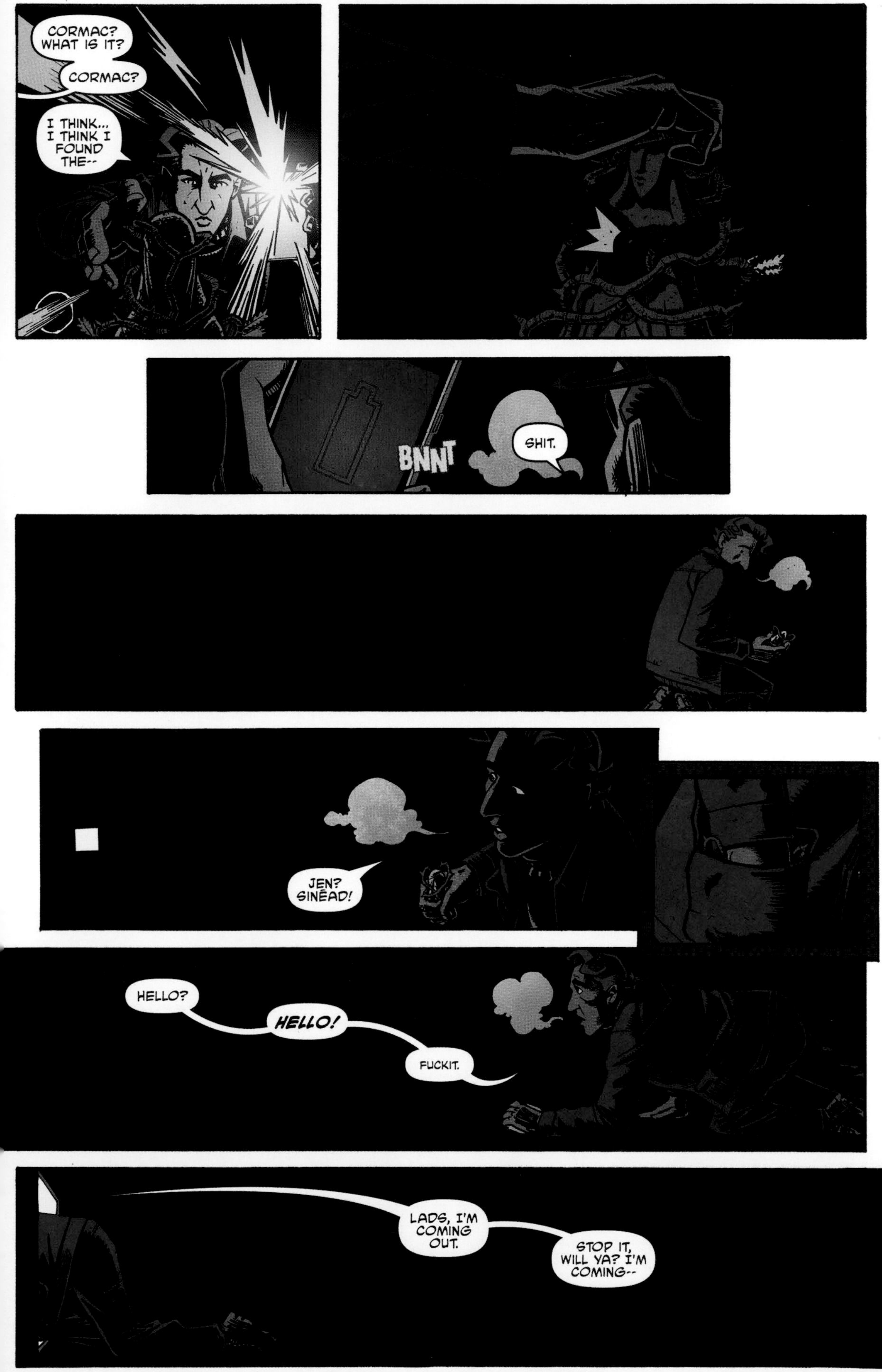
CORMAC? WHAT IS IT?
CORMAC?
I THINK... I THINK I FOUND THE--
BNNT
SHIT.
JEN? SINÉAD!
HELLO?
HELLO!
FUCKIT.
LADS, I'M COMING OUT.
STOP IT, WILL YA? I'M COMING--

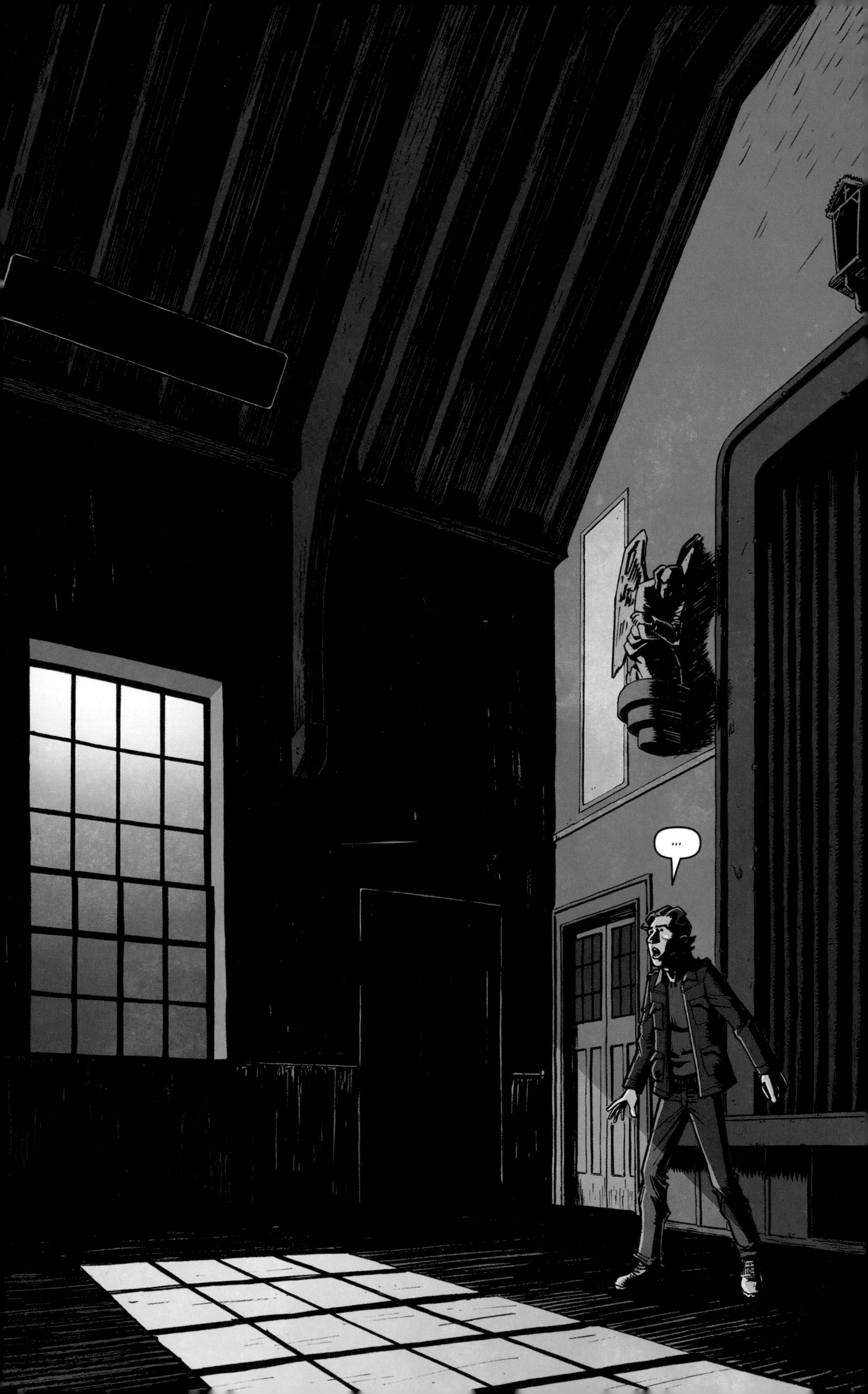
...

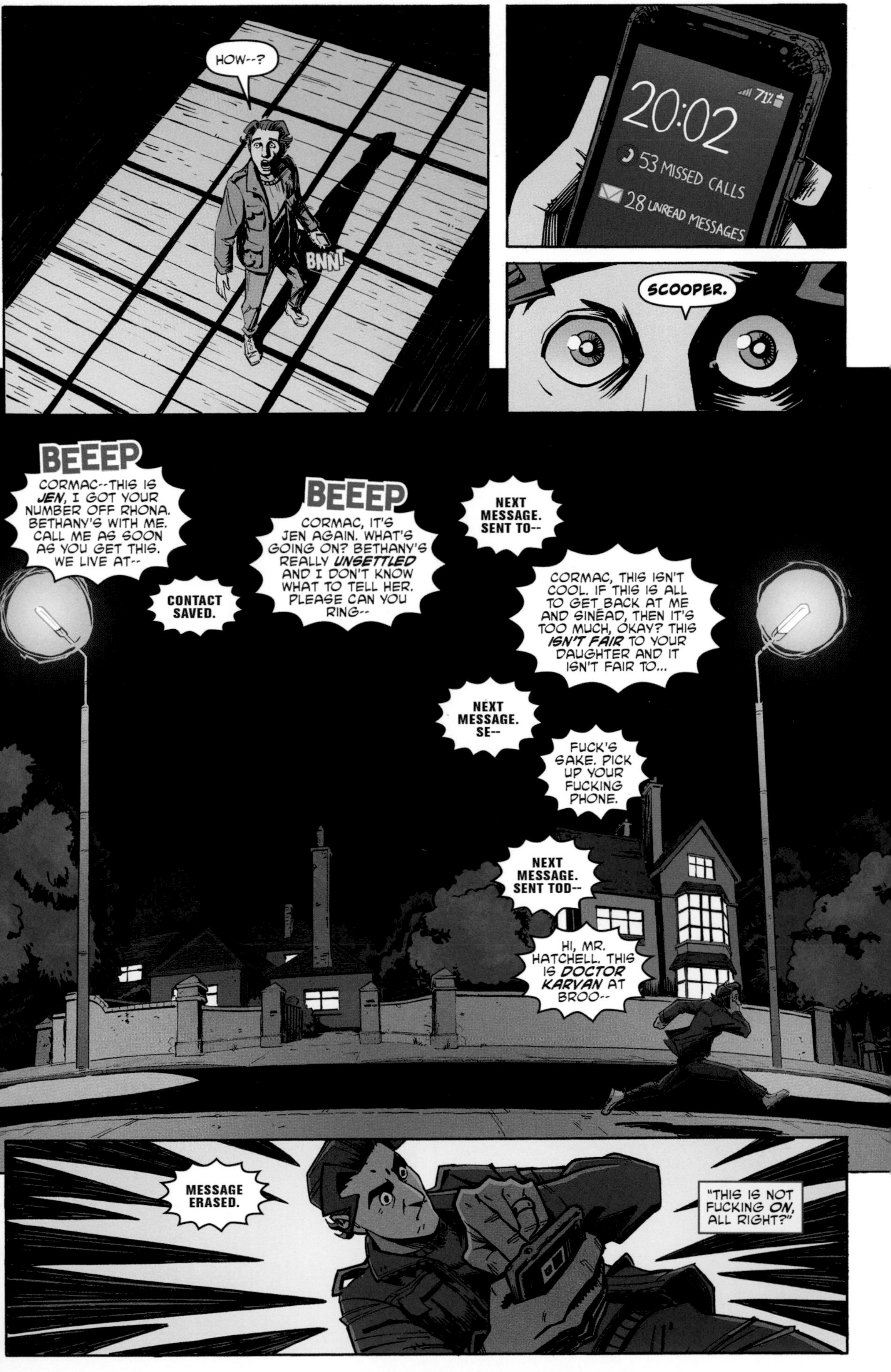
HOW--?
BNNT
20:02
71%
53 MISSED CALLS
28 UNREAD MESSAGES
SCOOPER.
BEEEP
CORMAC--THIS IS JEN, I GOT YOUR NUMBER OFF RHONA. BETHANY'S WITH ME. CALL ME AS SOON AS YOU GET THIS. WE LIVE AT--
CONTACT SAVED.
BEEEP
CORMAC, IT'S JEN AGAIN. WHAT'S GOING ON? BETHANY'S REALLY UNSETTLED AND I DON'T KNOW WHAT TO TELL HER. PLEASE CAN YOU RING--
NEXT MESSAGE. SENT TO--
CORMAC, THIS ISN'T COOL. IF THIS IS ALL TO GET BACK AT ME AND SINÉAD, THEN IT'S TOO MUCH, OKAY? THIS ISN'T FAIR TO YOUR DAUGHTER AND IT ISN'T FAIR TO...
NEXT MESSAGE. SE--
FUCK'S SAKE. PICK UP YOUR FUCKING PHONE.
NEXT MESSAGE. SENT TOD--
HI, MR. HATCHELL. THIS IS DOCTOR KARVAN AT BROO--
MESSAGE ERASED.
"THIS IS NOT FUCKING ON, ALL RIGHT?"

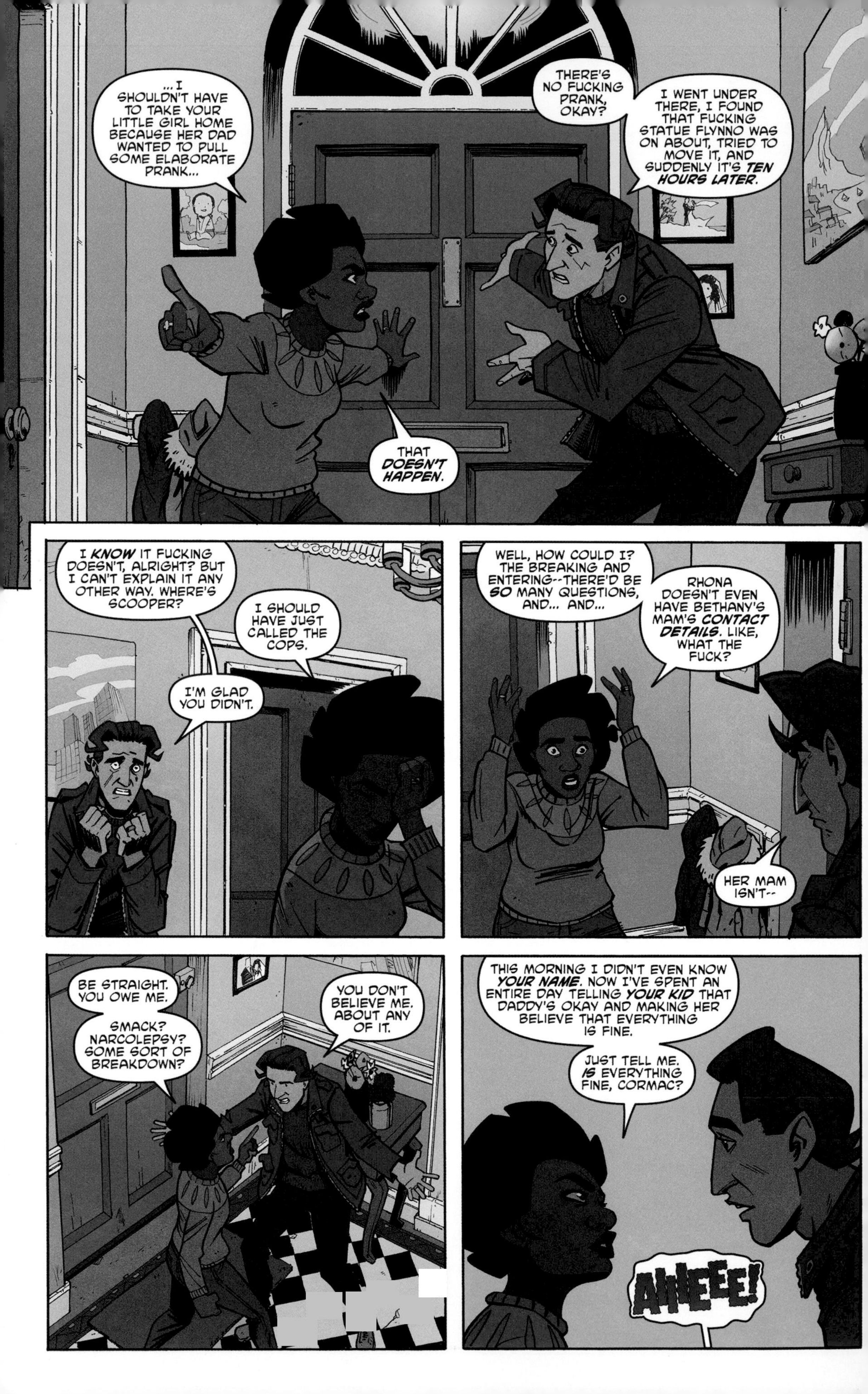
...I SHOULDN'T HAVE TO TAKE YOUR LITTLE GIRL HOME BECAUSE HER DAD WANTED TO PULL SOME ELABORATE PRANK...
THERE'S NO FUCKING PRANK, OKAY?
I WENT UNDER THERE, I FOUND THAT FUCKING STATUE FLYNNO WAS ON ABOUT, TRIED TO MOVE IT, AND SUDDENLY IT'S TEN HOURS LATER.
THAT DOESN'T HAPPEN.
I KNOW IT FUCKING DOESN'T, ALRIGHT? BUT I CAN'T EXPLAIN IT ANY OTHER WAY. WHERE'S SCOOPER?
I SHOULD HAVE JUST CALLED THE COPS.
I'M GLAD YOU DIDN'T.
WELL, HOW COULD I? THE BREAKING AND ENTERING--THERE'D BE SO MANY QUESTIONS, AND... AND...
RHONA DOESN'T EVEN HAVE BETHANY'S MAM'S CONTACT DETAILS. LIKE, WHAT THE FUCK?
HER MAM ISN'T--
BE STRAIGHT. YOU OWE ME.
SMACK? NARCOLEPSY? SOME SORT OF BREAKDOWN?
YOU DON'T BELIEVE ME. ABOUT ANY OF IT.
THIS MORNING I DIDN'T EVEN KNOW YOUR NAME. NOW I'VE SPENT AN ENTIRE DAY TELLING YOUR KID THAT DADDY'S OKAY AND MAKING HER BELIEVE THAT EVERYTHING IS FINE.
JUST TELL ME. IS EVERYTHING FINE, CORMAC?
AIIEEEE!

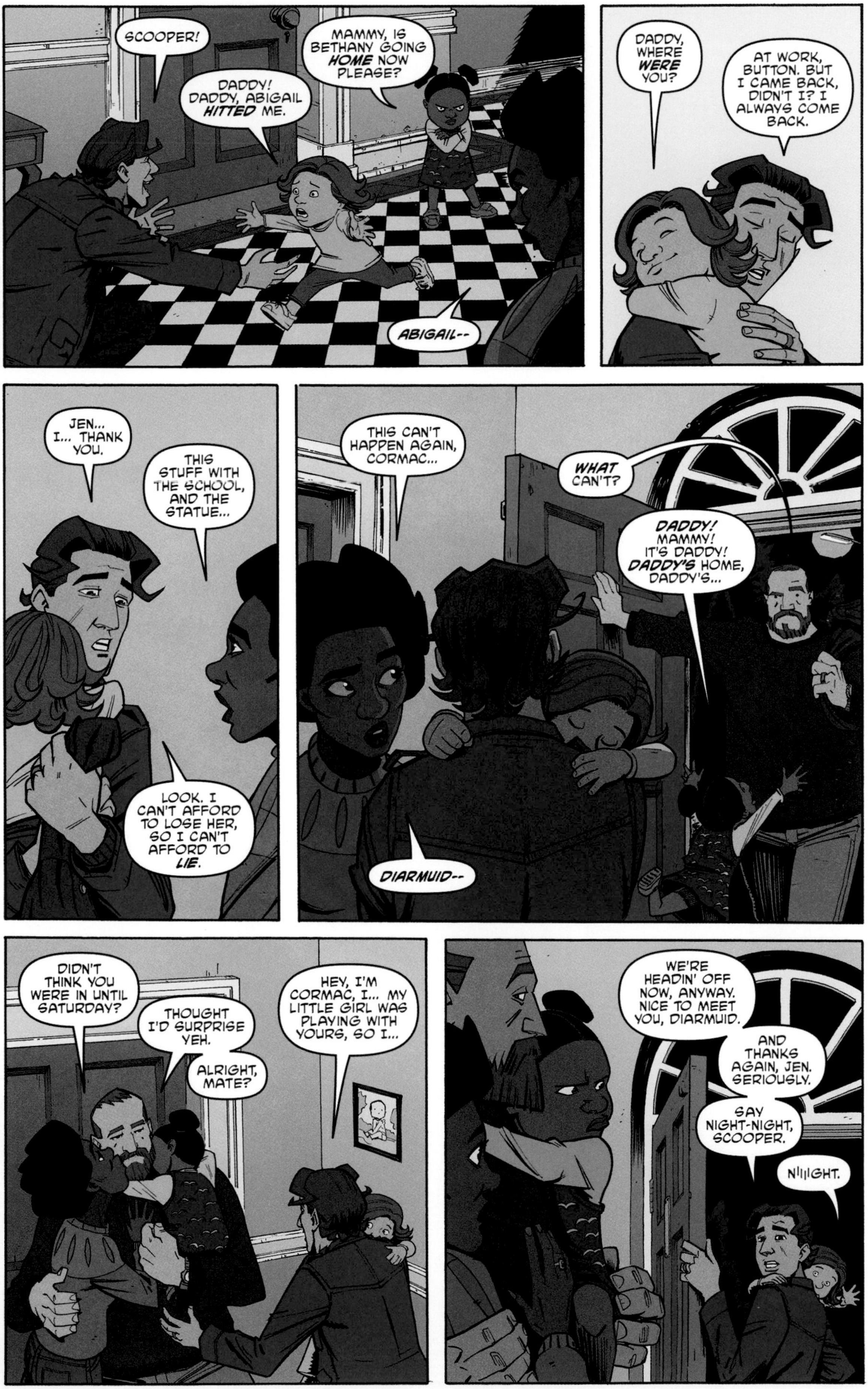
SCOOPER!
DADDY! DADDY, ABIGAIL HITTED ME.
MAMMY, IS BETHANY GOING HOME NOW PLEASE?
ABIGAIL--
DADDY, WHERE WERE YOU?
AT WORK, BUTTON. BUT I CAME BACK, DIDN'T I? I ALWAYS COME BACK.
JEN... I... THANK YOU.
THIS STUFF WITH THE SCHOOL, AND THE STATUE...
LOOK. I CAN'T AFFORD TO LOSE HER, SO I CAN'T AFFORD TO LIE.
THIS CAN'T HAPPEN AGAIN, CORMAC...
WHAT CAN'T?
DADDY! MAMMY! IT'S DADDY! DADDY'S HOME, DADDY'S...
DIARMUID--
DIDN'T THINK YOU WERE IN UNTIL SATURDAY?
THOUGHT I'D SURPRISE YEH.
ALRIGHT, MATE?
HEY, I'M CORMAC, I... MY LITTLE GIRL WAS PLAYING WITH YOURS, SO I...
WE'RE HEADIN' OFF NOW, ANYWAY. NICE TO MEET YOU, DIARMUID.
AND THANKS AGAIN, JEN. SERIOUSLY.
SAY NIGHT-NIGHT, SCOOPER.
NIIIIGHT.

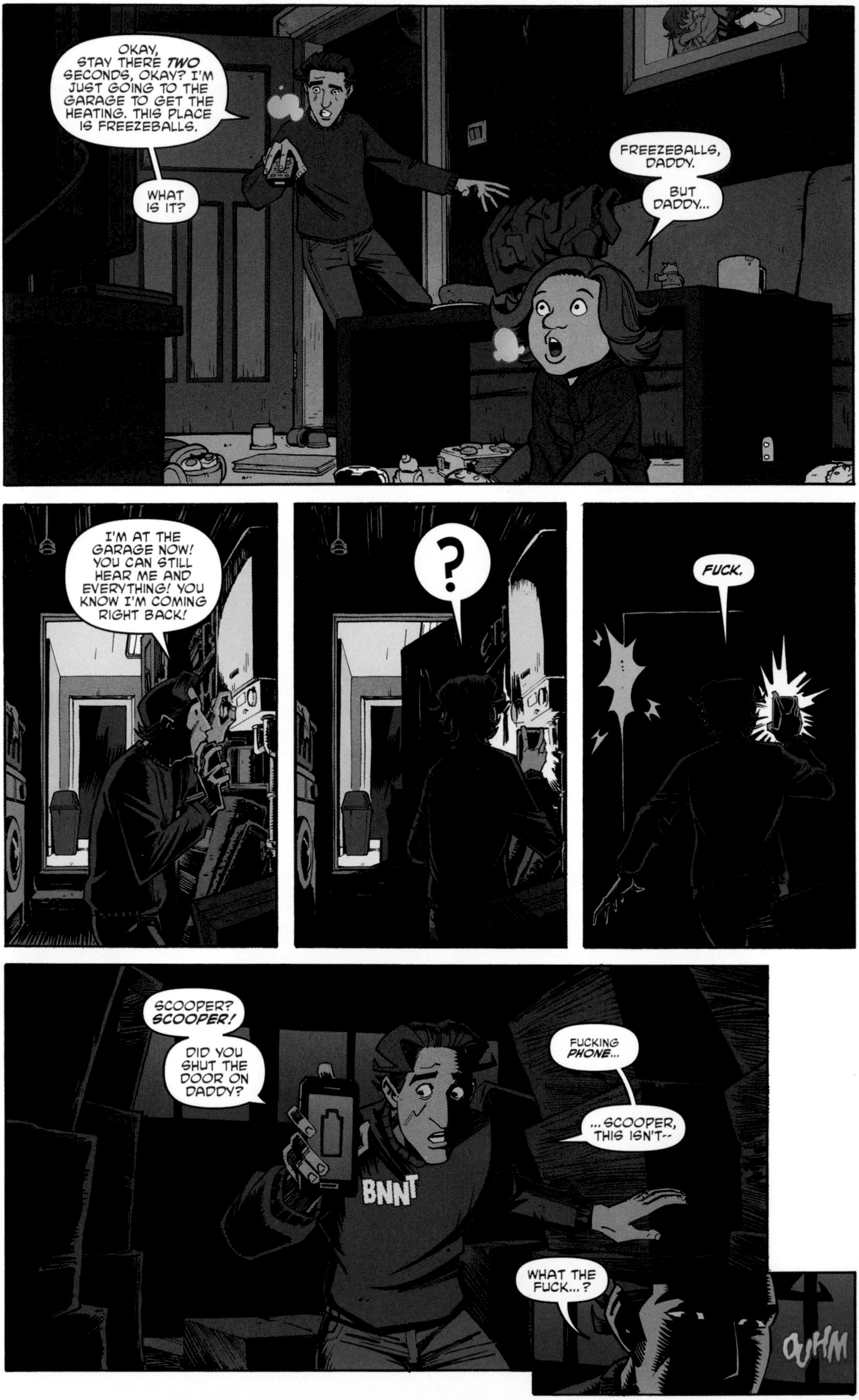

OKAY, STAY THERE *TWO* SECONDS, OKAY? I'M JUST GOING TO THE GARAGE TO GET THE HEATING. THIS PLACE IS FREEZEBALLS.
WHAT IS IT?
FREEZEBALLS, DADDY.
BUT DADDY...
I'M AT THE GARAGE NOW! YOU CAN STILL HEAR ME AND EVERYTHING! YOU KNOW I'M COMING RIGHT BACK!
?
FUCK.
SCOOPER? *SCOOPER!*
DID YOU SHUT THE DOOR ON DADDY?
FUCKING *PHONE...*
...SCOOPER, THIS ISN'T--
BNNT
WHAT THE FUCK...?
OUHM

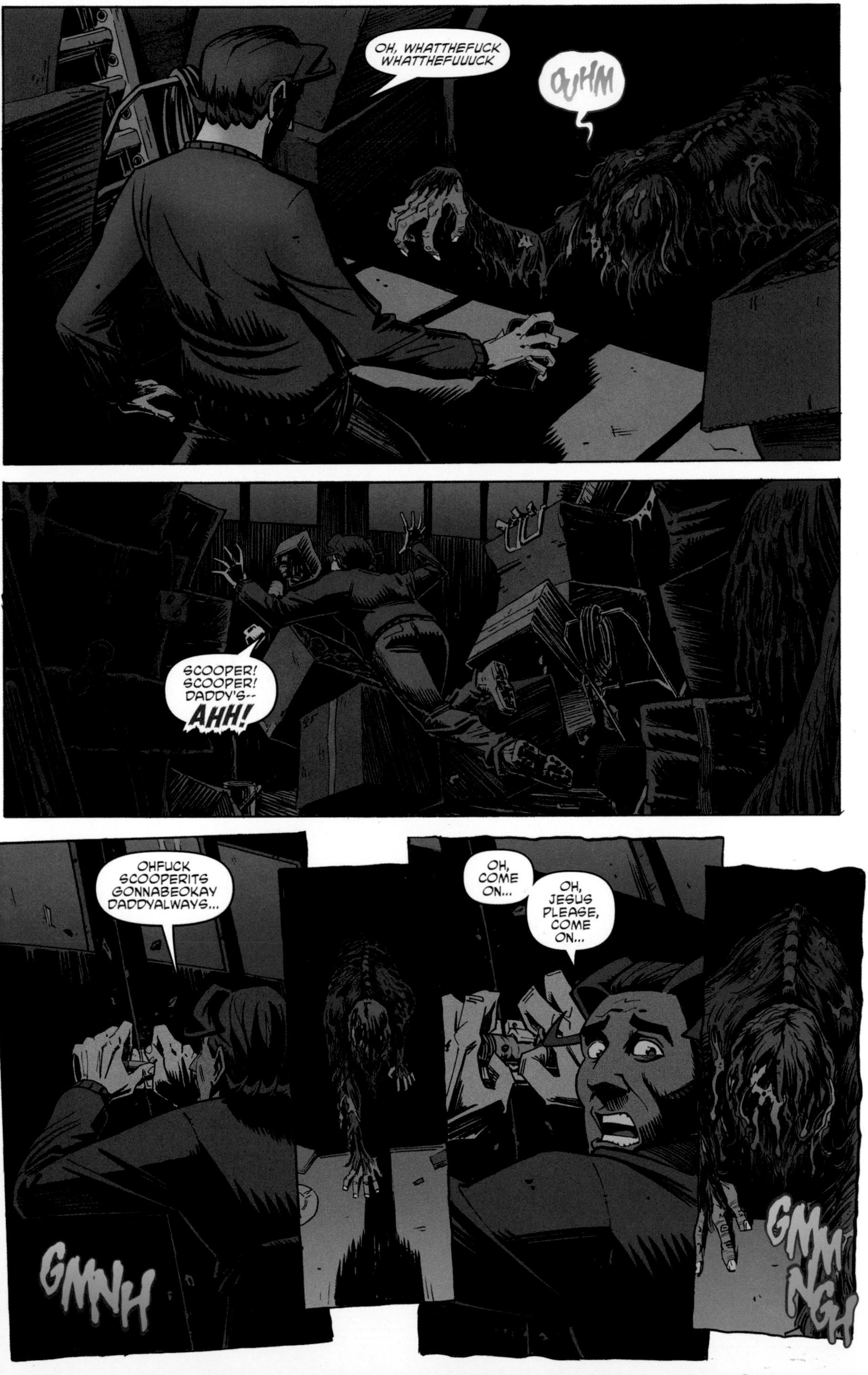
OH, WHATTHEFUCK WHATTHEFUUUCK
OUHM
SCOOPER! SCOOPER! DADDY'S-- AHH!
OHFUCK SCOOPERITS GONNABEOKAY DADDYALWAYS...
OH, COME ON...
OH, JESUS PLEASE, COME ON...
GMNH
GMMNGH

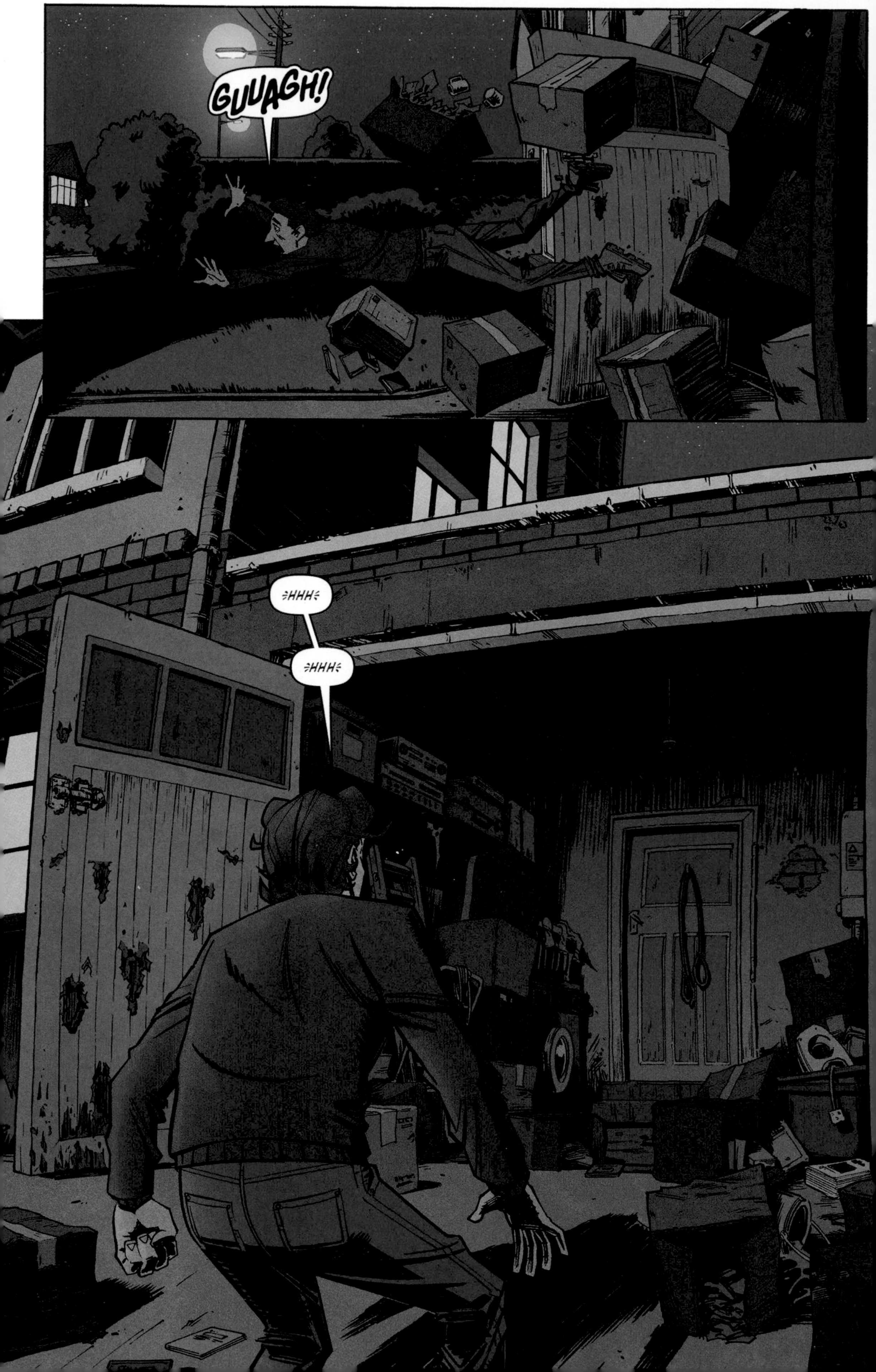
GUUAGH!
HHH
HHH

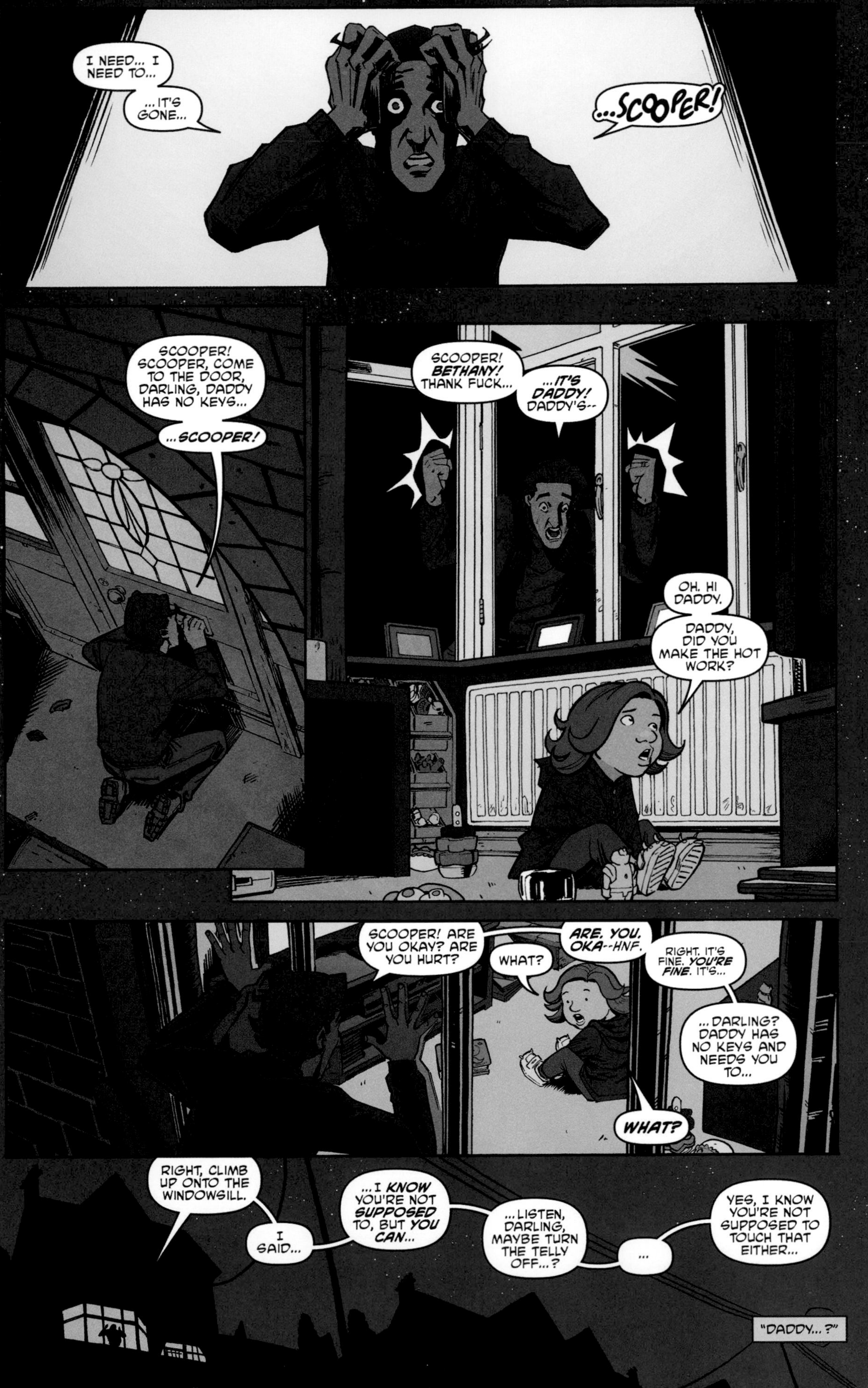
I NEED... I NEED TO...
...IT'S GONE...
...SCOOPER!
SCOOPER! SCOOPER, COME TO THE DOOR, DARLING, DADDY HAS NO KEYS...
...SCOOPER!
SCOOPER! BETHANY! THANK FUCK...
...IT'S DADDY! DADDY'S--
OH. HI DADDY.
DADDY, DID YOU MAKE THE HOT WORK?
SCOOPER! ARE YOU OKAY? ARE YOU HURT?
WHAT?
ARE. YOU. OKA--HNF.
RIGHT. IT'S FINE. YOU'RE FINE. IT'S...
...DARLING? DADDY HAS NO KEYS AND NEEDS YOU TO...
WHAT?
RIGHT, CLIMB UP ONTO THE WINDOWSILL.
I SAID...
...I KNOW YOU'RE NOT SUPPOSED TO, BUT YOU CAN...
...LISTEN, DARLING, MAYBE TURN THE TELLY OFF...?
...
YES, I KNOW YOU'RE NOT SUPPOSED TO TOUCH THAT EITHER...
"DADDY...?"

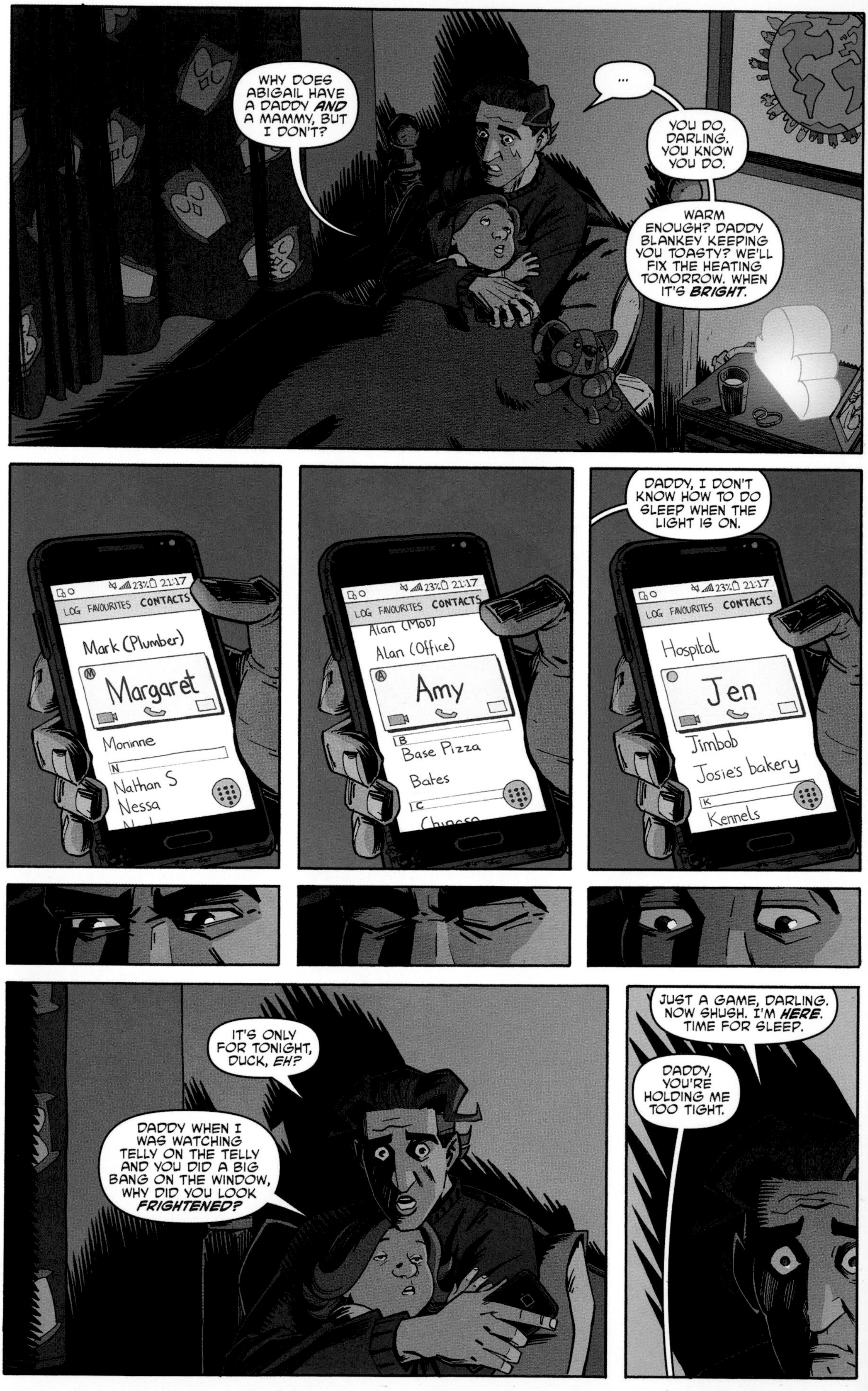
WHY DOES ABIGAIL HAVE A DADDY *AND* A MAMMY, BUT I DON'T?
...
YOU DO, DARLING. YOU KNOW YOU DO.
WARM ENOUGH? DADDY BLANKEY KEEPING YOU TOASTY? WE'LL FIX THE HEATING TOMORROW. WHEN IT'S ***BRIGHT.***
23% 21:17
LOG FAVOURITES CONTACTS
Mark (Plumber)
Margaret
Moninne
N
Nathan S
Nessa
23% 21:17
LOG FAVOURITES CONTACTS
Alan (Office)
Amy
B
Base Pizza
Bates
C
DADDY, I DON'T KNOW HOW TO DO SLEEP WHEN THE LIGHT IS ON.
23% 21:17
LOG FAVOURITES CONTACTS
Hospital
Jen
Jimbob
Josie's bakery
K
Kennels
IT'S ONLY FOR TONIGHT, DUCK, *EH?*
DADDY WHEN I WAS WATCHING TELLY ON THE TELLY AND YOU DID A BIG BANG ON THE WINDOW, WHY DID YOU LOOK ***FRIGHTENED?***
JUST A GAME, DARLING. NOW SHUSH. I'M ***HERE.*** TIME FOR SLEEP.
DADDY, YOU'RE HOLDING ME TOO TIGHT.

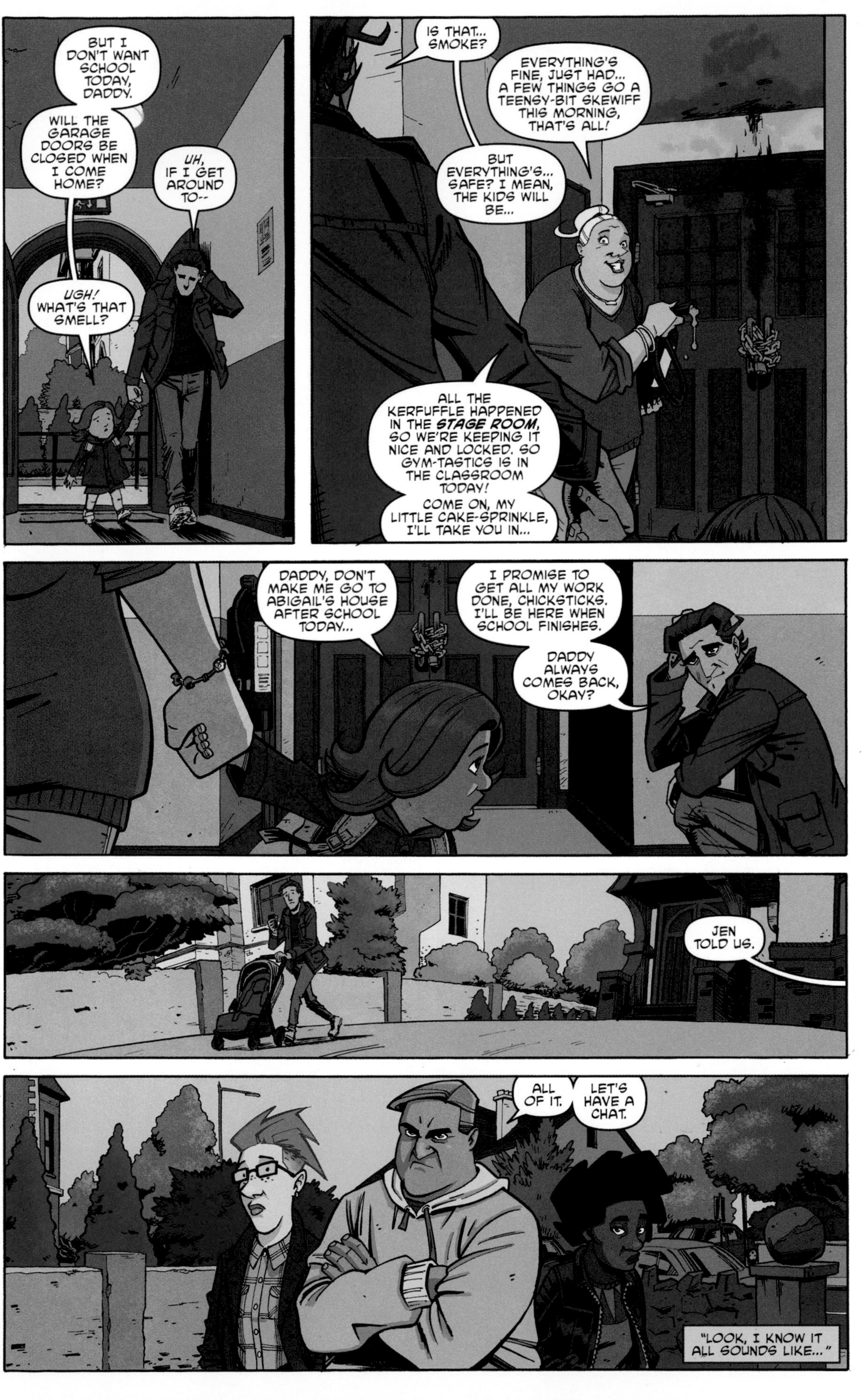
BUT I DON'T WANT SCHOOL TODAY, DADDY.
WILL THE GARAGE DOORS BE CLOSED WHEN I COME HOME?
UH, IF I GET AROUND TO--
UGH! WHAT'S THAT SMELL?
IS THAT... SMOKE?
EVERYTHING'S FINE, JUST HAD... A FEW THINGS GO A TEENSY-BIT SKEWIFF THIS MORNING, THAT'S ALL!
BUT EVERYTHING'S... SAFE? I MEAN, THE KIDS WILL BE...
ALL THE KERFUFFLE HAPPENED IN THE STAGE ROOM, SO WE'RE KEEPING IT NICE AND LOCKED. SO GYM-TASTICS IS IN THE CLASSROOM TODAY!
COME ON, MY LITTLE CAKE-SPRINKLE, I'LL TAKE YOU IN...
DADDY, DON'T MAKE ME GO TO ABIGAIL'S HOUSE AFTER SCHOOL TODAY...
I PROMISE TO GET ALL MY WORK DONE, CHICKSTICKS. I'LL BE HERE WHEN SCHOOL FINISHES.
DADDY ALWAYS COMES BACK, OKAY?
JEN TOLD US.
ALL OF IT.
LET'S HAVE A CHAT.
"LOOK, I KNOW IT ALL SOUNDS LIKE..."

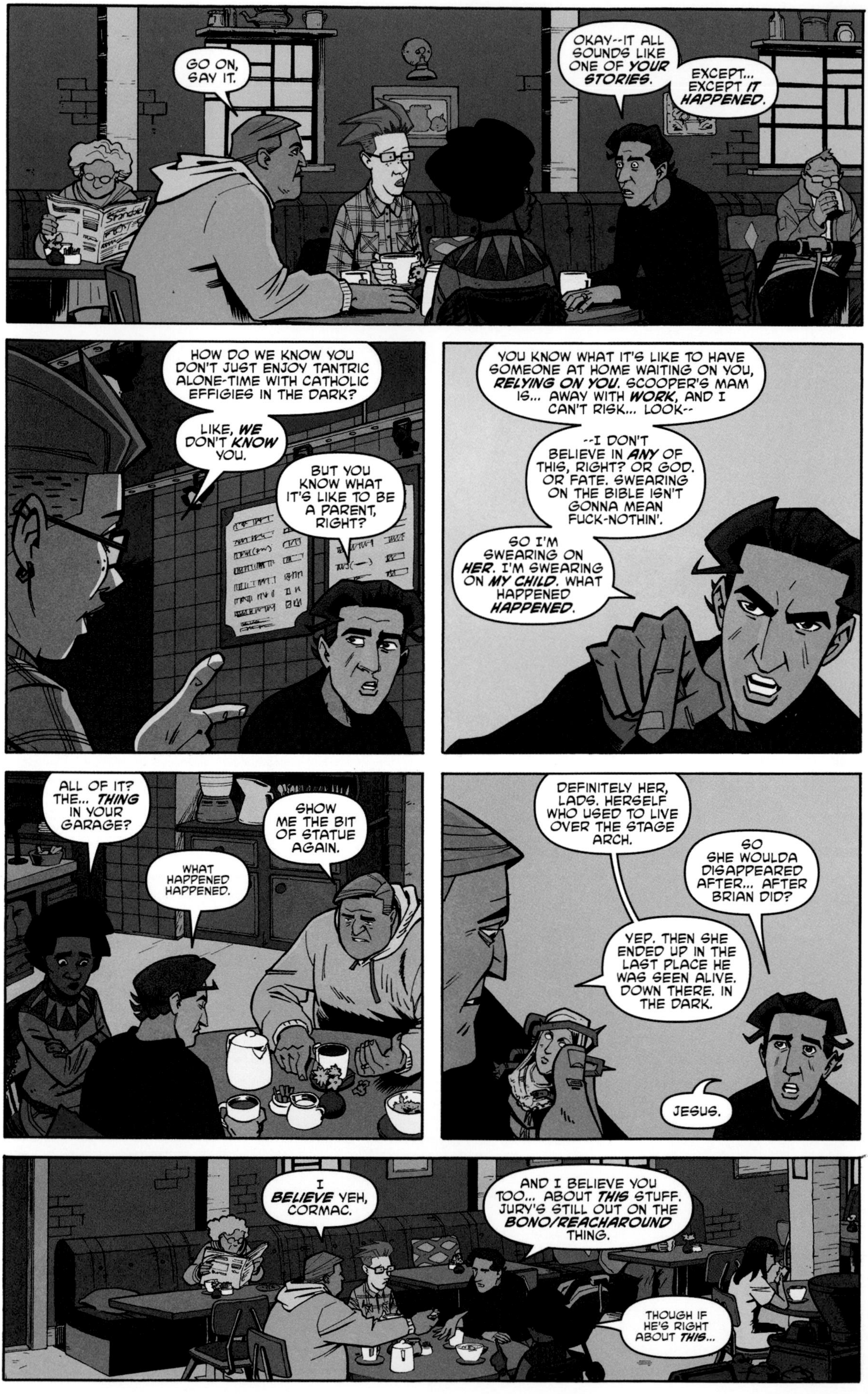

GO ON, SAY IT.
OKAY--IT ALL SOUNDS LIKE ONE OF YOUR STORIES.
EXCEPT... EXCEPT IT HAPPENED.
HOW DO WE KNOW YOU DON'T JUST ENJOY TANTRIC ALONE-TIME WITH CATHOLIC EFFIGIES IN THE DARK?
LIKE, WE DON'T KNOW YOU.
BUT YOU KNOW WHAT IT'S LIKE TO BE A PARENT, RIGHT?
YOU KNOW WHAT IT'S LIKE TO HAVE SOMEONE AT HOME WAITING ON YOU, RELYING ON YOU. SCOOPER'S MAM IS... AWAY WITH WORK, AND I CAN'T RISK... LOOK--
--I DON'T BELIEVE IN ANY OF THIS, RIGHT? OR GOD. OR FATE. SWEARING ON THE BIBLE ISN'T GONNA MEAN FUCK-NOTHIN'.
SO I'M SWEARING ON HER. I'M SWEARING ON MY CHILD. WHAT HAPPENED HAPPENED.
ALL OF IT? THE... THING IN YOUR GARAGE?
WHAT HAPPENED HAPPENED.
SHOW ME THE BIT OF STATUE AGAIN.
DEFINITELY HER, LADS. HERSELF WHO USED TO LIVE OVER THE STAGE ARCH.
SO SHE WOULDA DISAPPEARED AFTER... AFTER BRIAN DID?
YEP. THEN SHE ENDED UP IN THE LAST PLACE HE WAS SEEN ALIVE. DOWN THERE. IN THE DARK.
JESUS.
I BELIEVE YEH, CORMAC.
AND I BELIEVE YOU TOO... ABOUT THIS STUFF. JURY'S STILL OUT ON THE BONO/REACHAROUND THING.
THOUGH IF HE'S RIGHT ABOUT THIS...

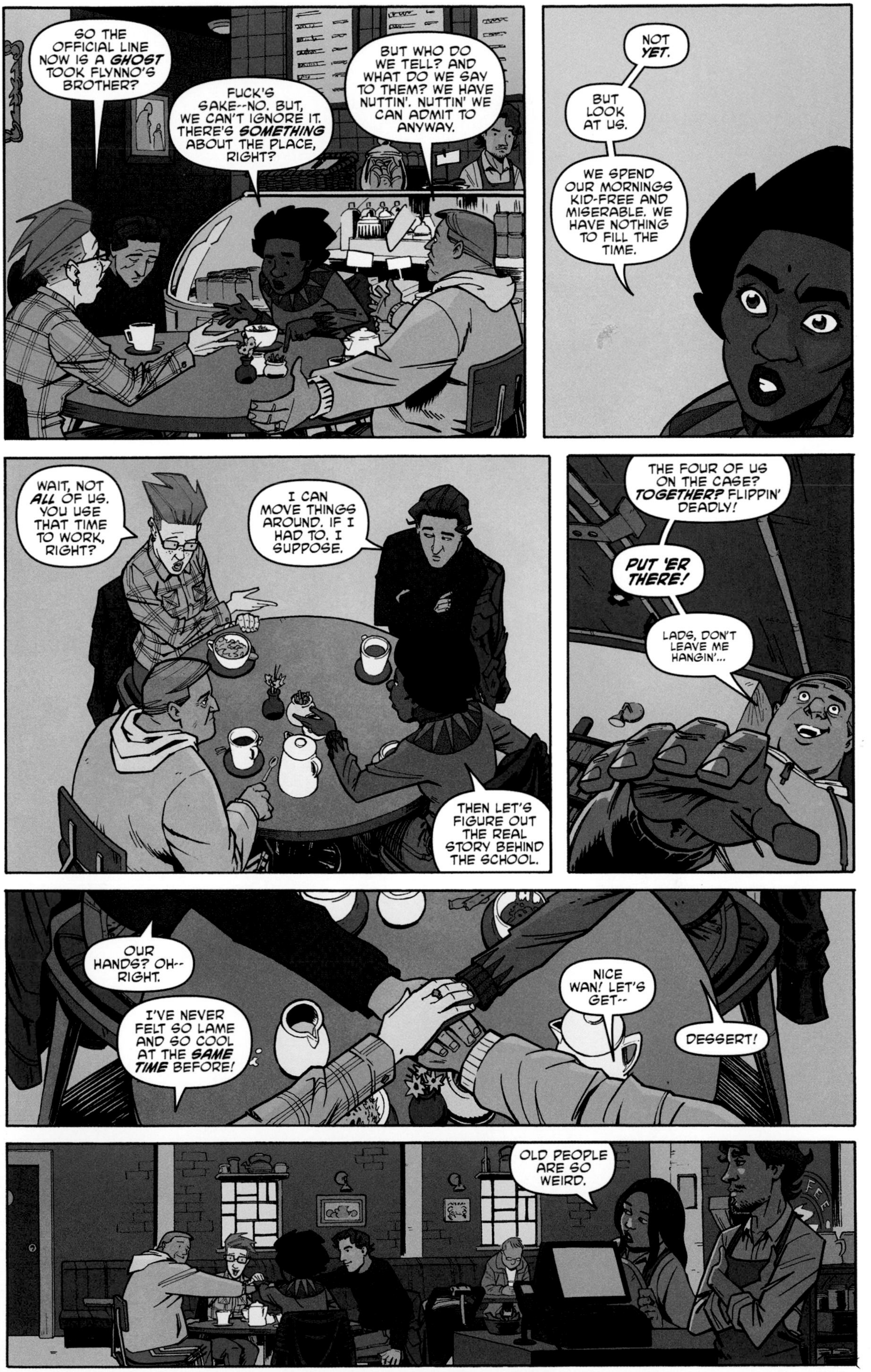
SO THE OFFICIAL LINE NOW IS A **GHOST** TOOK FLYNNO'S BROTHER?
FUCK'S SAKE--NO. BUT, WE CAN'T IGNORE IT. THERE'S **SOMETHING** ABOUT THE PLACE, RIGHT?
BUT WHO DO WE TELL? AND WHAT DO WE SAY TO THEM? WE HAVE NUTTIN'. NUTTIN' WE CAN ADMIT TO ANYWAY.
NOT **YET**.
BUT LOOK AT US.
WE SPEND OUR MORNINGS KID-FREE AND MISERABLE. WE HAVE NOTHING TO FILL THE TIME.
WAIT, NOT **ALL** OF US. YOU USE THAT TIME TO WORK, RIGHT?
I CAN MOVE THINGS AROUND. IF I HAD TO. I SUPPOSE.
THEN LET'S FIGURE OUT THE REAL STORY BEHIND THE SCHOOL.
THE FOUR OF US ON THE CASE? **TOGETHER?** FLIPPIN' DEADLY!
PUT 'ER THERE!
LADS, DON'T LEAVE ME HANGIN'...
OUR HANDS? OH-- RIGHT.
I'VE NEVER FELT SO LAME AND SO COOL AT THE **SAME TIME** BEFORE!
NICE WAN! LET'S GET--
DESSERT!
OLD PEOPLE ARE SO WEIRD.

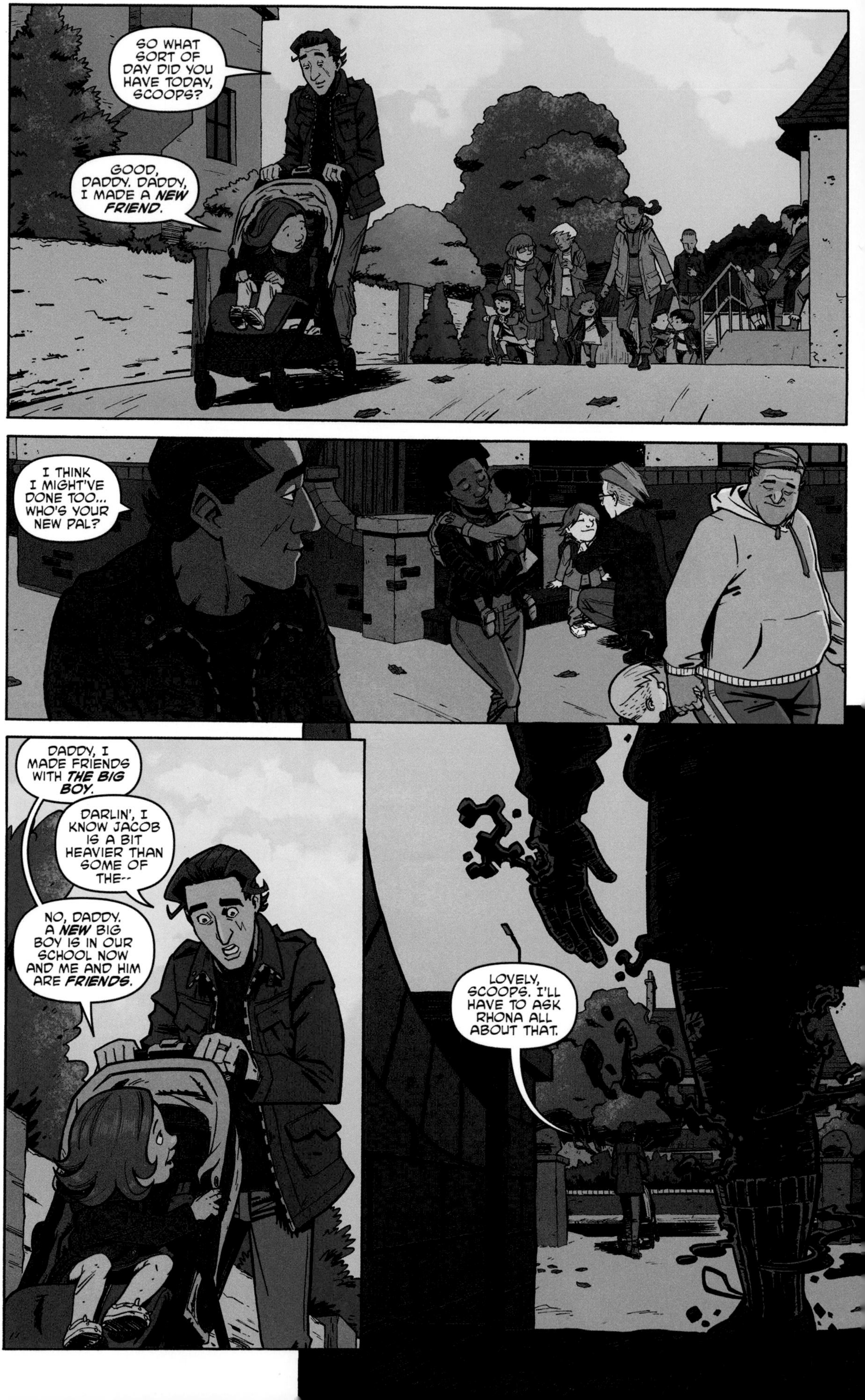
SO WHAT SORT OF DAY DID YOU HAVE TODAY, SCOOPS?
GOOD, DADDY. DADDY, I MADE A NEW FRIEND.
I THINK I MIGHT'VE DONE TOO... WHO'S YOUR NEW PAL?
DADDY, I MADE FRIENDS WITH THE BIG BOY.
DARLIN', I KNOW JACOB IS A BIT HEAVIER THAN SOME OF THE--
NO, DADDY. A NEW BIG BOY IS IN OUR SCHOOL NOW AND ME AND HIM ARE FRIENDS.
LOVELY, SCOOPS. I'LL HAVE TO ASK RHONA ALL ABOUT THAT.

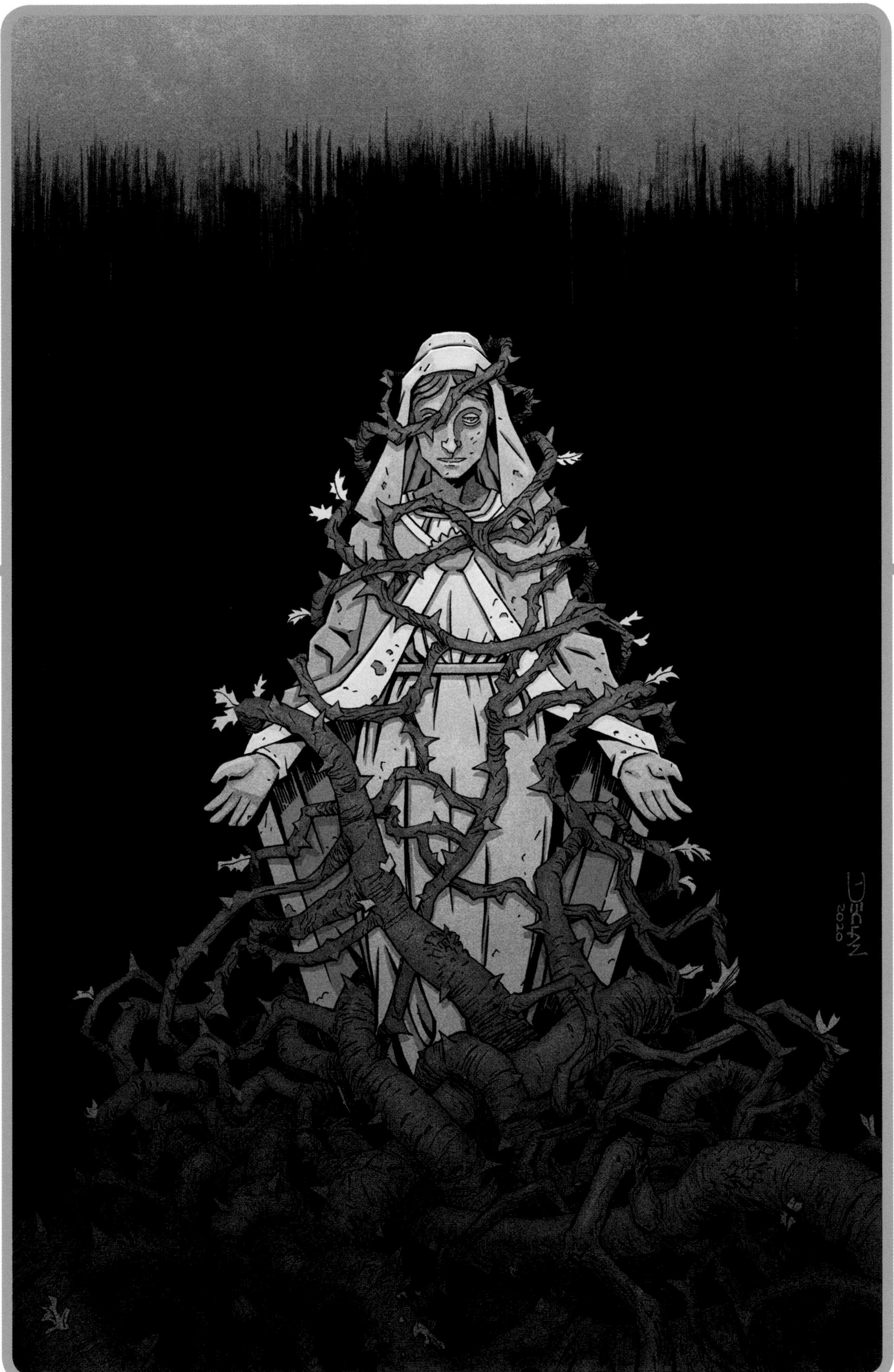
DECLAN
2020

Art by
DECLAN SHALVEY

Colors by
CHRIS O'HALLORAN

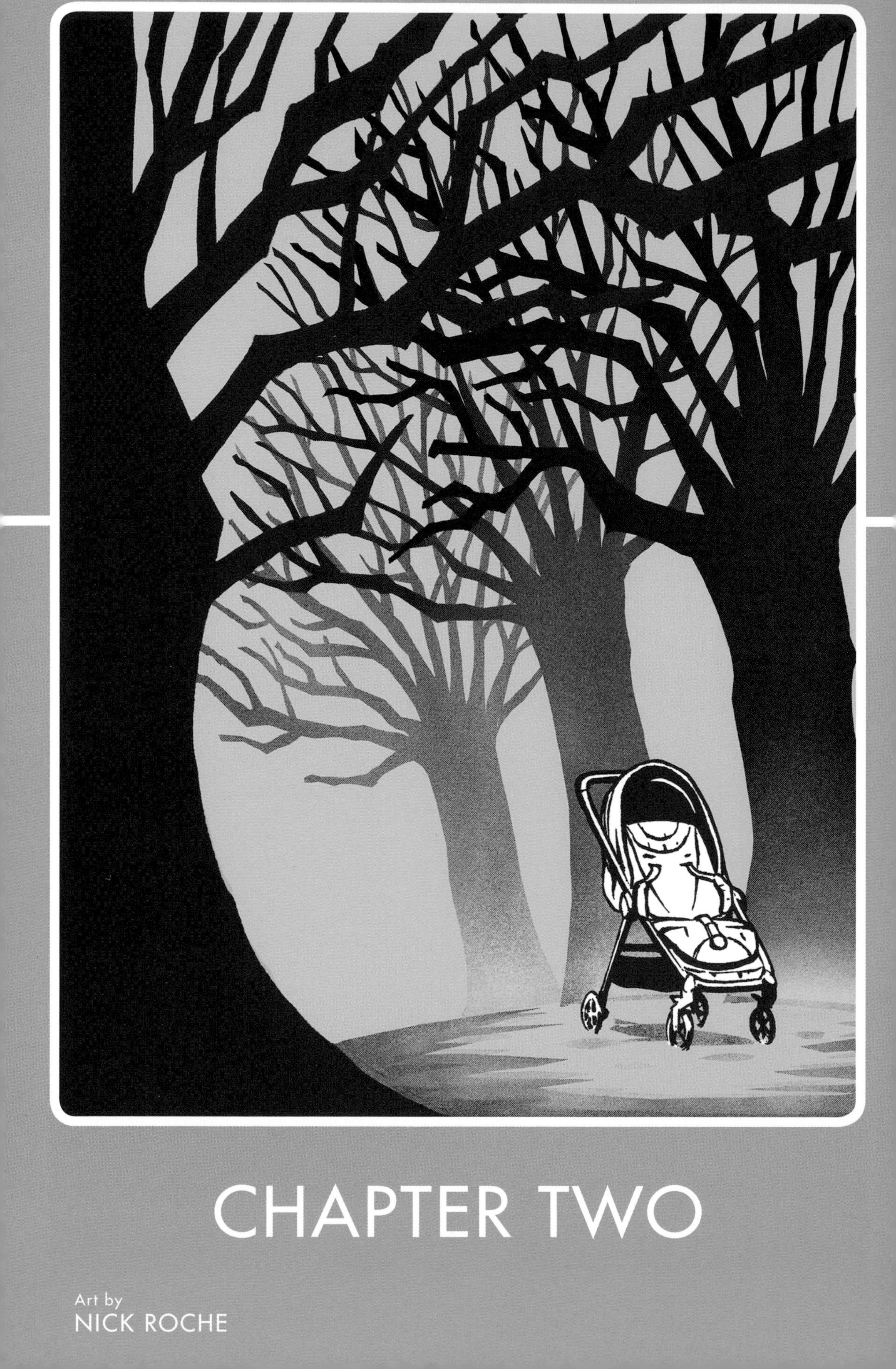

CHAPTER TWO

Art by
NICK ROCHE

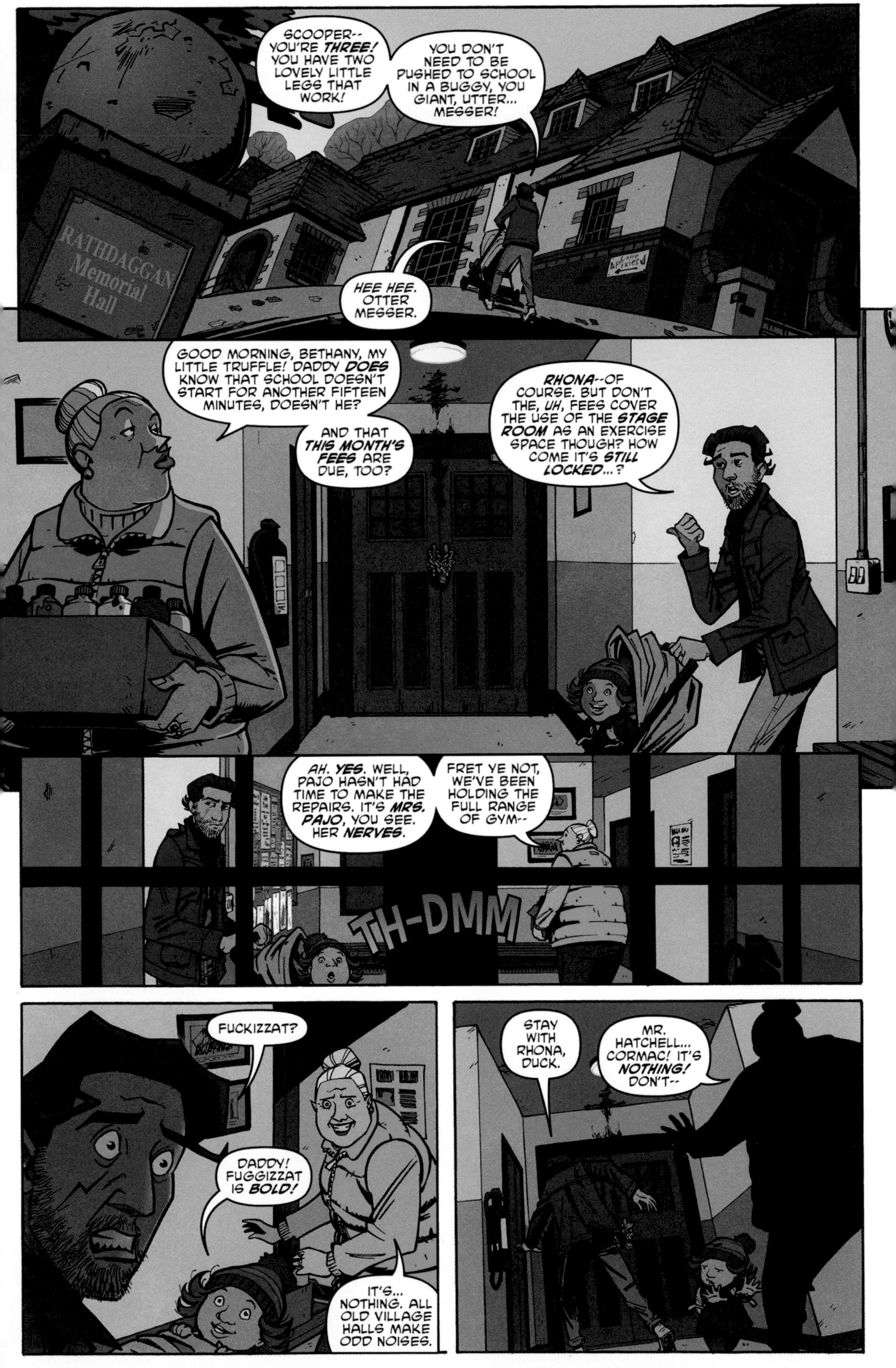
SCOOPER-- YOU'RE THREE! YOU HAVE TWO LOVELY LITTLE LEGS THAT WORK!
YOU DON'T NEED TO BE PUSHED TO SCHOOL IN A BUGGY, YOU GIANT, UTTER... MESSER!
RATHDAGGAN Memorial Hall
HEE HEE. OTTER MESSER.
GOOD MORNING, BETHANY, MY LITTLE TRUFFLE! DADDY DOES KNOW THAT SCHOOL DOESN'T START FOR ANOTHER FIFTEEN MINUTES, DOESN'T HE?
AND THAT THIS MONTH'S FEES ARE DUE, TOO?
RHONA--OF COURSE. BUT DON'T THE, UH, FEES COVER THE USE OF THE STAGE ROOM AS AN EXERCISE SPACE THOUGH? HOW COME IT'S STILL LOCKED...?
AH. YES. WELL, PAJO HASN'T HAD TIME TO MAKE THE REPAIRS. IT'S MRS. PAJO, YOU SEE. HER NERVES.
FRET YE NOT, WE'VE BEEN HOLDING THE FULL RANGE OF GYM--
TH-DMM
FUCKIZZAT?
DADDY! FUGGIZZAT IS BOLD!
IT'S... NOTHING. ALL OLD VILLAGE HALLS MAKE ODD NOISES.
STAY WITH RHONA, DUCK.
MR. HATCHELL... CORMAC! IT'S NOTHING! DON'T--

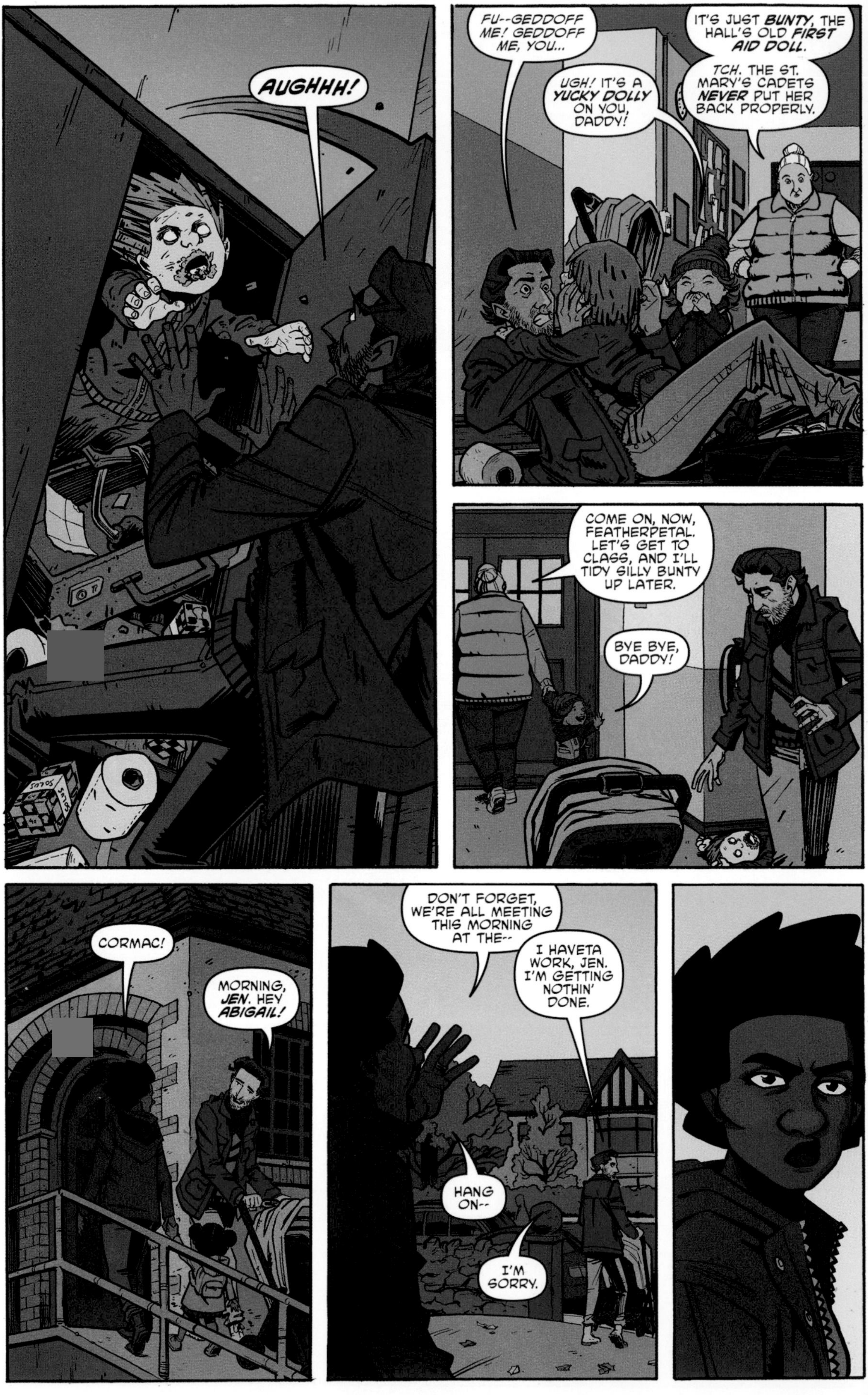
AUGHHH!
FU--GEDDOFF ME! GEDDOFF ME, YOU...
UGH! IT'S A YUCKY DOLLY ON YOU, DADDY!
IT'S JUST BUNTY, THE HALL'S OLD FIRST AID DOLL.
TCH. THE ST. MARY'S CADETS NEVER PUT HER BACK PROPERLY.
COME ON, NOW, FEATHERPETAL. LET'S GET TO CLASS, AND I'LL TIDY SILLY BUNTY UP LATER.
BYE BYE, DADDY!
CORMAC!
MORNING, JEN. HEY ABIGAIL!
DON'T FORGET, WE'RE ALL MEETING THIS MORNING AT THE--
I HAVETA WORK, JEN. I'M GETTING NOTHIN' DONE.
HANG ON--
I'M SORRY.

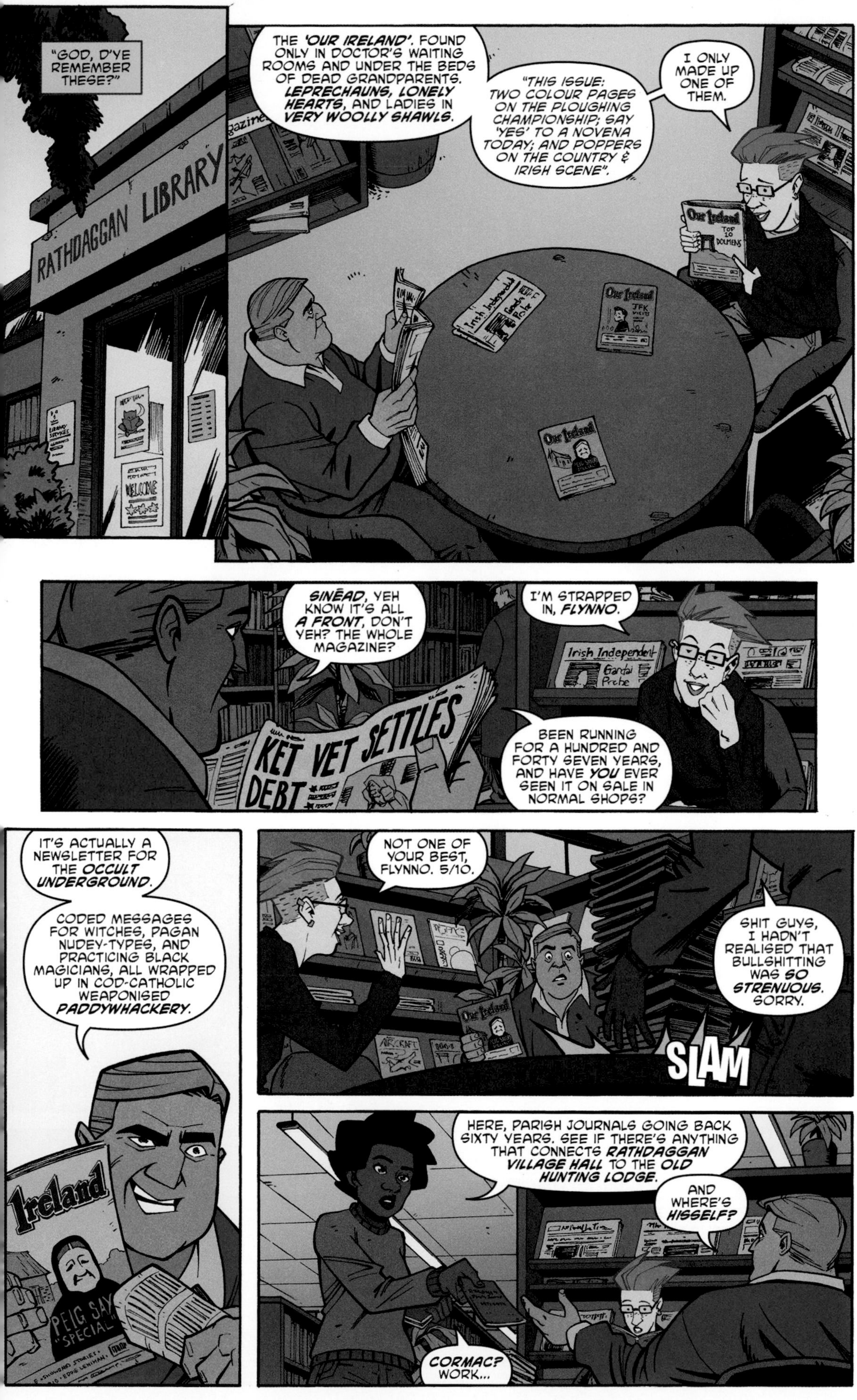
"GOD, D'YE REMEMBER THESE?"
RATHDAGGAN LIBRARY
THE 'OUR IRELAND'. FOUND ONLY IN DOCTOR'S WAITING ROOMS AND UNDER THE BEDS OF DEAD GRANDPARENTS. LEPRECHAUNS, LONELY HEARTS, AND LADIES IN VERY WOOLLY SHAWLS.
"THIS ISSUE: TWO COLOUR PAGES ON THE PLOUGHING CHAMPIONSHIP; SAY 'YES' TO A NOVENA TODAY; AND POPPERS ON THE COUNTRY & IRISH SCENE".
I ONLY MADE UP ONE OF THEM.
Our Ireland TOP 10 DOLMENS
SINÉAD, YEH KNOW IT'S ALL A FRONT, DON'T YEH? THE WHOLE MAGAZINE?
I'M STRAPPED IN, FLYNNO.
Irish Independent Gardai Probe
KET VET SETTLES DEBT
BEEN RUNNING FOR A HUNDRED AND FORTY SEVEN YEARS, AND HAVE YOU EVER SEEN IT ON SALE IN NORMAL SHOPS?
IT'S ACTUALLY A NEWSLETTER FOR THE OCCULT UNDERGROUND.
CODED MESSAGES FOR WITCHES, PAGAN NUDEY-TYPES, AND PRACTICING BLACK MAGICIANS, ALL WRAPPED UP IN COD-CATHOLIC WEAPONISED PADDYWHACKERY.
Ireland
PEIG SAY "SPECIAL"
NOT ONE OF YOUR BEST, FLYNNO. 5/10.
SHIT GUYS, I HADN'T REALISED THAT BULLSHITTING WAS SO STRENUOUS. SORRY.
SLAM
HERE, PARISH JOURNALS GOING BACK SIXTY YEARS. SEE IF THERE'S ANYTHING THAT CONNECTS RATHDAGGAN VILLAGE HALL TO THE OLD HUNTING LODGE.
AND WHERE'S HISSELF?
CORMAC? WORK...

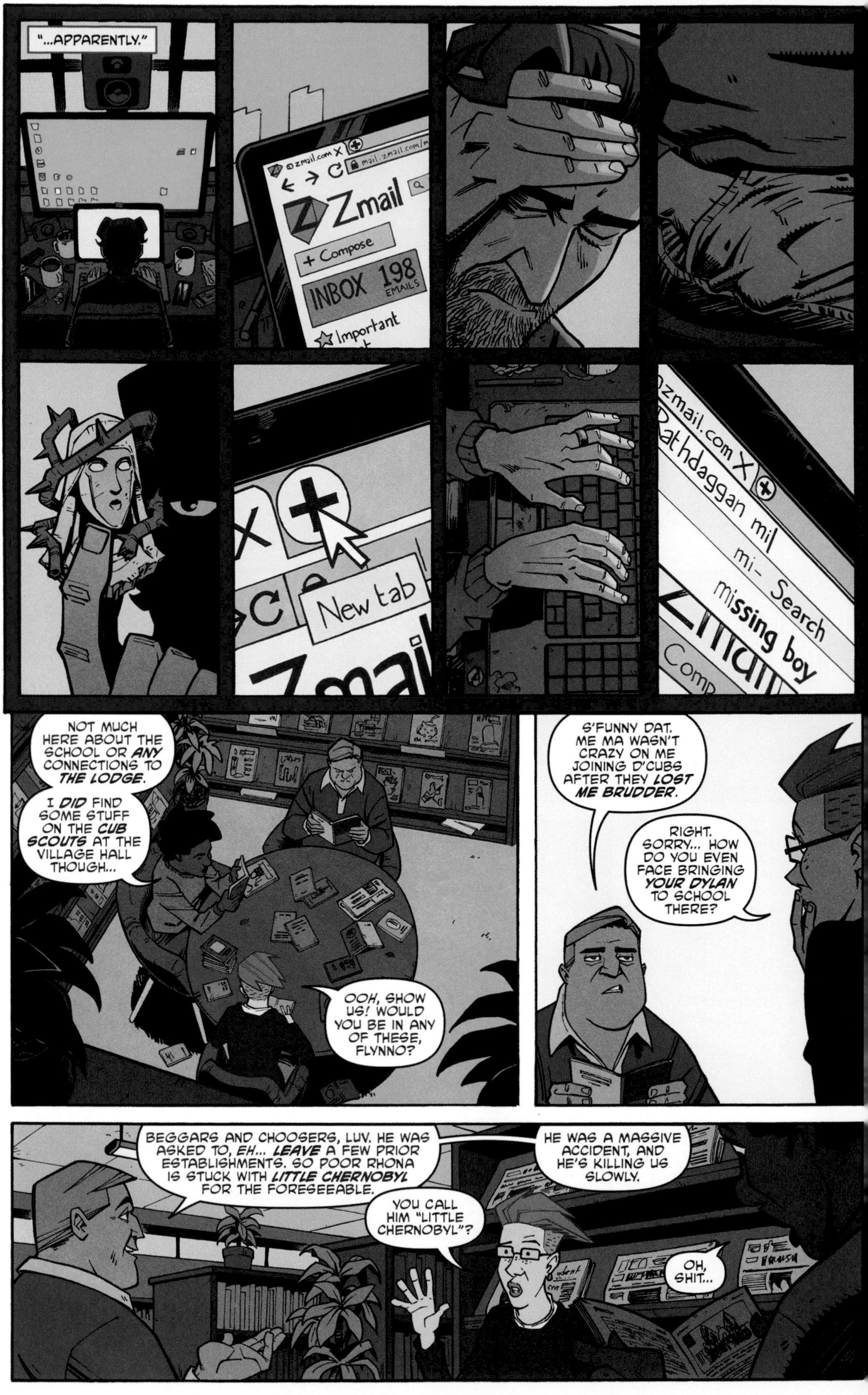

"...APPARENTLY."
zmail.com
mail.zmail.com
Zmail
+ Compose
INBOX 198 EMAILS
Important
New tab
Zmail
zmail.com
Rathdaggan mil
mi- Search
missing boy
Comp
NOT MUCH HERE ABOUT THE SCHOOL OR ANY CONNECTIONS TO THE LODGE.
I DID FIND SOME STUFF ON THE CUB SCOUTS AT THE VILLAGE HALL THOUGH...
OOH, SHOW US! WOULD YOU BE IN ANY OF THESE, FLYNNO?
S'FUNNY DAT. ME MA WASN'T CRAZY ON ME JOINING D'CUBS AFTER THEY LOST ME BRUDDER.
RIGHT. SORRY... HOW DO YOU EVEN FACE BRINGING YOUR DYLAN TO SCHOOL THERE?
BEGGARS AND CHOOSERS, LUV. HE WAS ASKED TO, EH... LEAVE A FEW PRIOR ESTABLISHMENTS. SO POOR RHONA IS STUCK WITH LITTLE CHERNOBYL FOR THE FORESEEABLE.
HE WAS A MASSIVE ACCIDENT, AND HE'S KILLING US SLOWLY.
YOU CALL HIM "LITTLE CHERNOBYL"?
OH, SHIT...

WHAT IS IT, JEN?

IT'S JUST...

YOUR *BROTHER*, FLYNNO...

...I FOUND A PICTURE OF *BRIAN*.

osey, Brian Flynn

...ish archive

...anoir... X | Haunted Ire... X | Celtic

...land%-unsolved/

UNSOLVED

07,837 Views!

Guestbook

Fr Mannix Sinnott offering mass for the missing Brian Flynn

...ts-of-dublin-list/

Cubs... | Cubs... | Churc... | Parish...

Tak... | Lost... | Churc... | Aw...

https:// hiddenireland

Hidden Irelan

The Devil and The Disappeared

Ghosts of Rathdoggan

13:01

SHIT.

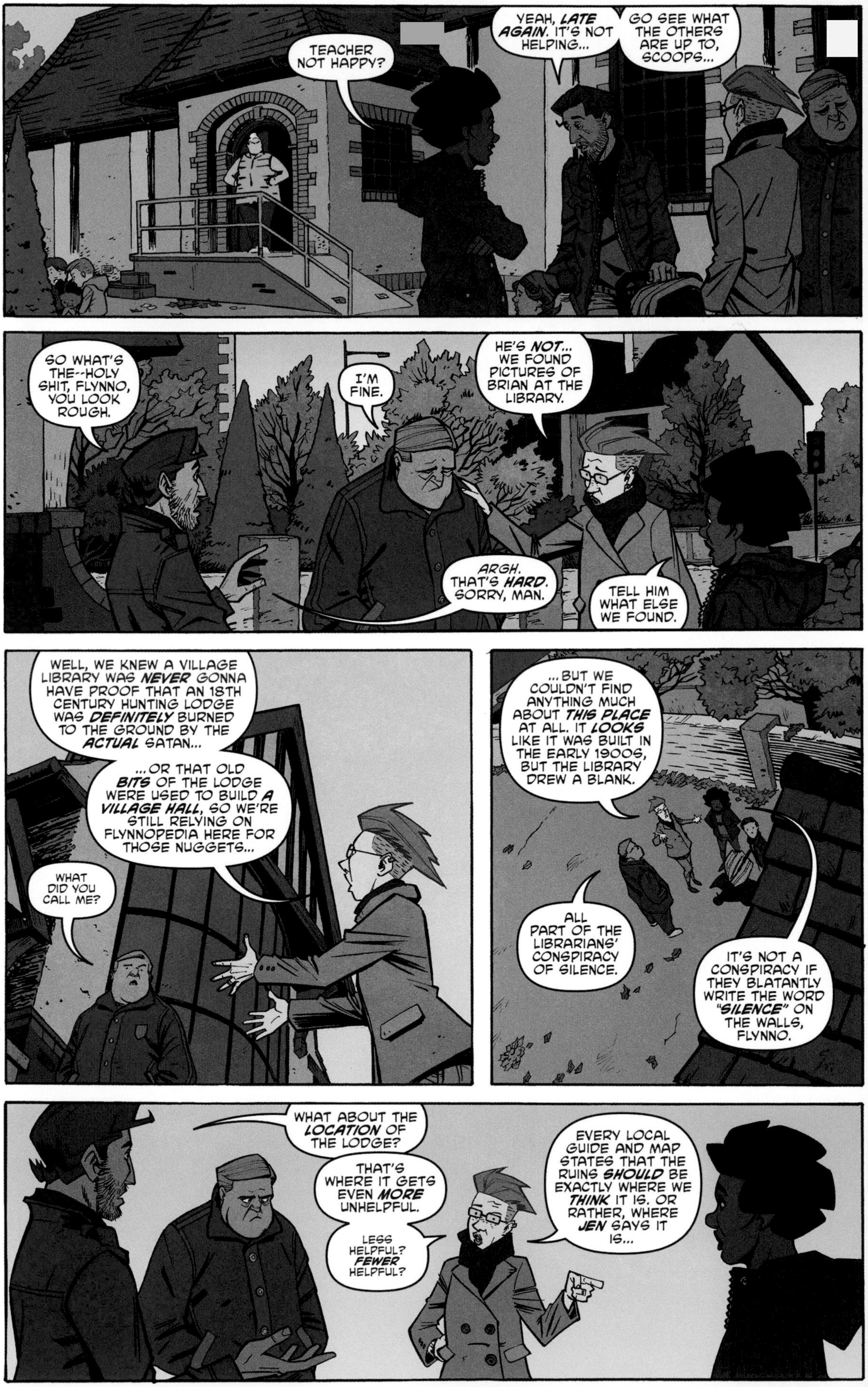
TEACHER NOT HAPPY?
YEAH, LATE AGAIN. IT'S NOT HELPING...
GO SEE WHAT THE OTHERS ARE UP TO, SCOOPS...
SO WHAT'S THE--HOLY SHIT, FLYNNO, YOU LOOK ROUGH.
I'M FINE.
HE'S NOT... WE FOUND PICTURES OF BRIAN AT THE LIBRARY.
ARGH. THAT'S HARD. SORRY, MAN.
TELL HIM WHAT ELSE WE FOUND.
WELL, WE KNEW A VILLAGE LIBRARY WAS NEVER GONNA HAVE PROOF THAT AN 18TH CENTURY HUNTING LODGE WAS DEFINITELY BURNED TO THE GROUND BY THE ACTUAL SATAN...
...OR THAT OLD BITS OF THE LODGE WERE USED TO BUILD A VILLAGE HALL, SO WE'RE STILL RELYING ON FLYNNOPEDIA HERE FOR THOSE NUGGETS...
WHAT DID YOU CALL ME?
...BUT WE COULDN'T FIND ANYTHING MUCH ABOUT THIS PLACE AT ALL. IT LOOKS LIKE IT WAS BUILT IN THE EARLY 1900S, BUT THE LIBRARY DREW A BLANK.
ALL PART OF THE LIBRARIANS' CONSPIRACY OF SILENCE.
IT'S NOT A CONSPIRACY IF THEY BLATANTLY WRITE THE WORD "SILENCE" ON THE WALLS, FLYNNO.
WHAT ABOUT THE LOCATION OF THE LODGE?
THAT'S WHERE IT GETS EVEN MORE UNHELPFUL.
LESS HELPFUL? FEWER HELPFUL?
EVERY LOCAL GUIDE AND MAP STATES THAT THE RUINS SHOULD BE EXACTLY WHERE WE THINK IT IS. OR RATHER, WHERE JEN SAYS IT IS...

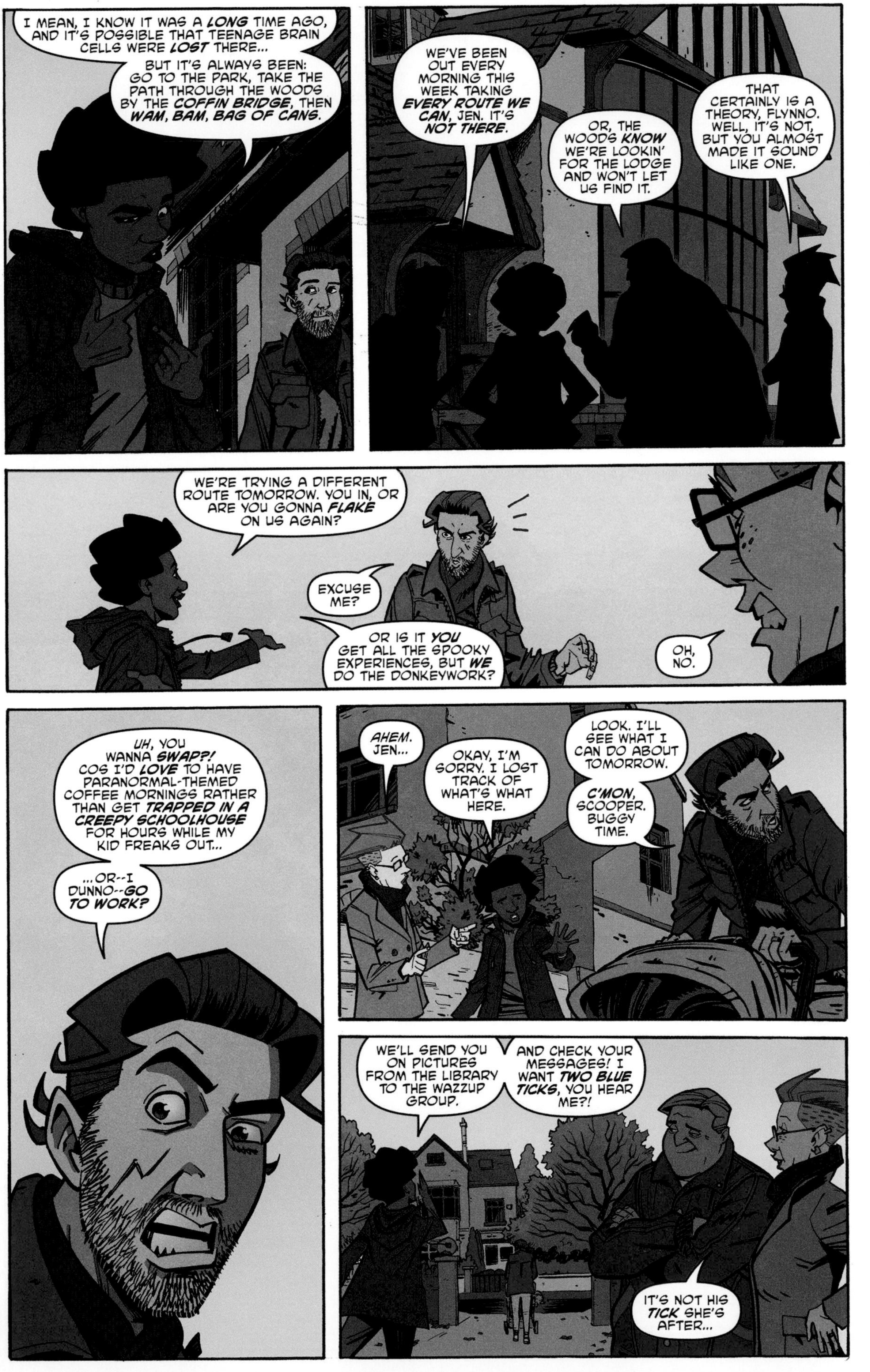

I MEAN, I KNOW IT WAS A LONG TIME AGO, AND IT'S POSSIBLE THAT TEENAGE BRAIN CELLS WERE LOST THERE...
BUT IT'S ALWAYS BEEN: GO TO THE PARK, TAKE THE PATH THROUGH THE WOODS BY THE COFFIN BRIDGE, THEN WAM, BAM, BAG OF CANS.
WE'VE BEEN OUT EVERY MORNING THIS WEEK TAKING EVERY ROUTE WE CAN, JEN. IT'S NOT THERE.
OR, THE WOODS KNOW WE'RE LOOKIN' FOR THE LODGE AND WON'T LET US FIND IT.
THAT CERTAINLY IS A THEORY, FLYNNO. WELL, IT'S NOT, BUT YOU ALMOST MADE IT SOUND LIKE ONE.
WE'RE TRYING A DIFFERENT ROUTE TOMORROW. YOU IN, OR ARE YOU GONNA FLAKE ON US AGAIN?
EXCUSE ME?
OR IS IT YOU GET ALL THE SPOOKY EXPERIENCES, BUT WE DO THE DONKEYWORK?
OH, NO.
UH, YOU WANNA SWAP?! COS I'D LOVE TO HAVE PARANORMAL-THEMED COFFEE MORNINGS RATHER THAN GET TRAPPED IN A CREEPY SCHOOLHOUSE FOR HOURS WHILE MY KID FREAKS OUT...
...OR--I DUNNO--GO TO WORK?
AHEM. JEN...
OKAY, I'M SORRY. I LOST TRACK OF WHAT'S WHAT HERE.
LOOK. I'LL SEE WHAT I CAN DO ABOUT TOMORROW.
C'MON, SCOOPER. BUGGY TIME.
WE'LL SEND YOU ON PICTURES FROM THE LIBRARY TO THE WAZZUP GROUP.
AND CHECK YOUR MESSAGES! I WANT TWO BLUE TICKS, YOU HEAR ME?!
IT'S NOT HIS TICK SHE'S AFTER...

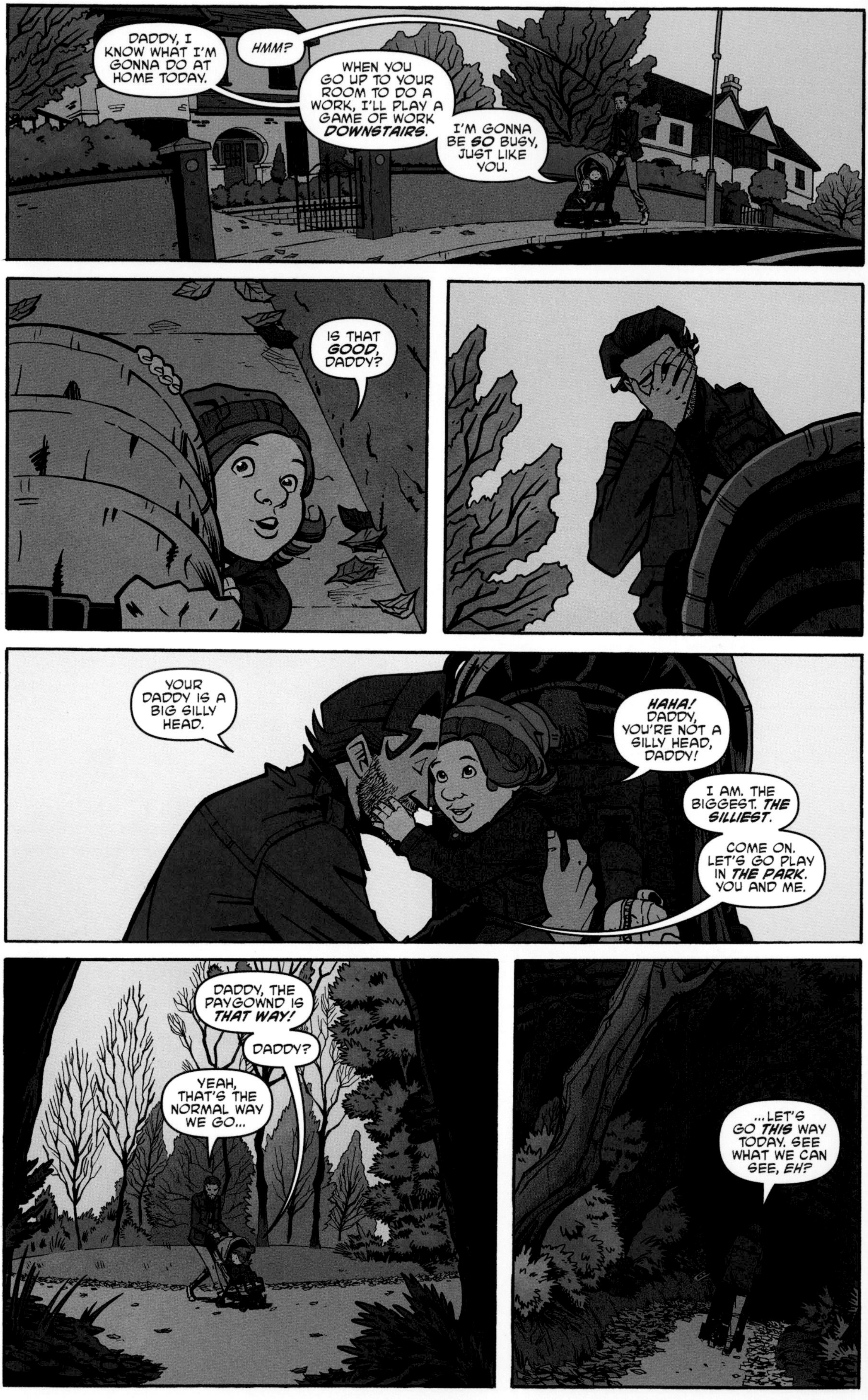
DADDY, I KNOW WHAT I'M GONNA DO AT HOME TODAY.
HMM?
WHEN YOU GO UP TO YOUR ROOM TO DO A WORK, I'LL PLAY A GAME OF WORK DOWNSTAIRS.
I'M GONNA BE SO BUSY, JUST LIKE YOU.
IS THAT GOOD, DADDY?
YOUR DADDY IS A BIG SILLY HEAD.
HAHA! DADDY, YOU'RE NOT A SILLY HEAD, DADDY!
I AM. THE BIGGEST. THE SILLIEST.
COME ON. LET'S GO PLAY IN THE PARK. YOU AND ME.
DADDY, THE PAYGOWND IS THAT WAY!
DADDY?
YEAH, THAT'S THE NORMAL WAY WE GO...
...LET'S GO THIS WAY TODAY. SEE WHAT WE CAN SEE, EH?

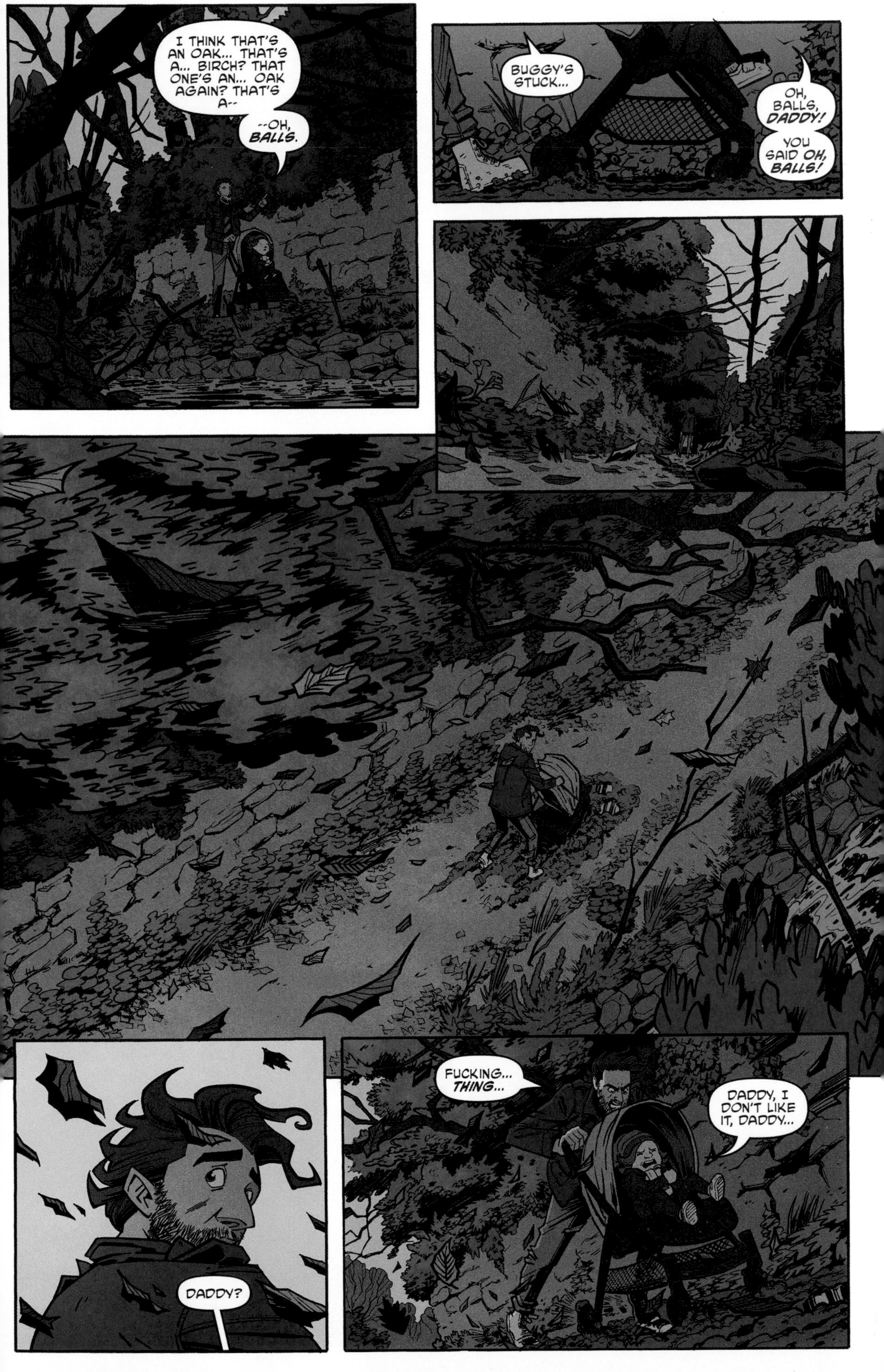
I THINK THAT'S AN OAK... THAT'S A... BIRCH? THAT ONE'S AN... OAK AGAIN? THAT'S A--
--OH, BALLS.
BUGGY'S STUCK...
OH, BALLS, DADDY!
YOU SAID OH, BALLS!
DADDY?
FUCKING... THING...
DADDY, I DON'T LIKE IT, DADDY...

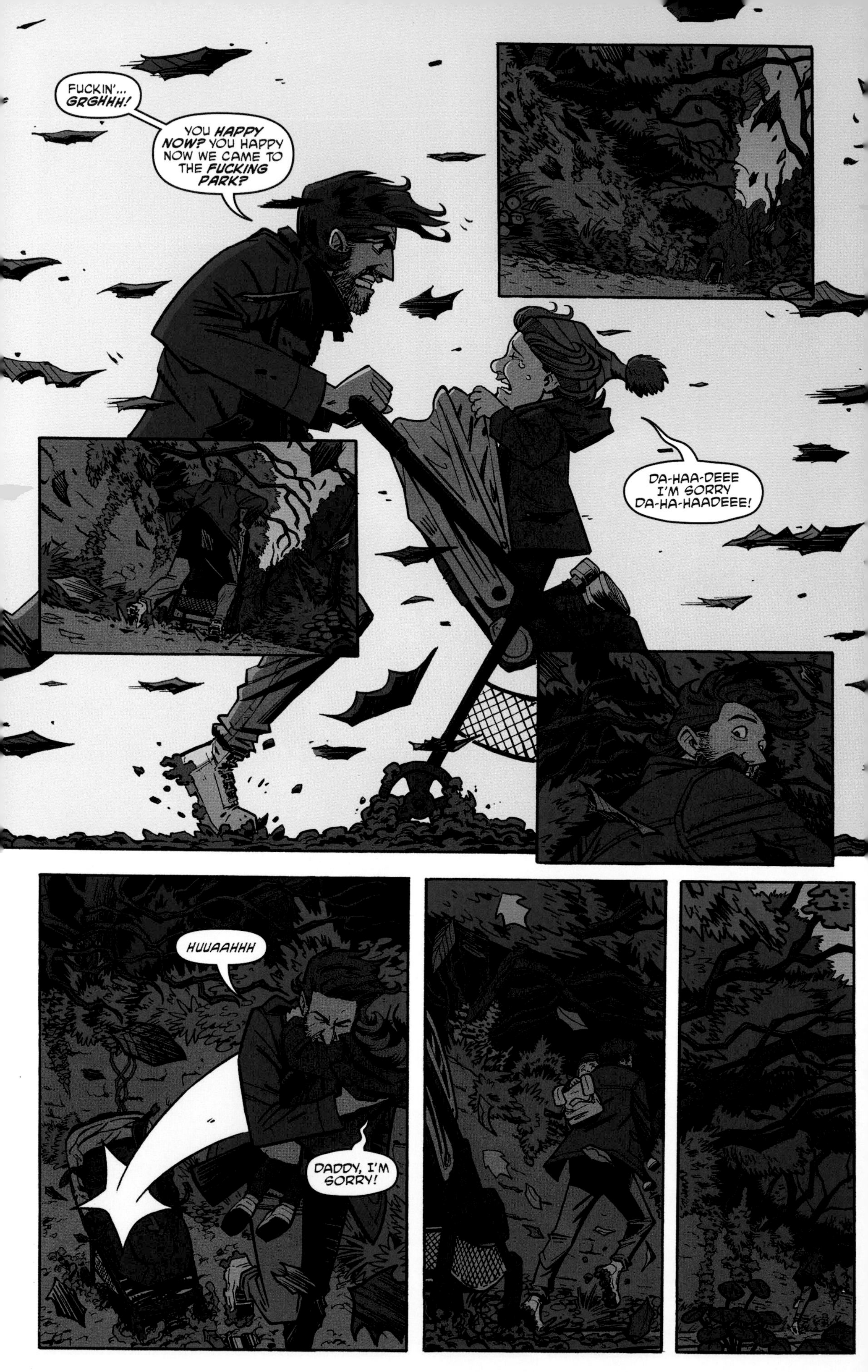
FUCKIN'... GRGHHH!
YOU HAPPY NOW? YOU HAPPY NOW WE CAME TO THE FUCKING PARK?
DA-HAA-DEEE I'M SORRY DA-HA-HAADEEE!
HUUAAHHH
DADDY, I'M SORRY!

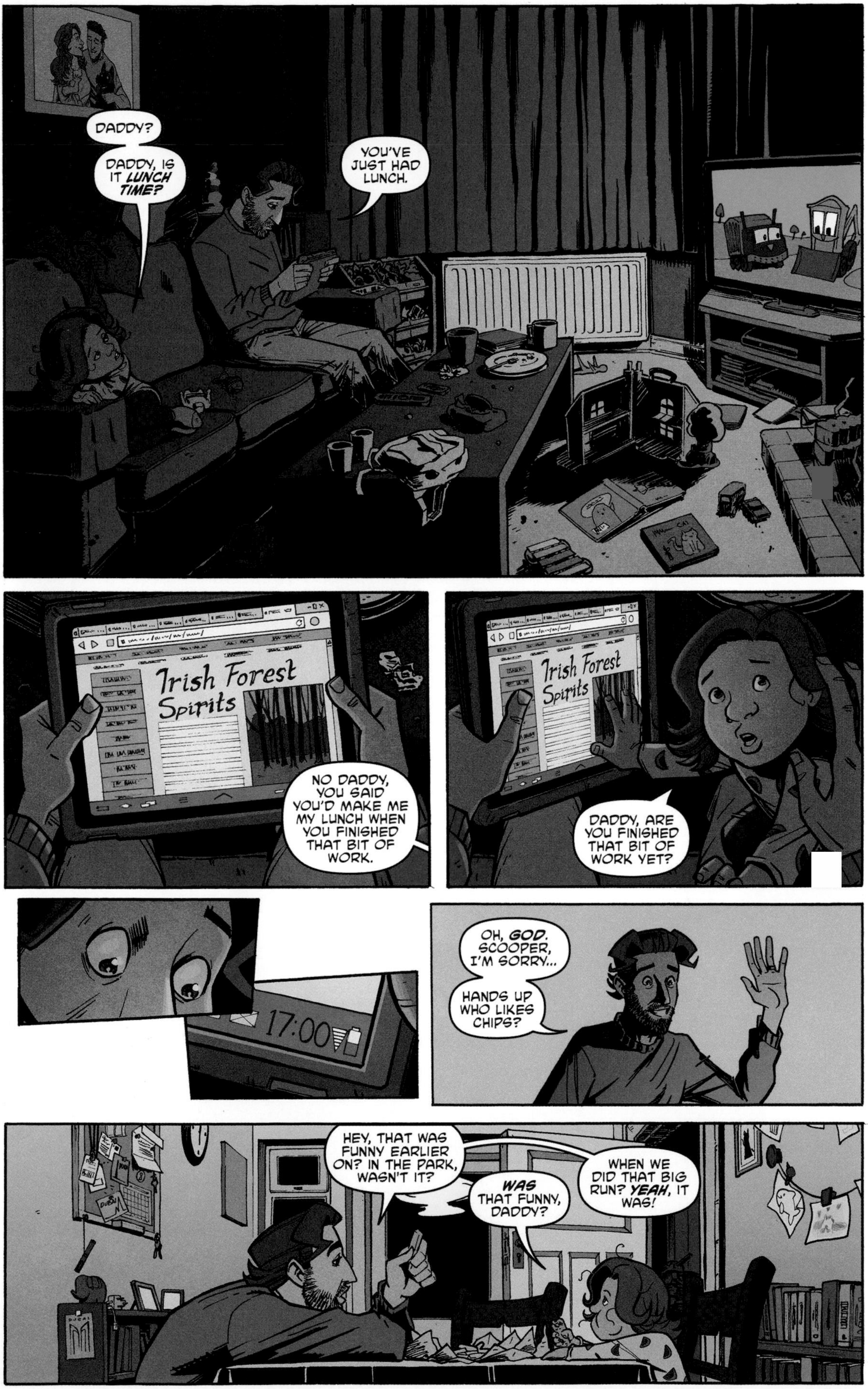
DADDY?
DADDY, IS IT LUNCH TIME?
YOU'VE JUST HAD LUNCH.
Irish Forest Spirits
NO DADDY, YOU SAID YOU'D MAKE ME MY LUNCH WHEN YOU FINISHED THAT BIT OF WORK.
Irish Forest Spirits
DADDY, ARE YOU FINISHED THAT BIT OF WORK YET?
17:00
OH, GOD. SCOOPER, I'M SORRY...
HANDS UP WHO LIKES CHIPS?
HEY, THAT WAS FUNNY EARLIER ON? IN THE PARK, WASN'T IT?
WAS THAT FUNNY, DADDY?
WHEN WE DID THAT BIG RUN? YEAH, IT WAS!

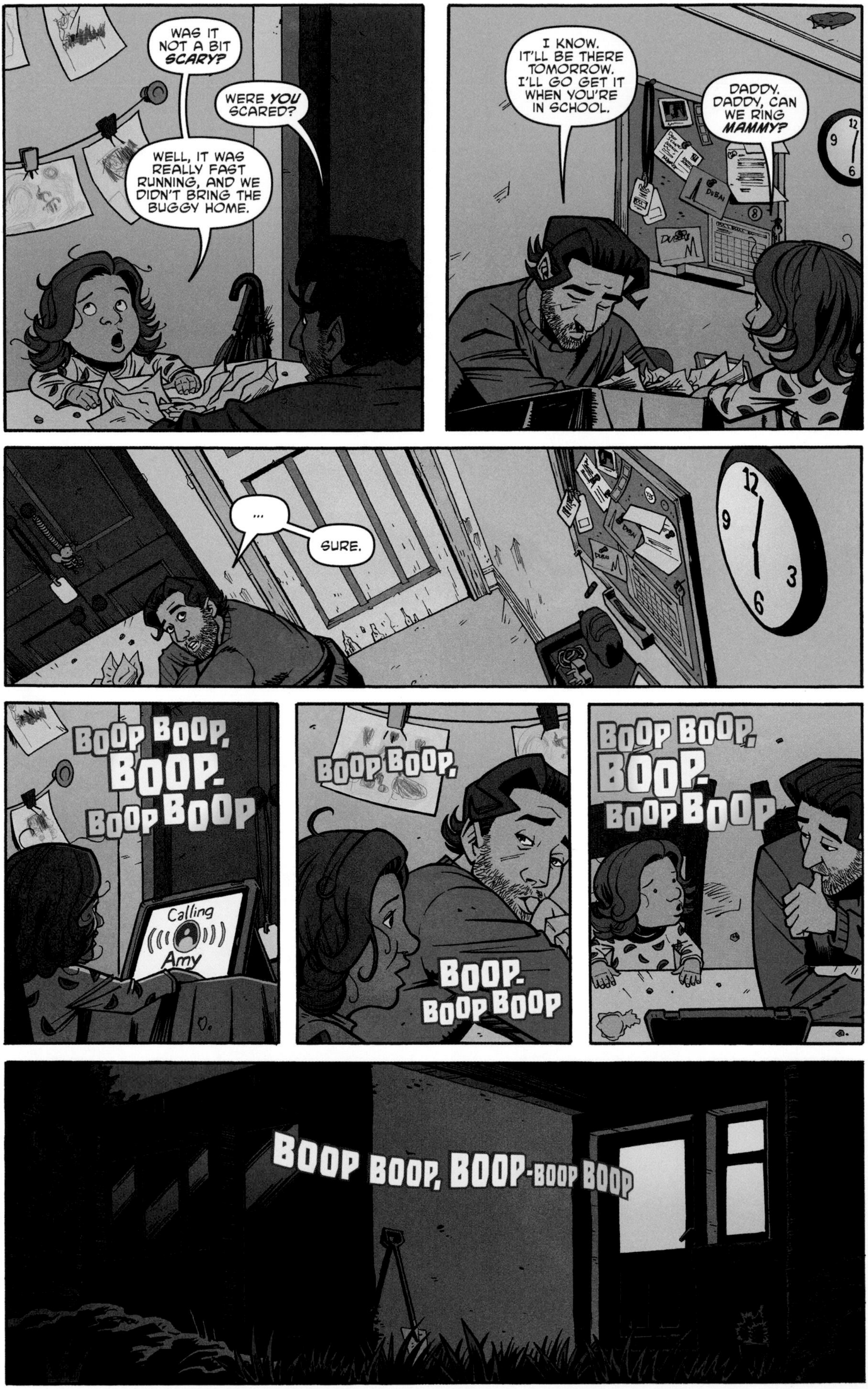
WAS IT NOT A BIT *SCARY?*
WERE *YOU* SCARED?
WELL, IT WAS REALLY FAST RUNNING, AND WE DIDN'T BRING THE BUGGY HOME.
DADDY. DADDY, CAN WE RING *MAMMY?*
I KNOW. IT'LL BE THERE TOMORROW. I'LL GO GET IT WHEN YOU'RE IN SCHOOL.
...
SURE.
BOOP BOOP, BOOP-BOOP BOOP
Calling
Amy
BOOP BOOP,
BOOP-BOOP BOOP
BOOP BOOP, BOOP-BOOP BOOP
BOOP BOOP, BOOP-BOOP BOOP

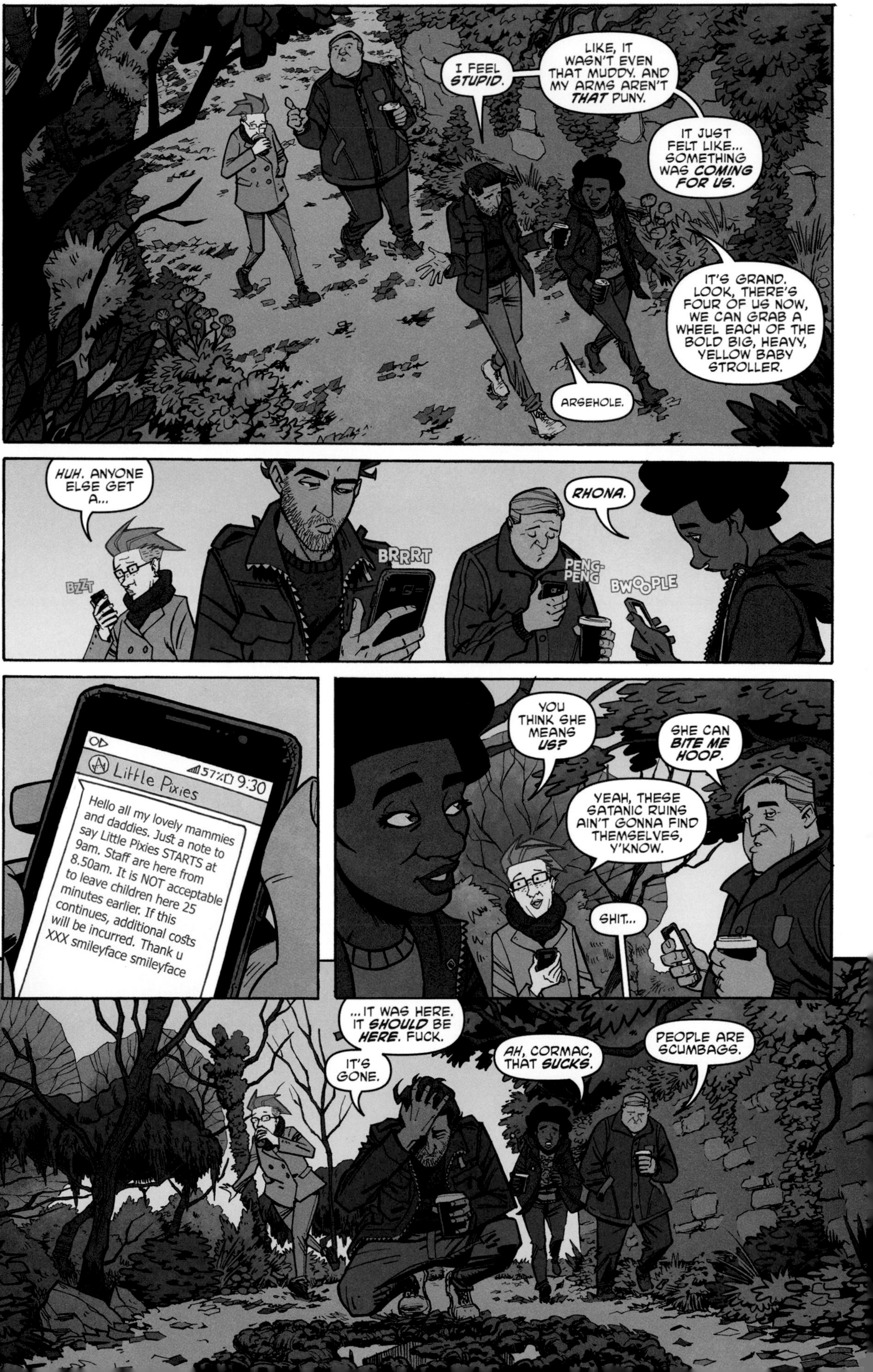
I FEEL *STUPID*.
LIKE, IT WASN'T EVEN THAT MUDDY. AND MY ARMS AREN'T *THAT* PUNY.
IT JUST FELT LIKE... SOMETHING WAS *COMING FOR US*.
IT'S GRAND. LOOK, THERE'S FOUR OF US NOW, WE CAN GRAB A WHEEL EACH OF THE BOLD BIG, HEAVY, YELLOW BABY STROLLER.
ARSEHOLE.
HUH. ANYONE ELSE GET A...
BZZT
BRRRT
RHONA.
PENG-PENG
BWOOPLE
Little Pixies
57% 9:30
Hello all my lovely mammies and daddies. Just a note to say Little Pixies STARTS at 9am. Staff are here from 8.50am. It is NOT acceptable to leave children here 25 minutes earlier. If this continues, additional costs will be incurred. Thank u XXX smileyface smileyface
YOU THINK SHE MEANS *US?*
SHE CAN *BITE ME HOOP*.
YEAH, THESE SATANIC RUINS AIN'T GONNA FIND THEMSELVES, Y'KNOW.
SHIT...
...IT WAS HERE. IT *SHOULD* BE *HERE*. FUCK.
IT'S GONE.
AH, CORMAC, THAT SUCKS.
PEOPLE ARE SCUMBAGS.

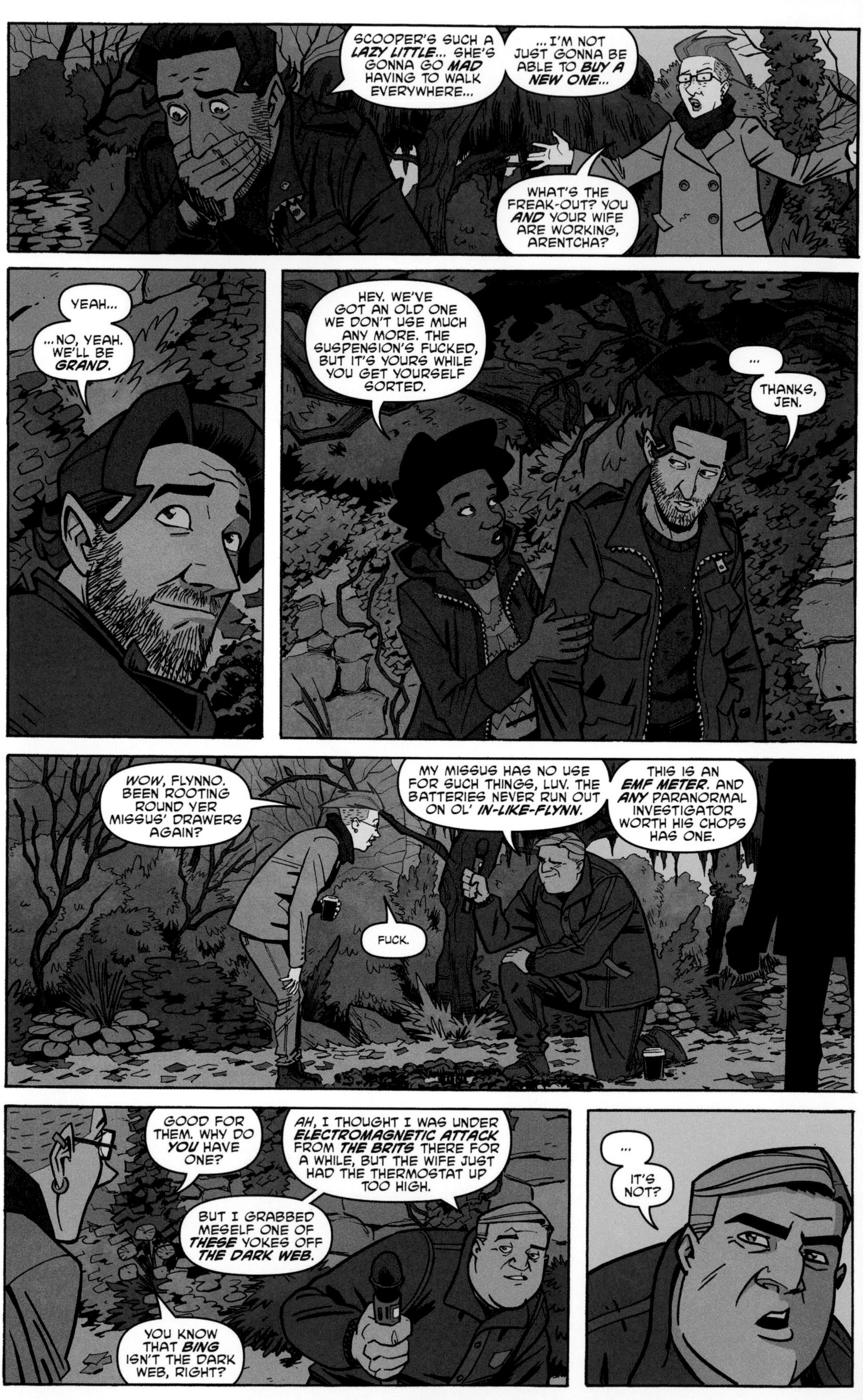
SCOOPER'S SUCH A LAZY LITTLE... SHE'S GONNA GO MAD HAVING TO WALK EVERYWHERE...
...I'M NOT JUST GONNA BE ABLE TO BUY A NEW ONE...
WHAT'S THE FREAK-OUT? YOU AND YOUR WIFE ARE WORKING, ARENTCHA?
YEAH...
...NO, YEAH. WE'LL BE GRAND.
HEY. WE'VE GOT AN OLD ONE WE DON'T USE MUCH ANY MORE. THE SUSPENSION'S FUCKED, BUT IT'S YOURS WHILE YOU GET YOURSELF SORTED.
...
THANKS, JEN.
WOW, FLYNNO. BEEN ROOTING ROUND YER MISSUS' DRAWERS AGAIN?
MY MISSUS HAS NO USE FOR SUCH THINGS, LUV. THE BATTERIES NEVER RUN OUT ON OL' IN-LIKE-FLYNN.
THIS IS AN EMF METER. AND ANY PARANORMAL INVESTIGATOR WORTH HIS CHOPS HAS ONE.
FUCK.
GOOD FOR THEM. WHY DO YOU HAVE ONE?
AH, I THOUGHT I WAS UNDER ELECTROMAGNETIC ATTACK FROM THE BRITS THERE FOR A WHILE, BUT THE WIFE JUST HAD THE THERMOSTAT UP TOO HIGH.
BUT I GRABBED MESELF ONE OF THESE YOKES OFF THE DARK WEB.
YOU KNOW THAT BING ISN'T THE DARK WEB, RIGHT?
...
IT'S NOT?

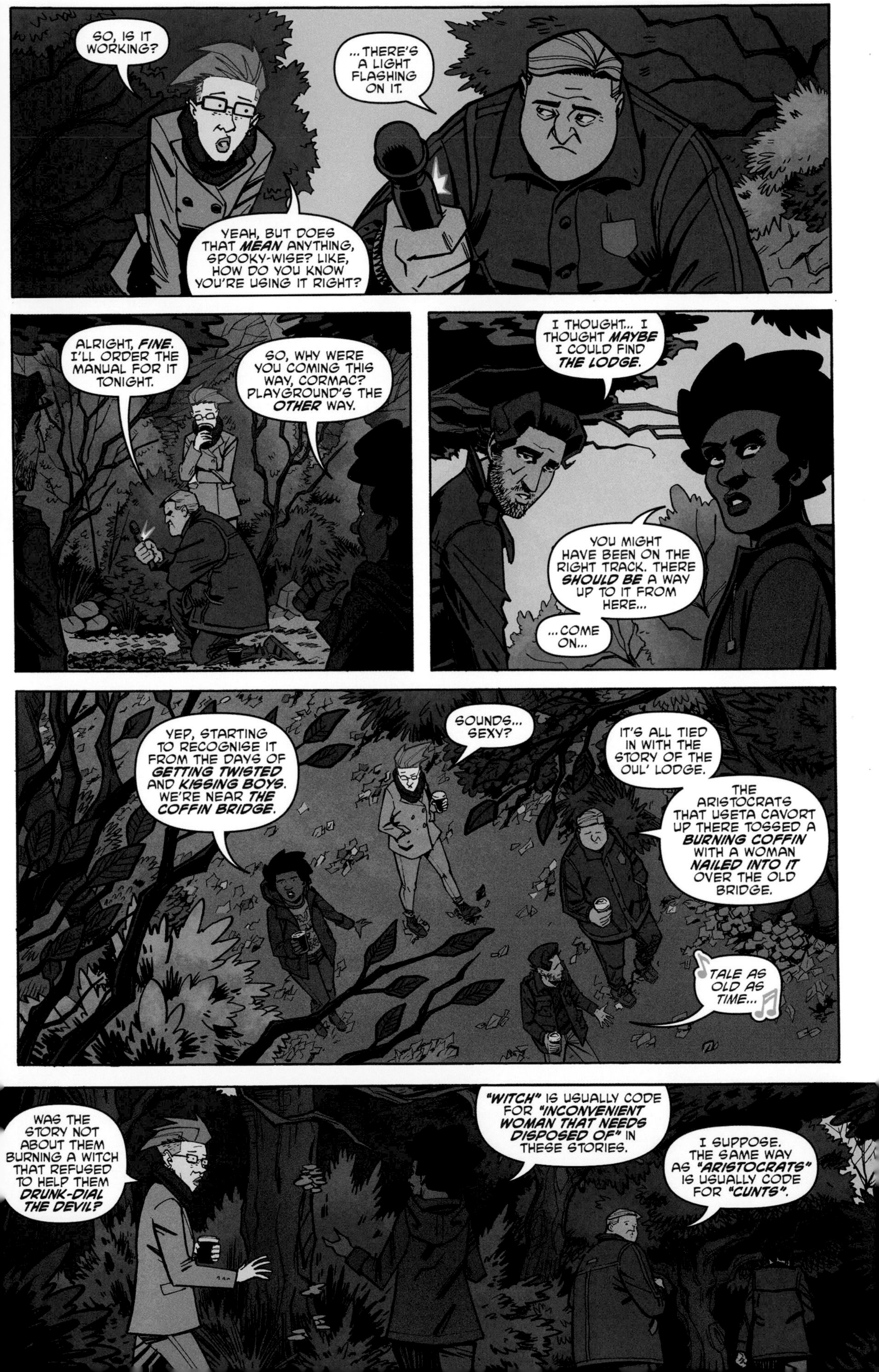
SO, IS IT WORKING?
...THERE'S A LIGHT FLASHING ON IT.
YEAH, BUT DOES THAT MEAN ANYTHING, SPOOKY-WISE? LIKE, HOW DO YOU KNOW YOU'RE USING IT RIGHT?
ALRIGHT, FINE. I'LL ORDER THE MANUAL FOR IT TONIGHT.
SO, WHY WERE YOU COMING THIS WAY, CORMAC? PLAYGROUND'S THE OTHER WAY.
I THOUGHT... I THOUGHT MAYBE I COULD FIND THE LODGE.
YOU MIGHT HAVE BEEN ON THE RIGHT TRACK. THERE SHOULD BE A WAY UP TO IT FROM HERE...
...COME ON...
YEP, STARTING TO RECOGNISE IT FROM THE DAYS OF GETTING TWISTED AND KISSING BOYS. WE'RE NEAR THE COFFIN BRIDGE.
SOUNDS... SEXY?
IT'S ALL TIED IN WITH THE STORY OF THE OUL' LODGE.
THE ARISTOCRATS THAT USETA CAVORT UP THERE TOSSED A BURNING COFFIN WITH A WOMAN NAILED INTO IT OVER THE OLD BRIDGE.
TALE AS OLD AS TIME...
WAS THE STORY NOT ABOUT THEM BURNING A WITCH THAT REFUSED TO HELP THEM DRUNK-DIAL THE DEVIL?
"WITCH" IS USUALLY CODE FOR "INCONVENIENT WOMAN THAT NEEDS DISPOSED OF" IN THESE STORIES.
I SUPPOSE. THE SAME WAY AS "ARISTOCRATS" IS USUALLY CODE FOR "CUNTS".

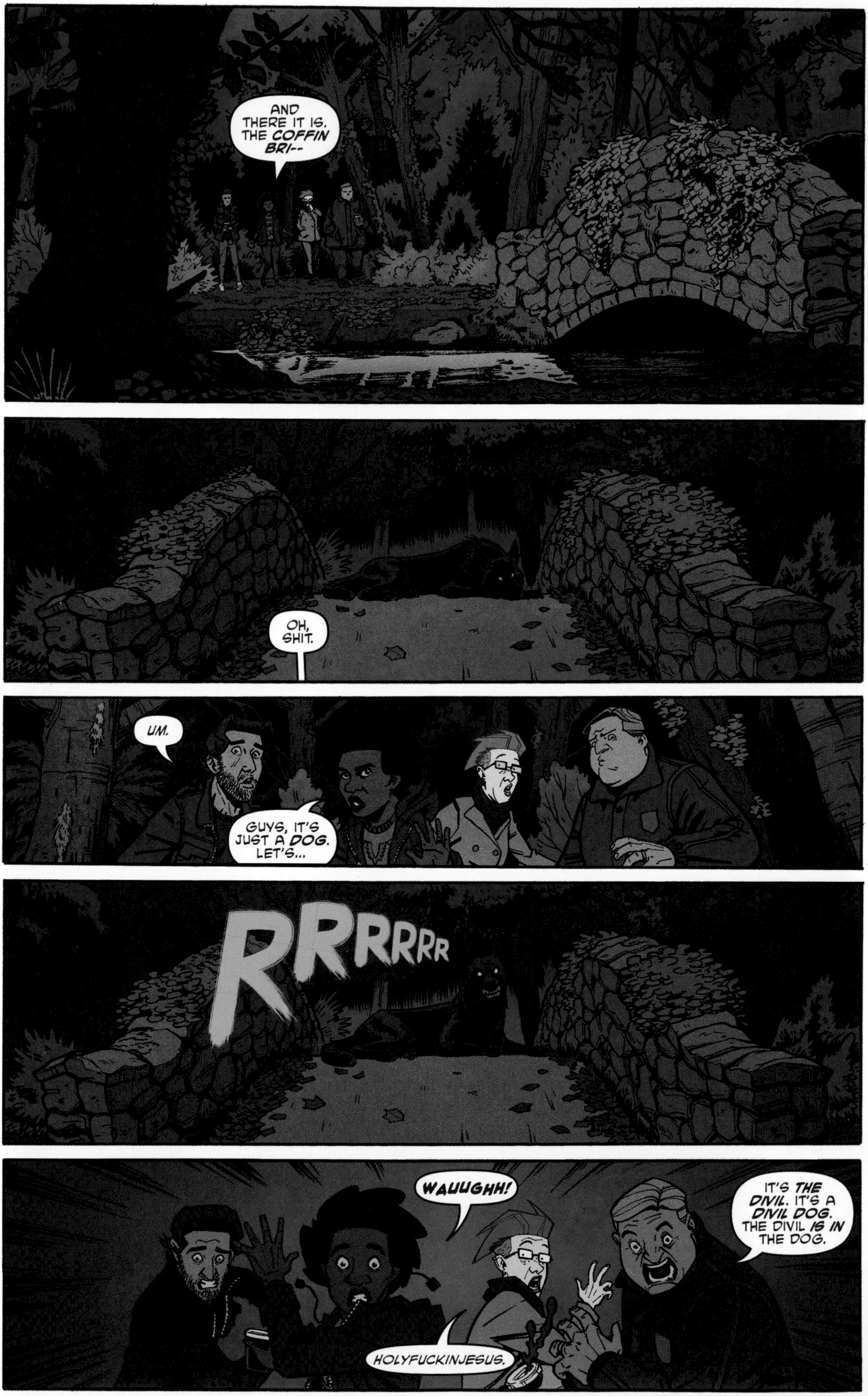
AND THERE IT IS. THE COFFIN BRI--
OH, SHIT.
UM.
GUYS, IT'S JUST A DOG. LET'S...
RRRRRR
WAUUGHH!
IT'S THE DIVIL. IT'S A DIVIL DOG. THE DIVIL IS IN THE DOG.
HOLYFUCKINJESUS.

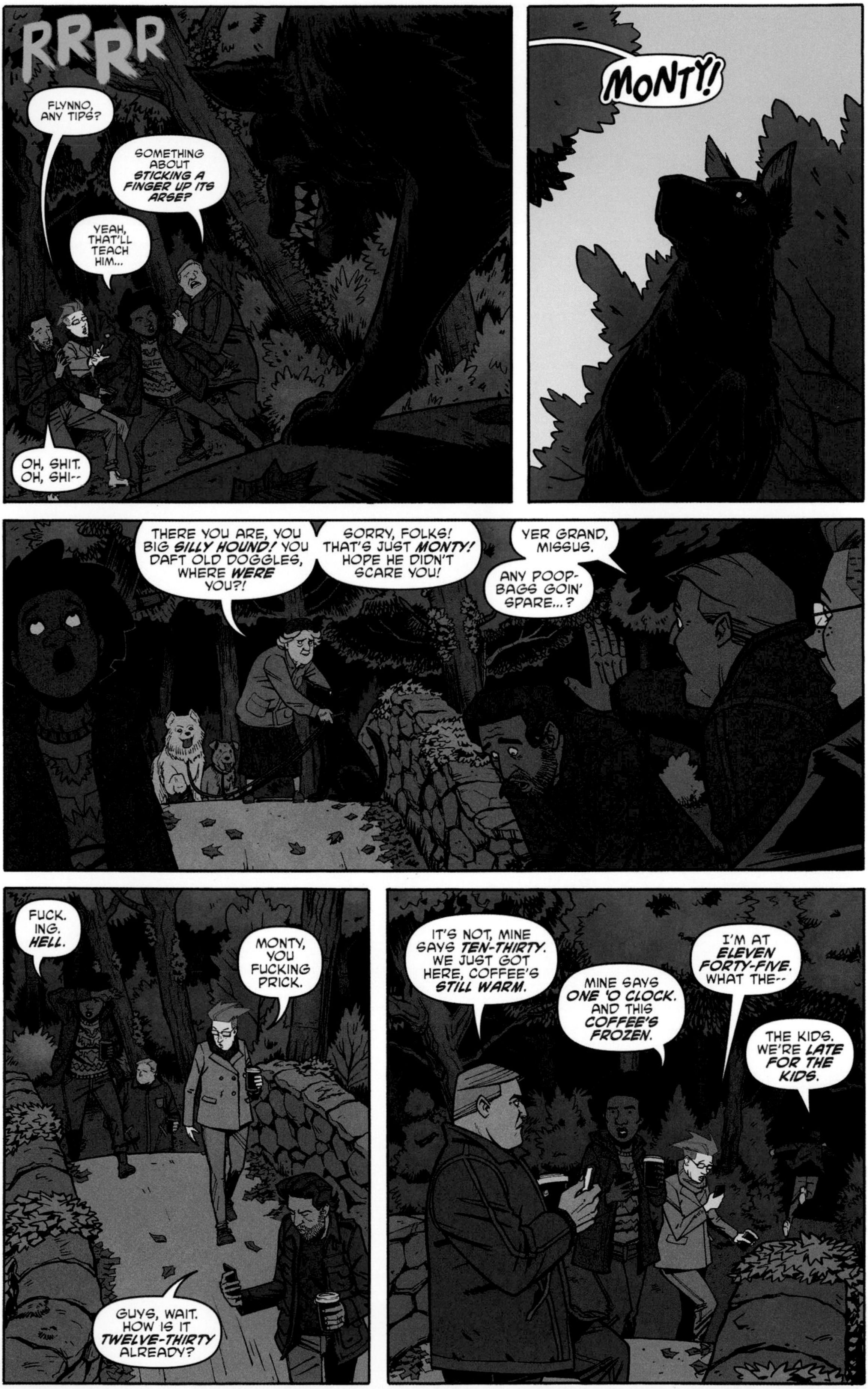
RRRR
FLYNNO, ANY TIPS?
SOMETHING ABOUT *STICKING A FINGER UP ITS ARSE?*
YEAH, THAT'LL TEACH HIM...
OH, SHIT. OH, SHI--
MONTY!
THERE YOU ARE, YOU BIG *SILLY HOUND!* YOU DAFT OLD DOGGLES, WHERE *WERE* YOU?!
SORRY, FOLKS! THAT'S JUST *MONTY!* HOPE HE DIDN'T SCARE YOU!
YER GRAND, MISSUS.
ANY POOP-BAGS GOIN' SPARE...?
FUCK. ING. *HELL*.
MONTY, YOU FUCKING PRICK.
GUYS, WAIT. HOW IS IT *TWELVE-THIRTY* ALREADY?
IT'S NOT, MINE SAYS *TEN-THIRTY*. WE JUST GOT HERE, COFFEE'S *STILL WARM*.
MINE SAYS *ONE 'O CLOCK*. AND THIS *COFFEE'S FROZEN*.
I'M AT *ELEVEN FORTY-FIVE*. WHAT THE--
THE KIDS. WE'RE *LATE FOR THE KIDS*.

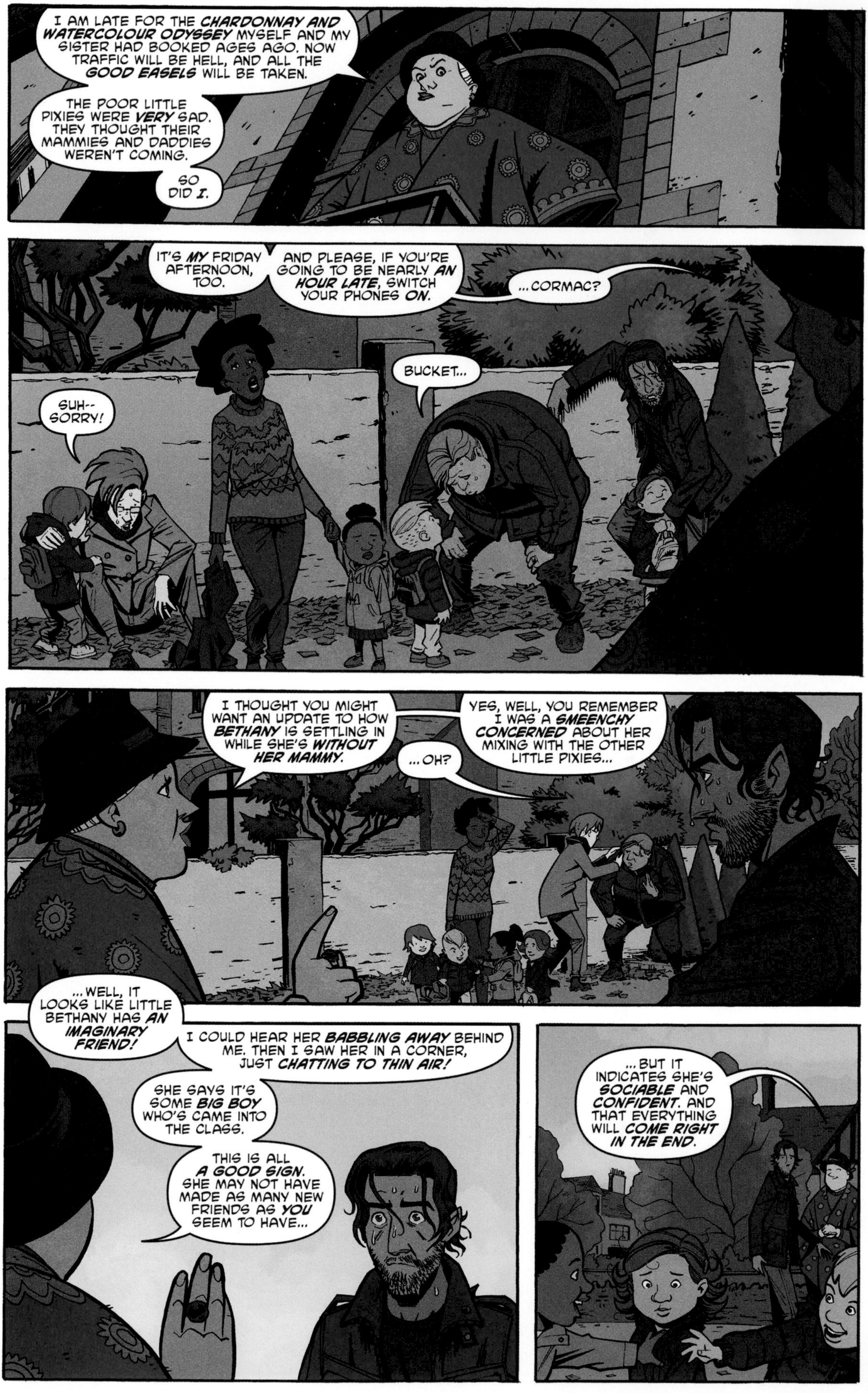
I AM LATE FOR THE CHARDONNAY AND WATERCOLOUR ODYSSEY MYSELF AND MY SISTER HAD BOOKED AGES AGO. NOW TRAFFIC WILL BE HELL, AND ALL THE GOOD EASELS WILL BE TAKEN.
THE POOR LITTLE PIXIES WERE VERY SAD. THEY THOUGHT THEIR MAMMIES AND DADDIES WEREN'T COMING.
SO DID I.
IT'S MY FRIDAY AFTERNOON, TOO.
AND PLEASE, IF YOU'RE GOING TO BE NEARLY AN HOUR LATE, SWITCH YOUR PHONES ON.
...CORMAC?
SUH-- SORRY!
BUCKET...
I THOUGHT YOU MIGHT WANT AN UPDATE TO HOW BETHANY IS SETTLING IN WHILE SHE'S WITHOUT HER MAMMY.
...OH?
YES, WELL, YOU REMEMBER I WAS A SMEENCHY CONCERNED ABOUT HER MIXING WITH THE OTHER LITTLE PIXIES...
...WELL, IT LOOKS LIKE LITTLE BETHANY HAS AN IMAGINARY FRIEND!
I COULD HEAR HER BABBLING AWAY BEHIND ME. THEN I SAW HER IN A CORNER, JUST CHATTING TO THIN AIR!
SHE SAYS IT'S SOME BIG BOY WHO'S CAME INTO THE CLASS.
THIS IS ALL A GOOD SIGN. SHE MAY NOT HAVE MADE AS MANY NEW FRIENDS AS YOU SEEM TO HAVE...
...BUT IT INDICATES SHE'S SOCIABLE AND CONFIDENT. AND THAT EVERYTHING WILL COME RIGHT IN THE END.

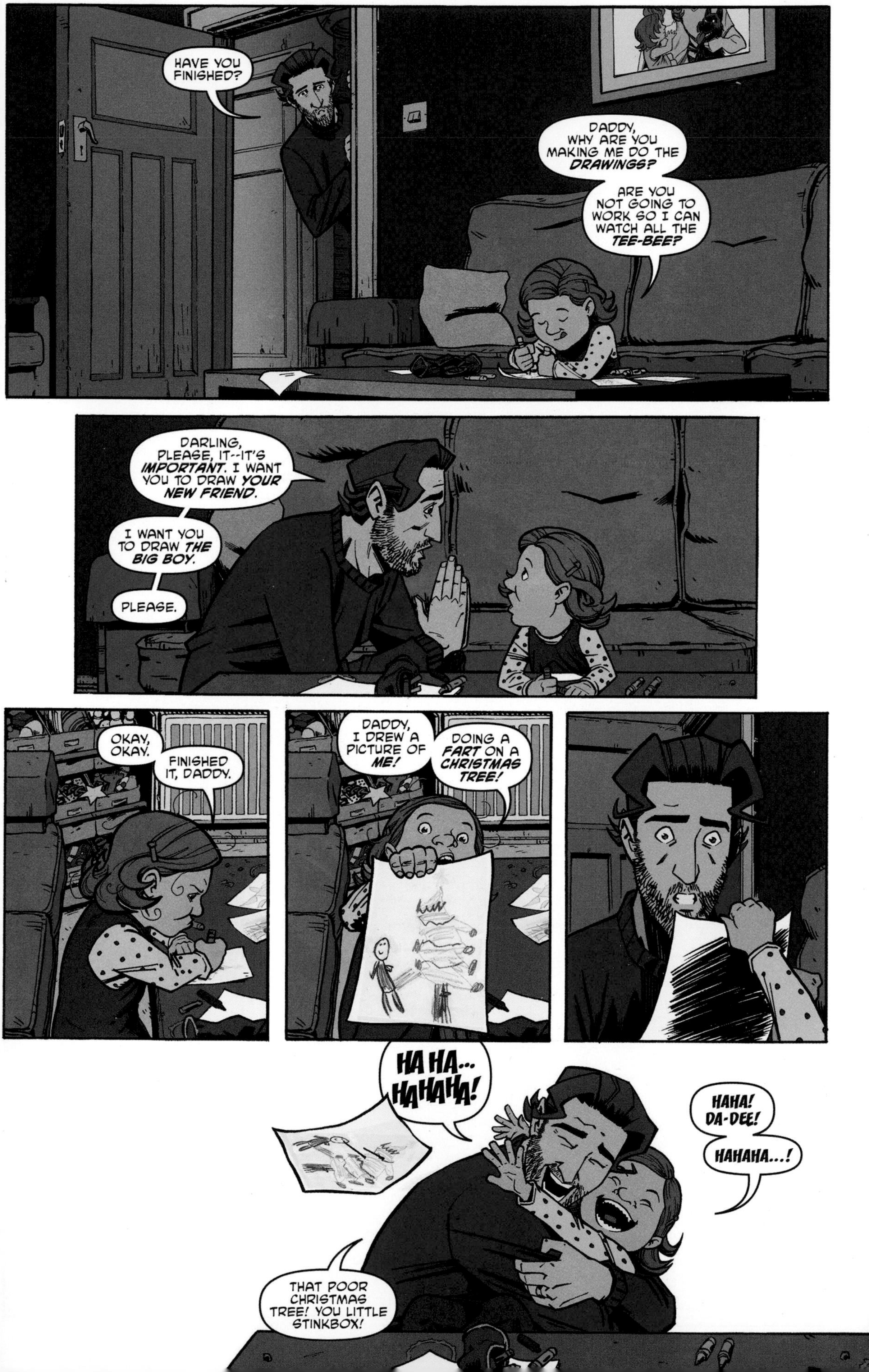
HAVE YOU FINISHED?
DADDY, WHY ARE YOU MAKING ME DO THE DRAWINGS?
ARE YOU NOT GOING TO WORK SO I CAN WATCH ALL THE TEE-BEE?
DARLING, PLEASE, IT--IT'S IMPORTANT. I WANT YOU TO DRAW YOUR NEW FRIEND.
I WANT YOU TO DRAW THE BIG BOY.
PLEASE.
OKAY, OKAY.
FINISHED IT, DADDY.
DADDY, I DREW A PICTURE OF ME!
DOING A FART ON A CHRISTMAS TREE!
HA HA... HAHAHA!
HAHA! DA-DEE!
HAHAHA...!
THAT POOR CHRISTMAS TREE! YOU LITTLE STINKBOX!

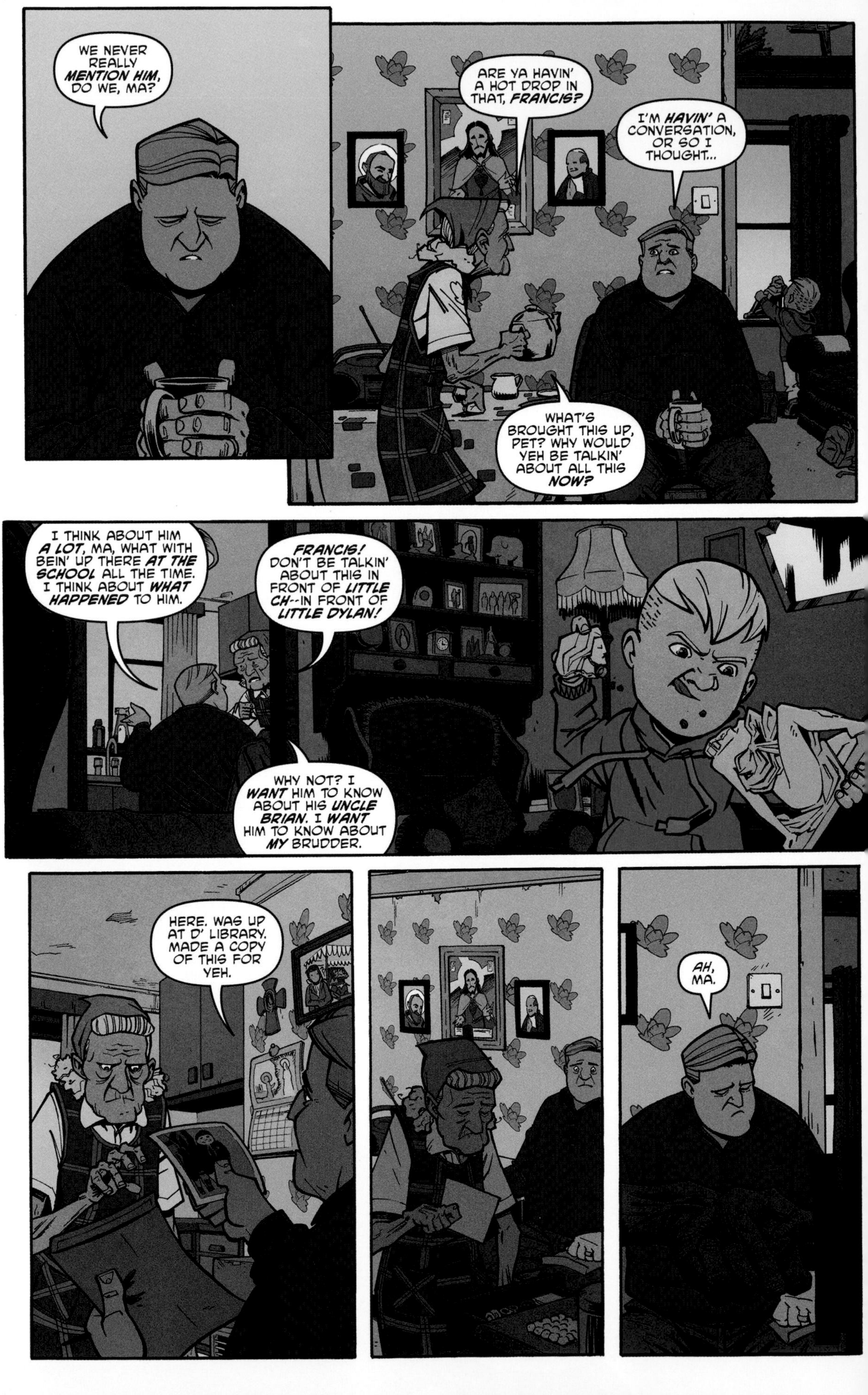
WE NEVER REALLY MENTION HIM, DO WE, MA?
ARE YA HAVIN' A HOT DROP IN THAT, FRANCIS?
I'M HAVIN' A CONVERSATION, OR SO I THOUGHT...
WHAT'S BROUGHT THIS UP, PET? WHY WOULD YEH BE TALKIN' ABOUT ALL THIS NOW?
I THINK ABOUT HIM A LOT, MA, WHAT WITH BEIN' UP THERE AT THE SCHOOL ALL THE TIME. I THINK ABOUT WHAT HAPPENED TO HIM.
FRANCIS! DON'T BE TALKIN' ABOUT THIS IN FRONT OF LITTLE CH--IN FRONT OF LITTLE DYLAN!
WHY NOT? I WANT HIM TO KNOW ABOUT HIS UNCLE BRIAN. I WANT HIM TO KNOW ABOUT MY BRUDDER.
HERE. WAS UP AT D' LIBRARY. MADE A COPY OF THIS FOR YEH.
AH, MA.

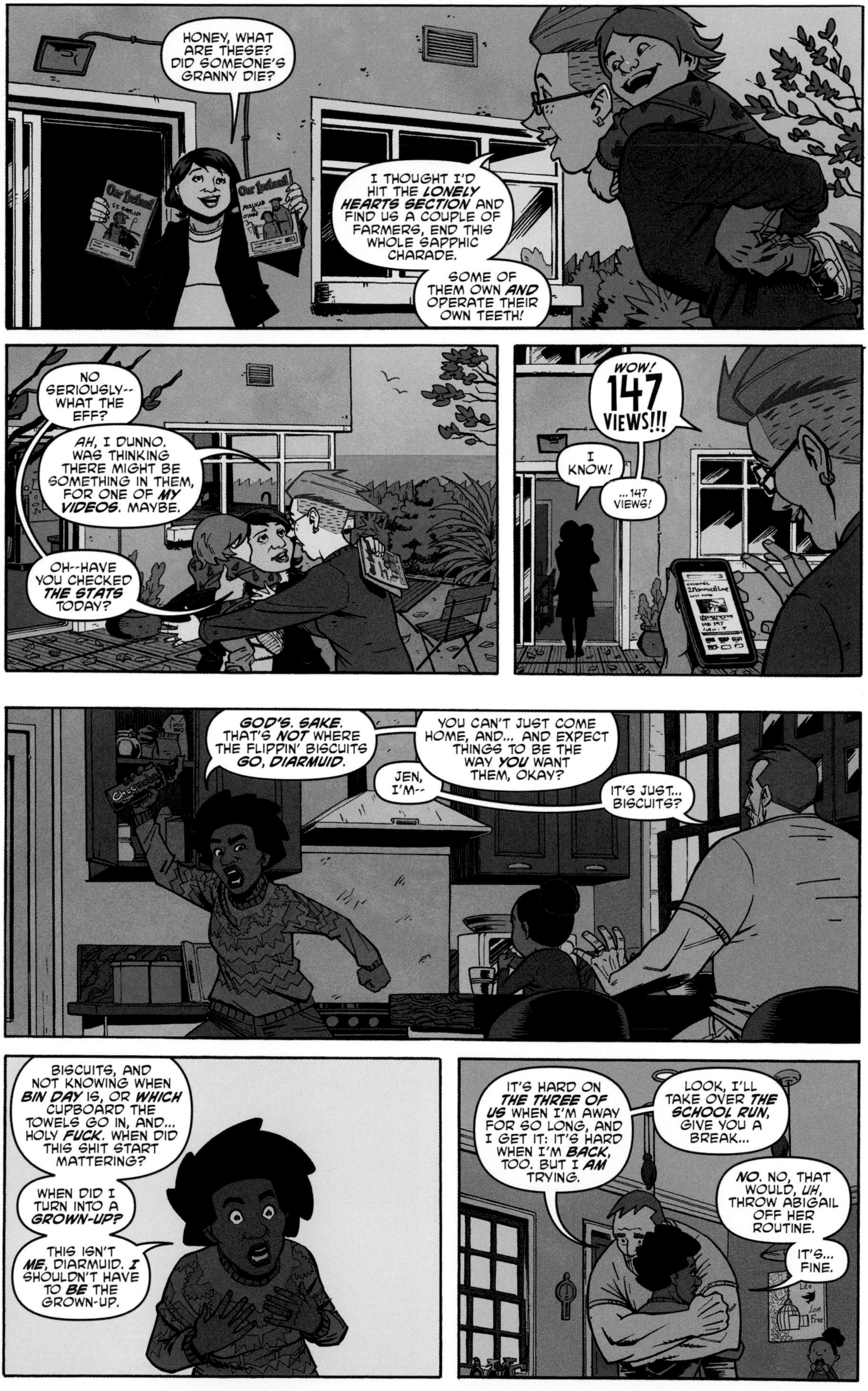
HONEY, WHAT ARE THESE? DID SOMEONE'S GRANNY DIE?
I THOUGHT I'D HIT THE LONELY HEARTS SECTION AND FIND US A COUPLE OF FARMERS, END THIS WHOLE SAPPHIC CHARADE.
SOME OF THEM OWN AND OPERATE THEIR OWN TEETH!
NO SERIOUSLY-- WHAT THE EFF?
AH, I DUNNO. WAS THINKING THERE MIGHT BE SOMETHING IN THEM, FOR ONE OF MY VIDEOS. MAYBE.
OH--HAVE YOU CHECKED THE STATS TODAY?
WOW! 147 VIEWS!!!
I KNOW!
...147 VIEWS!
GOD'S. SAKE. THAT'S NOT WHERE THE FLIPPIN' BISCUITS GO, DIARMUID.
JEN, I'M--
YOU CAN'T JUST COME HOME, AND... AND EXPECT THINGS TO BE THE WAY YOU WANT THEM, OKAY?
IT'S JUST... BISCUITS?
BISCUITS, AND NOT KNOWING WHEN BIN DAY IS, OR WHICH CUPBOARD THE TOWELS GO IN, AND... HOLY FUCK. WHEN DID THIS SHIT START MATTERING?
WHEN DID I TURN INTO A GROWN-UP?
THIS ISN'T ME, DIARMUID. I SHOULDN'T HAVE TO BE THE GROWN-UP.
IT'S HARD ON THE THREE OF US WHEN I'M AWAY FOR SO LONG, AND I GET IT: IT'S HARD WHEN I'M BACK, TOO. BUT I AM TRYING.
LOOK, I'LL TAKE OVER THE SCHOOL RUN, GIVE YOU A BREAK...
NO. NO, THAT WOULD, UH, THROW ABIGAIL OFF HER ROUTINE.
IT'S... FINE.

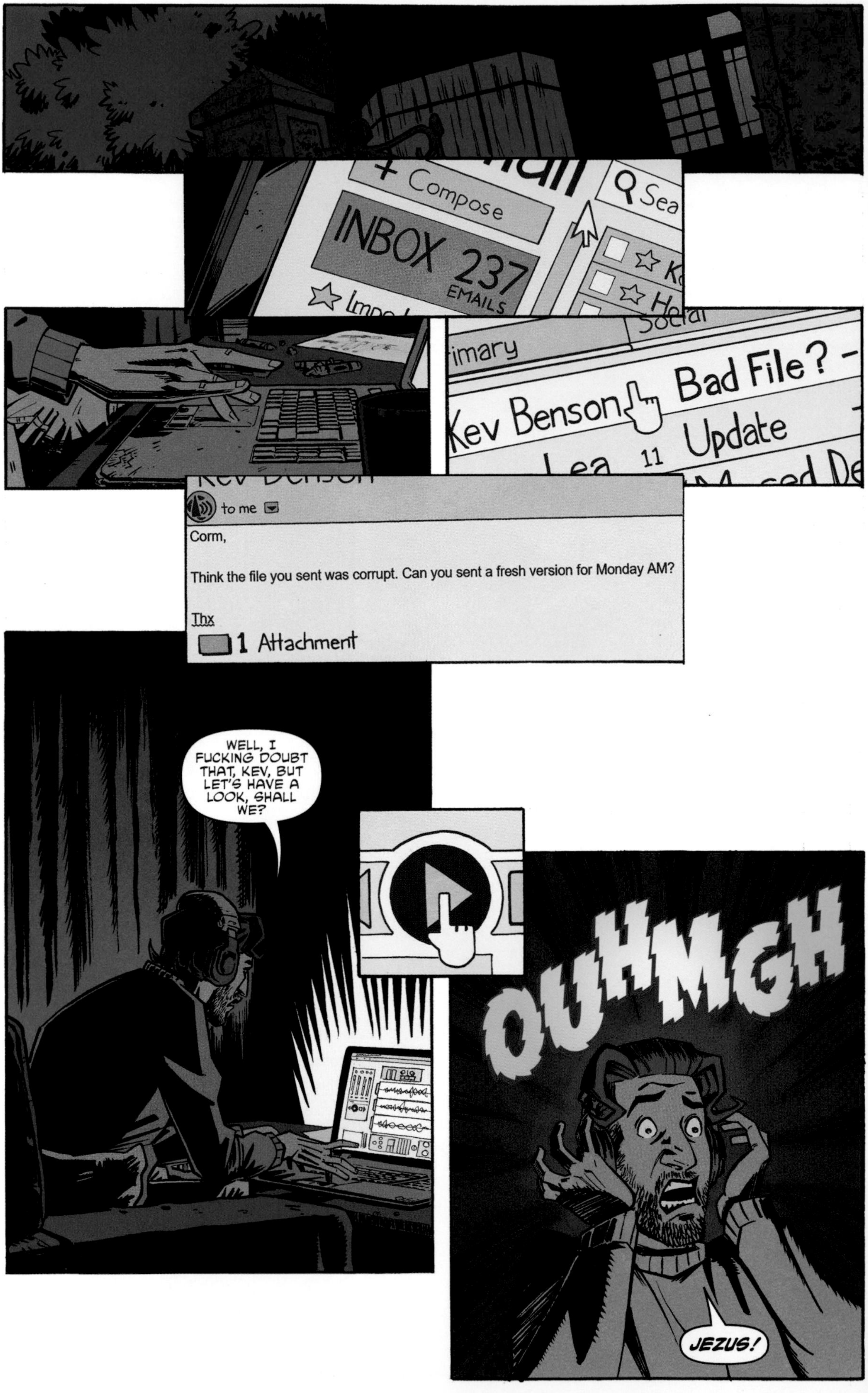
+ Compose
INBOX 237
EMAILS
Primary
Social
Kev Benson
Bad File? -
Update
11
to me
Corm,
Think the file you sent was corrupt. Can you sent a fresh version for Monday AM?
Thx
1 Attachment
WELL, I FUCKING DOUBT THAT, KEV, BUT LET'S HAVE A LOOK, SHALL WE?
OUHMGH
JEZUS!

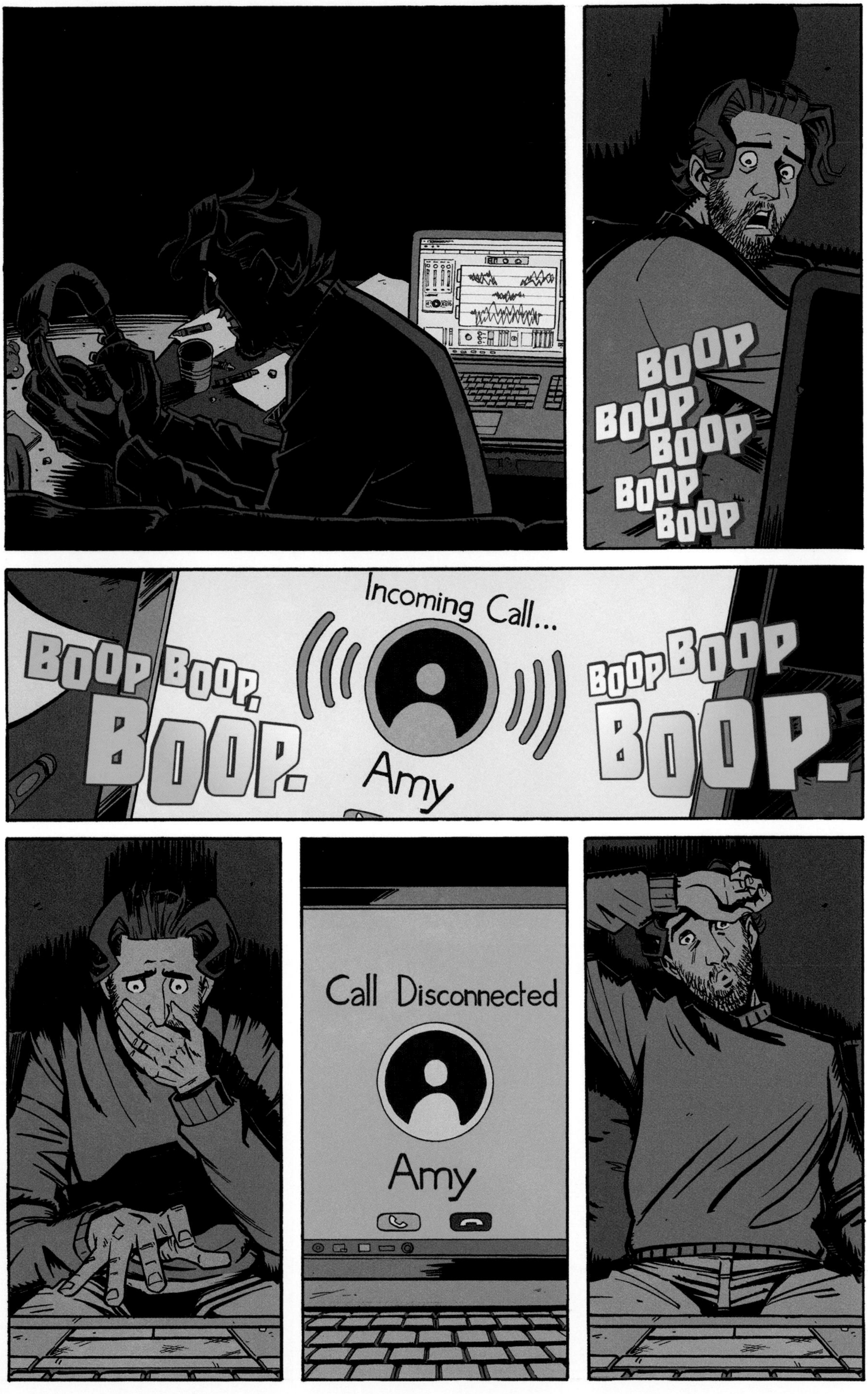
BOOP
BOOP
BOOP
BOOP
BOOP
Incoming Call...
BOOP BOOP,
BOOP.
Amy
BOOP BOOP
BOOP.
Call Disconnected
Amy

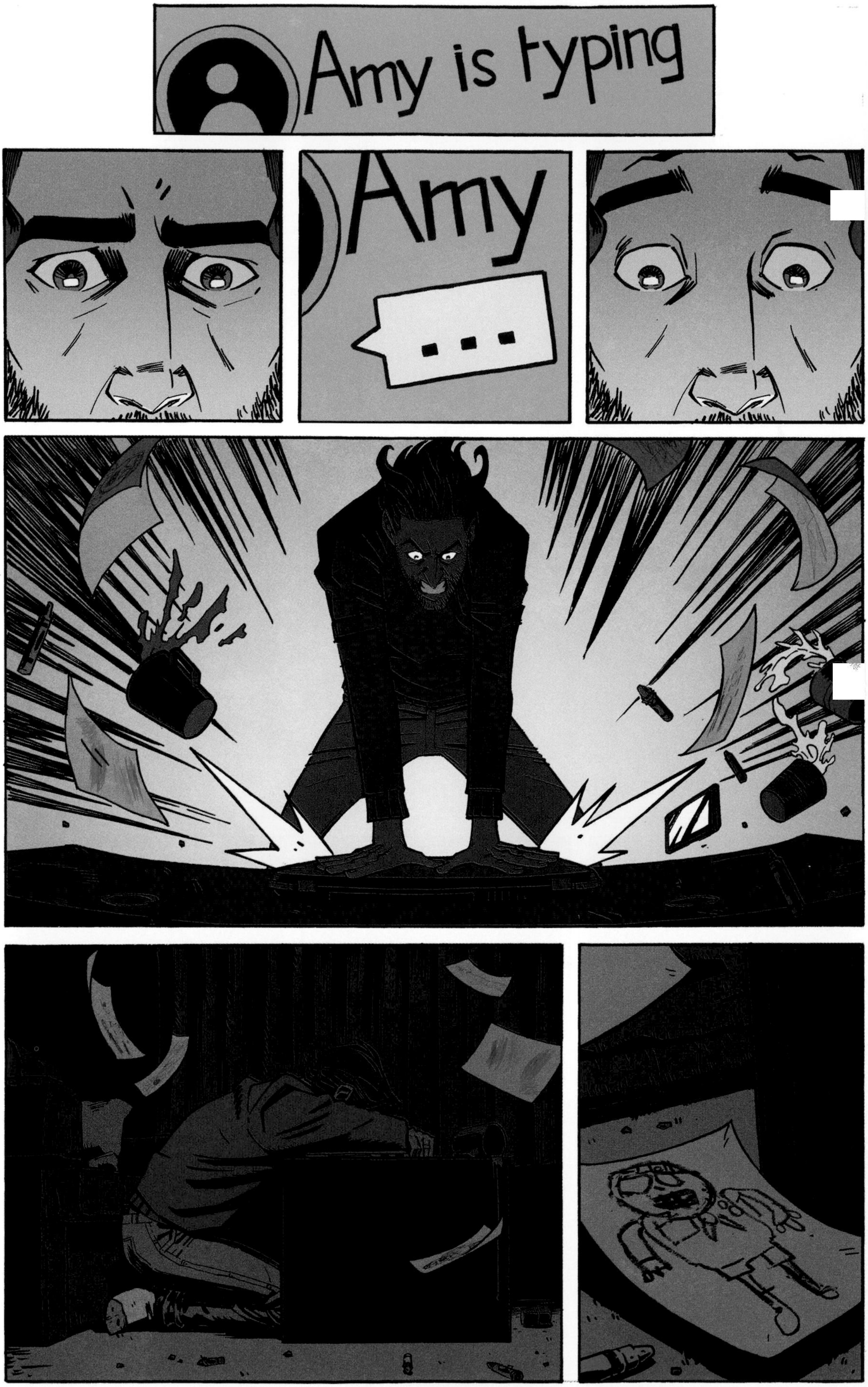
Amy is typing
Amy
...

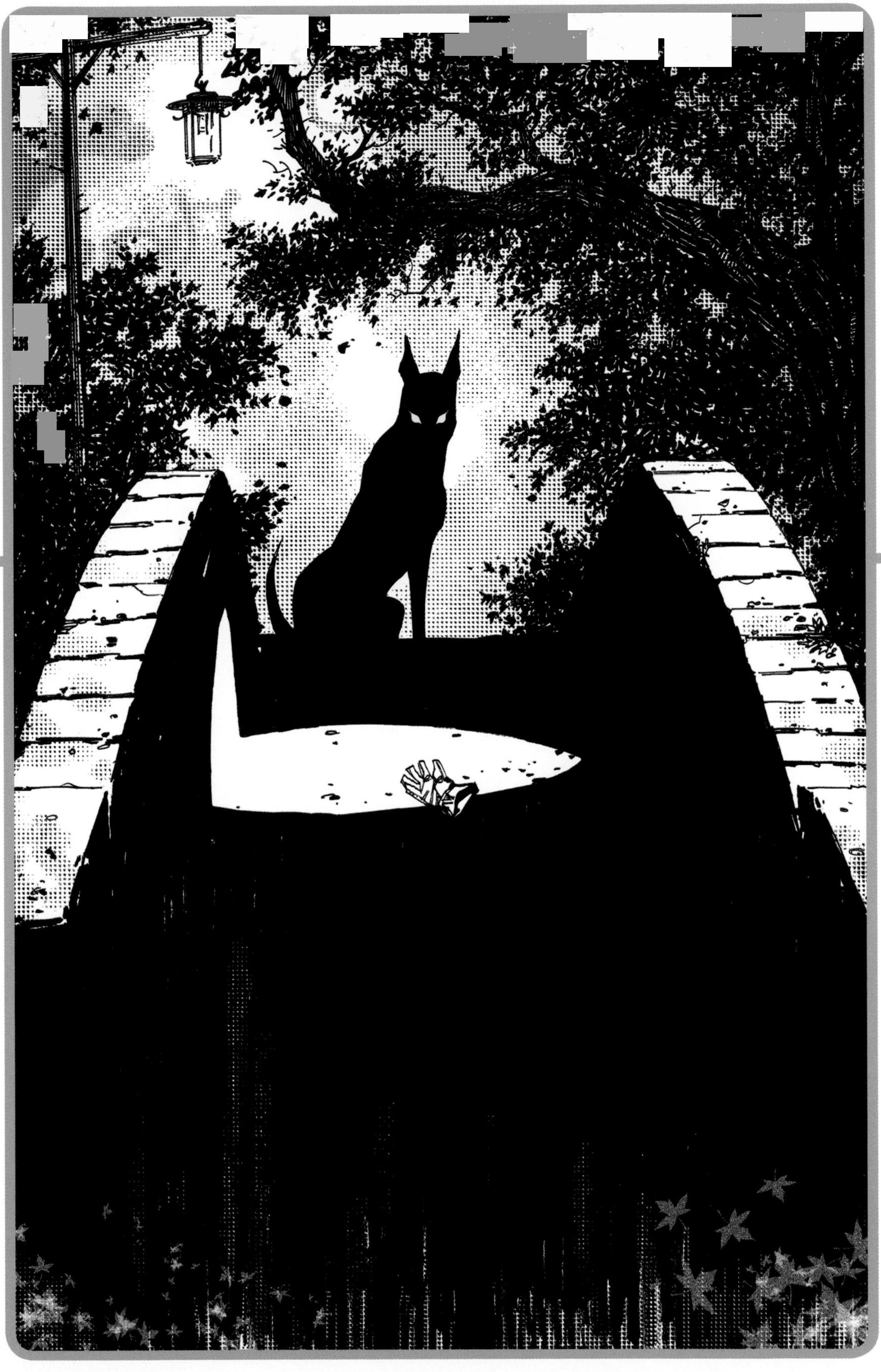

Art by
JOHN McCREA

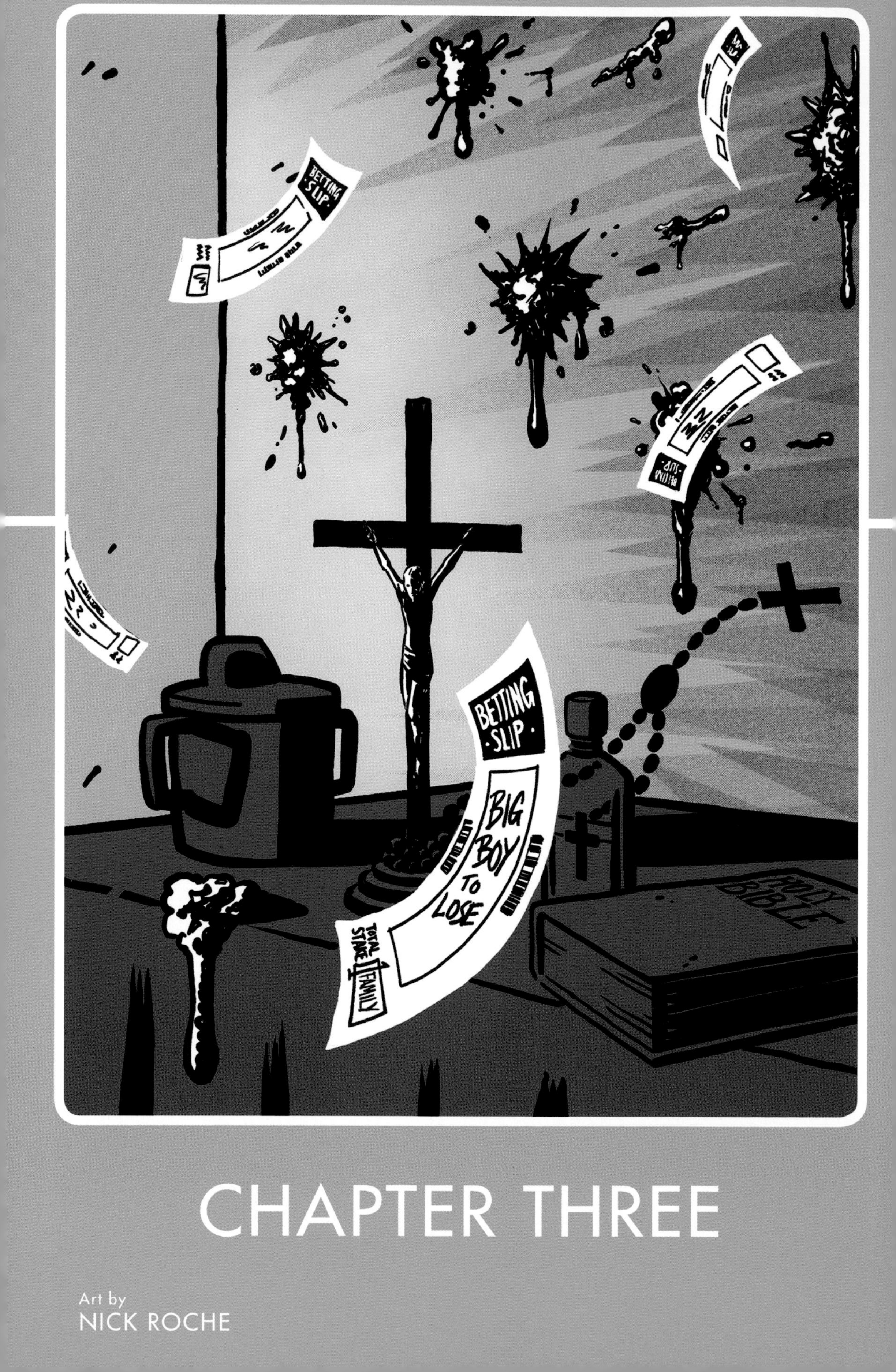
BETTING SLIP
BETTING SLIP
BIG BOY TO LOSE
TOTAL STAKE
1 FAMILY
HOLY BIBLE

CHAPTER THREE

Art by
NICK ROCHE

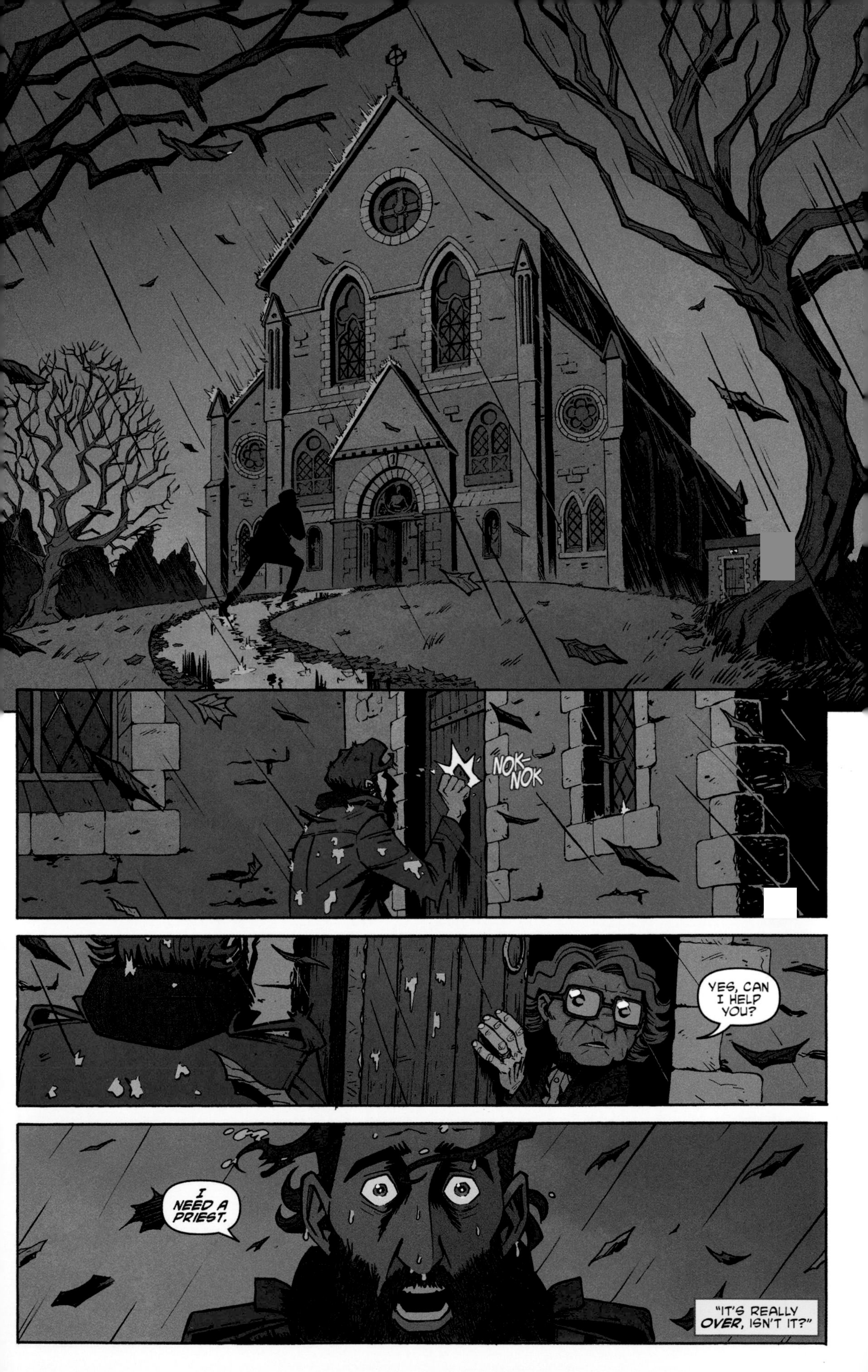
NOK-
NOK
YES, CAN I HELP YOU?
I NEED A PRIEST.
"IT'S REALLY OVER, ISN'T IT?"

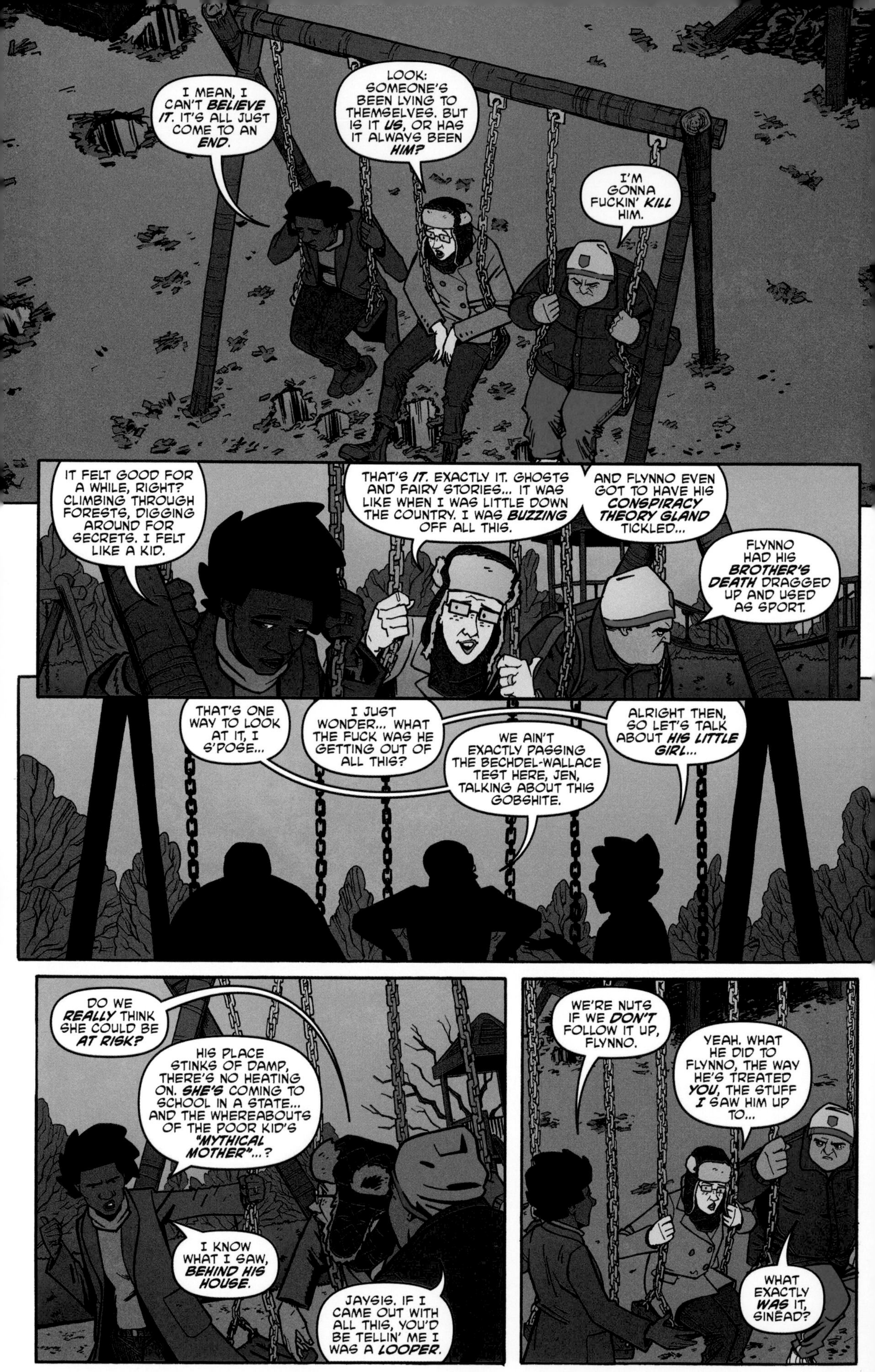
I MEAN, I CAN'T BELIEVE IT. IT'S ALL JUST COME TO AN END.
LOOK: SOMEONE'S BEEN LYING TO THEMSELVES. BUT IS IT US, OR HAS IT ALWAYS BEEN HIM?
I'M GONNA FUCKIN' KILL HIM.
IT FELT GOOD FOR A WHILE, RIGHT? CLIMBING THROUGH FORESTS, DIGGING AROUND FOR SECRETS. I FELT LIKE A KID.
THAT'S IT. EXACTLY IT. GHOSTS AND FAIRY STORIES... IT WAS LIKE WHEN I WAS LITTLE DOWN THE COUNTRY. I WAS BUZZING OFF ALL THIS.
AND FLYNNO EVEN GOT TO HAVE HIS CONSPIRACY THEORY GLAND TICKLED...
FLYNNO HAD HIS BROTHER'S DEATH DRAGGED UP AND USED AS SPORT.
THAT'S ONE WAY TO LOOK AT IT, I S'POSE...
I JUST WONDER... WHAT THE FUCK WAS HE GETTING OUT OF ALL THIS?
WE AIN'T EXACTLY PASSING THE BECHDEL-WALLACE TEST HERE, JEN, TALKING ABOUT THIS GOBSHITE.
ALRIGHT THEN, SO LET'S TALK ABOUT HIS LITTLE GIRL...
DO WE REALLY THINK SHE COULD BE AT RISK?
HIS PLACE STINKS OF DAMP, THERE'S NO HEATING ON. SHE'S COMING TO SCHOOL IN A STATE... AND THE WHEREABOUTS OF THE POOR KID'S "MYTHICAL MOTHER"...?
I KNOW WHAT I SAW, BEHIND HIS HOUSE.
JAYSIS. IF I CAME OUT WITH ALL THIS, YOU'D BE TELLIN' ME I WAS A LOOPER.
WE'RE NUTS IF WE DON'T FOLLOW IT UP, FLYNNO.
YEAH. WHAT HE DID TO FLYNNO, THE WAY HE'S TREATED YOU, THE STUFF I SAW HIM UP TO...
WHAT EXACTLY WAS IT, SINEAD?

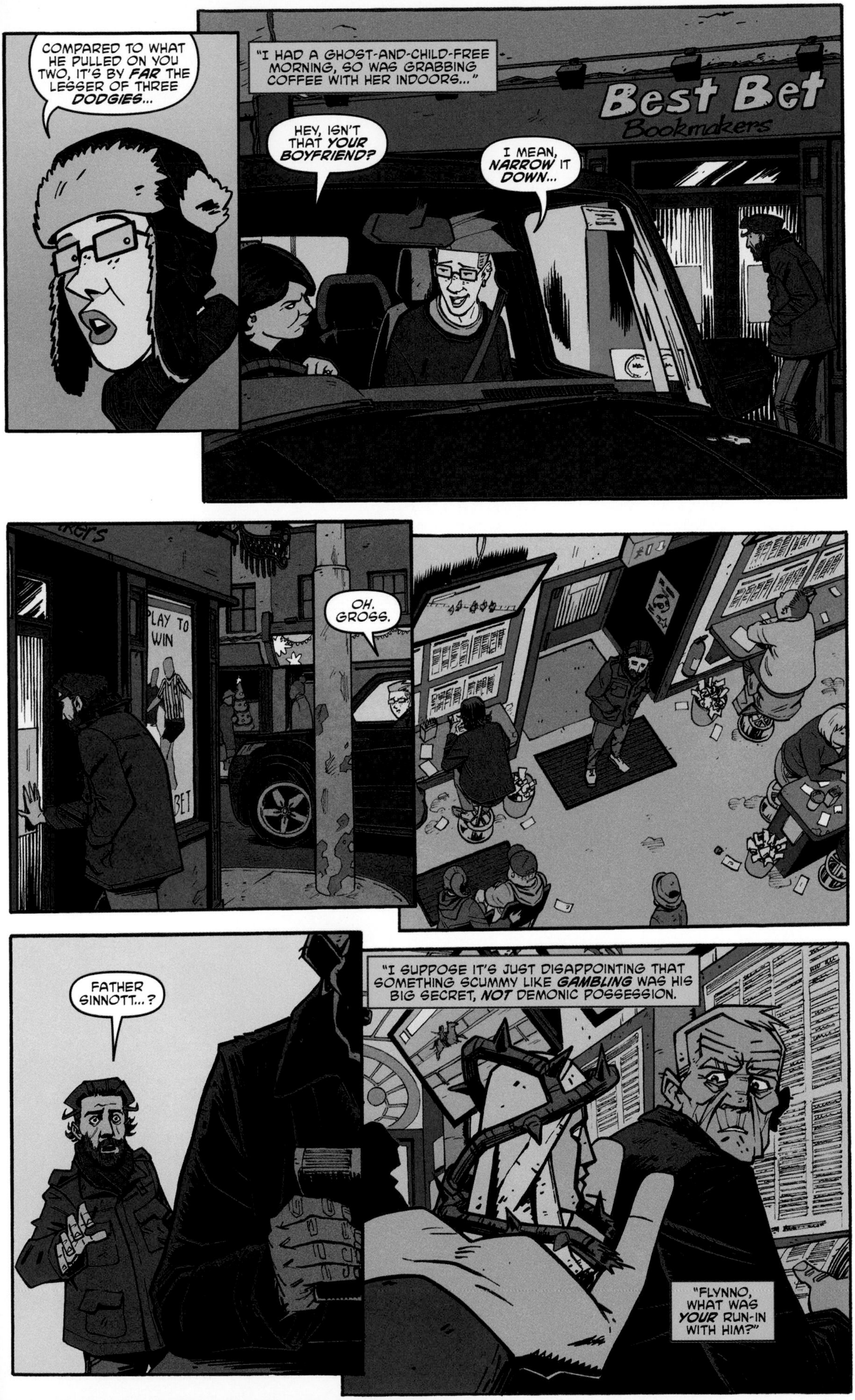
COMPARED TO WHAT HE PULLED ON YOU TWO, IT'S BY FAR THE LESSER OF THREE DODGIES...
"I HAD A GHOST-AND-CHILD-FREE MORNING, SO WAS GRABBING COFFEE WITH HER INDOORS..."
Best Bet
Bookmakers
HEY, ISN'T THAT YOUR BOYFRIEND?
I MEAN, NARROW IT DOWN...
PLAY TO WIN
OH. GROSS.
FATHER SINNOTT...?
"I SUPPOSE IT'S JUST DISAPPOINTING THAT SOMETHING SCUMMY LIKE GAMBLING WAS HIS BIG SECRET, NOT DEMONIC POSSESSION.
"FLYNNO, WHAT WAS YOUR RUN-IN WITH HIM?"

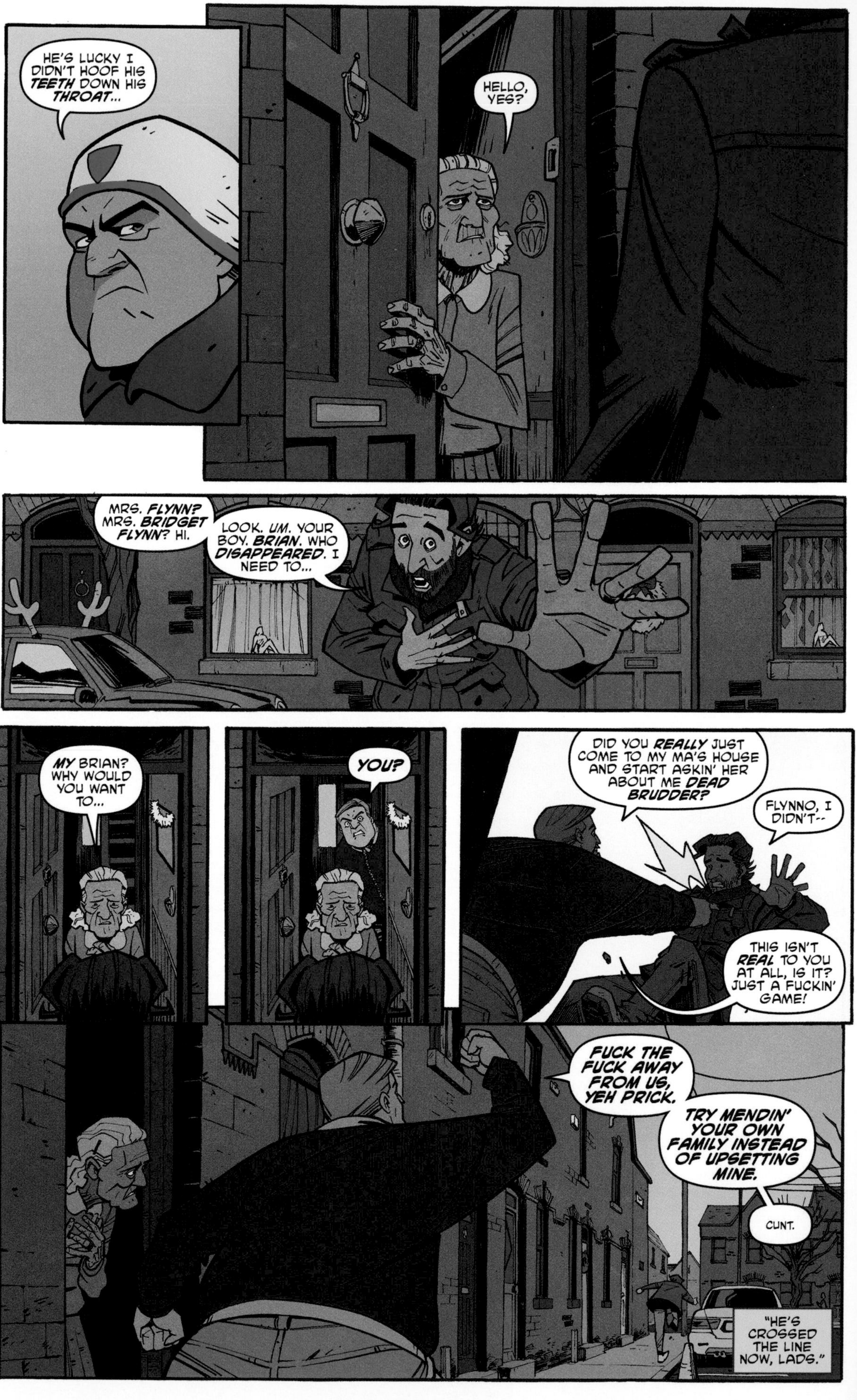
HE'S LUCKY I DIDN'T HOOF HIS *TEETH* DOWN HIS *THROAT*...
HELLO, YES?
MRS. *FLYNN*? MRS. *BRIDGET FLYNN*? HI.
LOOK. *UM*. YOUR BOY. *BRIAN*. WHO *DISAPPEARED*. I NEED TO...
MY BRIAN? WHY WOULD YOU WANT TO...
YOU?
DID YOU *REALLY* JUST COME TO MY MA'S HOUSE AND START ASKIN' HER ABOUT ME *DEAD BRUDDER?*
FLYNNO, I DIDN'T--
THIS ISN'T *REAL* TO YOU AT ALL, IS IT? JUST A FUCKIN' GAME!
FUCK THE FUCK AWAY FROM US, YEH PRICK.
TRY MENDIN' YOUR OWN FAMILY INSTEAD OF UPSETTING MINE.
CUNT.
"HE'S CROSSED THE LINE NOW, LADS."

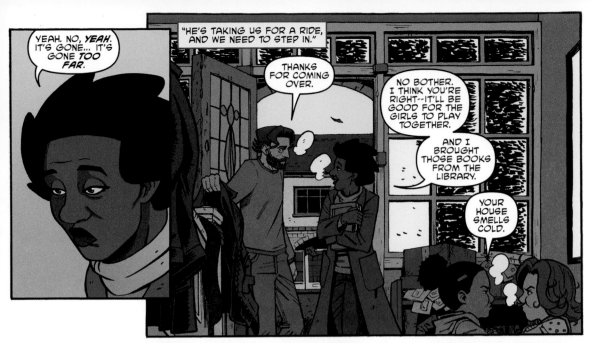

YEAH. NO, *YEAH.* IT'S GONE... IT'S GONE *TOO FAR.*

"HE'S TAKING US FOR A RIDE, AND WE NEED TO STEP IN."

THANKS FOR COMING OVER.

NO BOTHER. I THINK YOU'RE RIGHT--IT'LL BE GOOD FOR THE GIRLS TO PLAY TOGETHER.

AND I BROUGHT THOSE BOOKS FROM THE LIBRARY.

YOUR HOUSE SMELLS COLD.

ACE. LOOK, I HAVE TO POP OUT FOR A WHILE. ARE YOU OKAY TO...?

WHAT?! NO, THIS WASN'T--

PLEASE, JEN. THERE'S SOMETHING I *HAVE* TO DO.

CORMAC, YOU *CAN'T* KEEP DOING THIS.

CORMAC.

NO WONDER *YOU* DIDN'T STICK AROUND...

OH SHIT.

"I'D NEVER BEEN TO HIS HOUSE BEFORE. BUT I BET IT WASN'T ALWAYS IN SUCH A STATE.

"AND I BET THE GARDEN DIDN'T USED TO LOOK LIKE *THAT...*"

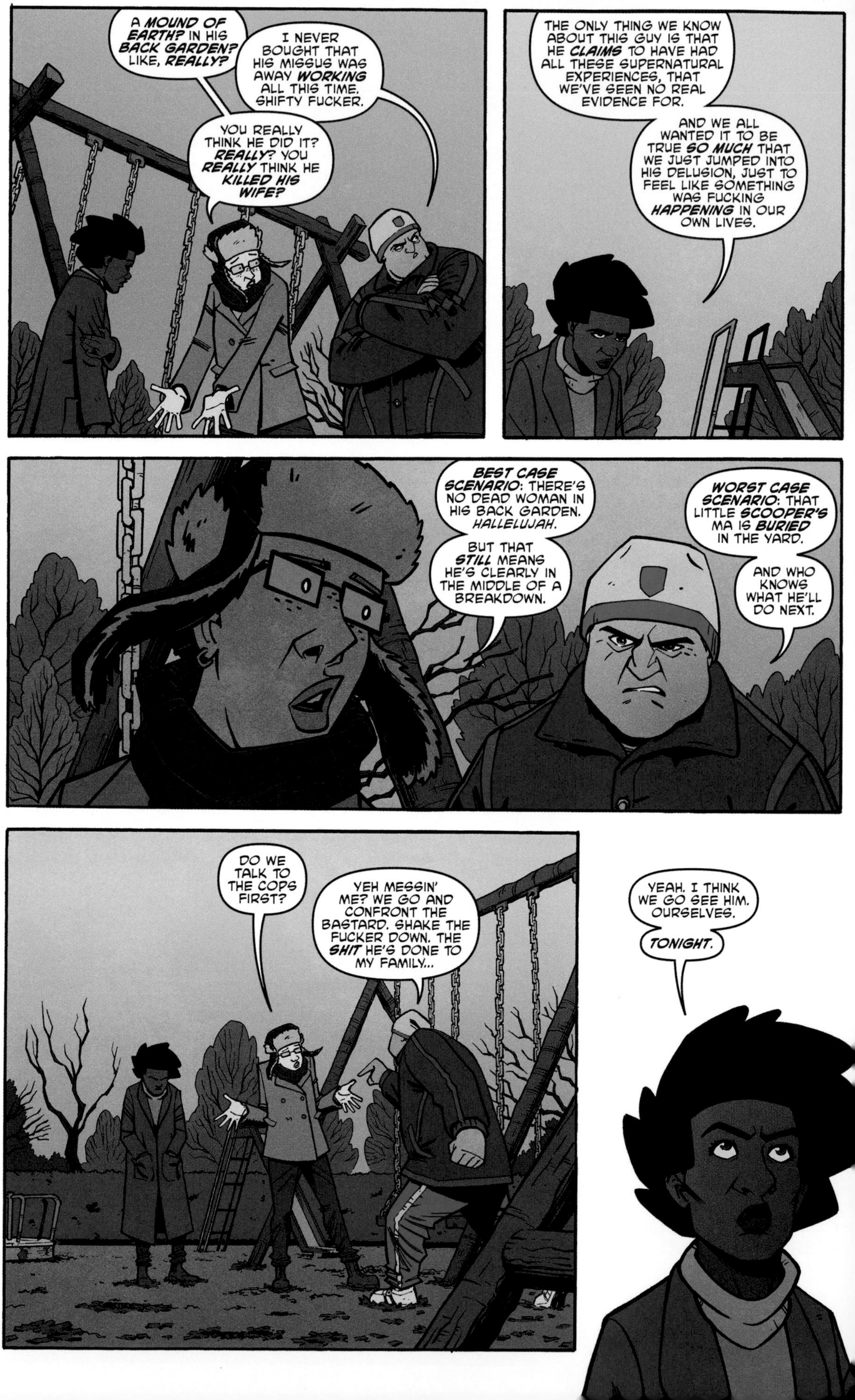
A MOUND OF EARTH? IN HIS BACK GARDEN? LIKE, REALLY?
I NEVER BOUGHT THAT HIS MISSUS WAS AWAY WORKING ALL THIS TIME. SHIFTY FUCKER.
YOU REALLY THINK HE DID IT? REALLY? YOU REALLY THINK HE KILLED HIS WIFE?
THE ONLY THING WE KNOW ABOUT THIS GUY IS THAT HE CLAIMS TO HAVE HAD ALL THESE SUPERNATURAL EXPERIENCES, THAT WE'VE SEEN NO REAL EVIDENCE FOR.
AND WE ALL WANTED IT TO BE TRUE SO MUCH THAT WE JUST JUMPED INTO HIS DELUSION, JUST TO FEEL LIKE SOMETHING WAS FUCKING HAPPENING IN OUR OWN LIVES.
BEST CASE SCENARIO: THERE'S NO DEAD WOMAN IN HIS BACK GARDEN. HALLELUJAH.
BUT THAT STILL MEANS HE'S CLEARLY IN THE MIDDLE OF A BREAKDOWN.
WORST CASE SCENARIO: THAT LITTLE SCOOPER'S MA IS BURIED IN THE YARD.
AND WHO KNOWS WHAT HE'LL DO NEXT.
DO WE TALK TO THE COPS FIRST?
YEH MESSIN' ME? WE GO AND CONFRONT THE BASTARD. SHAKE THE FUCKER DOWN. THE SHIT HE'S DONE TO MY FAMILY...
YEAH. I THINK WE GO SEE HIM. OURSELVES.
TONIGHT.

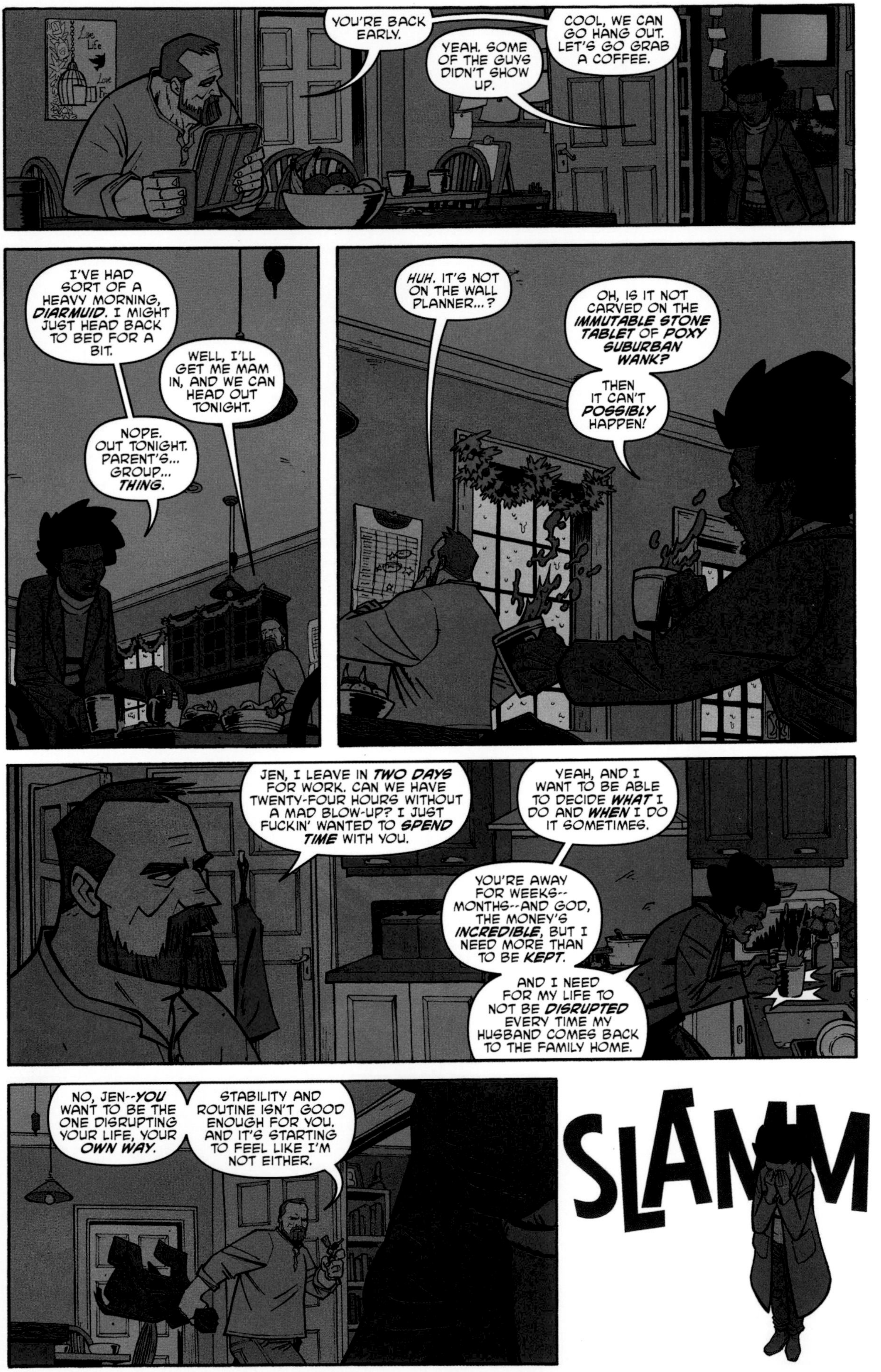
YOU'RE BACK EARLY.
YEAH. SOME OF THE GUYS DIDN'T SHOW UP.
COOL, WE CAN GO HANG OUT. LET'S GO GRAB A COFFEE.
I'VE HAD SORT OF A HEAVY MORNING, DIARMUID. I MIGHT JUST HEAD BACK TO BED FOR A BIT.
WELL, I'LL GET ME MAM IN, AND WE CAN HEAD OUT TONIGHT.
NOPE. OUT TONIGHT. PARENT'S... GROUP... THING.
HUH. IT'S NOT ON THE WALL PLANNER...?
OH, IS IT NOT CARVED ON THE IMMUTABLE STONE TABLET OF POXY SUBURBAN WANK?
THEN IT CAN'T POSSIBLY HAPPEN!
JEN, I LEAVE IN TWO DAYS FOR WORK. CAN WE HAVE TWENTY-FOUR HOURS WITHOUT A MAD BLOW-UP? I JUST FUCKIN' WANTED TO SPEND TIME WITH YOU.
YEAH, AND I WANT TO BE ABLE TO DECIDE WHAT I DO AND WHEN I DO IT SOMETIMES.
YOU'RE AWAY FOR WEEKS--MONTHS--AND GOD, THE MONEY'S INCREDIBLE, BUT I NEED MORE THAN TO BE KEPT.
AND I NEED FOR MY LIFE TO NOT BE DISRUPTED EVERY TIME MY HUSBAND COMES BACK TO THE FAMILY HOME.
NO, JEN--YOU WANT TO BE THE ONE DISRUPTING YOUR LIFE, YOUR OWN WAY.
STABILITY AND ROUTINE ISN'T GOOD ENOUGH FOR YOU. AND IT'S STARTING TO FEEL LIKE I'M NOT EITHER.
SLAMM

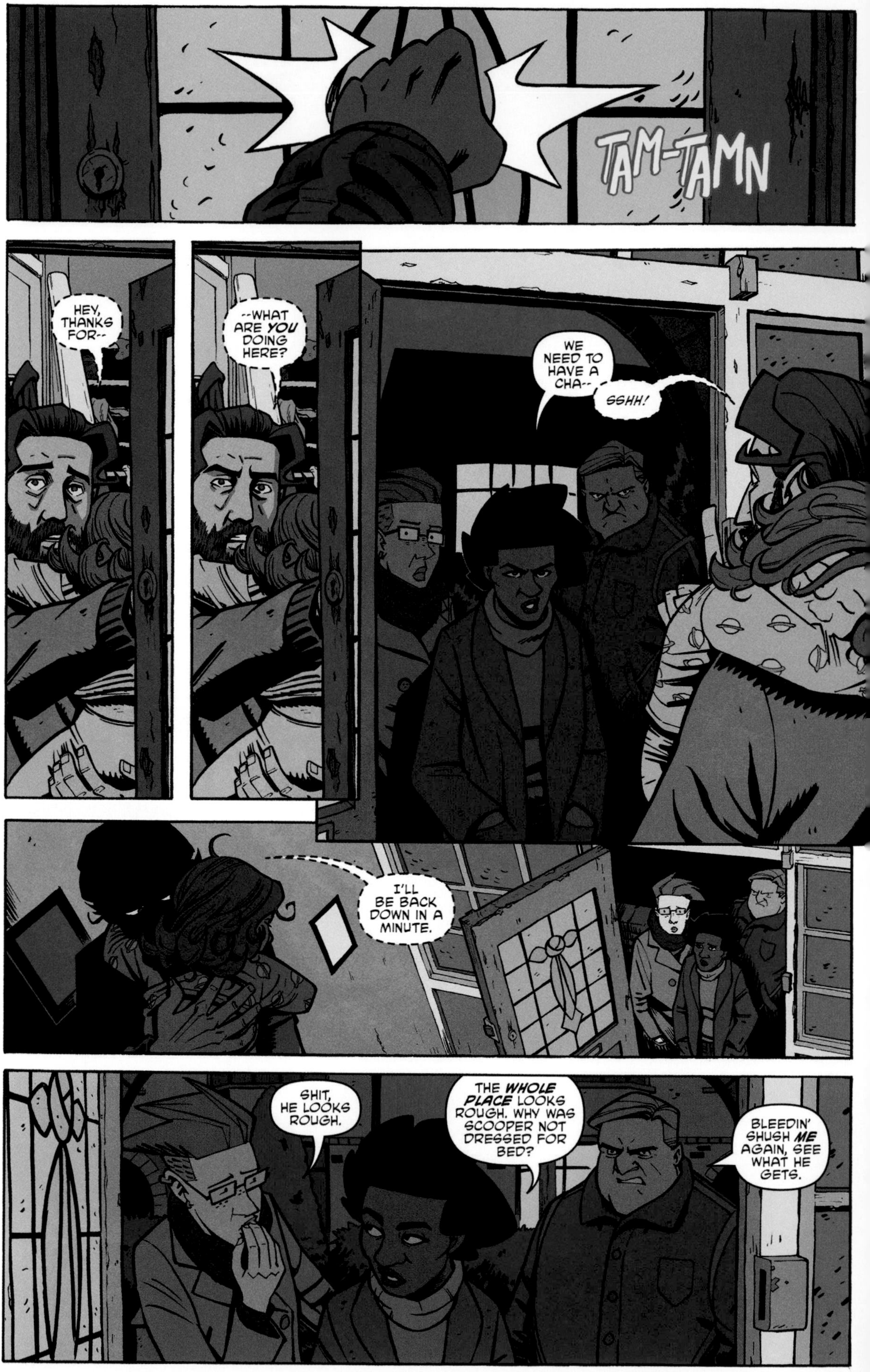
TAM-TAMN
HEY, THANKS FOR--
--WHAT ARE YOU DOING HERE?
WE NEED TO HAVE A CHA--
SSHH!
I'LL BE BACK DOWN IN A MINUTE.
SHIT, HE LOOKS ROUGH.
THE WHOLE PLACE LOOKS ROUGH. WHY WAS SCOOPER NOT DRESSED FOR BED?
BLEEDIN' SHUSH ME AGAIN, SEE WHAT HE GETS.

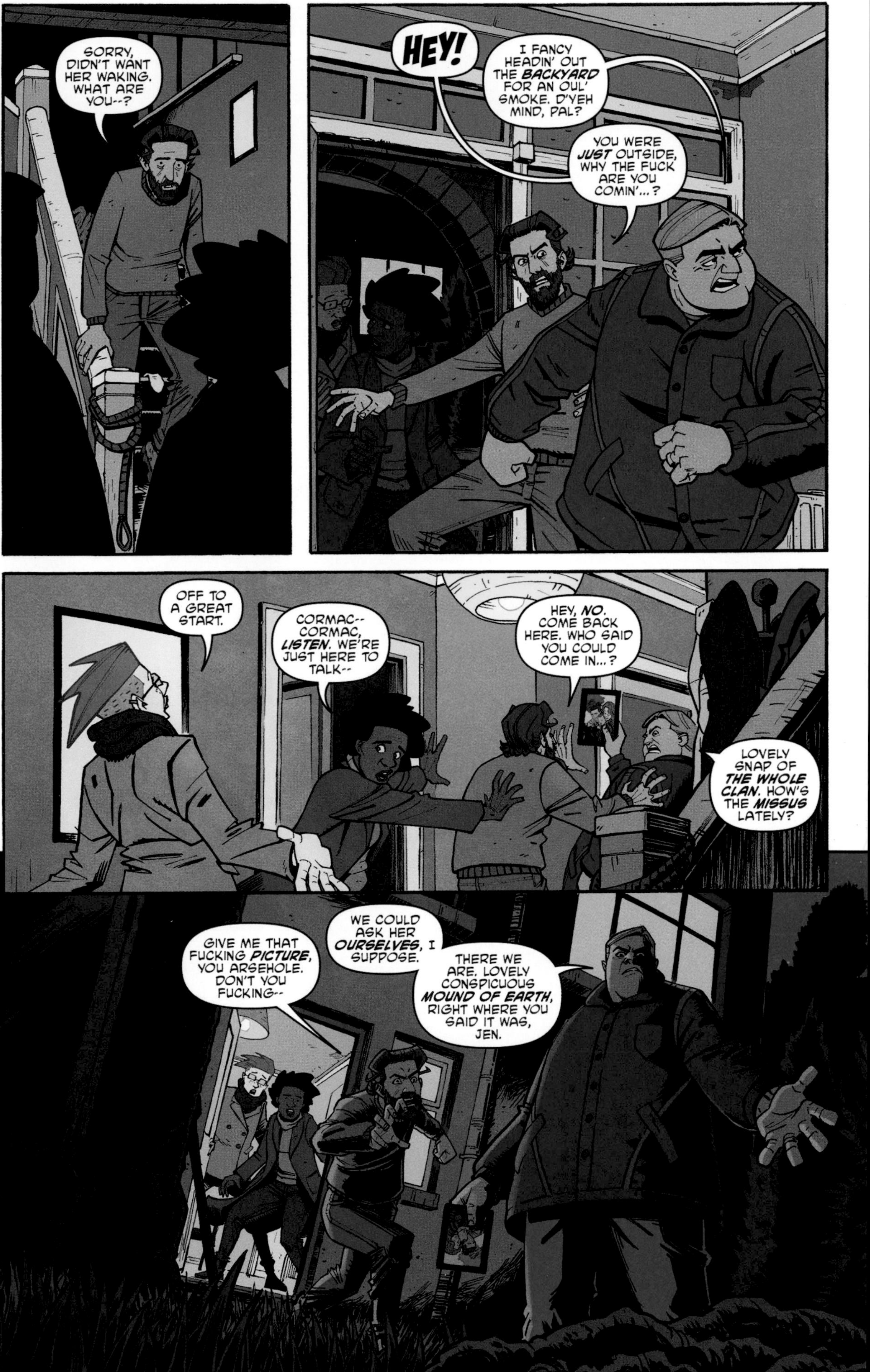
SORRY, DIDN'T WANT HER WAKING. WHAT ARE YOU--?
HEY!
I FANCY HEADIN' OUT THE BACKYARD FOR AN OUL' SMOKE. D'YEH MIND, PAL?
YOU WERE JUST OUTSIDE, WHY THE FUCK ARE YOU COMIN'...?
OFF TO A GREAT START.
CORMAC-- CORMAC, LISTEN. WE'RE JUST HERE TO TALK--
HEY, NO. COME BACK HERE. WHO SAID YOU COULD COME IN...?
LOVELY SNAP OF THE WHOLE CLAN. HOW'S THE MISSUS LATELY?
GIVE ME THAT FUCKING PICTURE, YOU ARSEHOLE. DON'T YOU FUCKING--
WE COULD ASK HER OURSELVES, I SUPPOSE.
THERE WE ARE. LOVELY CONSPICUOUS MOUND OF EARTH, RIGHT WHERE YOU SAID IT WAS, JEN.

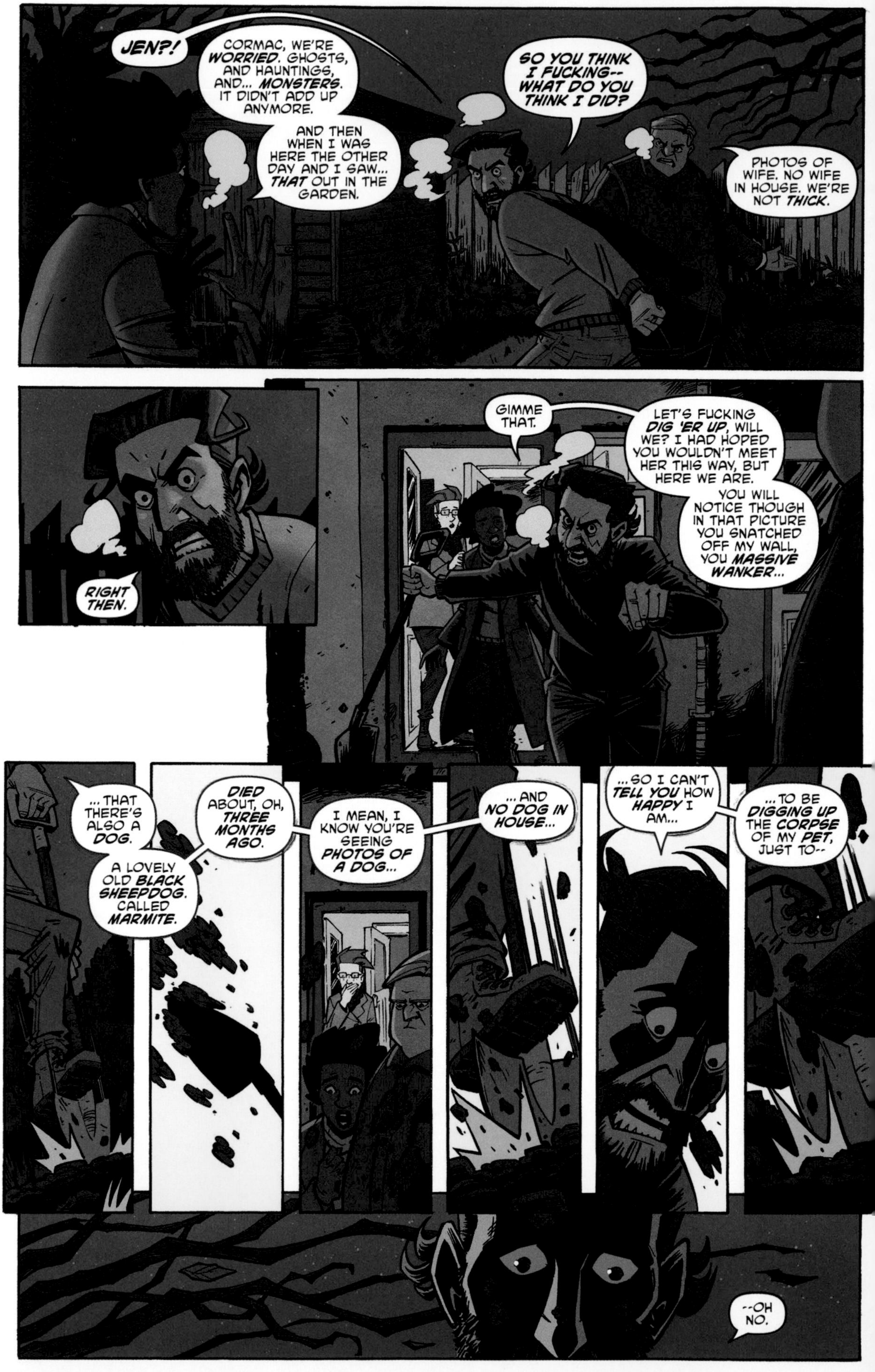

JEN?!
CORMAC, WE'RE WORRIED. GHOSTS, AND HAUNTINGS, AND... MONSTERS. IT DIDN'T ADD UP ANYMORE.
AND THEN WHEN I WAS HERE THE OTHER DAY AND I SAW... THAT OUT IN THE GARDEN.
SO YOU THINK I FUCKING-- WHAT DO YOU THINK I DID?
PHOTOS OF WIFE. NO WIFE IN HOUSE. WE'RE NOT THICK.
RIGHT THEN.
GIMME THAT.
LET'S FUCKING DIG 'ER UP, WILL WE? I HAD HOPED YOU WOULDN'T MEET HER THIS WAY, BUT HERE WE ARE.
YOU WILL NOTICE THOUGH IN THAT PICTURE YOU SNATCHED OFF MY WALL, YOU MASSIVE WANKER...
...THAT THERE'S ALSO A DOG.
A LOVELY OLD BLACK SHEEPDOG. CALLED MARMITE.
DIED ABOUT, OH, THREE MONTHS AGO.
I MEAN, I KNOW YOU'RE SEEING PHOTOS OF A DOG...
...AND NO DOG IN HOUSE...
...SO I CAN'T TELL YOU HOW HAPPY I AM...
...TO BE DIGGING UP THE CORPSE OF MY PET, JUST TO--
--OH NO.

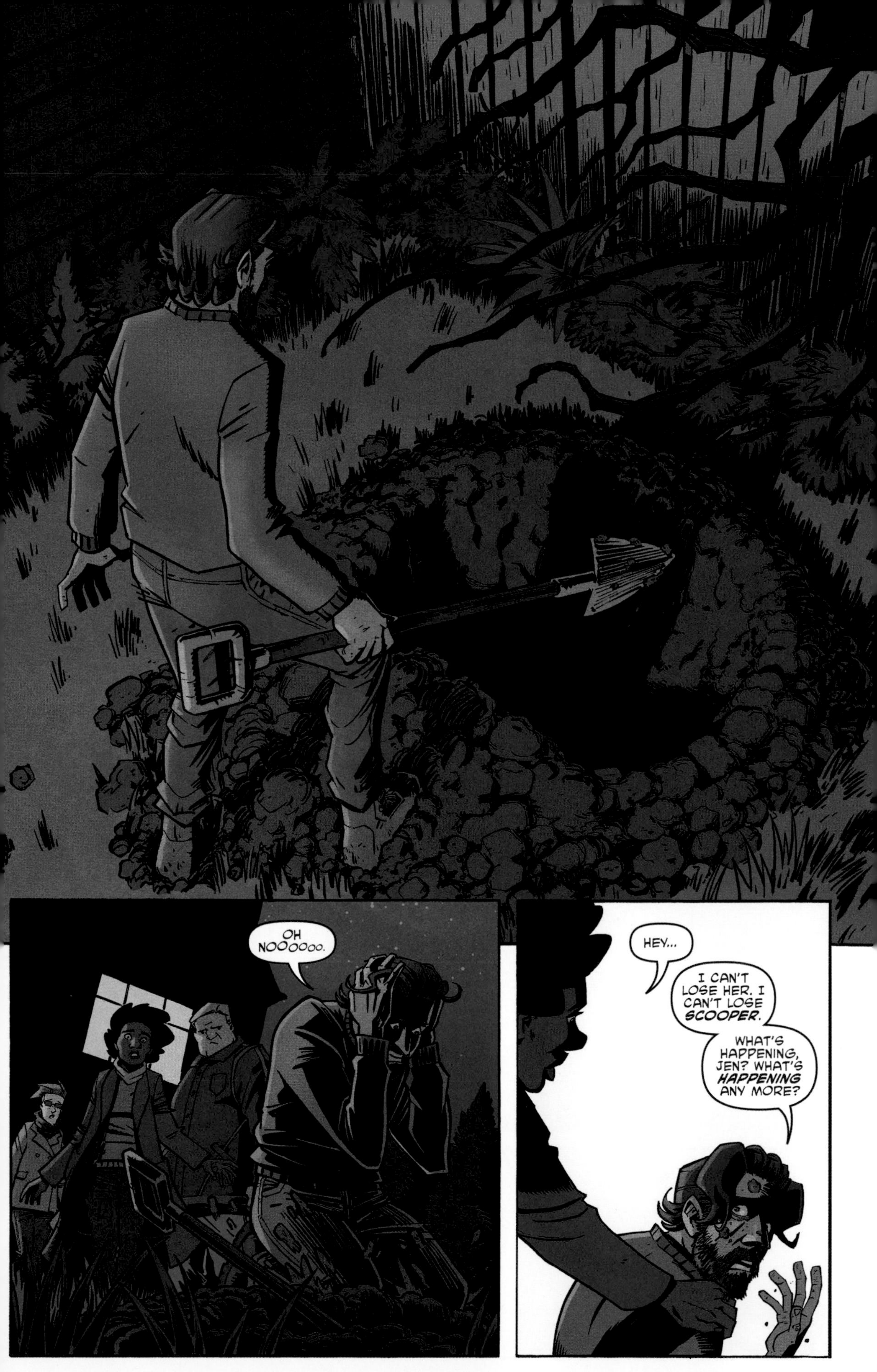
OH NOOOOOO.
HEY...
I CAN'T LOSE HER. I CAN'T LOSE SCOOPER.
WHAT'S HAPPENING, JEN? WHAT'S HAPPENING ANY MORE?

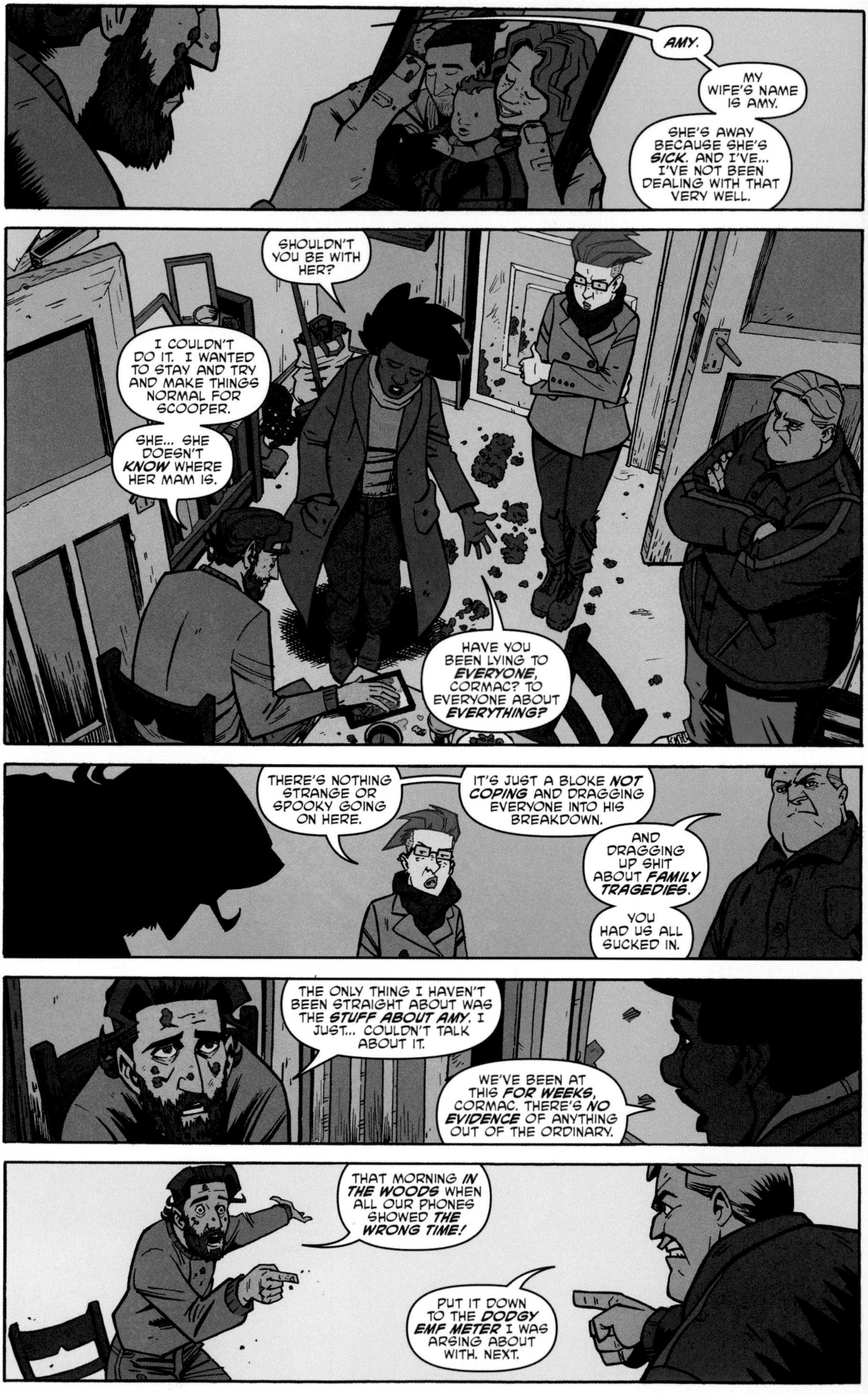
AMY.
MY WIFE'S NAME IS AMY.
SHE'S AWAY BECAUSE SHE'S SICK. AND I'VE... I'VE NOT BEEN DEALING WITH THAT VERY WELL.
SHOULDN'T YOU BE WITH HER?
I COULDN'T DO IT. I WANTED TO STAY AND TRY AND MAKE THINGS NORMAL FOR SCOOPER.
SHE... SHE DOESN'T KNOW WHERE HER MAM IS.
HAVE YOU BEEN LYING TO EVERYONE, CORMAC? TO EVERYONE ABOUT EVERYTHING?
THERE'S NOTHING STRANGE OR SPOOKY GOING ON HERE.
IT'S JUST A BLOKE NOT COPING AND DRAGGING EVERYONE INTO HIS BREAKDOWN.
AND DRAGGING UP SHIT ABOUT FAMILY TRAGEDIES.
YOU HAD US ALL SUCKED IN.
THE ONLY THING I HAVEN'T BEEN STRAIGHT ABOUT WAS THE STUFF ABOUT AMY. I JUST... COULDN'T TALK ABOUT IT.
WE'VE BEEN AT THIS FOR WEEKS, CORMAC. THERE'S NO EVIDENCE OF ANYTHING OUT OF THE ORDINARY.
THAT MORNING IN THE WOODS WHEN ALL OUR PHONES SHOWED THE WRONG TIME!
PUT IT DOWN TO THE DODGY EMF METER I WAS ARSING ABOUT WITH. NEXT.

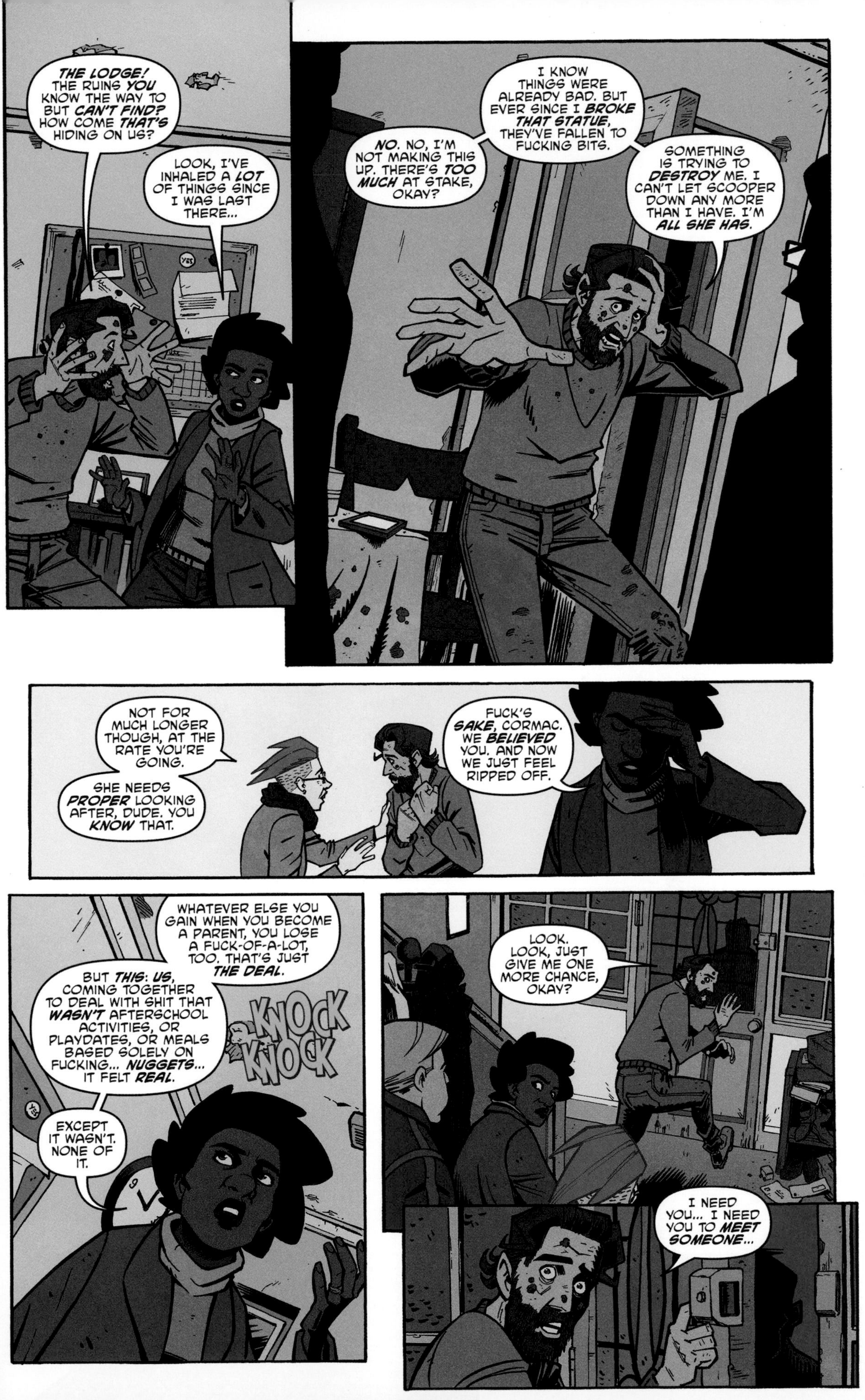
THE LODGE! THE RUINS YOU KNOW THE WAY TO BUT CAN'T FIND? HOW COME THAT'S HIDING ON US?
LOOK, I'VE INHALED A LOT OF THINGS SINCE I WAS LAST THERE...
NO. NO, I'M NOT MAKING THIS UP. THERE'S TOO MUCH AT STAKE, OKAY?
I KNOW THINGS WERE ALREADY BAD. BUT EVER SINCE I BROKE THAT STATUE, THEY'VE FALLEN TO FUCKING BITS.
SOMETHING IS TRYING TO DESTROY ME. I CAN'T LET SCOOPER DOWN ANY MORE THAN I HAVE. I'M ALL SHE HAS.
NOT FOR MUCH LONGER THOUGH, AT THE RATE YOU'RE GOING.
SHE NEEDS PROPER LOOKING AFTER, DUDE. YOU KNOW THAT.
FUCK'S SAKE, CORMAC. WE BELIEVED YOU. AND NOW WE JUST FEEL RIPPED OFF.
WHATEVER ELSE YOU GAIN WHEN YOU BECOME A PARENT, YOU LOSE A FUCK-OF-A-LOT, TOO. THAT'S JUST THE DEAL.
BUT THIS: US, COMING TOGETHER TO DEAL WITH SHIT THAT WASN'T AFTERSCHOOL ACTIVITIES, OR PLAYDATES, OR MEALS BASED SOLELY ON FUCKING... NUGGETS... IT FELT REAL.
KNOCK KNOCK
EXCEPT IT WASN'T. NONE OF IT.
LOOK. LOOK, JUST GIVE ME ONE MORE CHANCE, OKAY?
I NEED YOU... I NEED YOU TO MEET SOMEONE...

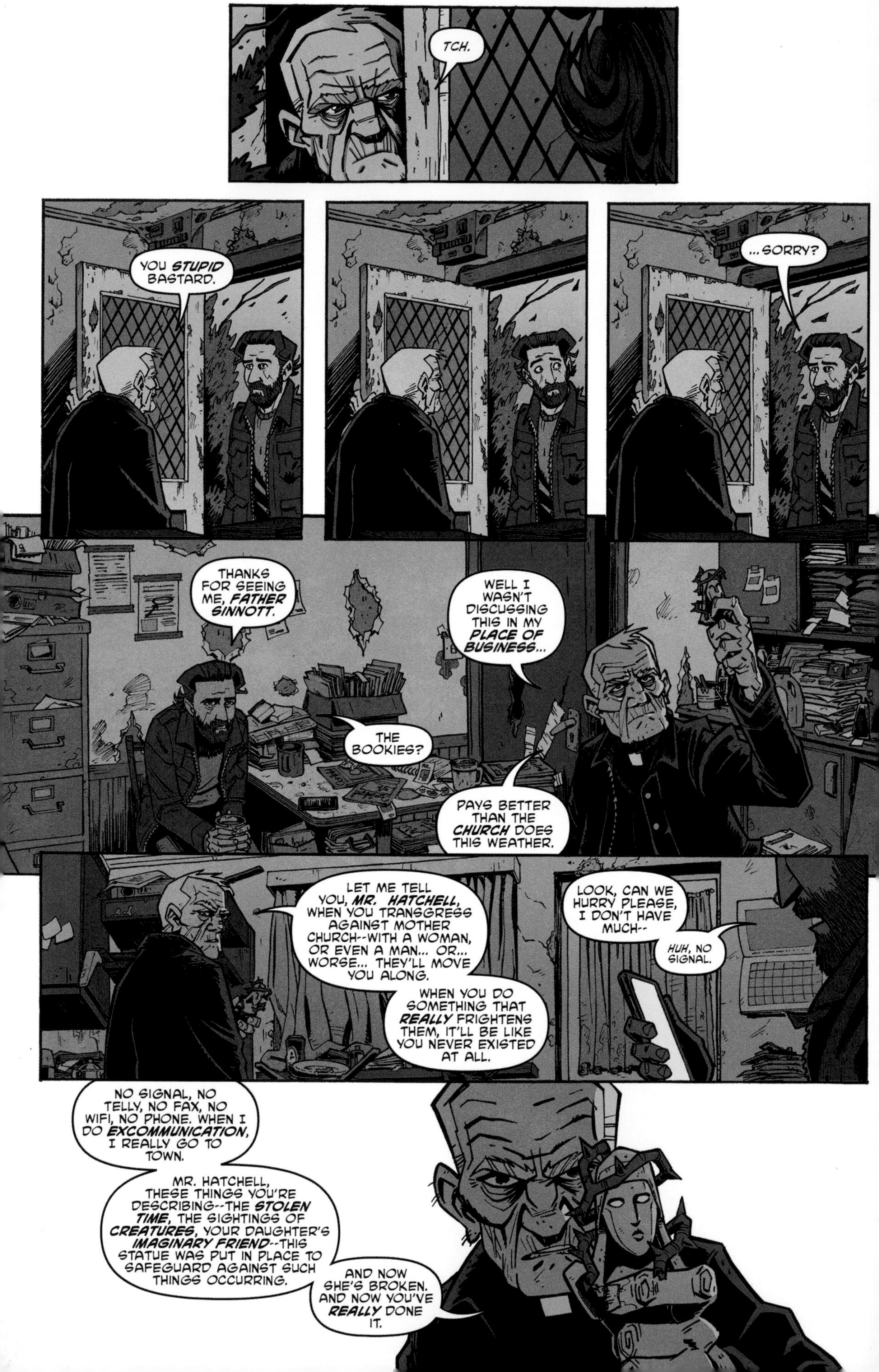
TCH.
YOU STUPID BASTARD.
...SORRY?
THANKS FOR SEEING ME, FATHER SINNOTT.
WELL I WASN'T DISCUSSING THIS IN MY PLACE OF BUSINESS...
THE BOOKIES?
PAYS BETTER THAN THE CHURCH DOES THIS WEATHER.
LET ME TELL YOU, MR. HATCHELL, WHEN YOU TRANSGRESS AGAINST MOTHER CHURCH--WITH A WOMAN, OR EVEN A MAN... OR... WORSE... THEY'LL MOVE YOU ALONG.
WHEN YOU DO SOMETHING THAT REALLY FRIGHTENS THEM, IT'LL BE LIKE YOU NEVER EXISTED AT ALL.
LOOK, CAN WE HURRY PLEASE, I DON'T HAVE MUCH--
HUH, NO SIGNAL.
NO SIGNAL, NO TELLY, NO FAX, NO WIFI, NO PHONE. WHEN I DO EXCOMMUNICATION, I REALLY GO TO TOWN.
MR. HATCHELL, THESE THINGS YOU'RE DESCRIBING--THE STOLEN TIME, THE SIGHTINGS OF CREATURES, YOUR DAUGHTER'S IMAGINARY FRIEND--THIS STATUE WAS PUT IN PLACE TO SAFEGUARD AGAINST SUCH THINGS OCCURRING.
AND NOW SHE'S BROKEN. AND NOW YOU'VE REALLY DONE IT.

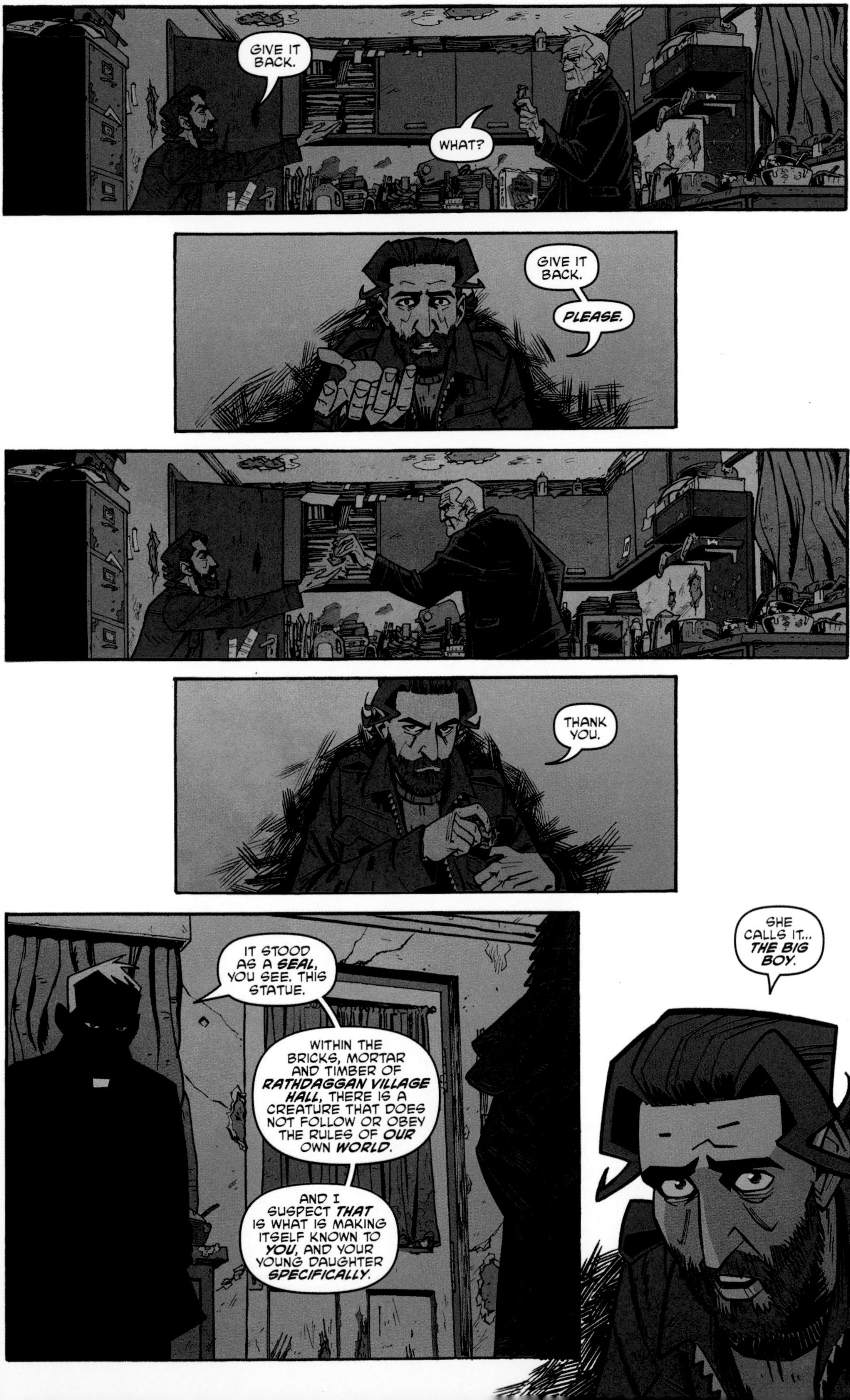
GIVE IT BACK.
WHAT?
GIVE IT BACK.
PLEASE.
THANK YOU.
IT STOOD AS A SEAL, YOU SEE. THIS STATUE.
WITHIN THE BRICKS, MORTAR AND TIMBER OF RATHDAGGAN VILLAGE HALL, THERE IS A CREATURE THAT DOES NOT FOLLOW OR OBEY THE RULES OF OUR OWN WORLD.
AND I SUSPECT THAT IS WHAT IS MAKING ITSELF KNOWN TO YOU, AND YOUR YOUNG DAUGHTER SPECIFICALLY.
SHE CALLS IT... THE BIG BOY.

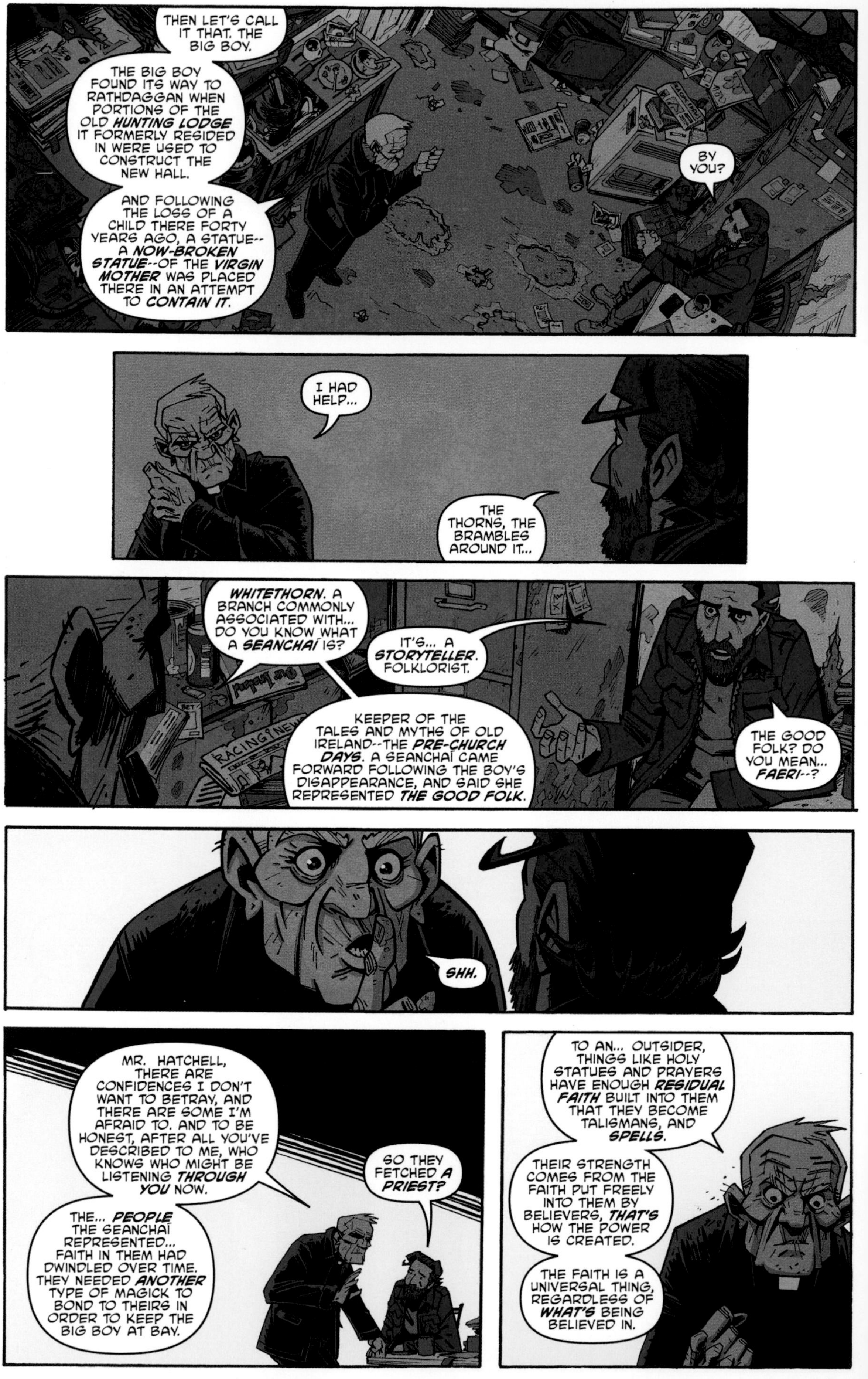
THEN LET'S CALL IT THAT. THE BIG BOY.
THE BIG BOY FOUND ITS WAY TO RATHDAGGAN WHEN PORTIONS OF THE OLD HUNTING LODGE IT FORMERLY RESIDED IN WERE USED TO CONSTRUCT THE NEW HALL.
AND FOLLOWING THE LOSS OF A CHILD THERE FORTY YEARS AGO, A STATUE-- A NOW-BROKEN STATUE--OF THE VIRGIN MOTHER WAS PLACED THERE IN AN ATTEMPT TO CONTAIN IT.
BY YOU?
I HAD HELP...
THE THORNS, THE BRAMBLES AROUND IT...
WHITETHORN. A BRANCH COMMONLY ASSOCIATED WITH... DO YOU KNOW WHAT A SEANCHAÍ IS?
IT'S... A STORYTELLER. FOLKLORIST.
KEEPER OF THE TALES AND MYTHS OF OLD IRELAND--THE PRE-CHURCH DAYS. A SEANCHAÍ CAME FORWARD FOLLOWING THE BOY'S DISAPPEARANCE, AND SAID SHE REPRESENTED THE GOOD FOLK.
THE GOOD FOLK? DO YOU MEAN... FAERI--?
SHH.
MR. HATCHELL, THERE ARE CONFIDENCES I DON'T WANT TO BETRAY, AND THERE ARE SOME I'M AFRAID TO. AND TO BE HONEST, AFTER ALL YOU'VE DESCRIBED TO ME, WHO KNOWS WHO MIGHT BE LISTENING THROUGH YOU NOW.
THE... PEOPLE THE SEANCHAÍ REPRESENTED... FAITH IN THEM HAD DWINDLED OVER TIME. THEY NEEDED ANOTHER TYPE OF MAGICK TO BOND TO THEIRS IN ORDER TO KEEP THE BIG BOY AT BAY.
SO THEY FETCHED A PRIEST?
TO AN... OUTSIDER, THINGS LIKE HOLY STATUES AND PRAYERS HAVE ENOUGH RESIDUAL FAITH BUILT INTO THEM THAT THEY BECOME TALISMANS, AND SPELLS.
THEIR STRENGTH COMES FROM THE FAITH PUT FREELY INTO THEM BY BELIEVERS, THAT'S HOW THE POWER IS CREATED.
THE FAITH IS A UNIVERSAL THING, REGARDLESS OF WHAT'S BEING BELIEVED IN.

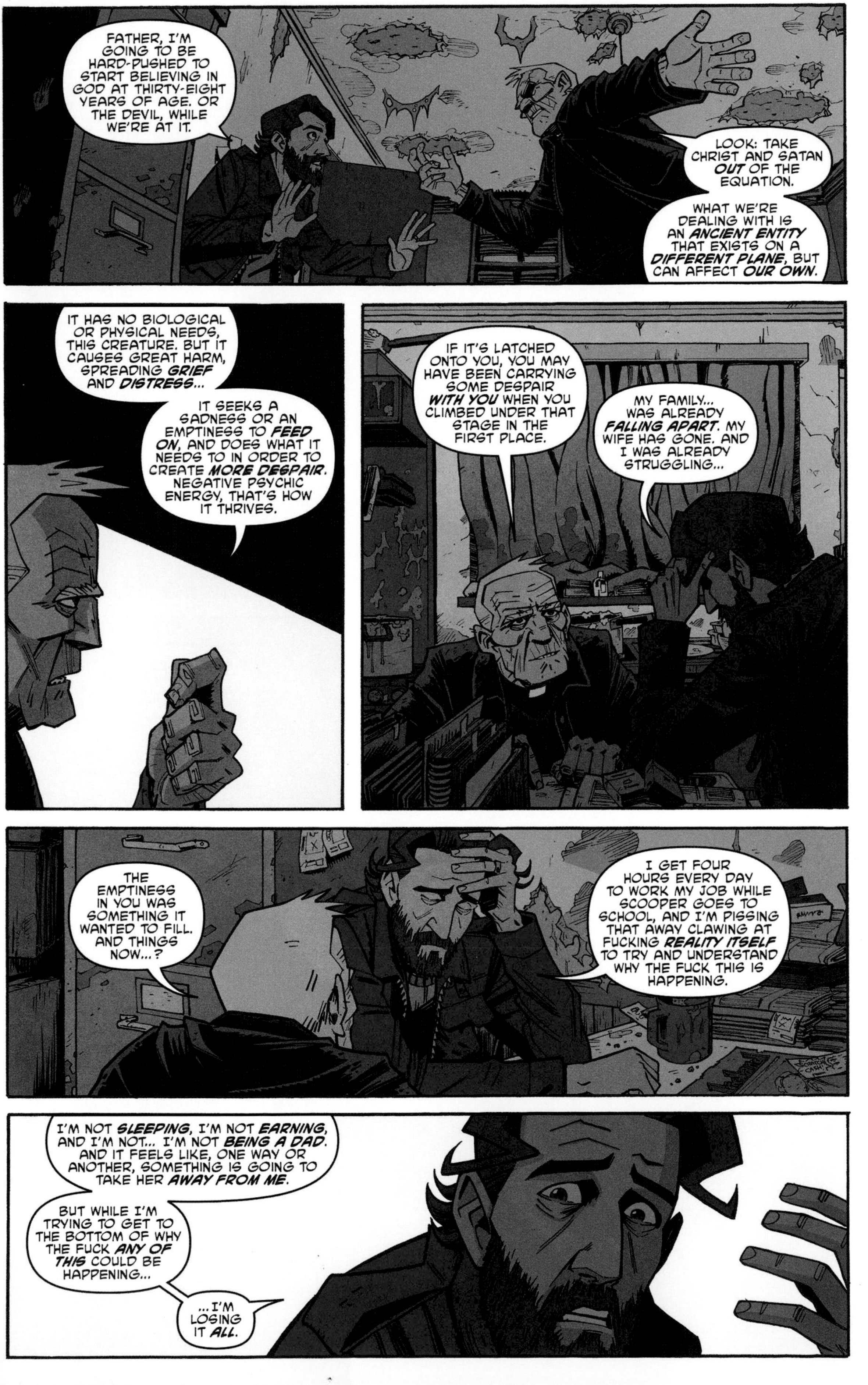
FATHER, I'M GOING TO BE HARD-PUSHED TO START BELIEVING IN GOD AT THIRTY-EIGHT YEARS OF AGE. OR THE DEVIL, WHILE WE'RE AT IT.
LOOK: TAKE CHRIST AND SATAN ***OUT*** OF THE EQUATION.
WHAT WE'RE DEALING WITH IS AN ***ANCIENT ENTITY*** THAT EXISTS ON A ***DIFFERENT PLANE***, BUT CAN AFFECT ***OUR OWN***.
IT HAS NO BIOLOGICAL OR PHYSICAL NEEDS, THIS CREATURE. BUT IT CAUSES GREAT HARM, SPREADING ***GRIEF*** AND ***DISTRESS***...
IT SEEKS A SADNESS OR AN EMPTINESS TO ***FEED ON***, AND DOES WHAT IT NEEDS TO IN ORDER TO CREATE ***MORE DESPAIR***. NEGATIVE PSYCHIC ENERGY, THAT'S HOW IT THRIVES.
IF IT'S LATCHED ONTO YOU, YOU MAY HAVE BEEN CARRYING SOME DESPAIR ***WITH YOU*** WHEN YOU CLIMBED UNDER THAT STAGE IN THE FIRST PLACE.
MY FAMILY... WAS ALREADY ***FALLING APART***. MY WIFE HAS GONE. AND I WAS ALREADY STRUGGLING...
THE EMPTINESS IN YOU WAS SOMETHING IT WANTED TO FILL. AND THINGS NOW...?
I GET FOUR HOURS EVERY DAY TO WORK MY JOB WHILE SCOOPER GOES TO SCHOOL, AND I'M PISSING THAT AWAY CLAWING AT FUCKING ***REALITY ITSELF*** TO TRY AND UNDERSTAND WHY THE FUCK THIS IS HAPPENING.
I'M NOT ***SLEEPING***, I'M NOT ***EARNING***, AND I'M NOT... I'M NOT ***BEING A DAD***. AND IT FEELS LIKE, ONE WAY OR ANOTHER, SOMETHING IS GOING TO TAKE HER ***AWAY FROM ME***.
BUT WHILE I'M TRYING TO GET TO THE BOTTOM OF WHY THE FUCK ***ANY OF THIS*** COULD BE HAPPENING...
...I'M LOSING IT ***ALL***.

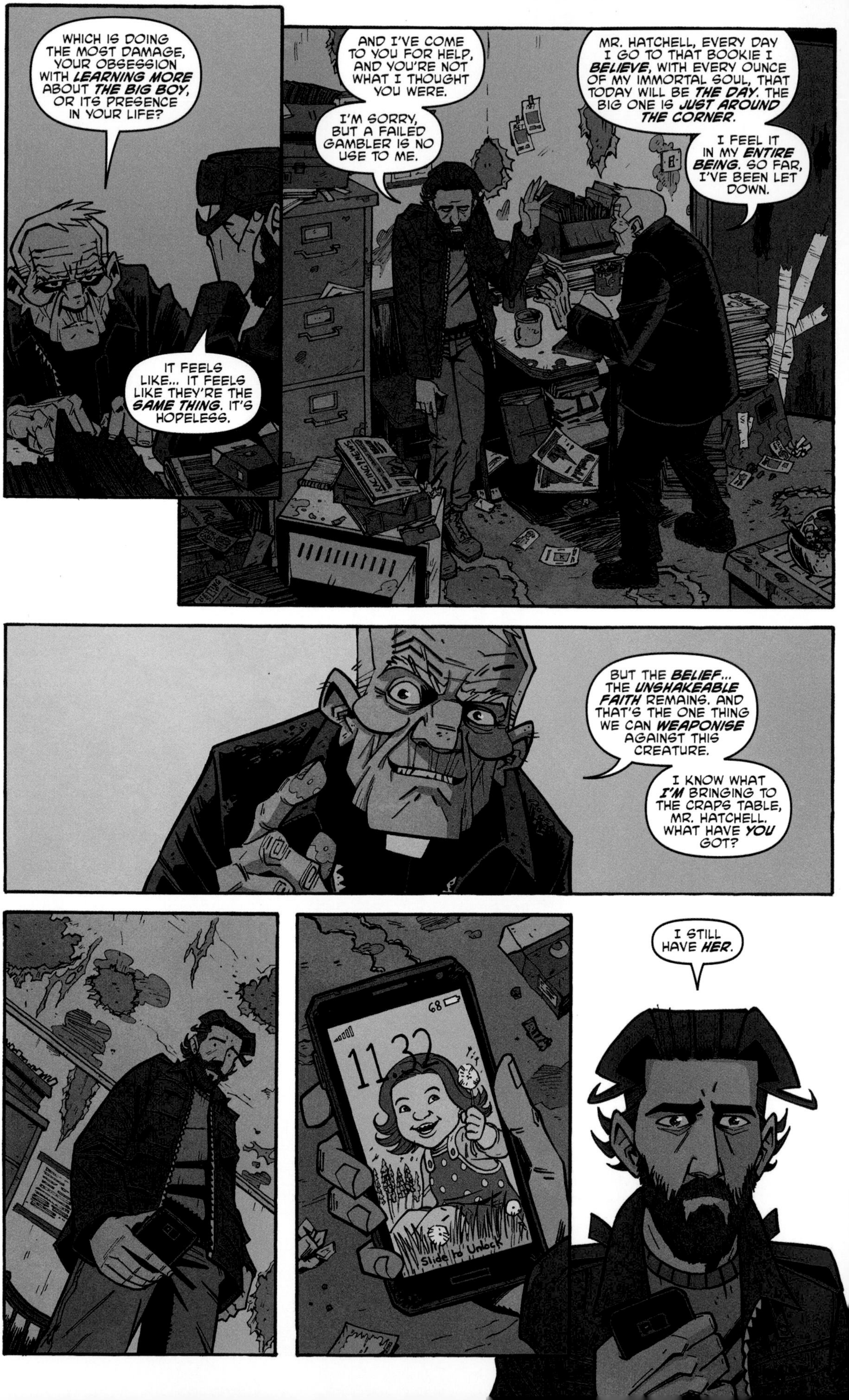
WHICH IS DOING THE MOST DAMAGE, YOUR OBSESSION WITH LEARNING MORE ABOUT THE BIG BOY, OR ITS PRESENCE IN YOUR LIFE?
IT FEELS LIKE... IT FEELS LIKE THEY'RE THE SAME THING. IT'S HOPELESS.
AND I'VE COME TO YOU FOR HELP, AND YOU'RE NOT WHAT I THOUGHT YOU WERE.
I'M SORRY, BUT A FAILED GAMBLER IS NO USE TO ME.
MR. HATCHELL, EVERY DAY I GO TO THAT BOOKIE I BELIEVE, WITH EVERY OUNCE OF MY IMMORTAL SOUL, THAT TODAY WILL BE THE DAY. THE BIG ONE IS JUST AROUND THE CORNER.
I FEEL IT IN MY ENTIRE BEING. SO FAR, I'VE BEEN LET DOWN.
BUT THE BELIEF... THE UNSHAKEABLE FAITH REMAINS. AND THAT'S THE ONE THING WE CAN WEAPONISE AGAINST THIS CREATURE.
I KNOW WHAT I'M BRINGING TO THE CRAPS TABLE, MR. HATCHELL. WHAT HAVE YOU GOT?
68
11 32
Slide to Unlock
I STILL HAVE HER.

SO YOU FOUND HIM IN A BOOKIE'S?

SHH. YEAH, I WAS *TOLD* HE'D BE THERE. I DIDN'T BUMP INTO HIM WHILE I WAS PUTTING A TENNER ON THE TWO-FORTY-FIVE.

YEAH... BUT YOU STILL FOUND THE PRIEST THAT'S GOING TO *SOLVE* THIS... IN *A BOOKIE'S*.

WILL YOU... WILL YOU GUYS STAY? PLEASE?

CORMAC, YOU TAKING ON SO MUCH OF THIS ALONE... THAT WASN'T THE DEAL.

YEAH, GOING ROGUE, AND RISKING *SUICIDE BY FLYNNO* BY ENDING UP ON HIS MA'S DOORSTEP. THAT'S JUST... THICK.

FUCKING *EEJIT*. ME MA DON'T TALK TO HER *OWN KIDS* ABOUT ME BRUDDER, SHE WAS NEVER GONNA OPEN UP TO A *STRANGER*.

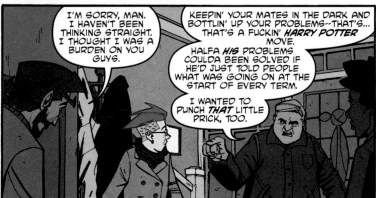

I'M SORRY, MAN. I HAVEN'T BEEN THINKING STRAIGHT. I THOUGHT I WAS A BURDEN ON YOU GUYS.

KEEPIN' YOUR MATES IN THE DARK AND BOTTLIN' UP YOUR PROBLEMS--THAT'S... THAT'S A FUCKIN' *HARRY POTTER* MOVE.

HALFA *HIS* PROBLEMS COULDA BEEN SOLVED IF HE'D JUST TOLD PEOPLE WHAT WAS GOING ON AT THE START OF EVERY TERM.

I WANTED TO PUNCH *THAT* LITTLE PRICK, TOO.

DIDN'T THINK THEY WERE YOUR TYPE OF MOVIE, DUDE.

SMOOCH ME GOOCH-- I'VE GOT THREE KIDS IN THEIR TWENTIES. I READ EVERY ONE A' DEM BOOKS *OUT LOUD*.

I'M THE NORTHSIDE STEPHEN FRY.

WE'LL STAY. OF COURSE WE'LL STAY. YOU *HAVE US*. YOU HAD US *ALL ALONG*, YOU TWAT.

AND HOPEFULLY, AFTER TONIGHT, WE CAN *ACTUALLY* JUST GO FOR COFFEE IN THE MORNINGS.

THAT SOUNDS GOOD.

AHEM.

WE'RE READY TO BEGIN.

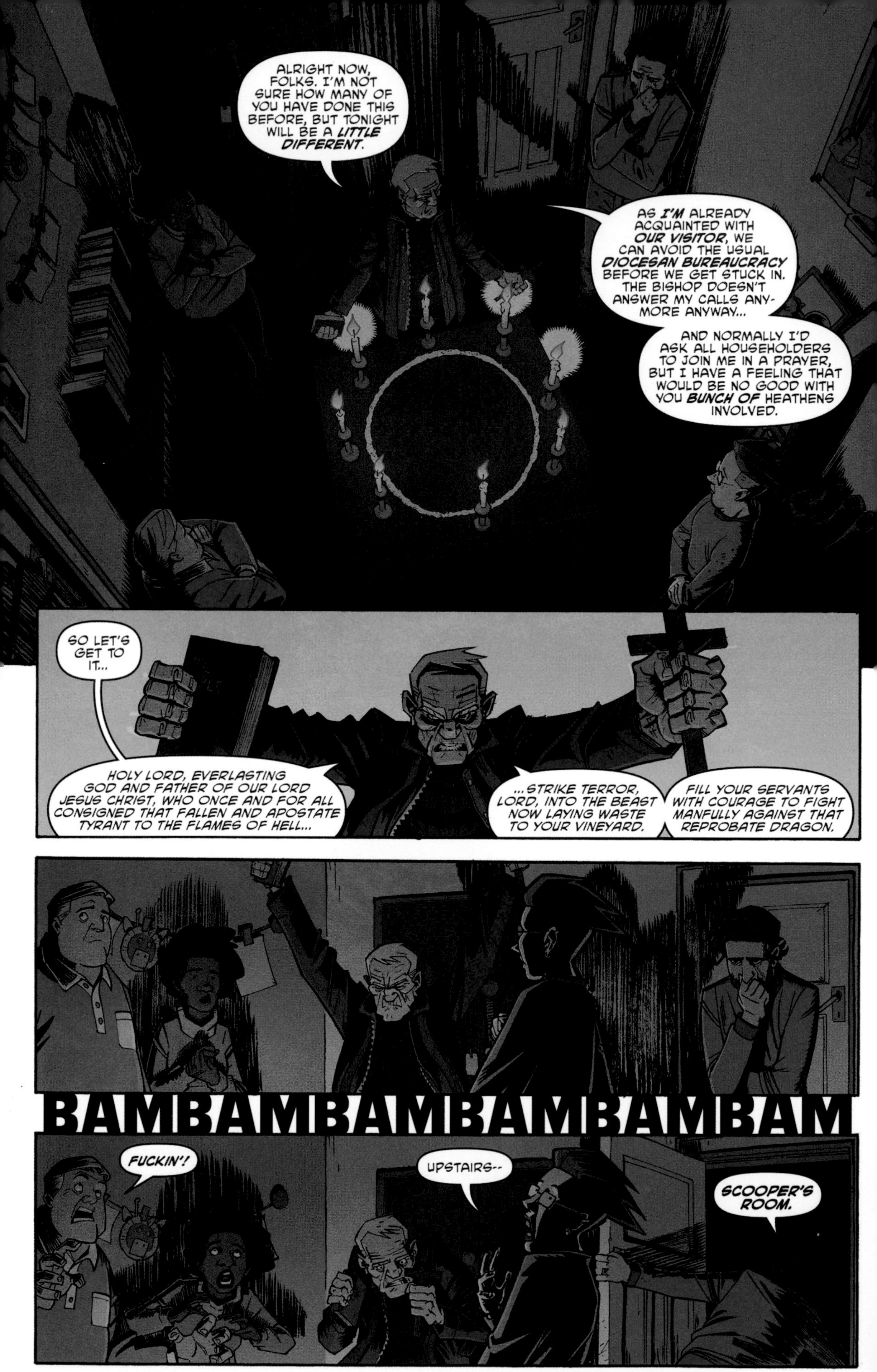
ALRIGHT NOW, FOLKS. I'M NOT SURE HOW MANY OF YOU HAVE DONE THIS BEFORE, BUT TONIGHT WILL BE A LITTLE DIFFERENT.
AS I'M ALREADY ACQUAINTED WITH OUR VISITOR, WE CAN AVOID THE USUAL DIOCESAN BUREAUCRACY BEFORE WE GET STUCK IN. THE BISHOP DOESN'T ANSWER MY CALLS ANY-MORE ANYWAY...
AND NORMALLY I'D ASK ALL HOUSEHOLDERS TO JOIN ME IN A PRAYER, BUT I HAVE A FEELING THAT WOULD BE NO GOOD WITH YOU BUNCH OF HEATHENS INVOLVED.
SO LET'S GET TO IT...
HOLY LORD, EVERLASTING GOD AND FATHER OF OUR LORD JESUS CHRIST, WHO ONCE AND FOR ALL CONSIGNED THAT FALLEN AND APOSTATE TYRANT TO THE FLAMES OF HELL...
...STRIKE TERROR, LORD, INTO THE BEAST NOW LAYING WASTE TO YOUR VINEYARD.
FILL YOUR SERVANTS WITH COURAGE TO FIGHT MANFULLY AGAINST THAT REPROBATE DRAGON.
BAMBAMBAMBAMBAMBAMBAM
FUCKIN'!
UPSTAIRS--
SCOOPER'S ROOM.

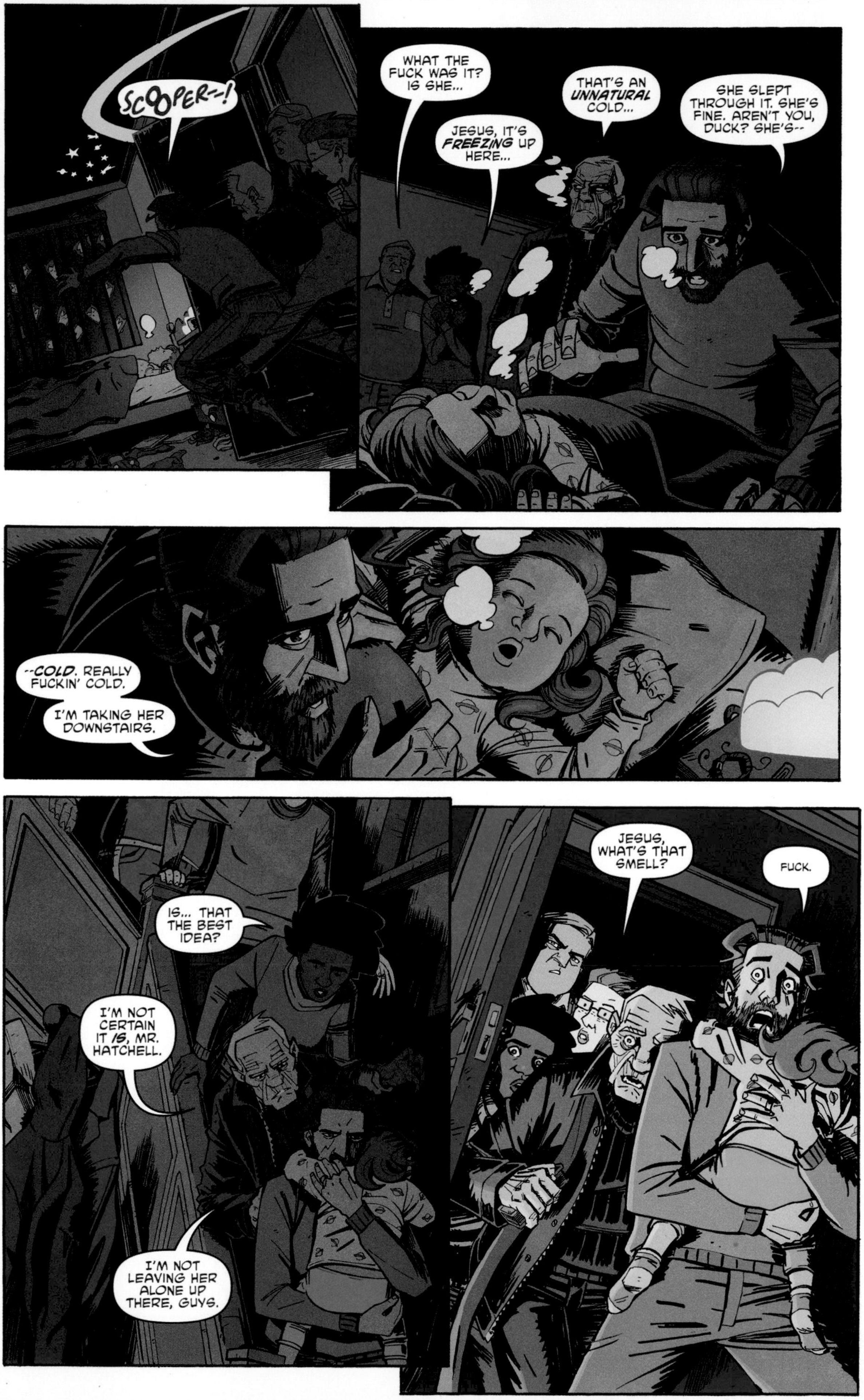
SCOOPER--!
WHAT THE FUCK WAS IT? IS SHE...
JESUS, IT'S FREEZING UP HERE...
THAT'S AN UNNATURAL COLD...
SHE SLEPT THROUGH IT. SHE'S FINE. AREN'T YOU, DUCK? SHE'S--
--COLD. REALLY FUCKIN' COLD.
I'M TAKING HER DOWNSTAIRS.
IS... THAT THE BEST IDEA?
I'M NOT CERTAIN IT IS, MR. HATCHELL.
I'M NOT LEAVING HER ALONE UP THERE, GUYS.
JESUS, WHAT'S THAT SMELL?
FUCK.

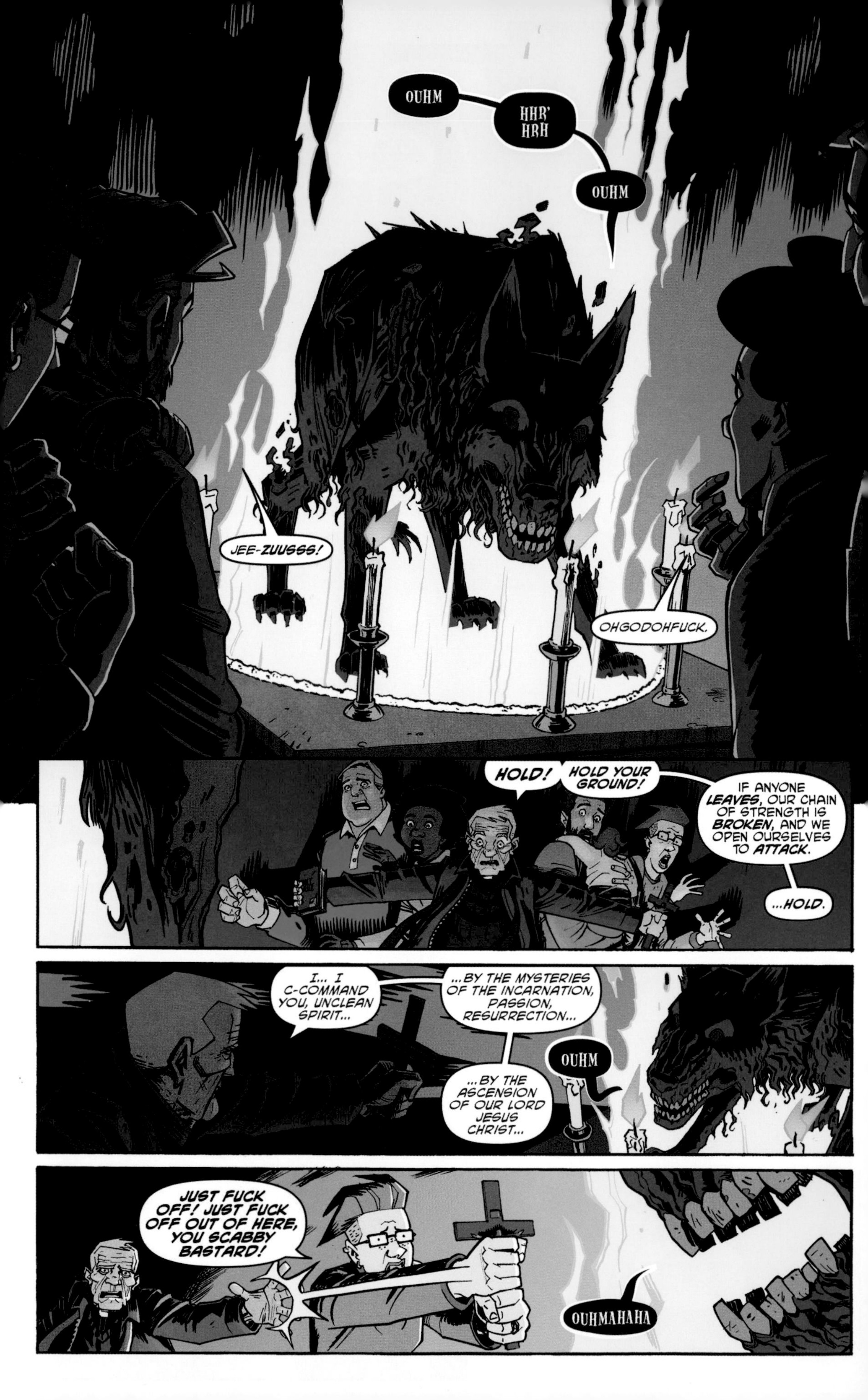
OUHM
HHR' HRH
OUHM
JEE-ZUUSSS!
OHGODOHFUCK.
HOLD!
HOLD YOUR GROUND!
IF ANYONE LEAVES, OUR CHAIN OF STRENGTH IS BROKEN, AND WE OPEN OURSELVES TO ATTACK.
...HOLD.
I... I C-COMMAND YOU, UNCLEAN SPIRIT...
...BY THE MYSTERIES OF THE INCARNATION, PASSION, RESURRECTION...
...BY THE ASCENSION OF OUR LORD JESUS CHRIST...
OUHM
JUST FUCK OFF! JUST FUCK OFF OUT OF HERE, YOU SCABBY BASTARD!
OUHMAHAHA

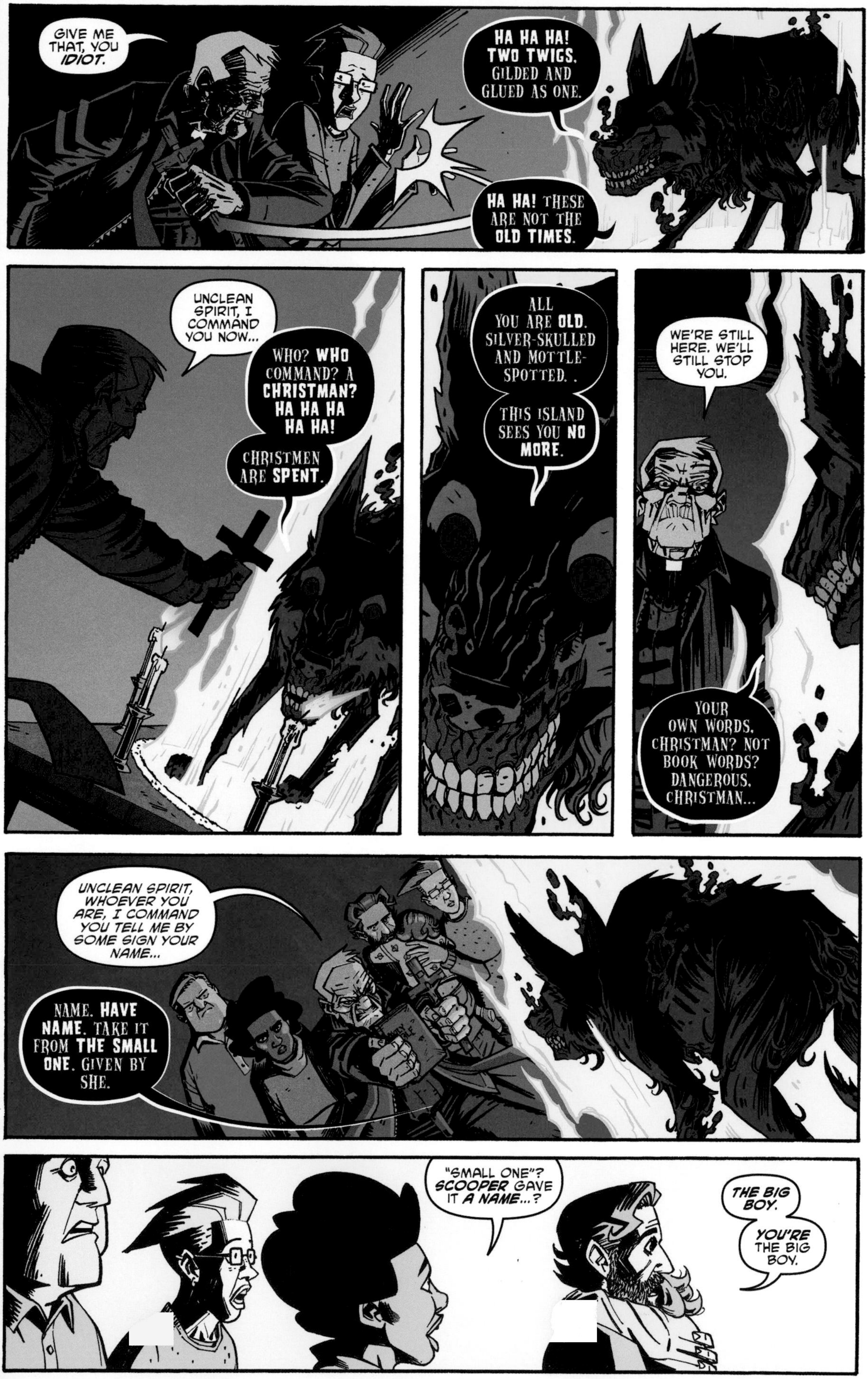
GIVE ME THAT, YOU IDIOT.
HA HA HA! TWO TWIGS, GILDED AND GLUED AS ONE.
HA HA! THESE ARE NOT THE OLD TIMES.
UNCLEAN SPIRIT, I COMMAND YOU NOW...
WHO? WHO COMMAND? A CHRISTMAN? HA HA HA HA HA!
CHRISTMEN ARE SPENT.
ALL YOU ARE OLD. SILVER-SKULLED AND MOTTLE-SPOTTED. .
THIS ISLAND SEES YOU NO MORE.
WE'RE STILL HERE. WE'LL STILL STOP YOU.
YOUR OWN WORDS, CHRISTMAN? NOT BOOK WORDS? DANGEROUS, CHRISTMAN...
UNCLEAN SPIRIT, WHOEVER YOU ARE, I COMMAND YOU TELL ME BY SOME SIGN YOUR NAME...
NAME. HAVE NAME. TAKE IT FROM THE SMALL ONE. GIVEN BY SHE.
"SMALL ONE"? SCOOPER GAVE IT A NAME...?
THE BIG BOY.
YOU'RE THE BIG BOY.

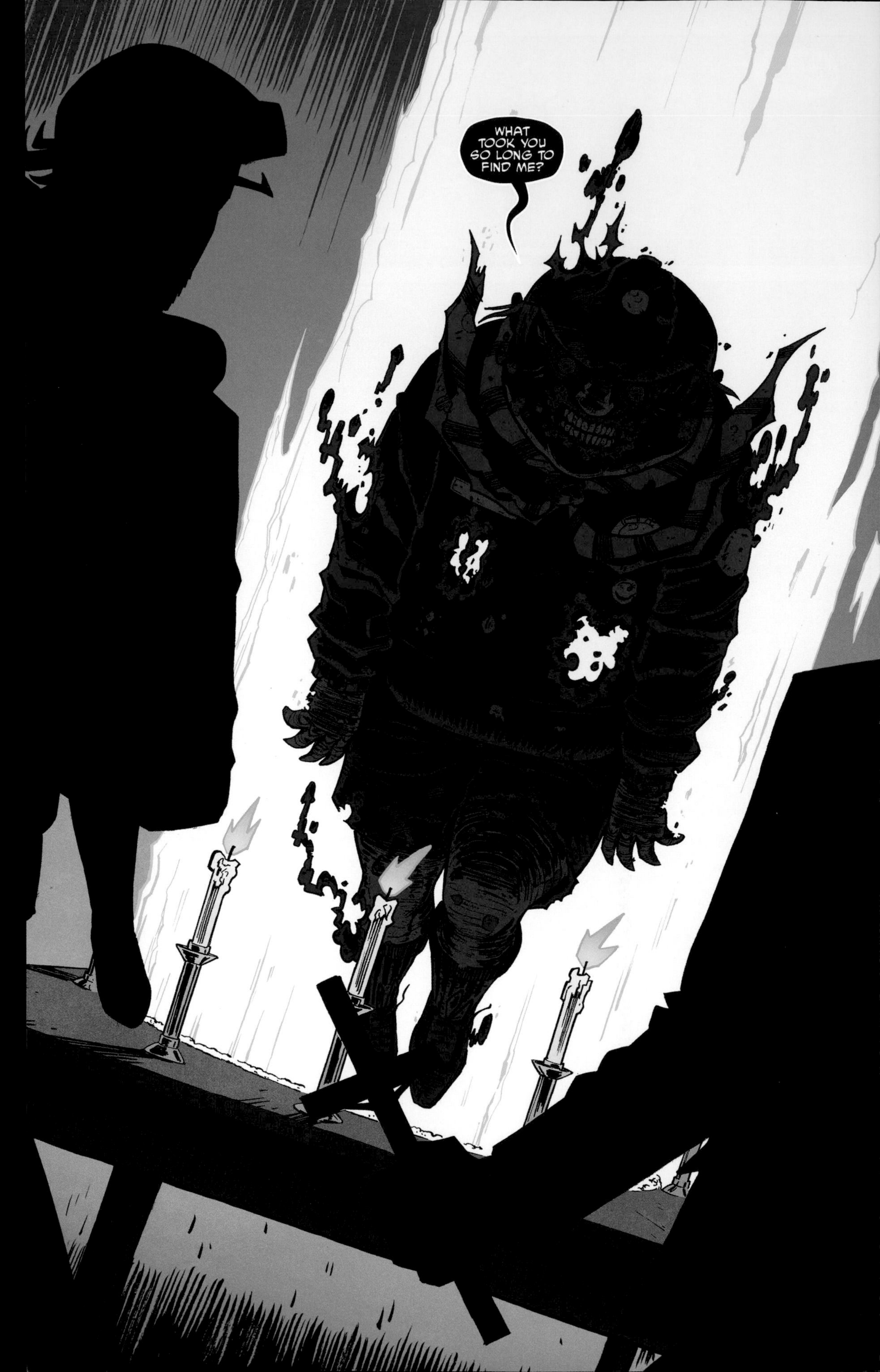
WHAT TOOK YOU SO LONG TO FIND ME?

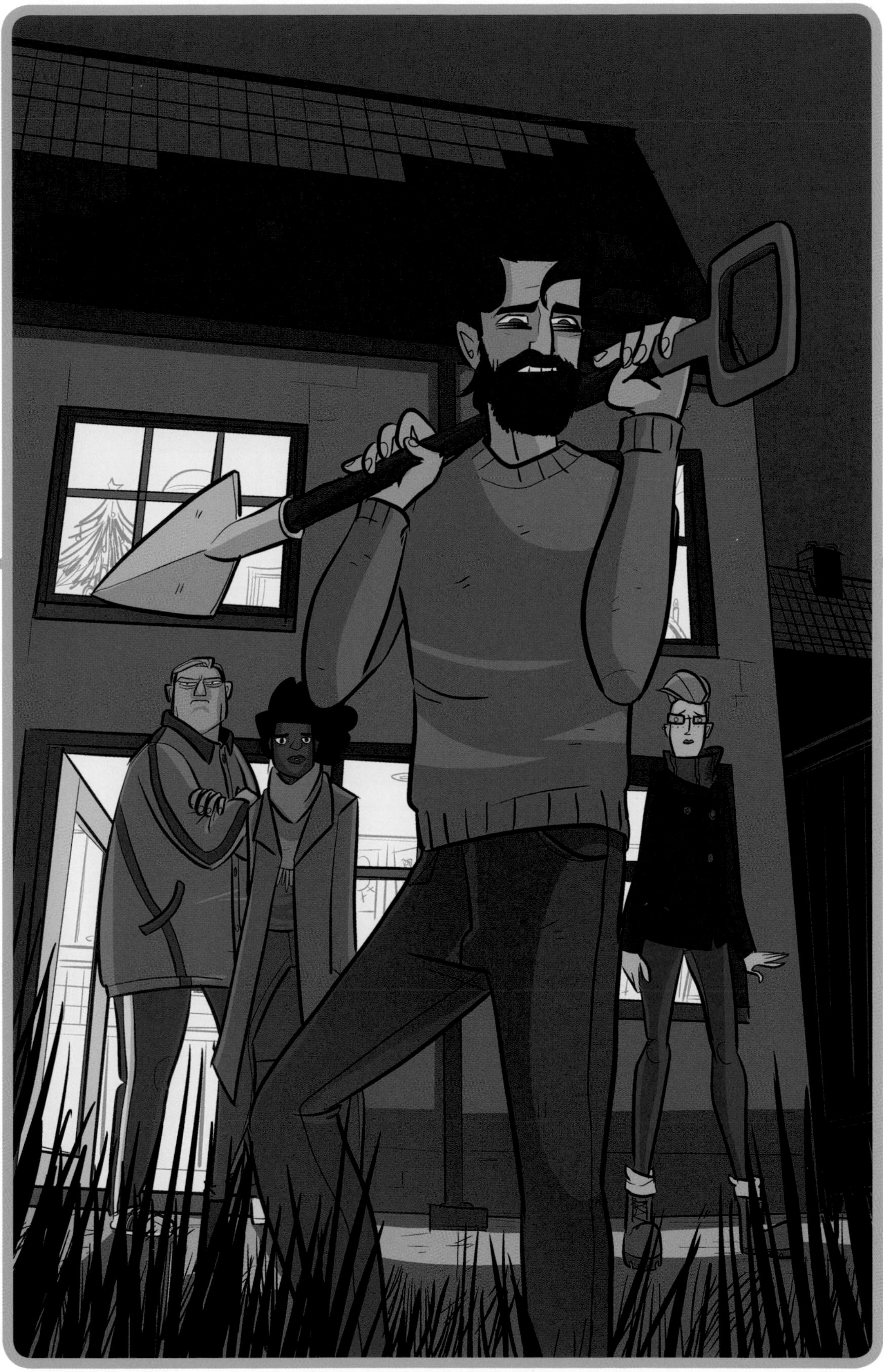

Art by
JOHN ALLISON

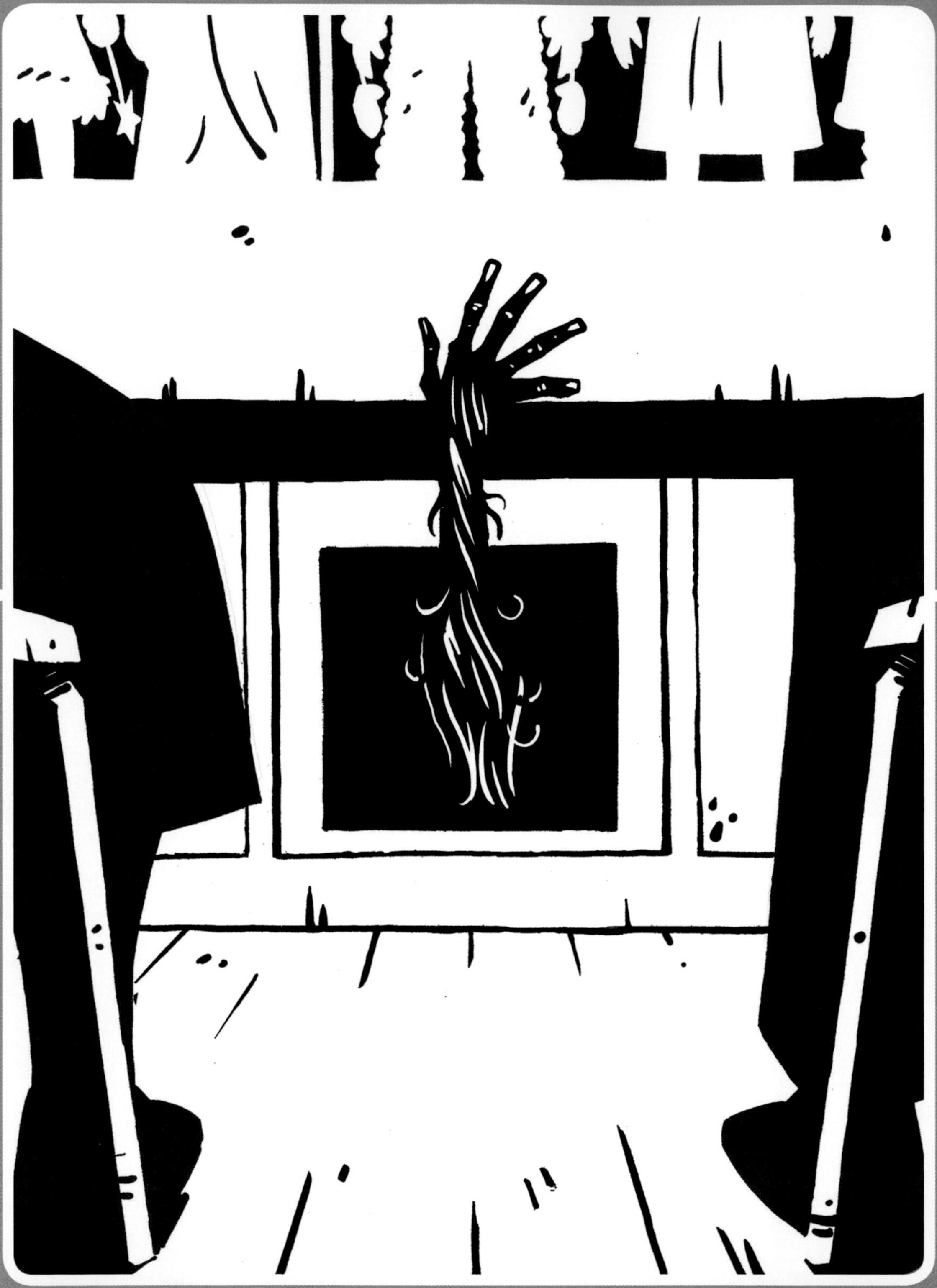

CHAPTER FOUR

Art by
NICK ROCHE

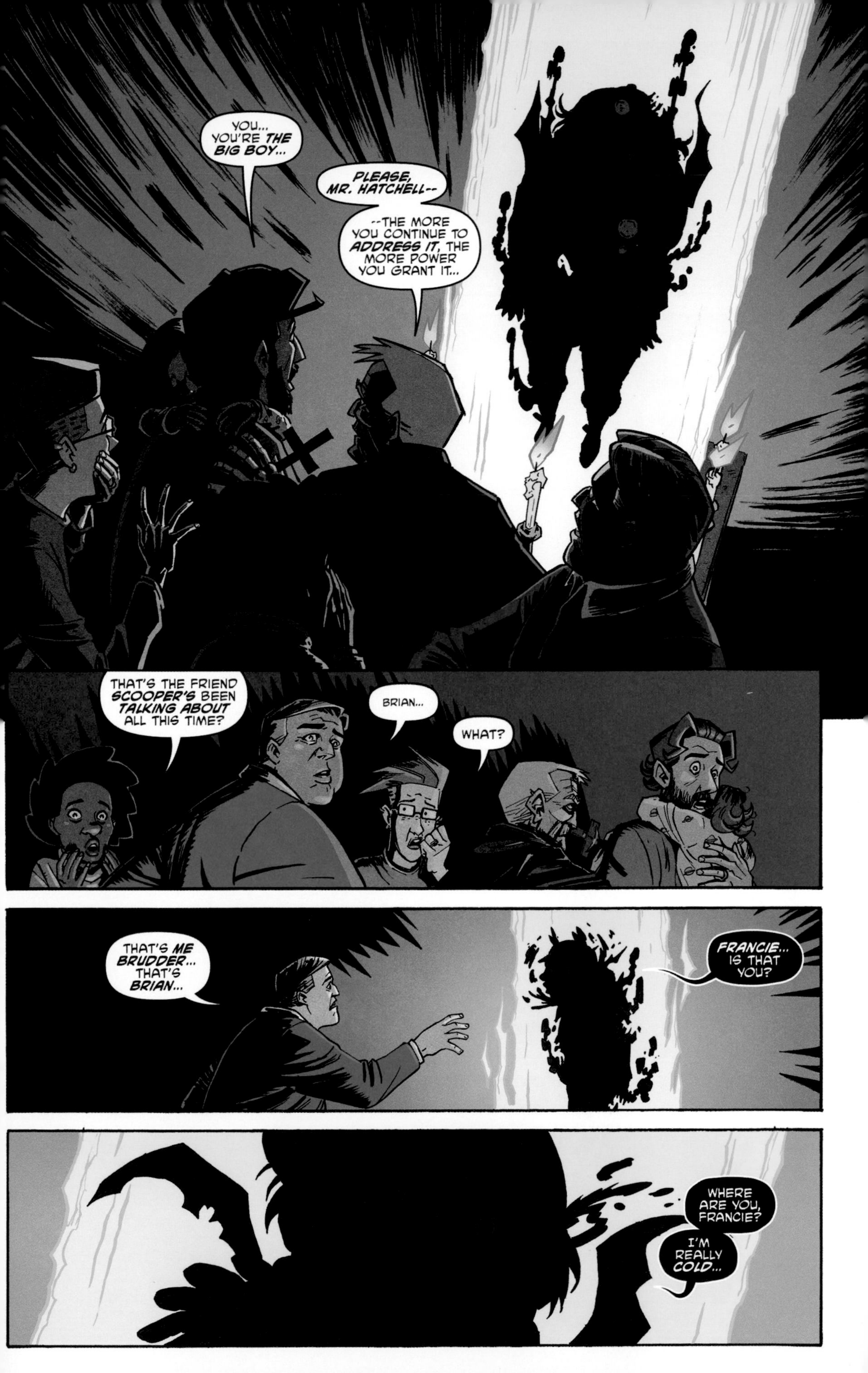
YOU... YOU'RE THE BIG BOY...
PLEASE, MR. HATCHELL--
--THE MORE YOU CONTINUE TO ADDRESS IT, THE MORE POWER YOU GRANT IT...
THAT'S THE FRIEND SCOOPER'S BEEN TALKING ABOUT ALL THIS TIME?
BRIAN...
WHAT?
THAT'S ME BRUDDER... THAT'S BRIAN...
FRANCIE... IS THAT YOU?
WHERE ARE YOU, FRANCIE?
I'M REALLY COLD...

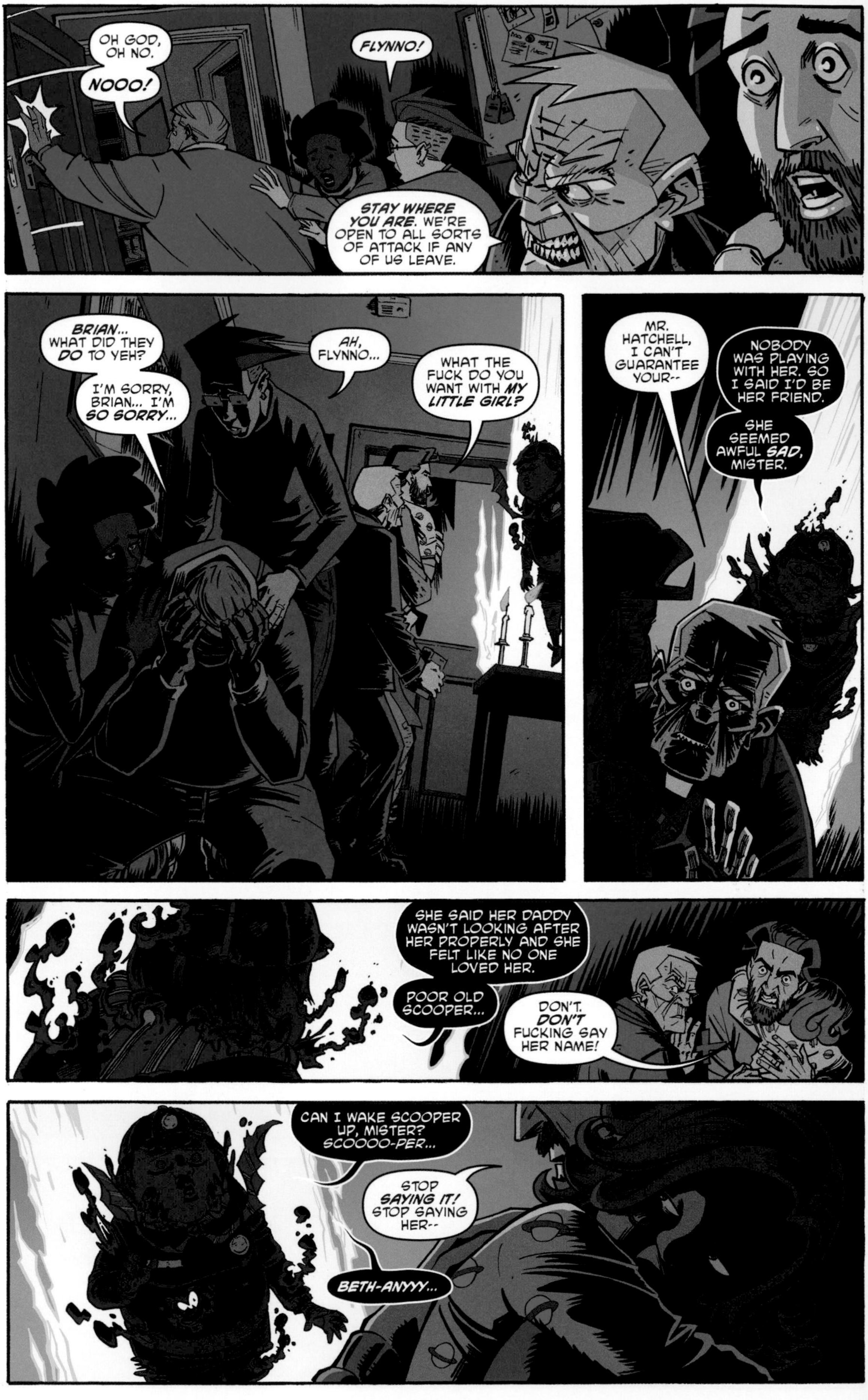
OH GOD, OH NO. NOOO!
FLYNNO!
STAY WHERE YOU ARE. WE'RE OPEN TO ALL SORTS OF ATTACK IF ANY OF US LEAVE.
BRIAN... WHAT DID THEY DO TO YEH?
I'M SORRY, BRIAN... I'M SO SORRY...
AH, FLYNNO...
WHAT THE FUCK DO YOU WANT WITH MY LITTLE GIRL?
MR. HATCHELL, I CAN'T GUARANTEE YOUR--
NOBODY WAS PLAYING WITH HER. SO I SAID I'D BE HER FRIEND.
SHE SEEMED AWFUL SAD, MISTER.
SHE SAID HER DADDY WASN'T LOOKING AFTER HER PROPERLY AND SHE FELT LIKE NO ONE LOVED HER.
POOR OLD SCOOPER...
DON'T. DON'T FUCKING SAY HER NAME!
CAN I WAKE SCOOPER UP, MISTER? SCOOOO-PER...
STOP SAYING IT! STOP SAYING HER--
BETH-ANYYY...

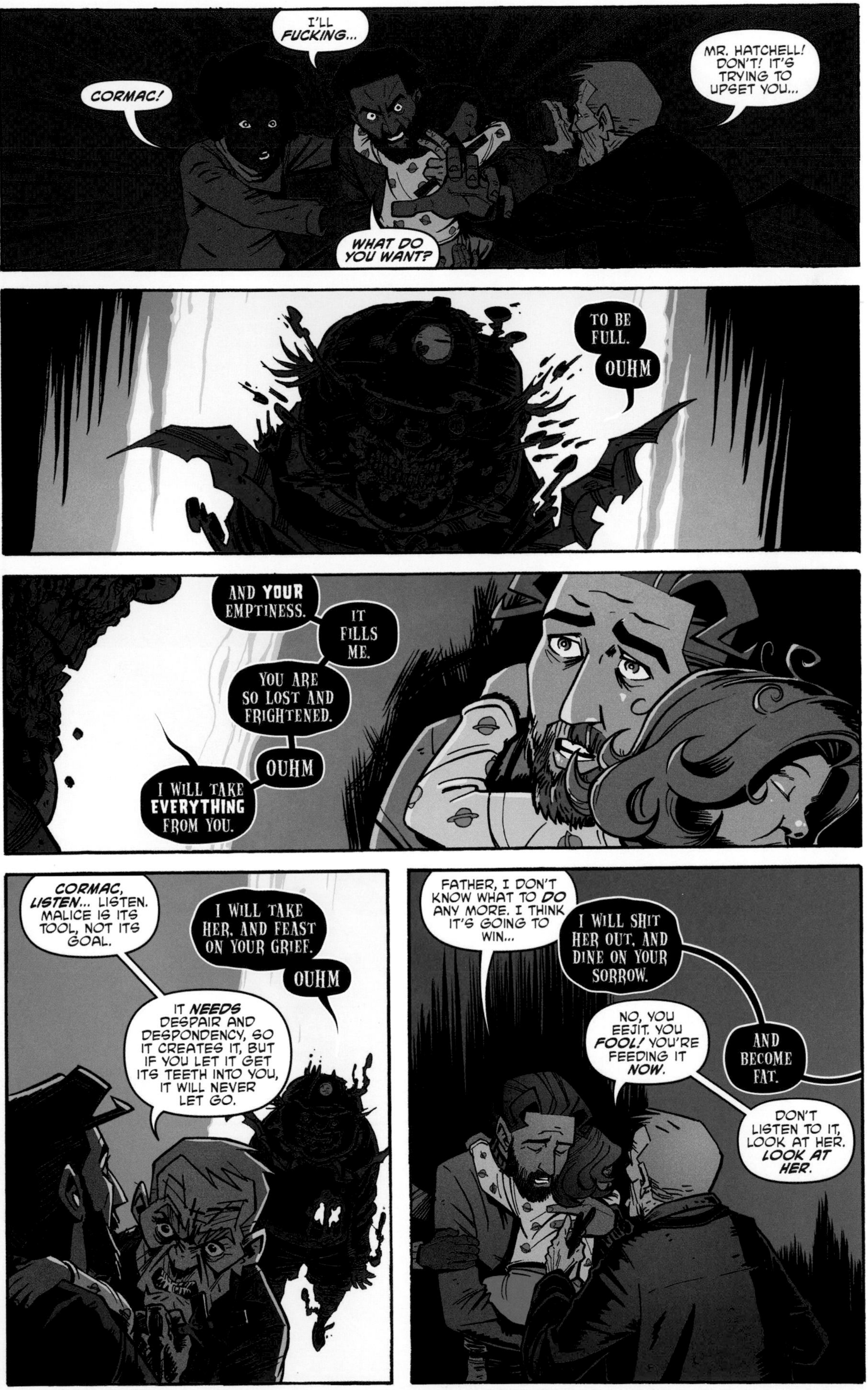
CORMAC!
I'LL FUCKING...
MR. HATCHELL! DON'T! IT'S TRYING TO UPSET YOU...
WHAT DO YOU WANT?
TO BE FULL.
OUHM
AND YOUR EMPTINESS.
IT FILLS ME.
YOU ARE SO LOST AND FRIGHTENED.
OUHM
I WILL TAKE EVERYTHING FROM YOU.
CORMAC, LISTEN... LISTEN. MALICE IS ITS TOOL, NOT ITS GOAL.
I WILL TAKE HER, AND FEAST ON YOUR GRIEF.
OUHM
IT NEEDS DESPAIR AND DESPONDENCY, SO IT CREATES IT, BUT IF YOU LET IT GET ITS TEETH INTO YOU, IT WILL NEVER LET GO.
FATHER, I DON'T KNOW WHAT TO DO ANY MORE. I THINK IT'S GOING TO WIN...
I WILL SHIT HER OUT, AND DINE ON YOUR SORROW.
NO, YOU EEJIT. YOU FOOL! YOU'RE FEEDING IT NOW.
AND BECOME FAT.
DON'T LISTEN TO IT, LOOK AT HER. LOOK AT HER.

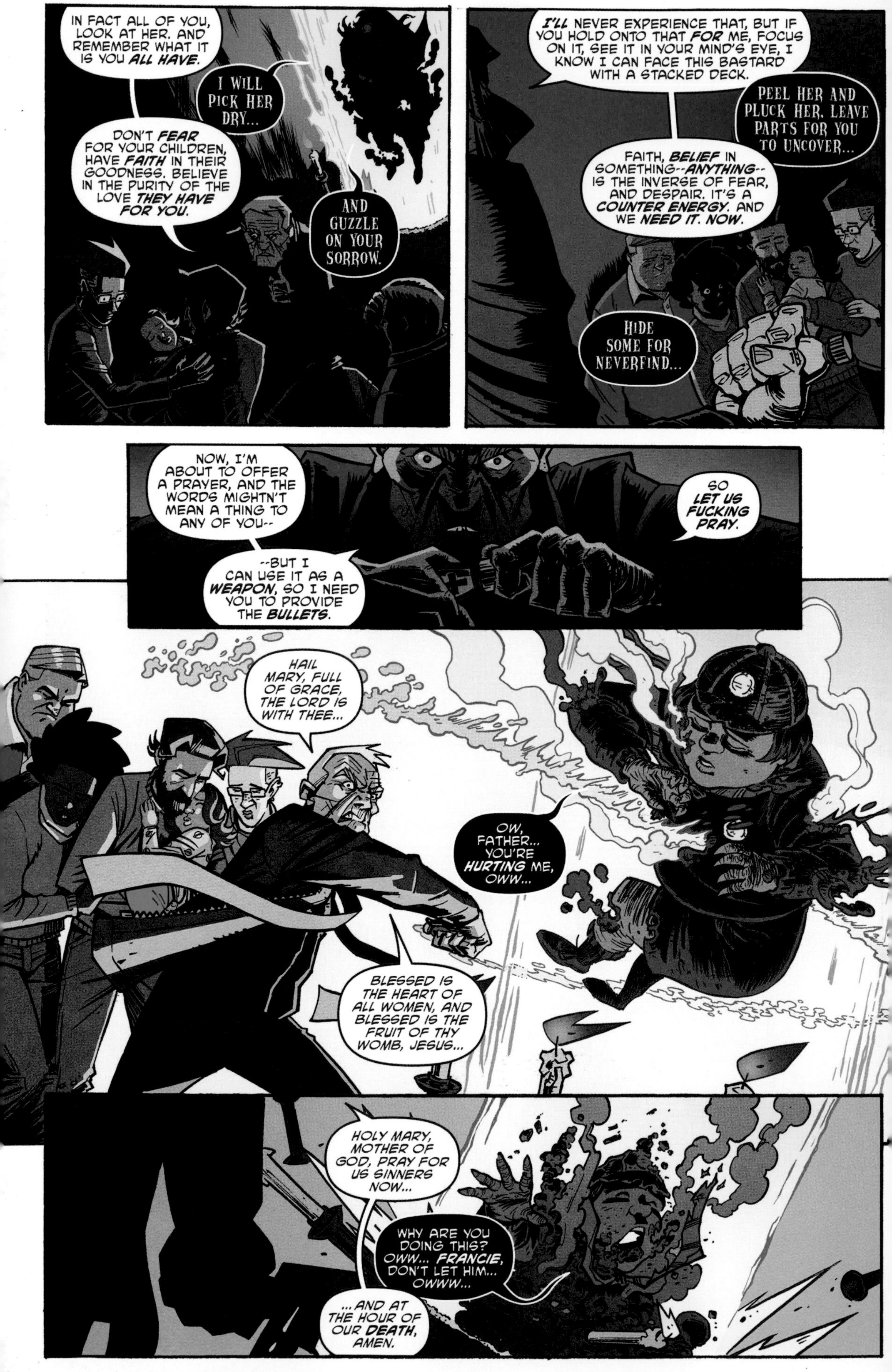

IN FACT ALL OF YOU, LOOK AT HER. AND REMEMBER WHAT IT IS YOU ALL HAVE.
I WILL PICK HER DRY...
DON'T FEAR FOR YOUR CHILDREN, HAVE FAITH IN THEIR GOODNESS. BELIEVE IN THE PURITY OF THE LOVE THEY HAVE FOR YOU.
AND GUZZLE ON YOUR SORROW.
I'LL NEVER EXPERIENCE THAT, BUT IF YOU HOLD ONTO THAT FOR ME, FOCUS ON IT, SEE IT IN YOUR MIND'S EYE, I KNOW I CAN FACE THIS BASTARD WITH A STACKED DECK.
PEEL HER AND PLUCK HER, LEAVE PARTS FOR YOU TO UNCOVER...
FAITH, BELIEF IN SOMETHING--ANYTHING--IS THE INVERSE OF FEAR, AND DESPAIR. IT'S A COUNTER ENERGY. AND WE NEED IT. NOW.
HIDE SOME FOR NEVERFIND...
NOW, I'M ABOUT TO OFFER A PRAYER, AND THE WORDS MIGHTN'T MEAN A THING TO ANY OF YOU--
--BUT I CAN USE IT AS A WEAPON, SO I NEED YOU TO PROVIDE THE BULLETS.
SO LET US FUCKING PRAY.
HAIL MARY, FULL OF GRACE, THE LORD IS WITH THEE...
OW, FATHER... YOU'RE HURTING ME, OWW...
BLESSED IS THE HEART OF ALL WOMEN, AND BLESSED IS THE FRUIT OF THY WOMB, JESUS...
HOLY MARY, MOTHER OF GOD, PRAY FOR US SINNERS NOW...
WHY ARE YOU DOING THIS? OWW... FRANCIE, DON'T LET HIM... OWWW...
...AND AT THE HOUR OF OUR DEATH, AMEN.

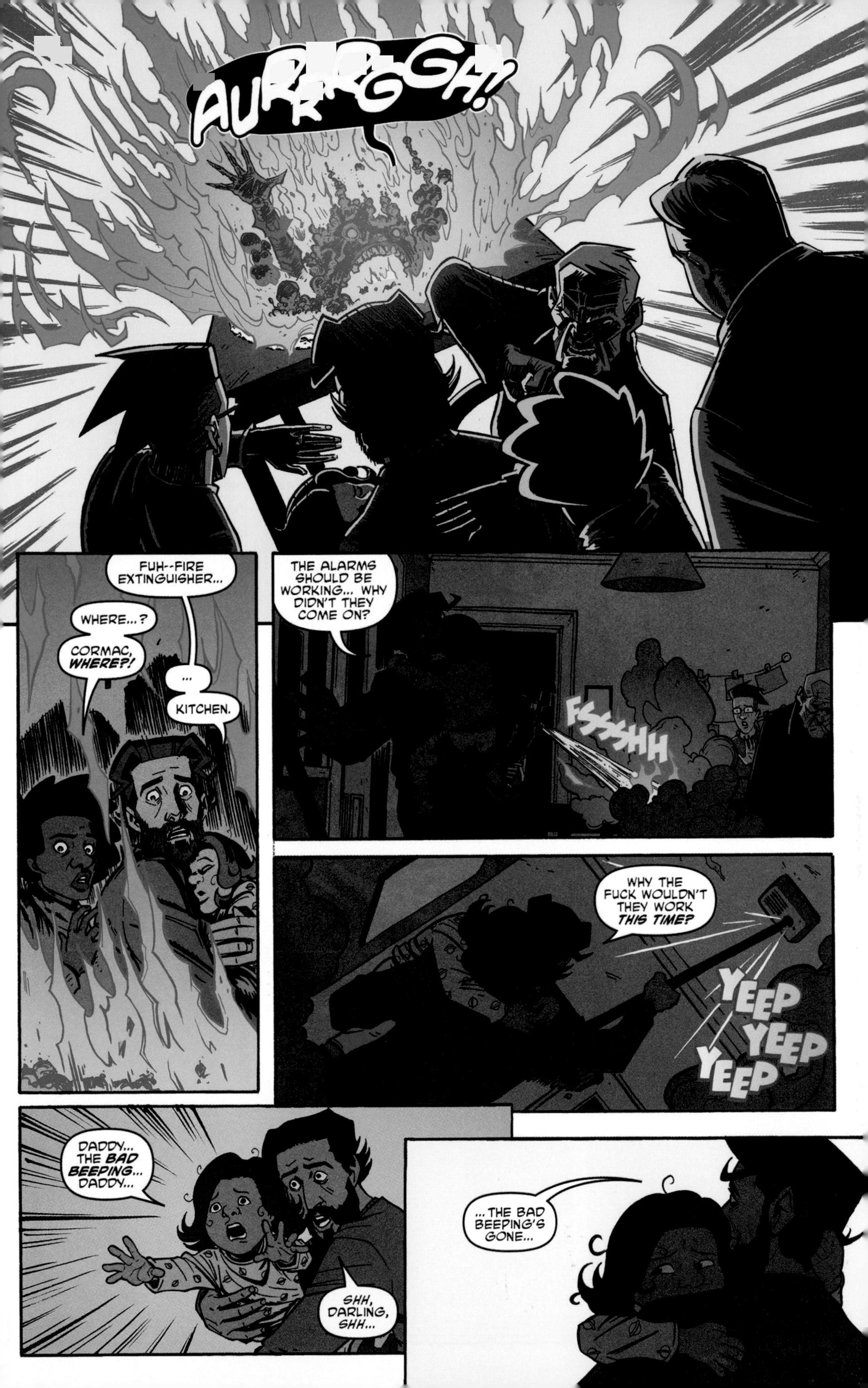
AURRGGH!
FUH--FIRE EXTINGUISHER...
WHERE...?
CORMAC, *WHERE?!*
...
KITCHEN.
THE ALARMS SHOULD BE WORKING... WHY DIDN'T THEY COME ON?
FSSSHH
WHY THE FUCK WOULDN'T THEY WORK *THIS TIME?*
YEEP YEEP YEEP
DADDY... THE *BAD BEEPING*... DADDY...
SHH, DARLING, SHH...
...THE BAD BEEPING'S GONE...

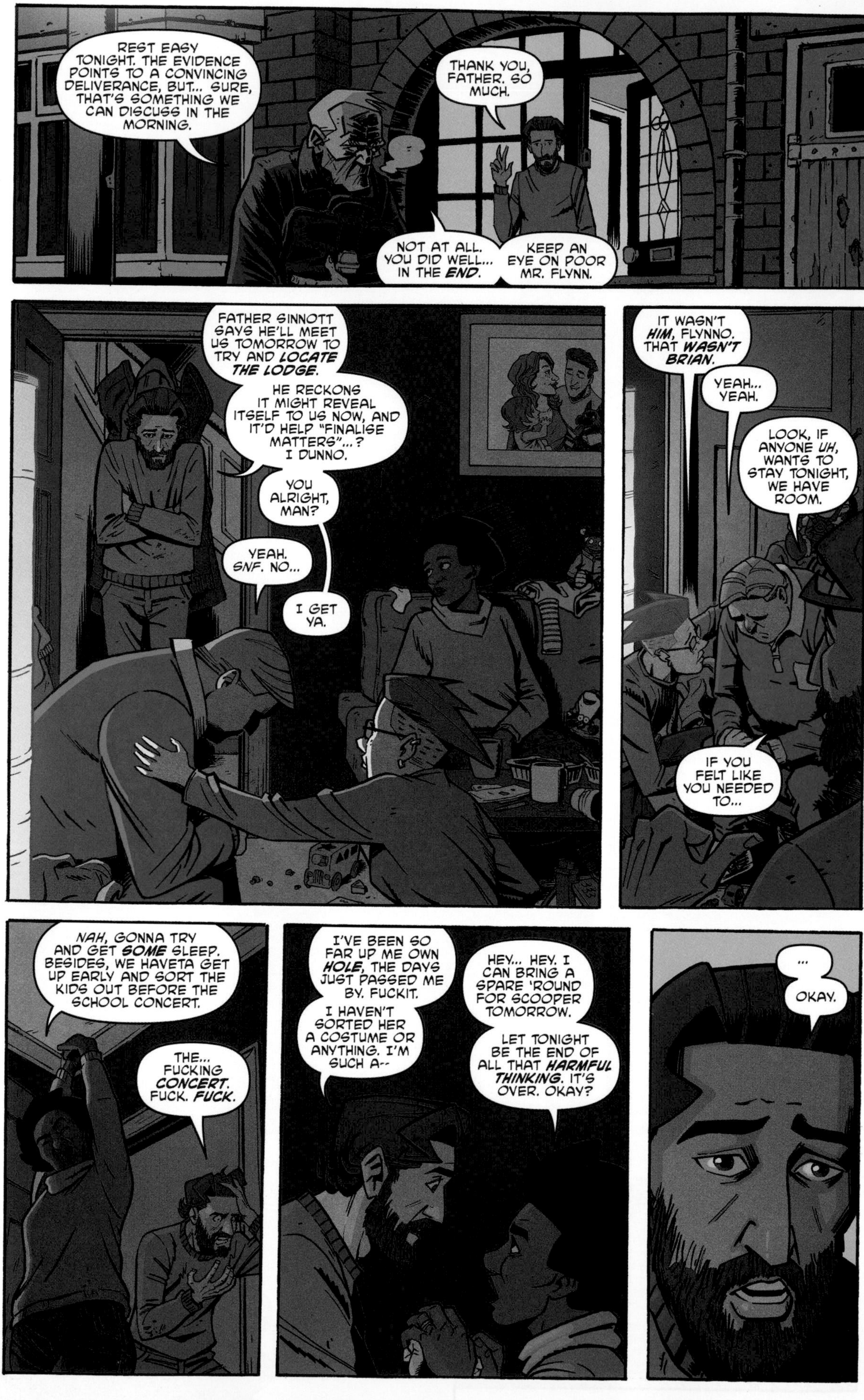
REST EASY TONIGHT. THE EVIDENCE POINTS TO A CONVINCING DELIVERANCE, BUT... SURE, THAT'S SOMETHING WE CAN DISCUSS IN THE MORNING.
THANK YOU, FATHER. SO MUCH.
NOT AT ALL. YOU DID WELL... IN THE *END*.
KEEP AN EYE ON POOR MR. FLYNN.
FATHER SINNOTT SAYS HE'LL MEET US TOMORROW TO TRY AND **LOCATE THE LODGE**.
HE RECKONS IT MIGHT REVEAL ITSELF TO US NOW, AND IT'D HELP "FINALISE MATTERS"...? I DUNNO.
YOU ALRIGHT, MAN?
YEAH. *SNF*. NO...
I GET YA.
IT WASN'T ***HIM***, FLYNNO. THAT ***WASN'T BRIAN***.
YEAH... YEAH.
LOOK, IF ANYONE *UH*, WANTS TO STAY TONIGHT, WE HAVE ROOM.
IF YOU FELT LIKE YOU NEEDED TO...
NAH, GONNA TRY AND GET **SOME** SLEEP. BESIDES, WE HAVETA GET UP EARLY AND SORT THE KIDS OUT BEFORE THE SCHOOL CONCERT.
THE... FUCKING ***CONCERT***. FUCK. ***FUCK***.
I'VE BEEN SO FAR UP ME OWN ***HOLE***, THE DAYS JUST PASSED ME BY. FUCKIT.
I HAVEN'T SORTED HER A COSTUME OR ANYTHING. I'M SUCH A--
HEY... HEY. I CAN BRING A SPARE 'ROUND FOR SCOOPER TOMORROW.
LET TONIGHT BE THE END OF ALL THAT ***HARMFUL THINKING***. IT'S OVER. OKAY?
...
OKAY.

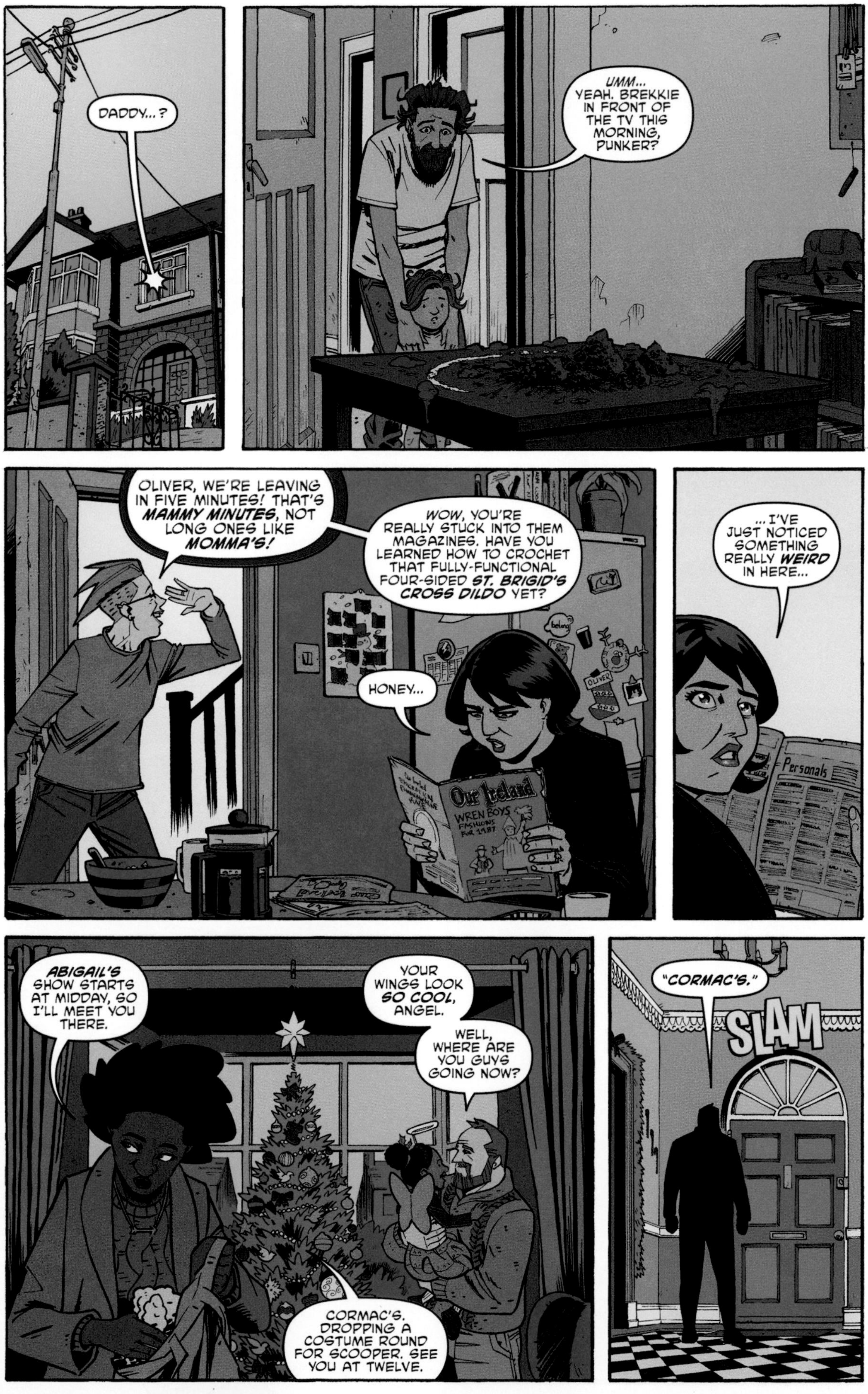
DADDY...?
UMM... YEAH. BREKKIE IN FRONT OF THE TV THIS MORNING, PUNKER?
OLIVER, WE'RE LEAVING IN FIVE MINUTES! THAT'S MAMMY MINUTES, NOT LONG ONES LIKE MOMMA'S!
WOW, YOU'RE REALLY STUCK INTO THEM MAGAZINES. HAVE YOU LEARNED HOW TO CROCHET THAT FULLY-FUNCTIONAL FOUR-SIDED ST. BRIGID'S CROSS DILDO YET?
HONEY...
Our Ireland
WREN BOYS FASHIONS FOR 1987
... I'VE JUST NOTICED SOMETHING REALLY WEIRD IN HERE...
Personals
ABIGAIL'S SHOW STARTS AT MIDDAY, SO I'LL MEET YOU THERE.
YOUR WINGS LOOK SO COOL, ANGEL.
WELL, WHERE ARE YOU GUYS GOING NOW?
CORMAC'S. DROPPING A COSTUME ROUND FOR SCOOPER. SEE YOU AT TWELVE.
"CORMAC'S."
SLAM

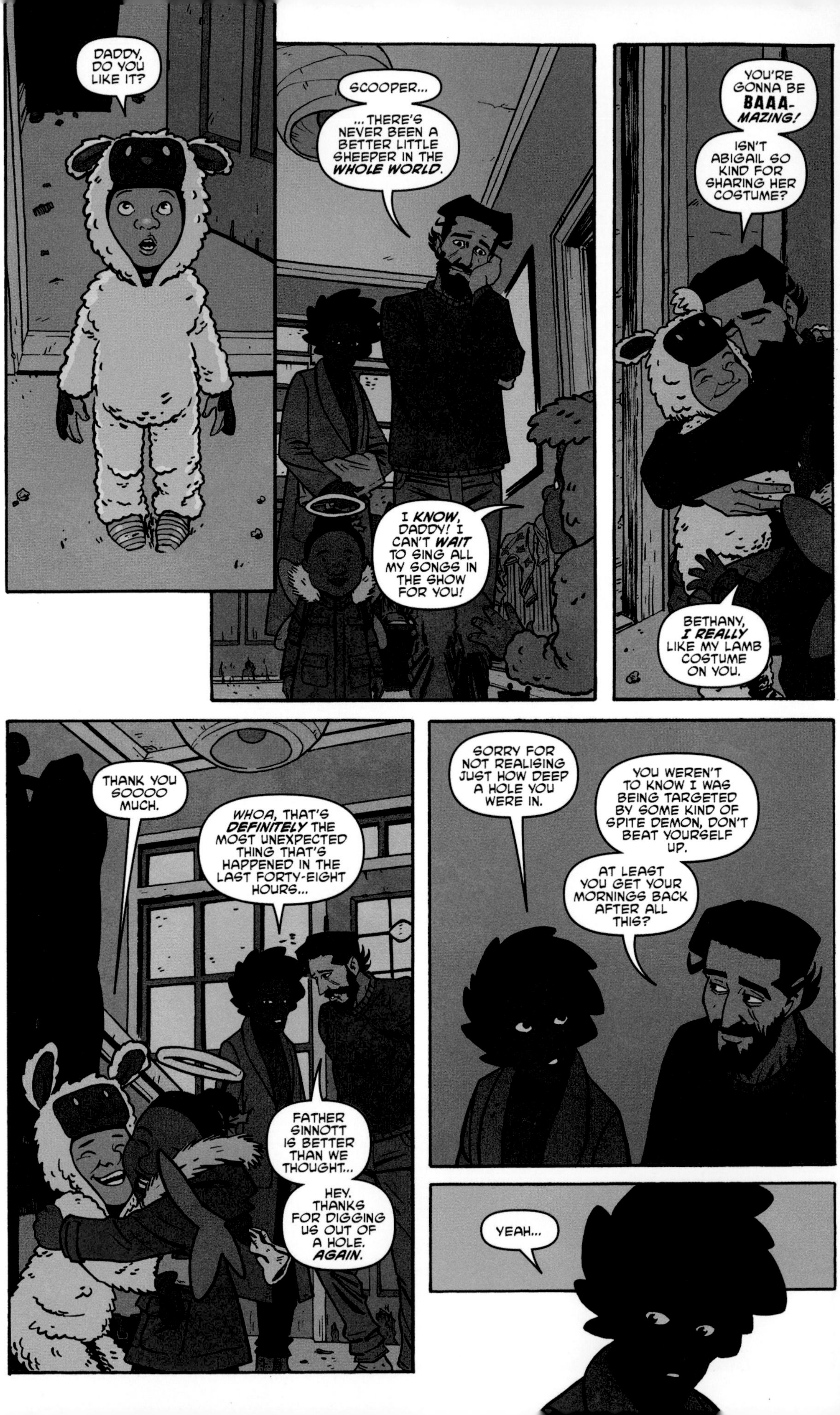
DADDY, DO YOU LIKE IT?
SCOOPER...
...THERE'S NEVER BEEN A BETTER LITTLE SHEEPER IN THE WHOLE WORLD.
I KNOW, DADDY! I CAN'T WAIT TO SING ALL MY SONGS IN THE SHOW FOR YOU!
YOU'RE GONNA BE BAAA-MAZING!
ISN'T ABIGAIL SO KIND FOR SHARING HER COSTUME?
BETHANY, I REALLY LIKE MY LAMB COSTUME ON YOU.
THANK YOU SOOOO MUCH.
WHOA, THAT'S DEFINITELY THE MOST UNEXPECTED THING THAT'S HAPPENED IN THE LAST FORTY-EIGHT HOURS...
FATHER SINNOTT IS BETTER THAN WE THOUGHT...
HEY. THANKS FOR DIGGING US OUT OF A HOLE. AGAIN.
SORRY FOR NOT REALISING JUST HOW DEEP A HOLE YOU WERE IN.
YOU WEREN'T TO KNOW I WAS BEING TARGETED BY SOME KIND OF SPITE DEMON, DON'T BEAT YOURSELF UP.
AT LEAST YOU GET YOUR MORNINGS BACK AFTER ALL THIS?
YEAH...

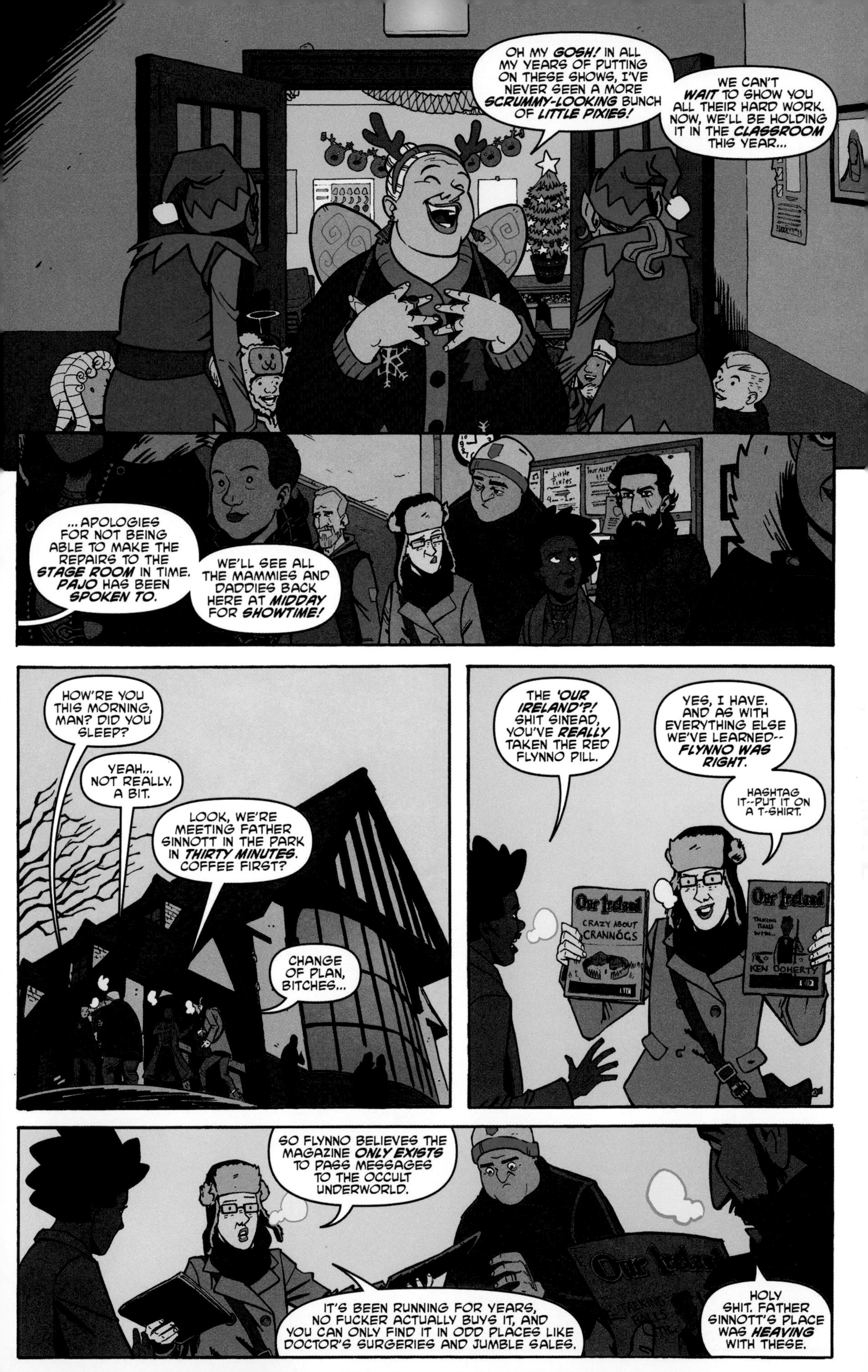
OH MY GOSH! IN ALL MY YEARS OF PUTTING ON THESE SHOWS, I'VE NEVER SEEN A MORE SCRUMMY-LOOKING BUNCH OF LITTLE PIXIES!
WE CAN'T WAIT TO SHOW YOU ALL THEIR HARD WORK. NOW, WE'LL BE HOLDING IT IN THE CLASSROOM THIS YEAR...
...APOLOGIES FOR NOT BEING ABLE TO MAKE THE REPAIRS TO THE STAGE ROOM IN TIME. PAJO HAS BEEN SPOKEN TO.
WE'LL SEE ALL THE MAMMIES AND DADDIES BACK HERE AT MIDDAY FOR SHOWTIME!
HOW'RE YOU THIS MORNING, MAN? DID YOU SLEEP?
YEAH... NOT REALLY. A BIT.
LOOK, WE'RE MEETING FATHER SINNOTT IN THE PARK IN THIRTY MINUTES. COFFEE FIRST?
CHANGE OF PLAN, BITCHES...
THE 'OUR IRELAND'?! SHIT SINEAD, YOU'VE REALLY TAKEN THE RED FLYNNO PILL.
YES, I HAVE. AND AS WITH EVERYTHING ELSE WE'VE LEARNED-- FLYNNO WAS RIGHT.
HASHTAG IT--PUT IT ON A T-SHIRT.
Our Ireland
CRAZY ABOUT CRANNÓGS
Our Ireland
KEN DOHERTY
SO FLYNNO BELIEVES THE MAGAZINE ONLY EXISTS TO PASS MESSAGES TO THE OCCULT UNDERWORLD.
IT'S BEEN RUNNING FOR YEARS, NO FUCKER ACTUALLY BUYS IT, AND YOU CAN ONLY FIND IT IN ODD PLACES LIKE DOCTOR'S SURGERIES AND JUMBLE SALES.
HOLY SHIT. FATHER SINNOTT'S PLACE WAS HEAVING WITH THESE.

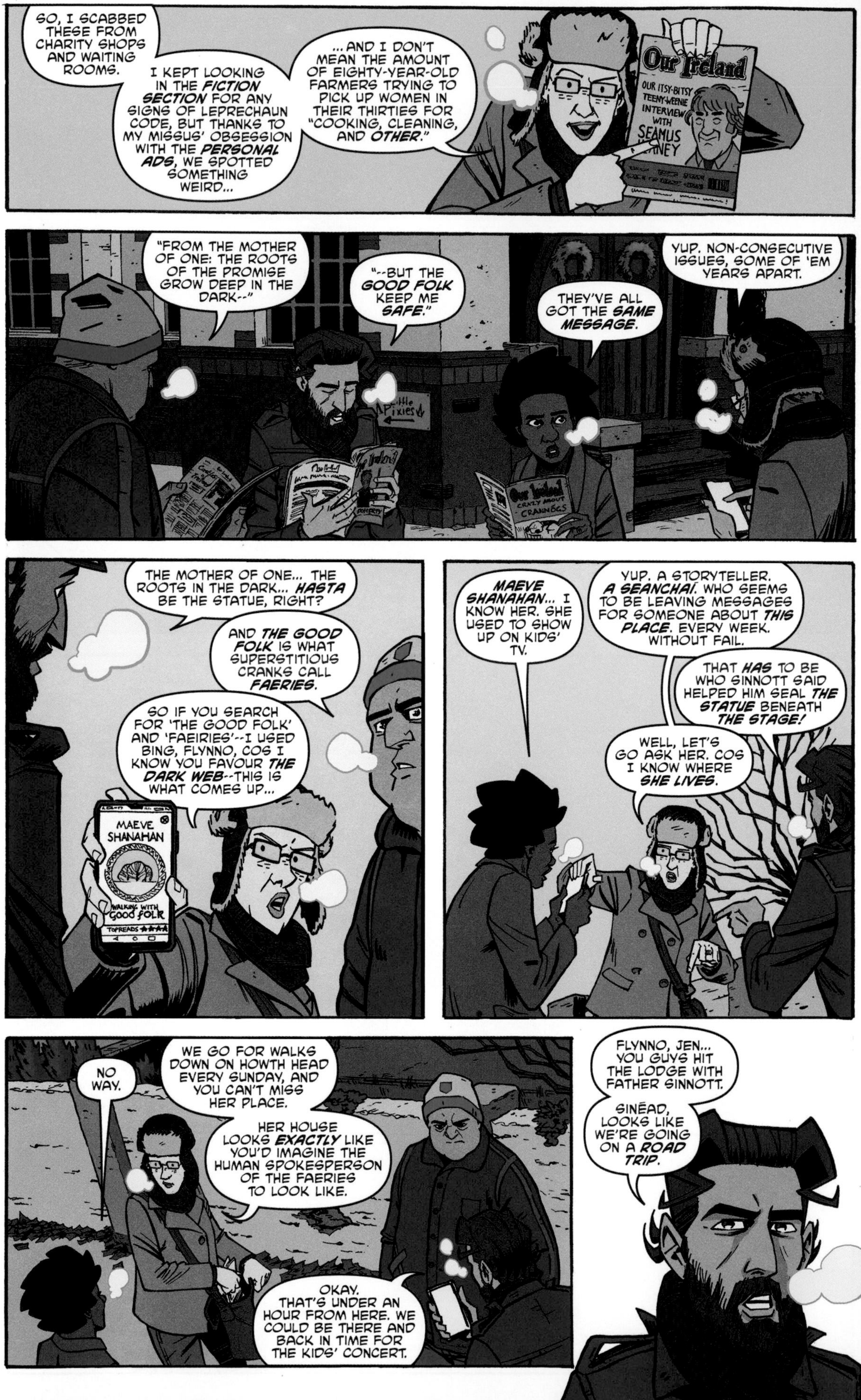
SO, I SCABBED THESE FROM CHARITY SHOPS AND WAITING ROOMS.
I KEPT LOOKING IN THE FICTION SECTION FOR ANY SIGNS OF LEPRECHAUN CODE, BUT THANKS TO MY MISSUS' OBSESSION WITH THE PERSONAL ADS, WE SPOTTED SOMETHING WEIRD...
...AND I DON'T MEAN THE AMOUNT OF EIGHTY-YEAR-OLD FARMERS TRYING TO PICK UP WOMEN IN THEIR THIRTIES FOR "COOKING, CLEANING, AND OTHER."
Our Ireland
OUR ITSY-BITSY TEENY-WEENIE INTERVIEW WITH SEAMUS
"FROM THE MOTHER OF ONE: THE ROOTS OF THE PROMISE GROW DEEP IN THE DARK--"
"--BUT THE GOOD FOLK KEEP ME SAFE."
THEY'VE ALL GOT THE SAME MESSAGE.
YUP. NON-CONSECUTIVE ISSUES, SOME OF 'EM YEARS APART.
Our Ireland
CRAZY ABOUT CRANNÓGS
THE MOTHER OF ONE... THE ROOTS IN THE DARK... HASTA BE THE STATUE, RIGHT?
AND THE GOOD FOLK IS WHAT SUPERSTITIOUS CRANKS CALL FAERIES.
SO IF YOU SEARCH FOR 'THE GOOD FOLK' AND 'FAERIES'--I USED BING, FLYNNO, COS I KNOW YOU FAVOUR THE DARK WEB--THIS IS WHAT COMES UP...
MAEVE SHANAHAN
WALKING WITH GOOD FOLK
TOPREADS
MAEVE SHANAHAN... I KNOW HER. SHE USED TO SHOW UP ON KIDS' TV.
YUP. A STORYTELLER. A SEANCHAÍ. WHO SEEMS TO BE LEAVING MESSAGES FOR SOMEONE ABOUT THIS PLACE. EVERY WEEK. WITHOUT FAIL.
THAT HAS TO BE WHO SINNOTT SAID HELPED HIM SEAL THE STATUE BENEATH THE STAGE!
WELL, LET'S GO ASK HER. COS I KNOW WHERE SHE LIVES.
NO WAY.
WE GO FOR WALKS DOWN ON HOWTH HEAD EVERY SUNDAY, AND YOU CAN'T MISS HER PLACE.
HER HOUSE LOOKS EXACTLY LIKE YOU'D IMAGINE THE HUMAN SPOKESPERSON OF THE FAERIES TO LOOK LIKE.
OKAY. THAT'S UNDER AN HOUR FROM HERE. WE COULD BE THERE AND BACK IN TIME FOR THE KIDS' CONCERT.
FLYNNO, JEN... YOU GUYS HIT THE LODGE WITH FATHER SINNOTT.
SINÉAD, LOOKS LIKE WE'RE GOING ON A ROAD TRIP.

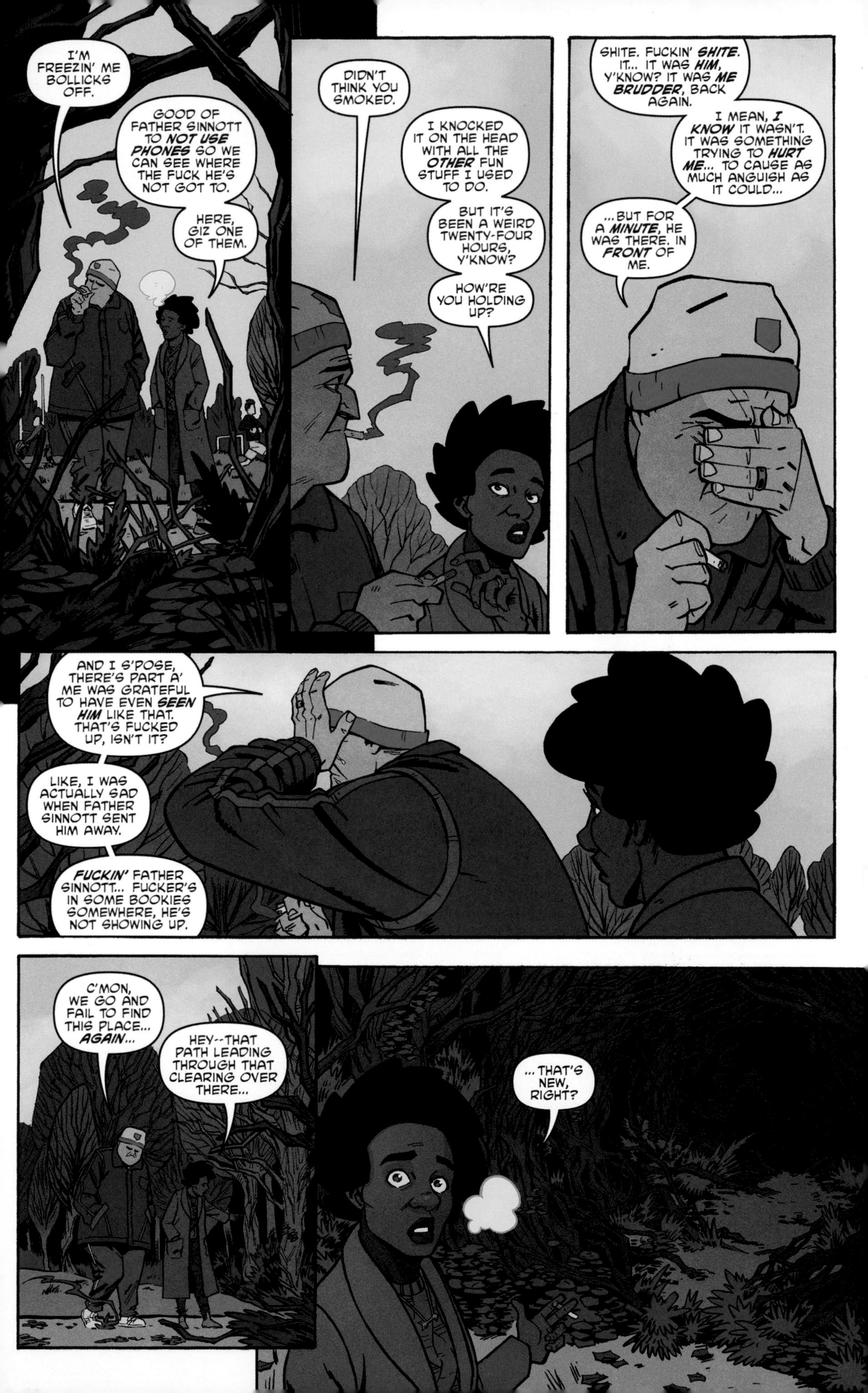
I'M FREEZIN' ME BOLLICKS OFF.
GOOD OF FATHER SINNOTT TO NOT USE PHONES SO WE CAN SEE WHERE THE FUCK HE'S NOT GOT TO.
HERE, GIZ ONE OF THEM.
DIDN'T THINK YOU SMOKED.
I KNOCKED IT ON THE HEAD WITH ALL THE OTHER FUN STUFF I USED TO DO.
BUT IT'S BEEN A WEIRD TWENTY-FOUR HOURS, Y'KNOW?
HOW'RE YOU HOLDING UP?
SHITE. FUCKIN' SHITE. IT... IT WAS HIM, Y'KNOW? IT WAS ME BRUDDER, BACK AGAIN.
I MEAN, I KNOW IT WASN'T. IT WAS SOMETHING TRYING TO HURT ME... TO CAUSE AS MUCH ANGUISH AS IT COULD...
...BUT FOR A MINUTE, HE WAS THERE. IN FRONT OF ME.
AND I S'POSE, THERE'S PART A' ME WAS GRATEFUL TO HAVE EVEN SEEN HIM LIKE THAT. THAT'S FUCKED UP, ISN'T IT?
LIKE, I WAS ACTUALLY SAD WHEN FATHER SINNOTT SENT HIM AWAY.
FUCKIN' FATHER SINNOTT... FUCKER'S IN SOME BOOKIES SOMEWHERE, HE'S NOT SHOWING UP.
C'MON, WE GO AND FAIL TO FIND THIS PLACE... AGAIN...
HEY--THAT PATH LEADING THROUGH THAT CLEARING OVER THERE...
...THAT'S NEW, RIGHT?

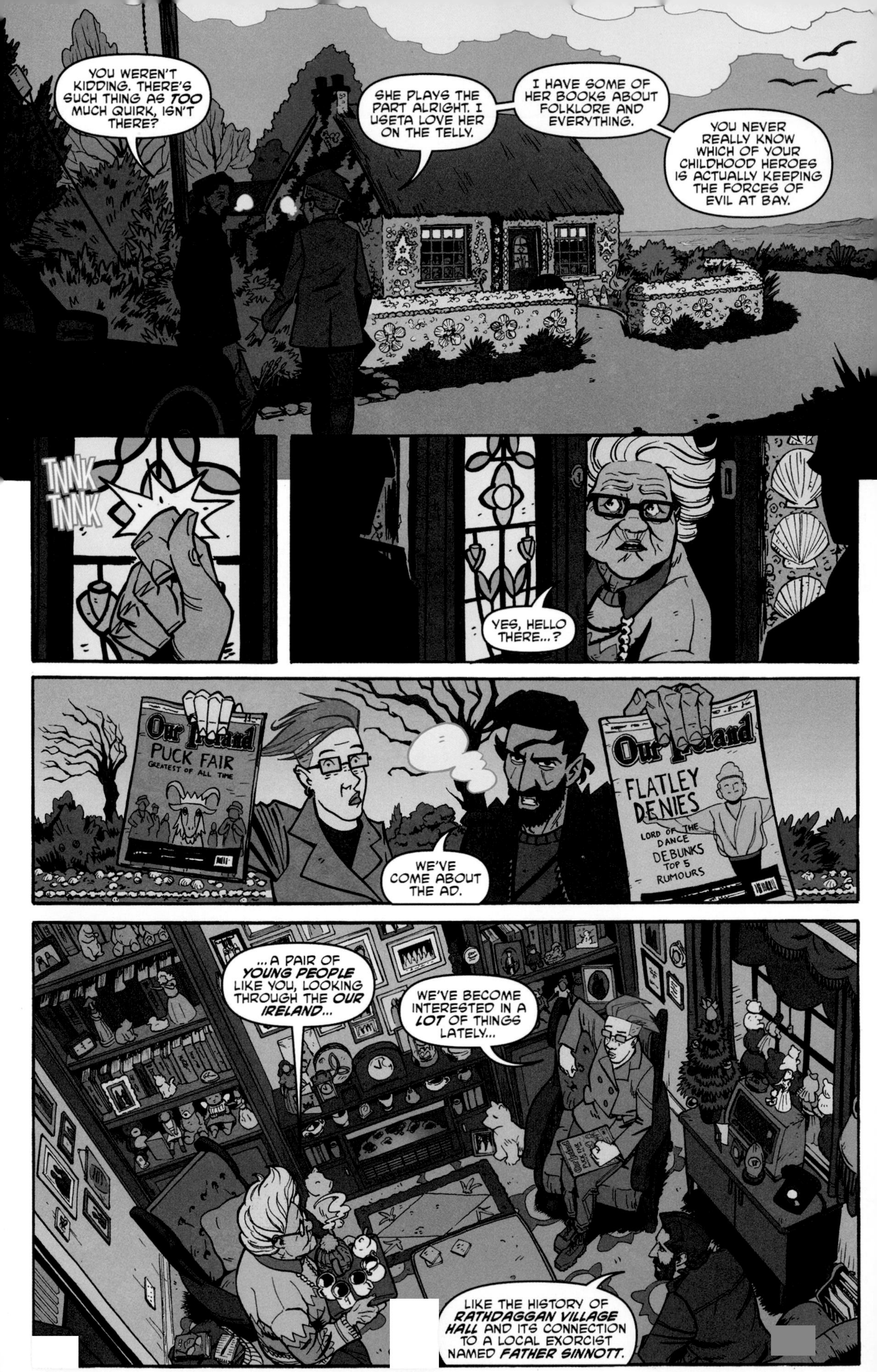
YOU WEREN'T KIDDING. THERE'S SUCH THING AS TOO MUCH QUIRK, ISN'T THERE?
SHE PLAYS THE PART ALRIGHT. I USETA LOVE HER ON THE TELLY.
I HAVE SOME OF HER BOOKS ABOUT FOLKLORE AND EVERYTHING.
YOU NEVER REALLY KNOW WHICH OF YOUR CHILDHOOD HEROES IS ACTUALLY KEEPING THE FORCES OF EVIL AT BAY.
TNNK TNNK
YES, HELLO THERE...?
Our Ireland
PUCK FAIR
GREATEST OF ALL TIME
Our Ireland
FLATLEY DENIES
LORD OF THE DANCE
DEBUNKS TOP 5 RUMOURS
WE'VE COME ABOUT THE AD.
...A PAIR OF YOUNG PEOPLE LIKE YOU, LOOKING THROUGH THE OUR IRELAND...
WE'VE BECOME INTERESTED IN A LOT OF THINGS LATELY...
LIKE THE HISTORY OF RATHDAGGAN VILLAGE HALL AND ITS CONNECTION TO A LOCAL EXORCIST NAMED FATHER SINNOTT.

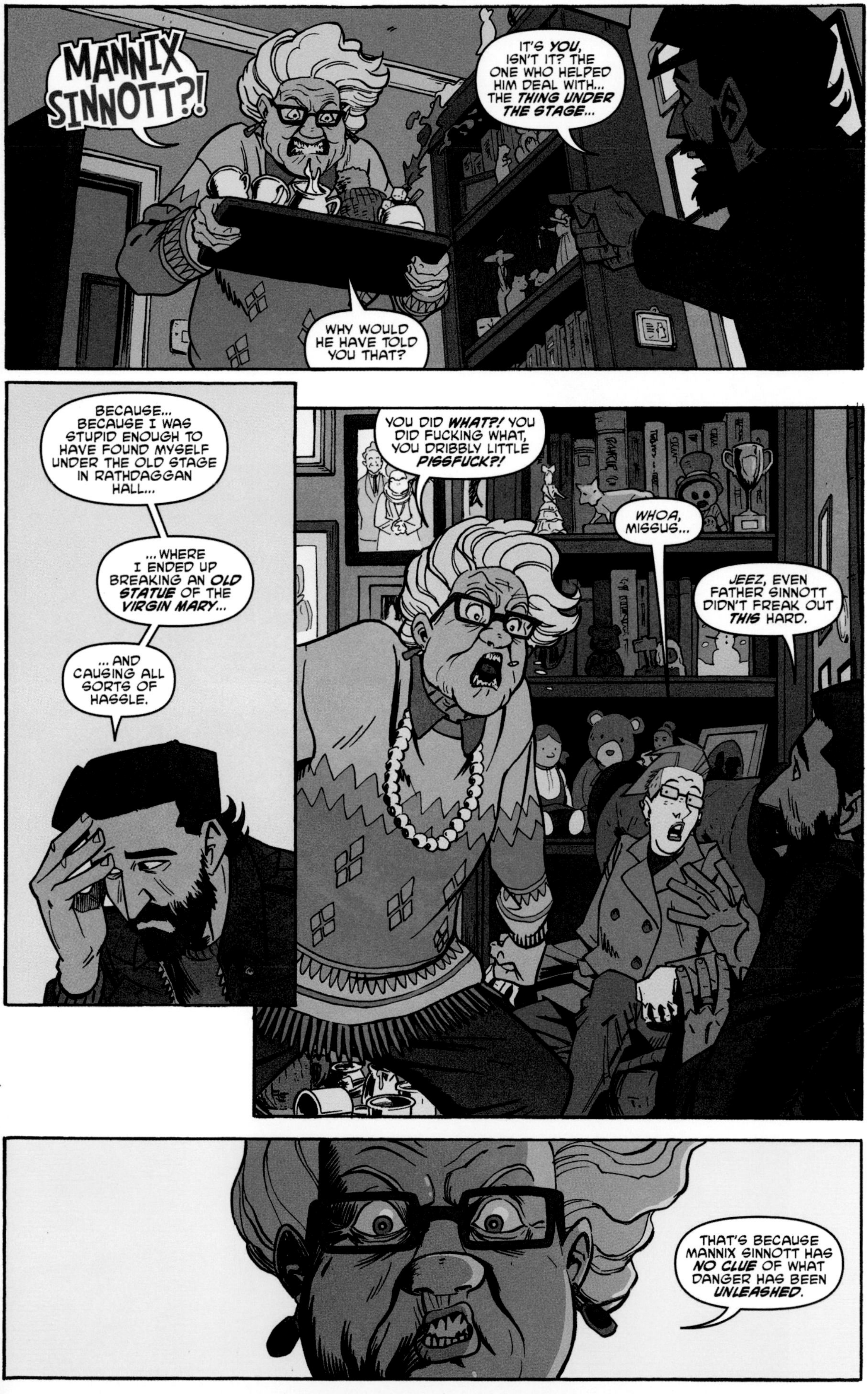
MANNIX SINNOTT?!
IT'S YOU, ISN'T IT? THE ONE WHO HELPED HIM DEAL WITH... THE THING UNDER THE STAGE...
WHY WOULD HE HAVE TOLD YOU THAT?
BECAUSE... BECAUSE I WAS STUPID ENOUGH TO HAVE FOUND MYSELF UNDER THE OLD STAGE IN RATHDAGGAN HALL...
...WHERE I ENDED UP BREAKING AN OLD STATUE OF THE VIRGIN MARY...
...AND CAUSING ALL SORTS OF HASSLE.
YOU DID WHAT?! YOU DID FUCKING WHAT, YOU DRIBBLY LITTLE PISSFUCK?!
WHOA, MISSUS...
JEEZ, EVEN FATHER SINNOTT DIDN'T FREAK OUT THIS HARD.
THAT'S BECAUSE MANNIX SINNOTT HAS NO CLUE OF WHAT DANGER HAS BEEN UNLEASHED.

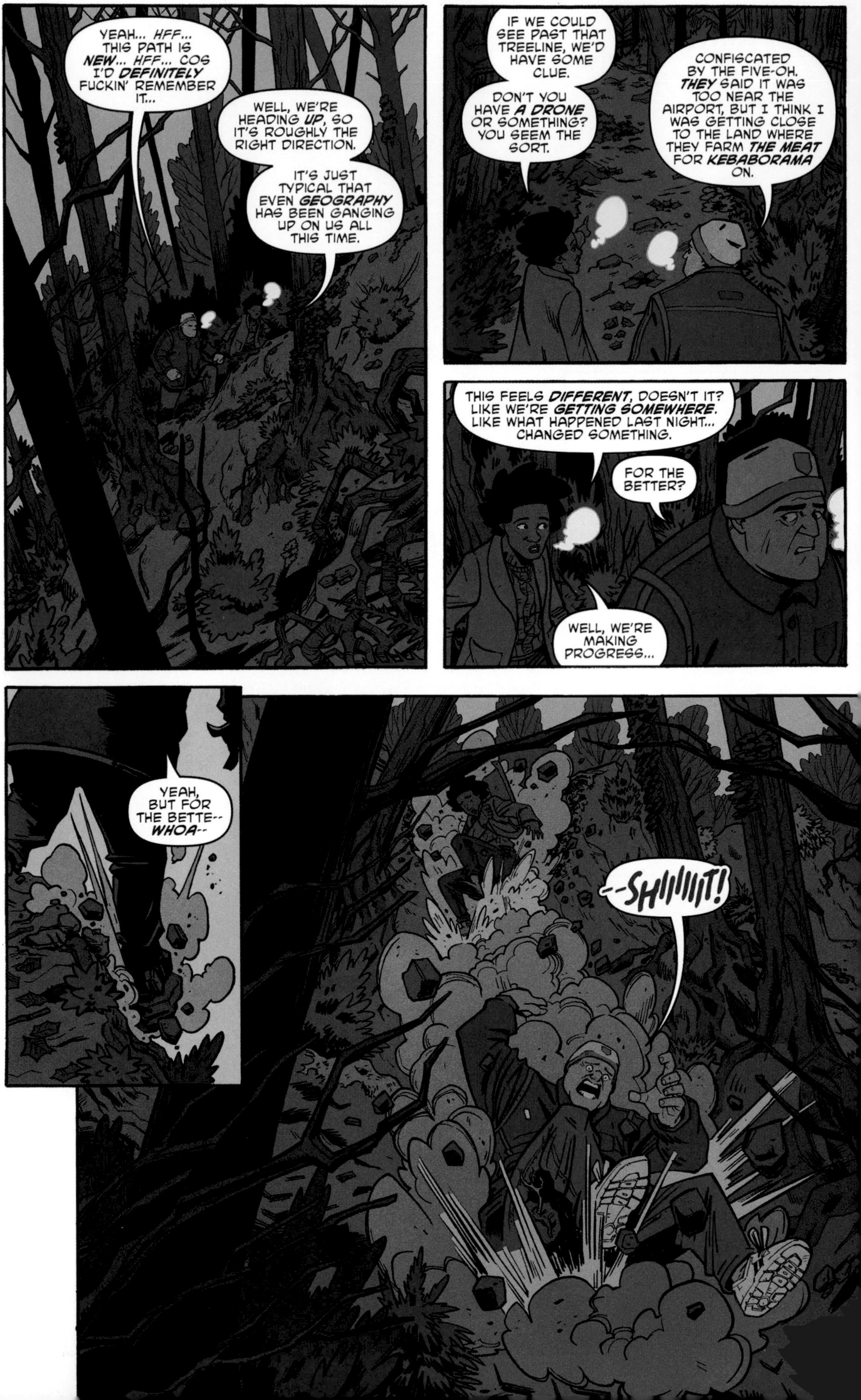

YEAH... *HFF*... THIS PATH IS *NEW*... *HFF*... COS I'D *DEFINITELY* FUCKIN' REMEMBER IT...
WELL, WE'RE HEADING *UP*, SO IT'S ROUGHLY THE RIGHT DIRECTION.
IT'S JUST TYPICAL THAT EVEN *GEOGRAPHY* HAS BEEN GANGING UP ON US ALL THIS TIME.
IF WE COULD SEE PAST THAT TREELINE, WE'D HAVE SOME CLUE.
DON'T YOU HAVE *A DRONE* OR SOMETHING? YOU SEEM THE SORT.
CONFISCATED BY THE FIVE-OH. *THEY* SAID IT WAS TOO NEAR THE AIRPORT, BUT I THINK I WAS GETTING CLOSE TO THE LAND WHERE THEY FARM *THE MEAT* FOR *KEBABORAMA* ON.
THIS FEELS *DIFFERENT*, DOESN'T IT? LIKE WE'RE *GETTING SOMEWHERE*. LIKE WHAT HAPPENED LAST NIGHT... CHANGED SOMETHING.
FOR THE BETTER?
WELL, WE'RE MAKING PROGRESS...
YEAH, BUT FOR THE BETTE-- *WHOA*--
--SHIIIIIT!

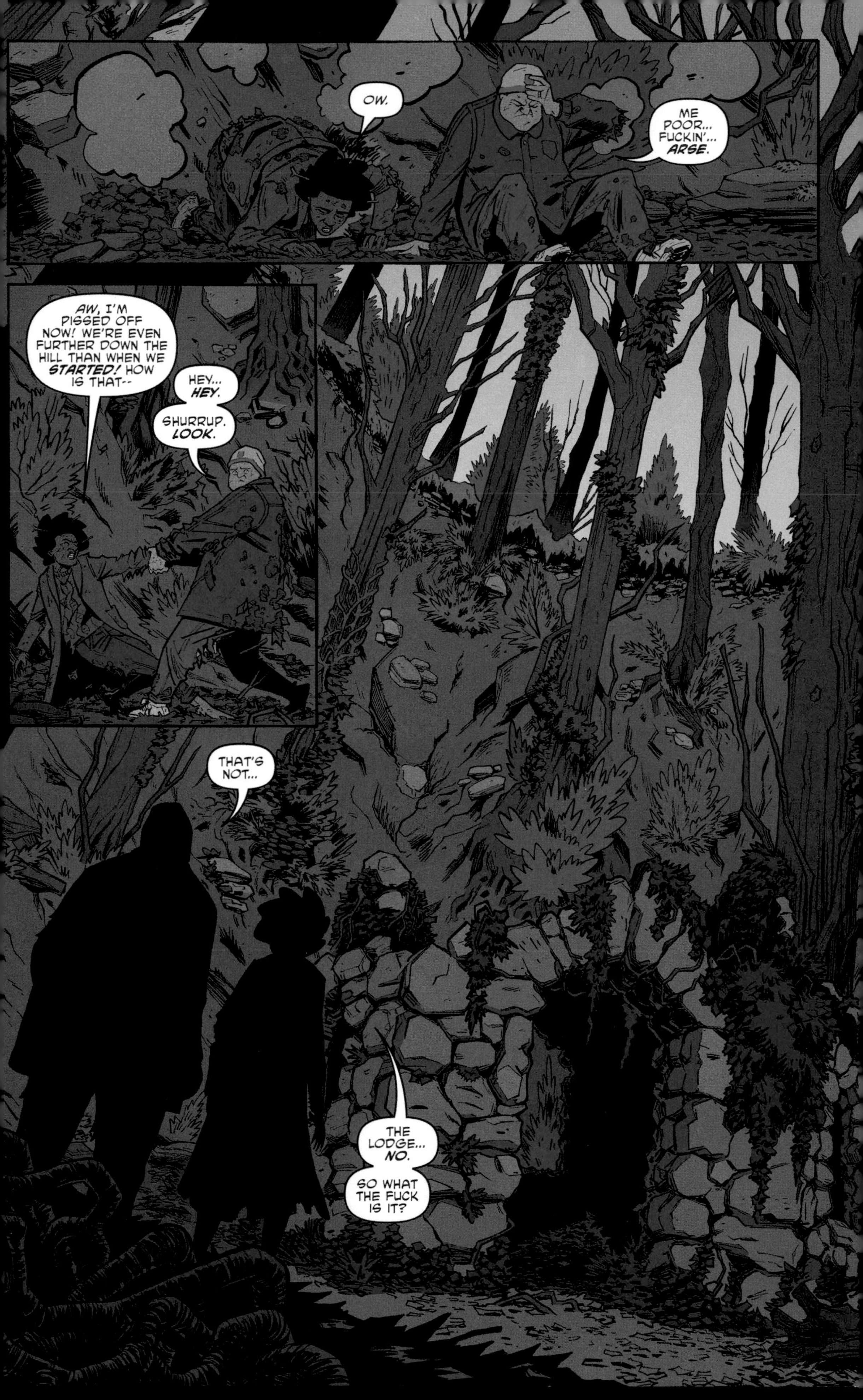
OW.
ME POOR... FUCKIN'... ARSE.
AW, I'M PISSED OFF NOW! WE'RE EVEN FURTHER DOWN THE HILL THAN WHEN WE STARTED! HOW IS THAT--
HEY... HEY.
SHURRUP. LOOK.
THAT'S NOT...
THE LODGE... NO.
SO WHAT THE FUCK IS IT?

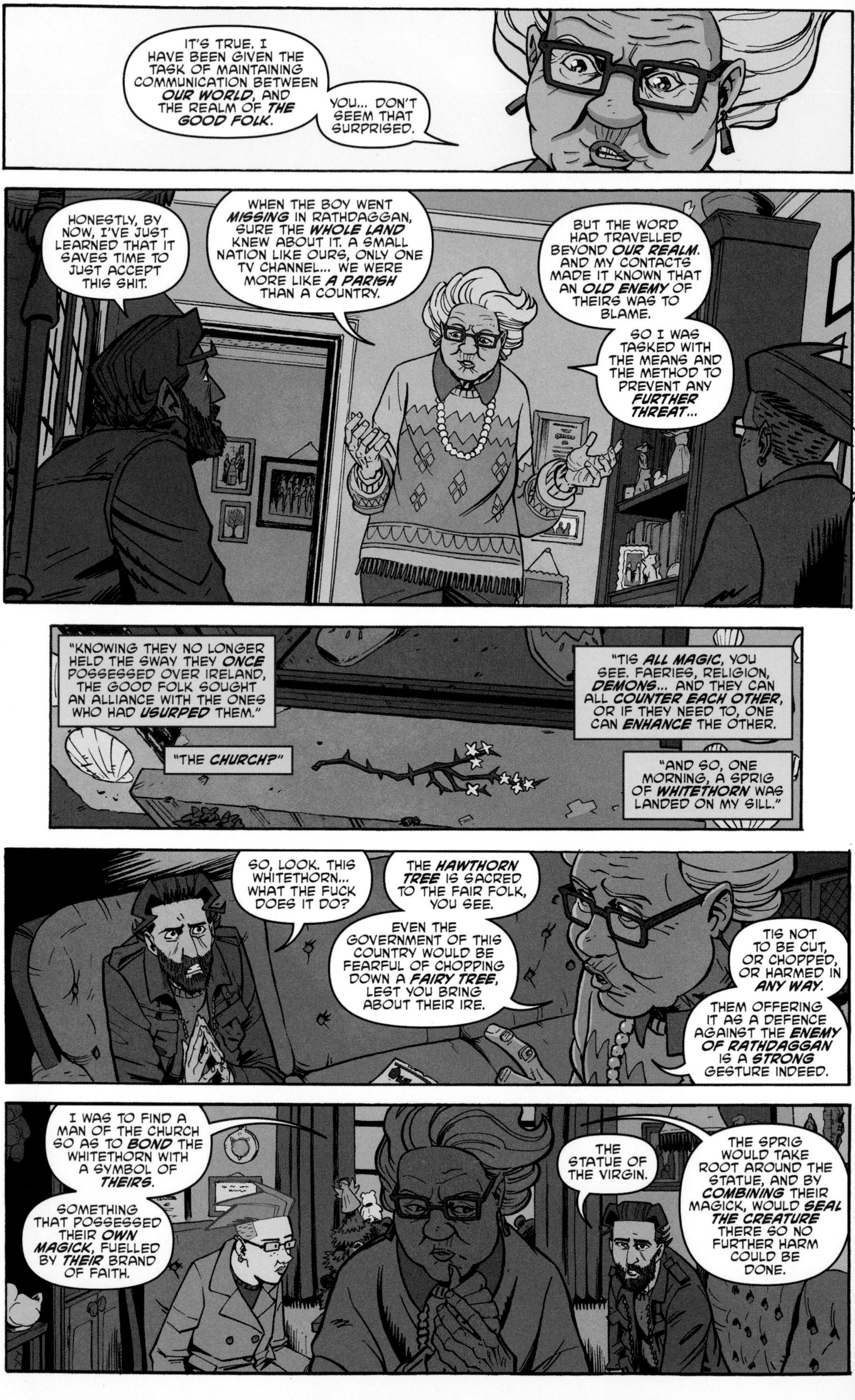
IT'S TRUE. I HAVE BEEN GIVEN THE TASK OF MAINTAINING COMMUNICATION BETWEEN OUR WORLD, AND THE REALM OF THE GOOD FOLK.
YOU... DON'T SEEM THAT SURPRISED.
HONESTLY, BY NOW, I'VE JUST LEARNED THAT IT SAVES TIME TO JUST ACCEPT THIS SHIT.
WHEN THE BOY WENT MISSING IN RATHDAGGAN, SURE THE WHOLE LAND KNEW ABOUT IT. A SMALL NATION LIKE OURS, ONLY ONE TV CHANNEL... WE WERE MORE LIKE A PARISH THAN A COUNTRY.
BUT THE WORD HAD TRAVELLED BEYOND OUR REALM. AND MY CONTACTS MADE IT KNOWN THAT AN OLD ENEMY OF THEIRS WAS TO BLAME.
SO I WAS TASKED WITH THE MEANS AND THE METHOD TO PREVENT ANY FURTHER THREAT...
"KNOWING THEY NO LONGER HELD THE SWAY THEY ONCE POSSESSED OVER IRELAND, THE GOOD FOLK SOUGHT AN ALLIANCE WITH THE ONES WHO HAD USURPED THEM."
"THE CHURCH?"
"TIS ALL MAGIC, YOU SEE. FAERIES, RELIGION, DEMONS... AND THEY CAN ALL COUNTER EACH OTHER, OR IF THEY NEED TO, ONE CAN ENHANCE THE OTHER.
"AND SO, ONE MORNING, A SPRIG OF WHITETHORN WAS LANDED ON MY SILL."
SO, LOOK. THIS WHITETHORN... WHAT THE FUCK DOES IT DO?
THE HAWTHORN TREE IS SACRED TO THE FAIR FOLK, YOU SEE.
EVEN THE GOVERNMENT OF THIS COUNTRY WOULD BE FEARFUL OF CHOPPING DOWN A FAIRY TREE, LEST YOU BRING ABOUT THEIR IRE.
TIS NOT TO BE CUT, OR CHOPPED, OR HARMED IN ANY WAY.
THEM OFFERING IT AS A DEFENCE AGAINST THE ENEMY OF RATHDAGGAN IS A STRONG GESTURE INDEED.
I WAS TO FIND A MAN OF THE CHURCH SO AS TO BOND THE WHITETHORN WITH A SYMBOL OF THEIRS.
SOMETHING THAT POSSESSED THEIR OWN MAGICK, FUELLED BY THEIR BRAND OF FAITH.
THE STATUE OF THE VIRGIN.
THE SPRIG WOULD TAKE ROOT AROUND THE STATUE, AND BY COMBINING THEIR MAGICK, WOULD SEAL THE CREATURE THERE SO NO FURTHER HARM COULD BE DONE.

"WE KNEW IT WOULD BE DANGEROUS. AN ALLIANCE BETWEEN THE CROSS AND THE GOOD FOLK CONTRAVENED AN *ANCIENT TREATY* BETWEEN THE DIFFERENT FORCES AT WORK IN IRELAND.

"TO BE HONEST, IT WOULD BE SEEN AS AN *ACT OF WAR.* SO WE HAD TO MAKE *FIERCE CERTAIN* IT'D WORK.

"AND SO AFTER, I BECAME A *LOOKOUT.* A SORT OF A GO-BETWEEN.

"THE *OUR IRELAND* HAS LONG BEEN USED TO PASS WORD BETWEEN THOSE WITH A FOOT *BETWEEN REALMS,* AND THOSE WHO WOULD HELP THEM.

- 80403 MOTHER OF ONE
The roots of the promise grow deep in the dark, but the good folk keep me safe.

80404 CORK MAN
Loves pastels and crayons making ice-cream detectorist

"AS LONG AS I PLACED THE SAME AD EVERY WEEK, *IN PERSON*--IT COULDN'T BE AUTOMATED; THAT'D GO AGIN' EVERYTHING ABOUT *THE OTHER CROWD*--IT WOULD BE SENDING A SIGN TO ALL THOSE WITH THE RIGHT EYES...

"...THAT *ALL WAS WELL.*"

SO, NOW YOU MUST BE TELLIN' ME... *IS* ALL WELL?

I THINK SO. FATHER SINNOTT PERFORMED A *RITUAL OF DELIVERANCE.* WE SAW THE CREATURE DISAPPEAR WITH OUR OWN EYES.

SO MAYBE NOW, I CAN GET RID OF *THE STATUE...*

BE THE HOKEY--YOU STILL *HAVE* IT?

...YEAH?

YOU HAVE IT *WITH* YOU?!

...YEAH? WHY?

YOU FECKING *GOBSHITE!* YOU'RE *NEVER* TO BRING THE FAIRY THORN *INDOORS!* HOUSE, CAR, SHED... YOU'LL BRING IRREPARABLE DAMAGE UPON US ALL!

STUPID BOLLOCKS!

HELLO? YES, IT'S ME. HAVE I MISSED THE PRINT DEADLINE?

I NEED TO CHANGE MY MESSAGE.

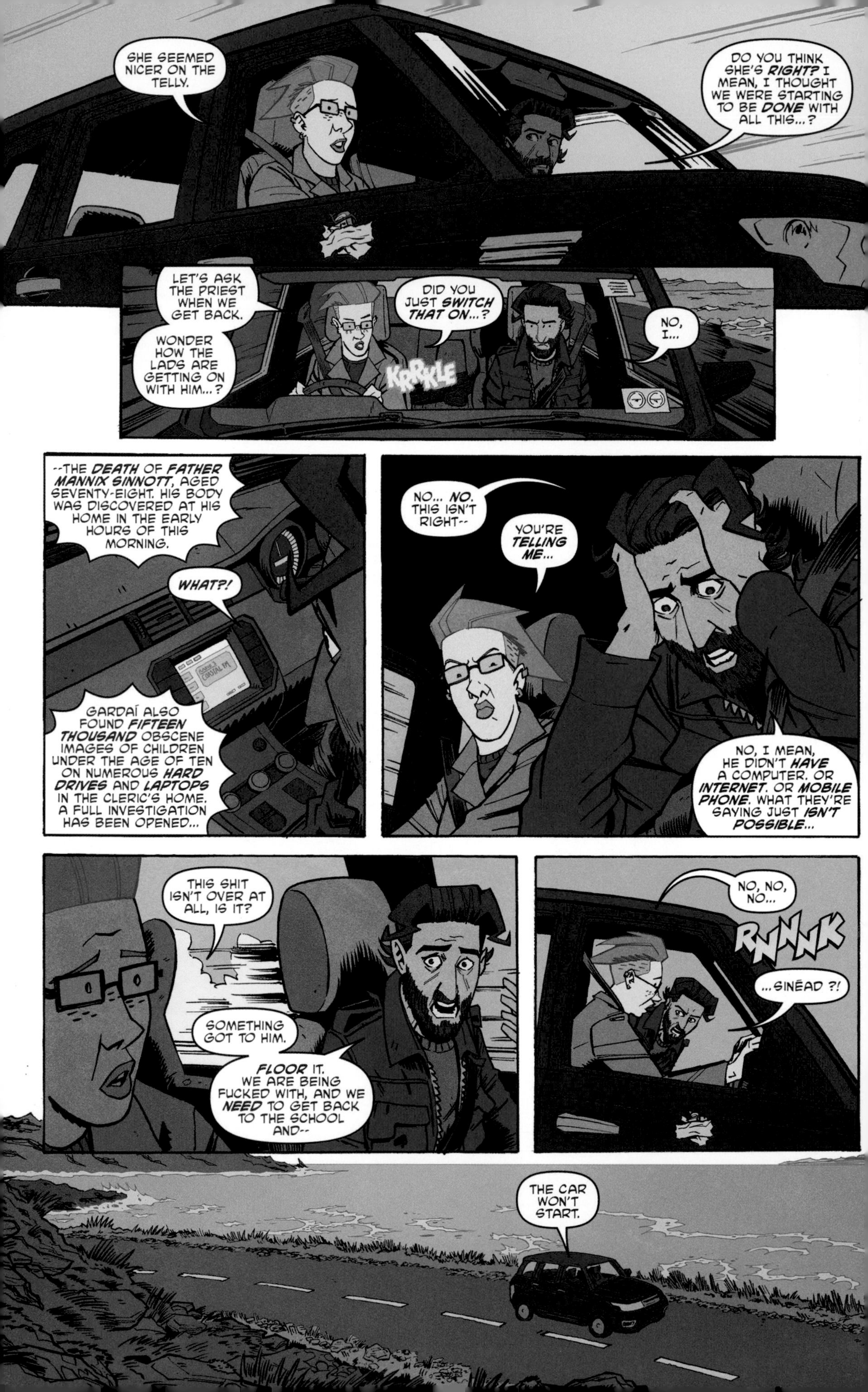
SHE SEEMED NICER ON THE TELLY.
DO YOU THINK SHE'S RIGHT? I MEAN, I THOUGHT WE WERE STARTING TO BE DONE WITH ALL THIS...?
LET'S ASK THE PRIEST WHEN WE GET BACK.
WONDER HOW THE LADS ARE GETTING ON WITH HIM...?
KRRKKLE
DID YOU JUST SWITCH THAT ON...?
NO, I...
--THE DEATH OF FATHER MANNIX SINNOTT, AGED SEVENTY-EIGHT. HIS BODY WAS DISCOVERED AT HIS HOME IN THE EARLY HOURS OF THIS MORNING.
WHAT?!
GARDAÍ ALSO FOUND FIFTEEN THOUSAND OBSCENE IMAGES OF CHILDREN UNDER THE AGE OF TEN ON NUMEROUS HARD DRIVES AND LAPTOPS IN THE CLERIC'S HOME. A FULL INVESTIGATION HAS BEEN OPENED...
NO... NO. THIS ISN'T RIGHT--
YOU'RE TELLING ME...
NO, I MEAN, HE DIDN'T HAVE A COMPUTER. OR INTERNET. OR MOBILE PHONE. WHAT THEY'RE SAYING JUST ISN'T POSSIBLE...
THIS SHIT ISN'T OVER AT ALL, IS IT?
SOMETHING GOT TO HIM.
FLOOR IT. WE ARE BEING FUCKED WITH, AND WE NEED TO GET BACK TO THE SCHOOL AND--
NO, NO, NO...
RNNNK
...SINÉAD ?!
THE CAR WON'T START.

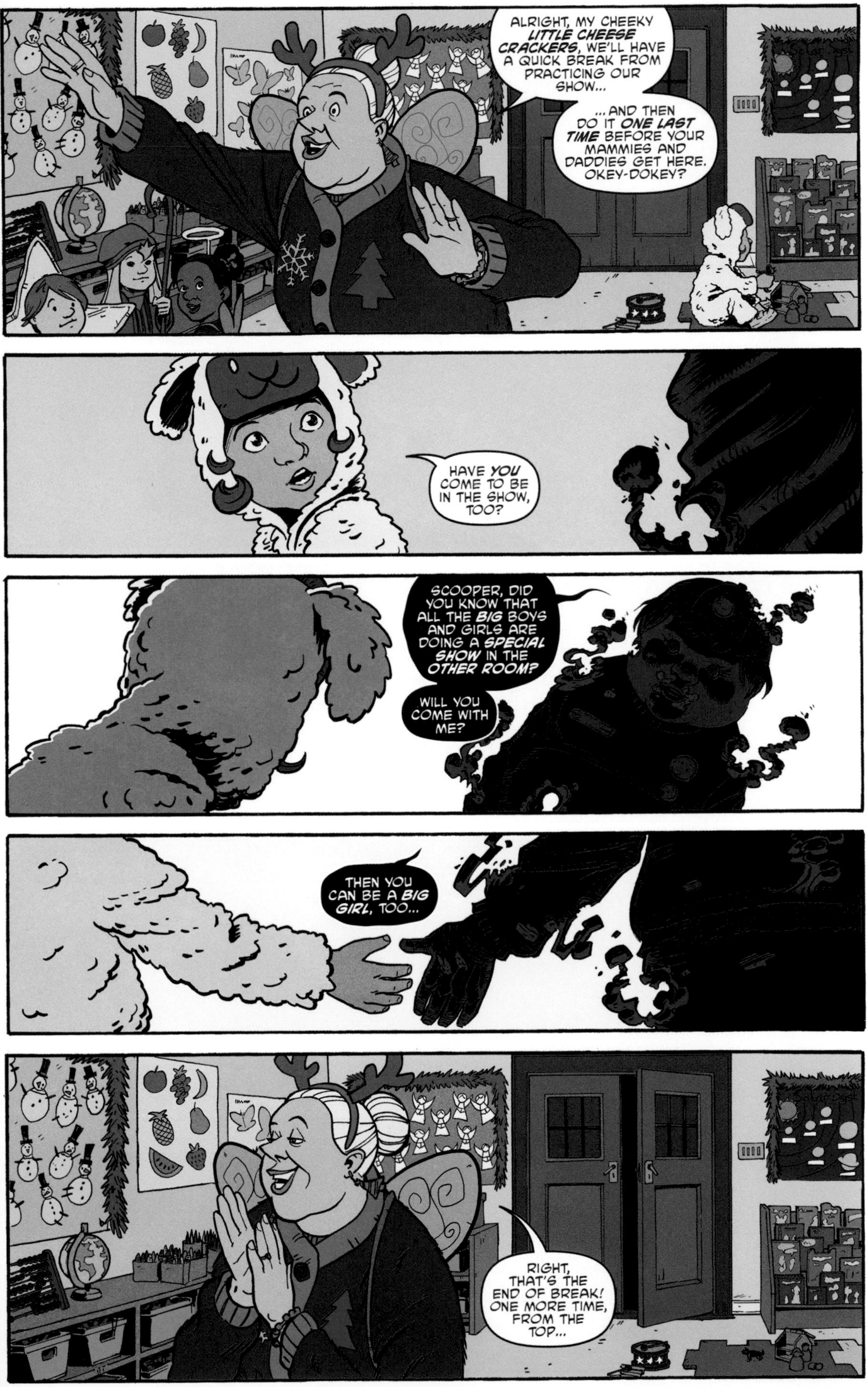
ALRIGHT, MY CHEEKY LITTLE CHEESE CRACKERS, WE'LL HAVE A QUICK BREAK FROM PRACTICING OUR SHOW...
...AND THEN DO IT ONE LAST TIME BEFORE YOUR MAMMIES AND DADDIES GET HERE. OKEY-DOKEY?
HAVE YOU COME TO BE IN THE SHOW, TOO?
SCOOPER, DID YOU KNOW THAT ALL THE BIG BOYS AND GIRLS ARE DOING A SPECIAL SHOW IN THE OTHER ROOM?
WILL YOU COME WITH ME?
THEN YOU CAN BE A BIG GIRL, TOO...
RIGHT, THAT'S THE END OF BREAK! ONE MORE TIME, FROM THE TOP...

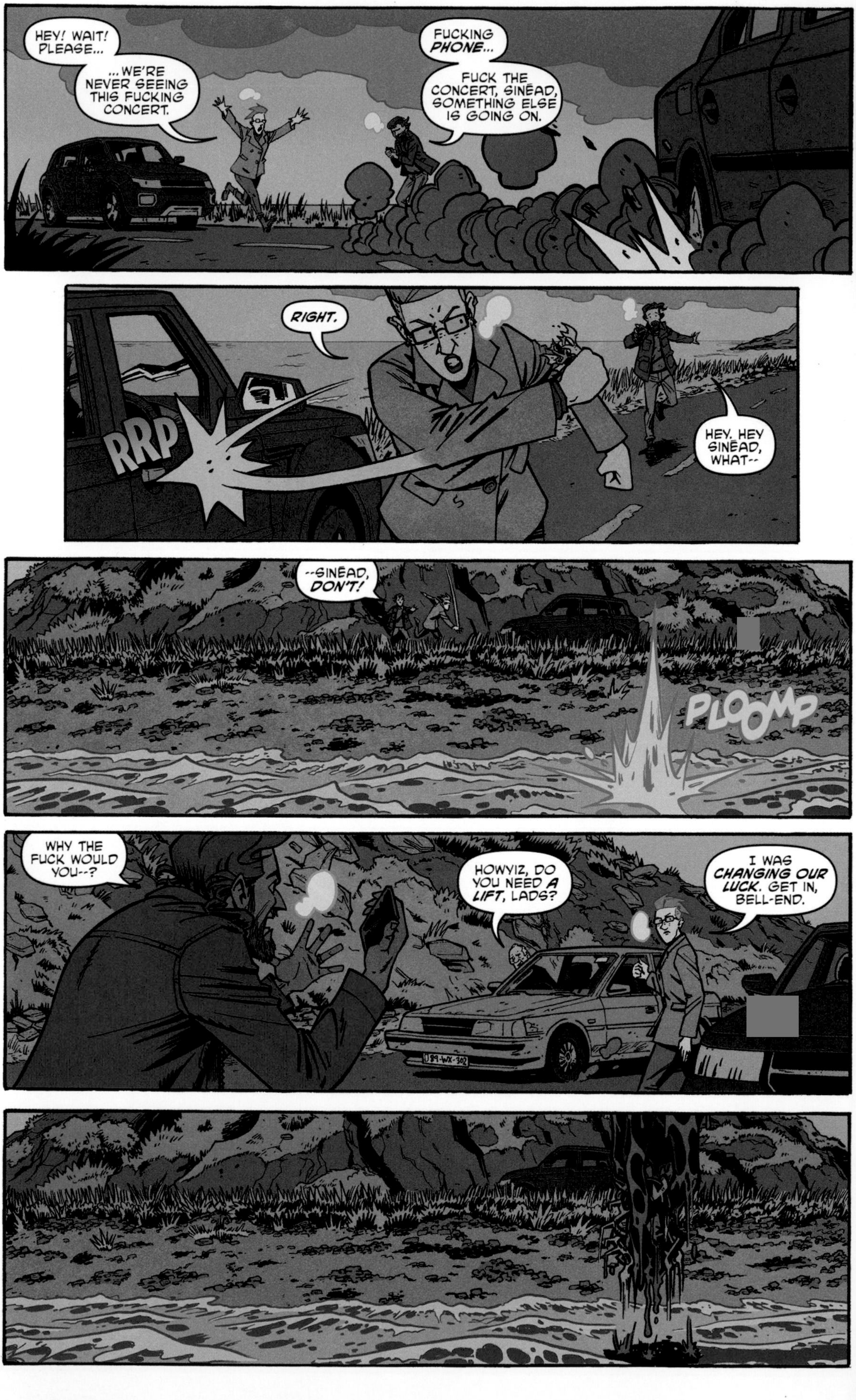
HEY! WAIT! PLEASE...
...WE'RE NEVER SEEING THIS FUCKING CONCERT.
FUCKING PHONE...
FUCK THE CONCERT, SINÉAD, SOMETHING ELSE IS GOING ON.
RIGHT.
RRP
HEY. HEY SINÉAD, WHAT--
--SINÉAD, DON'T!
PLOOMP
WHY THE FUCK WOULD YOU--?
HOWYIZ, DO YOU NEED A LIFT, LADS?
I WAS CHANGING OUR LUCK. GET IN, BELL-END.

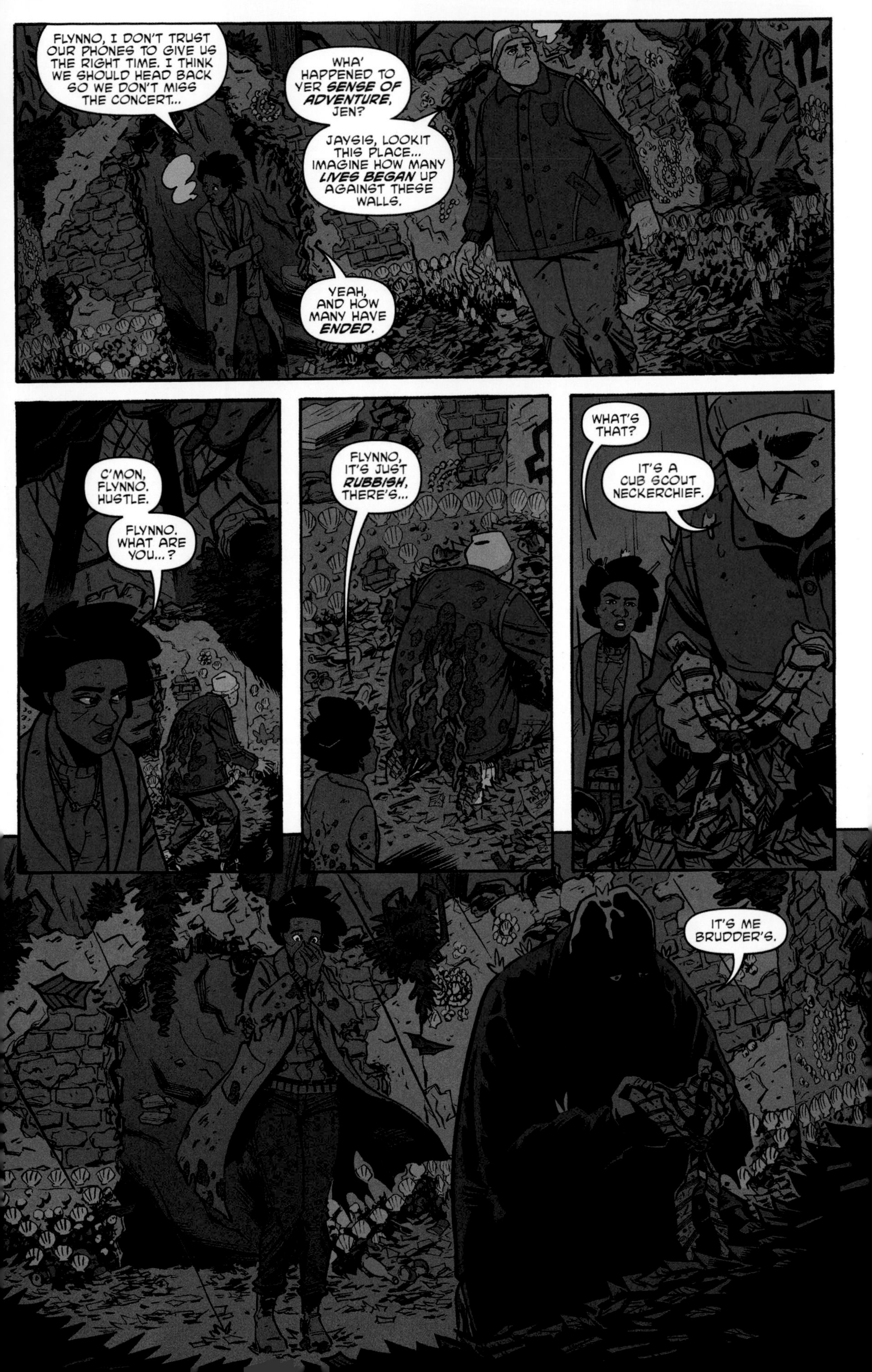
FLYNNO, I DON'T TRUST OUR PHONES TO GIVE US THE RIGHT TIME. I THINK WE SHOULD HEAD BACK SO WE DON'T MISS THE CONCERT...
WHA' HAPPENED TO YER **SENSE OF ADVENTURE**, JEN?
JAYSIS, LOOKIT THIS PLACE... IMAGINE HOW MANY **LIVES BEGAN** UP AGAINST THESE WALLS.
YEAH, AND HOW MANY HAVE **ENDED**.
C'MON, FLYNNO. HUSTLE.
FLYNNO. WHAT ARE YOU...?
FLYNNO, IT'S JUST **RUBBISH**, THERE'S...
WHAT'S THAT?
IT'S A CUB SCOUT NECKERCHIEF.
IT'S ME BRUDDER'S.

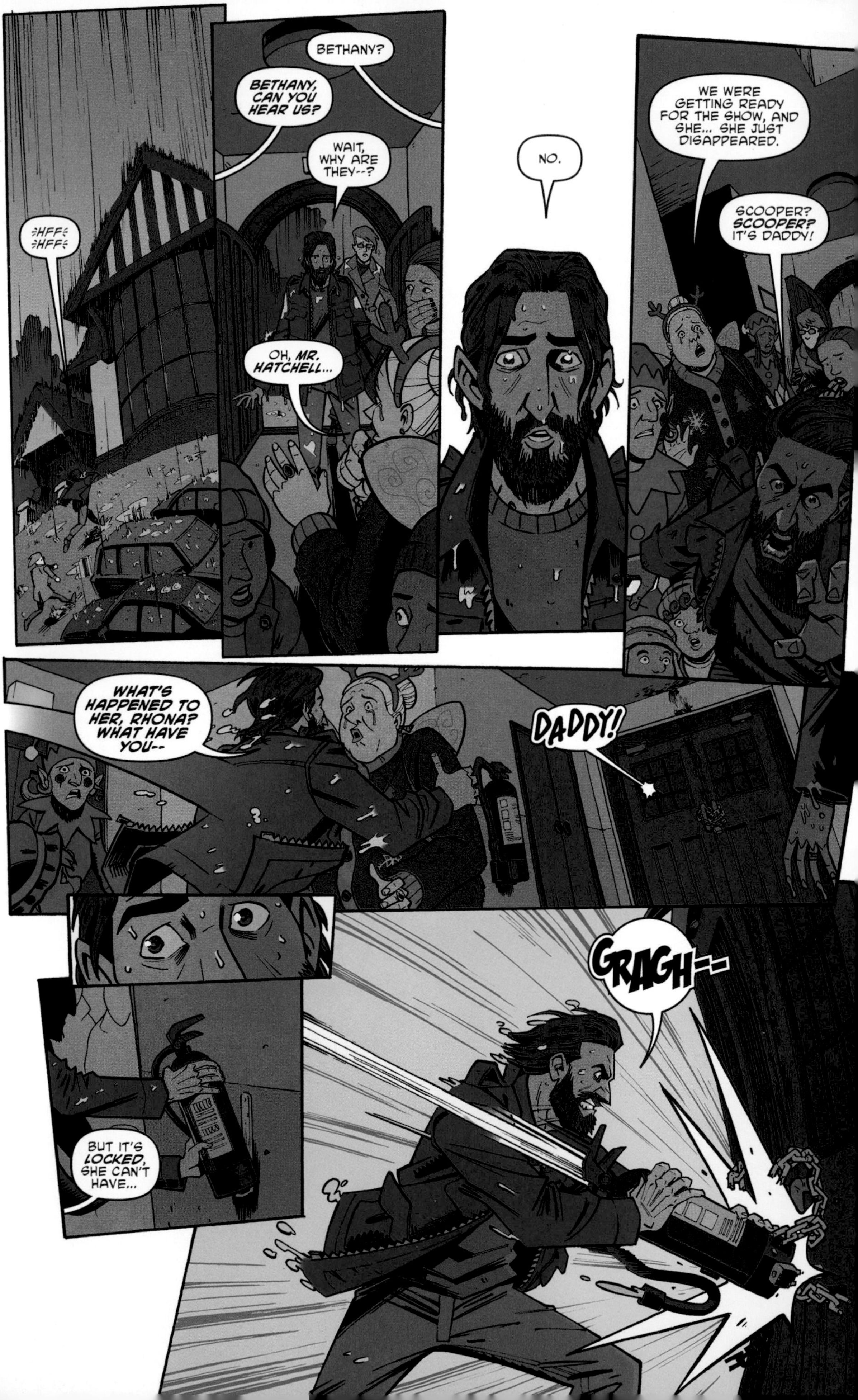

HFF HFF
BETHANY?
BETHANY, CAN YOU HEAR US?
WAIT, WHY ARE THEY--?
OH, MR. HATCHELL...
NO.
WE WERE GETTING READY FOR THE SHOW, AND SHE... SHE JUST DISAPPEARED.
SCOOPER? SCOOPER? IT'S DADDY!
WHAT'S HAPPENED TO HER, RHONA? WHAT HAVE YOU--
DADDY!
BUT IT'S LOCKED, SHE CAN'T HAVE...
GRAGH--

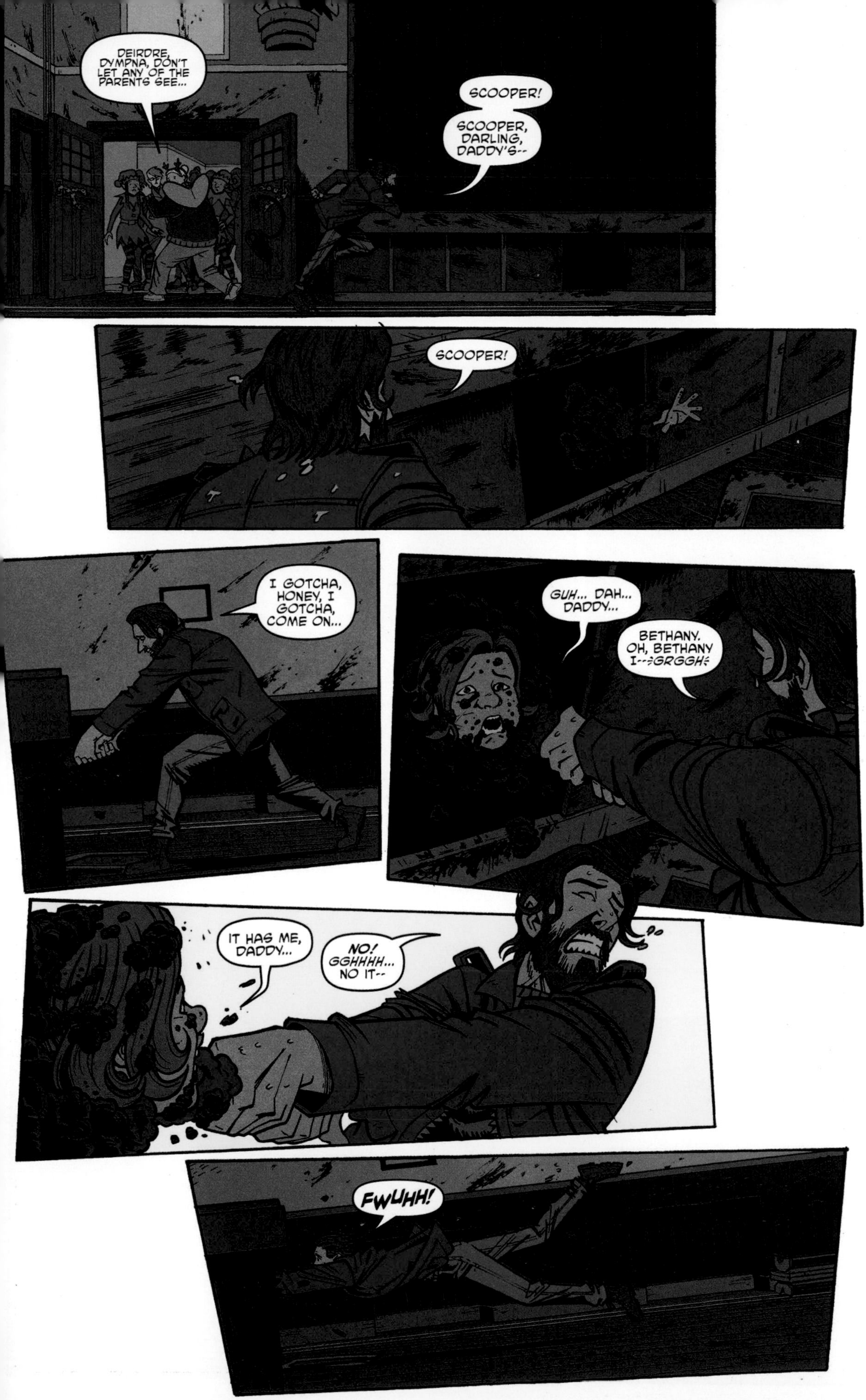
DEIRDRE, DYMPNA, DON'T LET ANY OF THE PARENTS SEE...
SCOOPER!
SCOOPER, DARLING, DADDY'S--
SCOOPER!
I GOTCHA, HONEY, I GOTCHA, COME ON...
GUH... DAH... DADDY...
BETHANY. OH, BETHANY I--GRGGH
IT HAS ME, DADDY...
NO! GGHHHH... NO IT--
FWUHH!

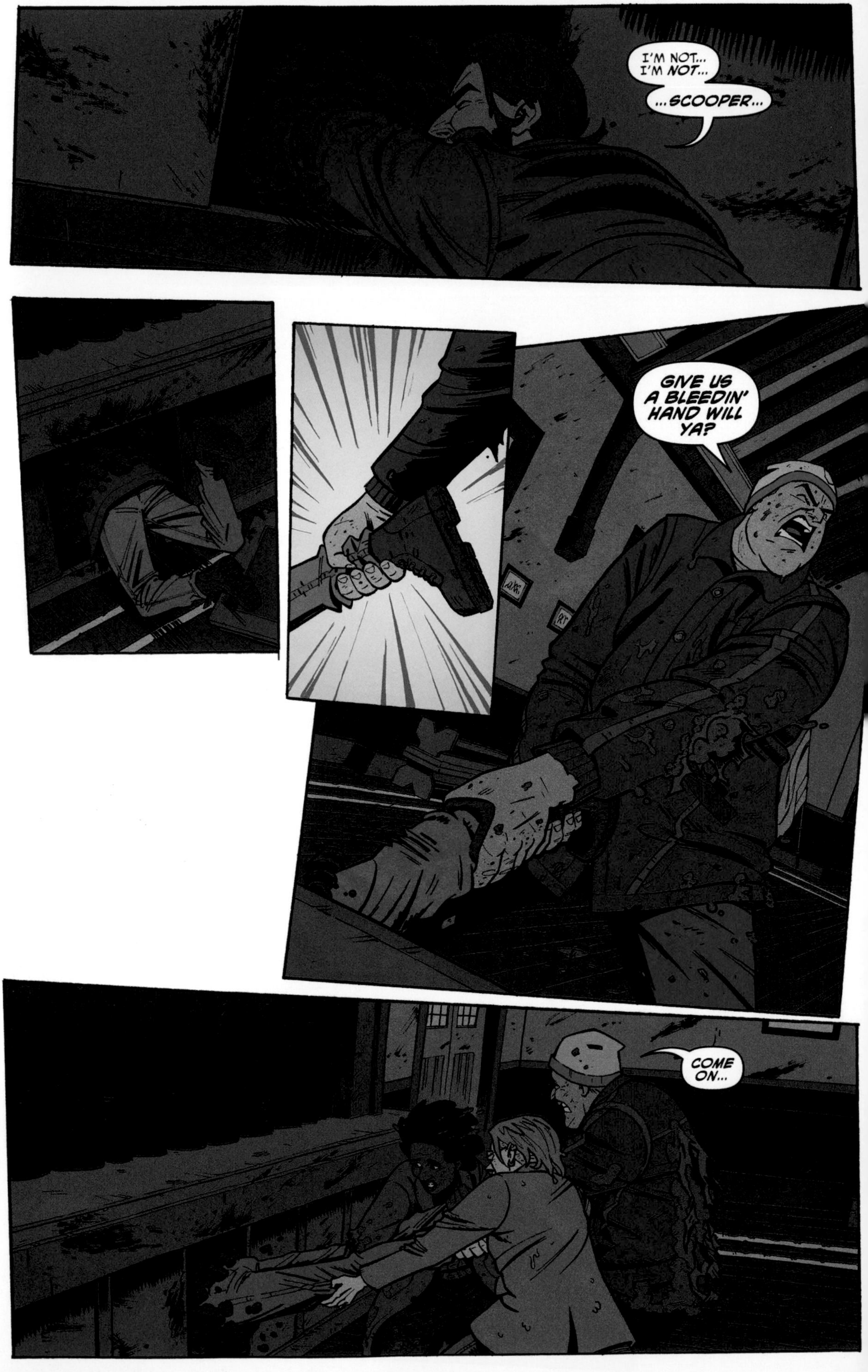
I'M NOT...
I'M NOT...
...SCOOPER...
GIVE US A BLEEDIN' HAND WILL YA?
COME ON...

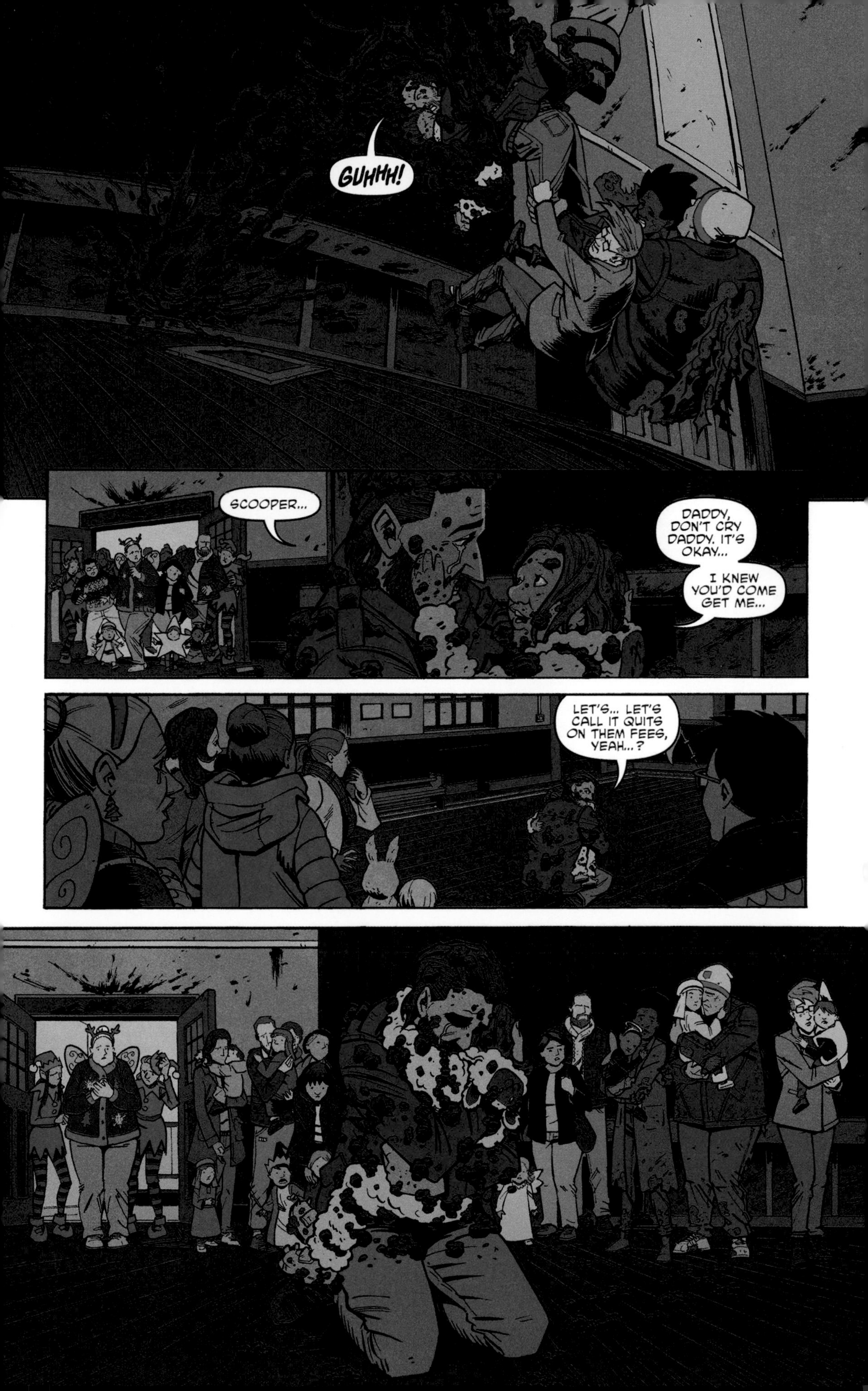
GUHHH!
SCOOPER...
DADDY, DON'T CRY DADDY. IT'S OKAY...
I KNEW YOU'D COME GET ME...
LET'S... LET'S CALL IT QUITS ON THEM FEES, YEAH...?

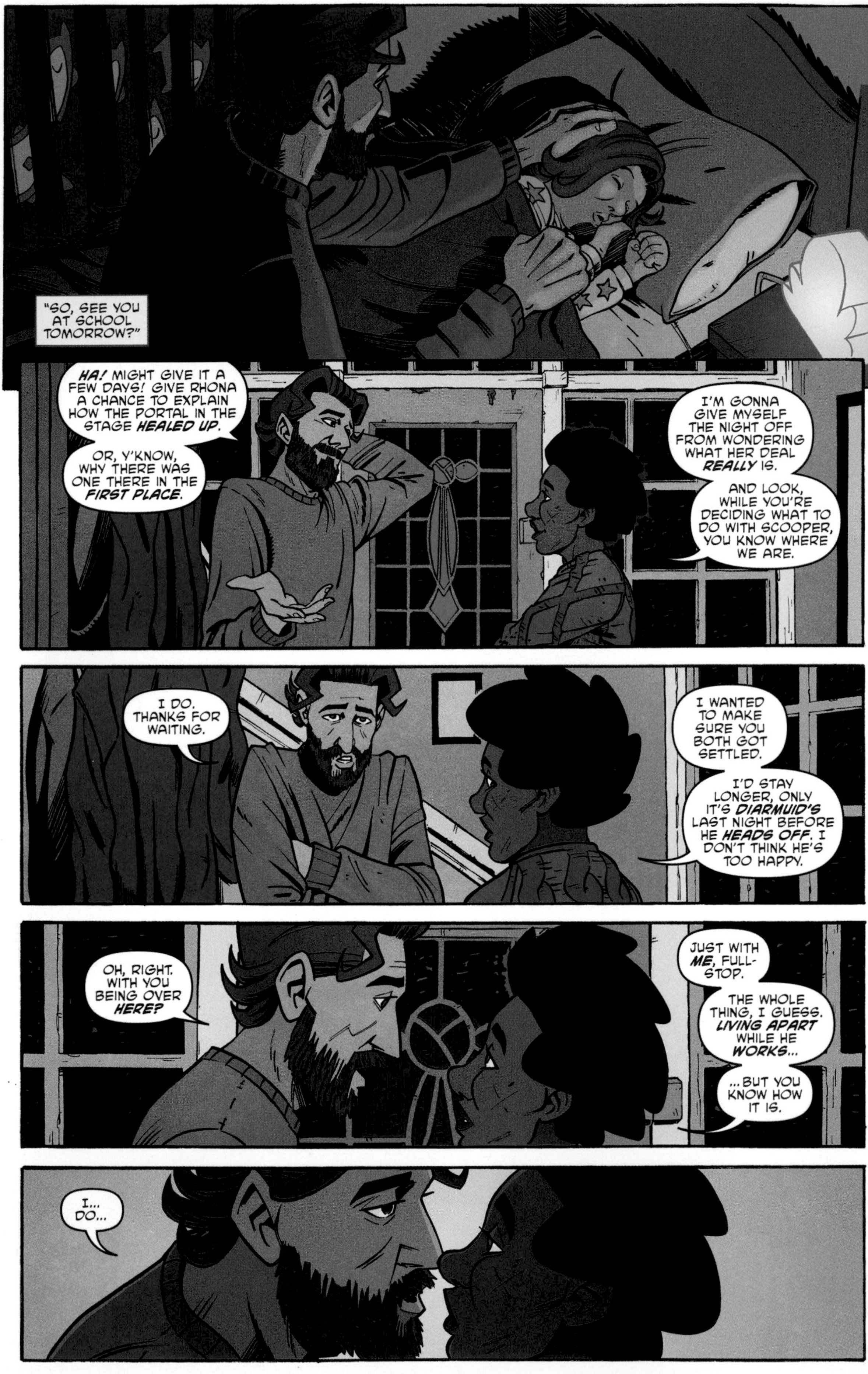
"SO, SEE YOU AT SCHOOL TOMORROW?"
HA! MIGHT GIVE IT A FEW DAYS! GIVE RHONA A CHANCE TO EXPLAIN HOW THE PORTAL IN THE STAGE HEALED UP.
OR, Y'KNOW, WHY THERE WAS ONE THERE IN THE FIRST PLACE.
I'M GONNA GIVE MYSELF THE NIGHT OFF FROM WONDERING WHAT HER DEAL REALLY IS.
AND LOOK, WHILE YOU'RE DECIDING WHAT TO DO WITH SCOOPER, YOU KNOW WHERE WE ARE.
I DO. THANKS FOR WAITING.
I WANTED TO MAKE SURE YOU BOTH GOT SETTLED.
I'D STAY LONGER, ONLY IT'S DIARMUID'S LAST NIGHT BEFORE HE HEADS OFF. I DON'T THINK HE'S TOO HAPPY.
OH, RIGHT. WITH YOU BEING OVER HERE?
JUST WITH ME, FULL-STOP.
THE WHOLE THING, I GUESS. LIVING APART WHILE HE WORKS...
...BUT YOU KNOW HOW IT IS.
I... DO...

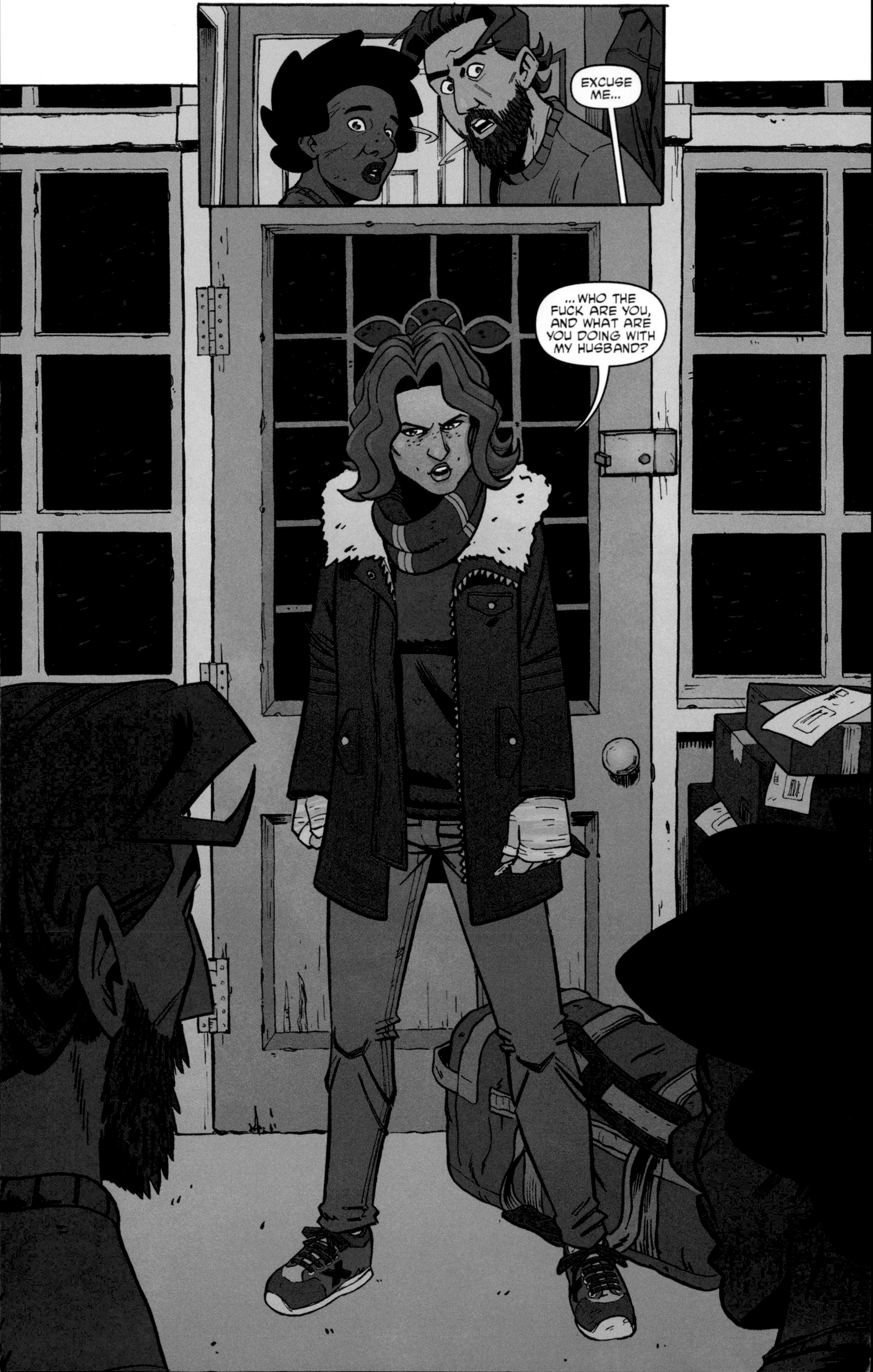
EXCUSE ME...
...WHO THE FUCK ARE YOU, AND WHAT ARE YOU DOING WITH MY HUSBAND?

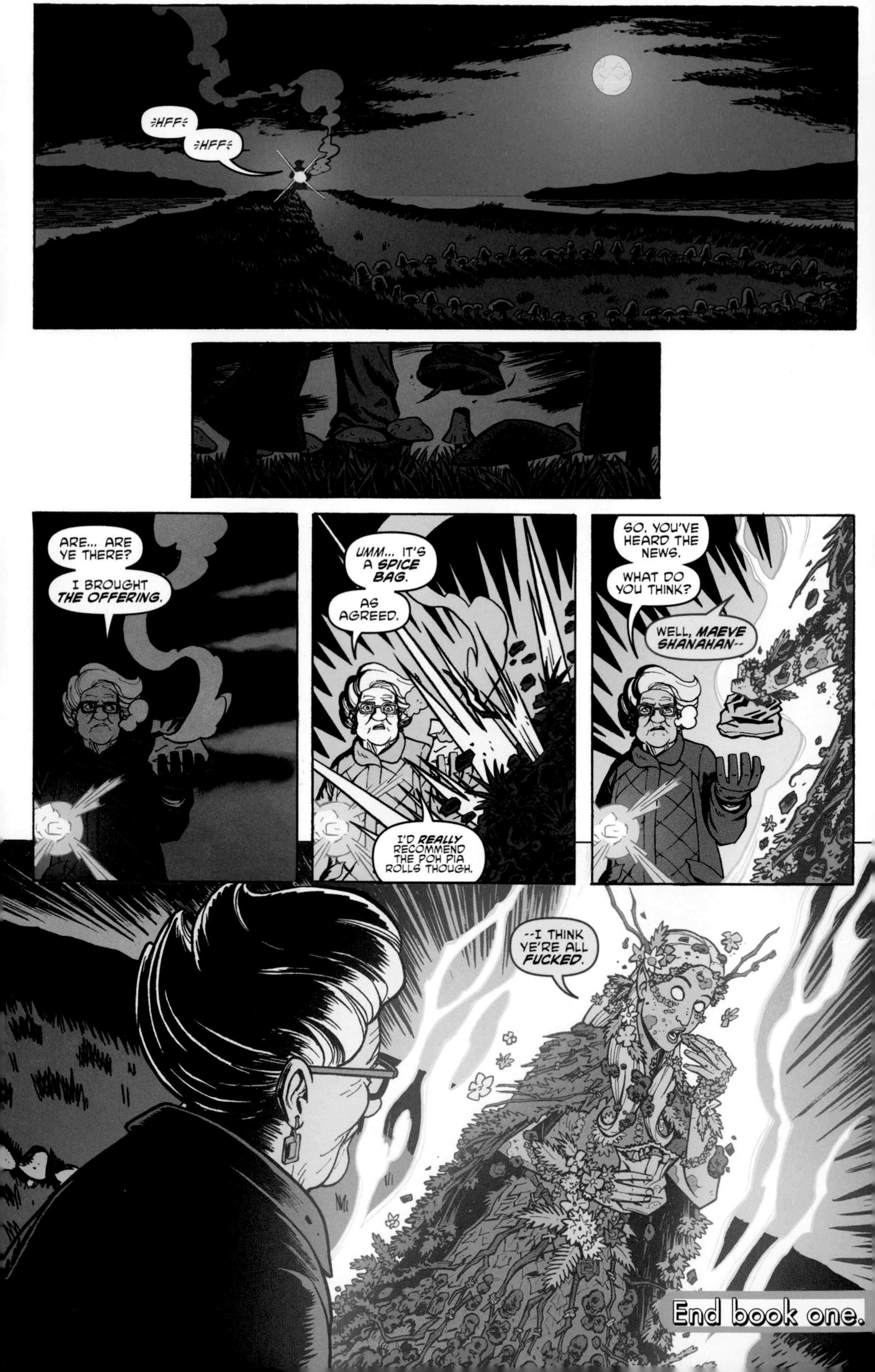
HFF
HFF
ARE... ARE YE THERE?
I BROUGHT THE OFFERING.
UMM... IT'S A SPICE BAG.
AS AGREED.
I'D REALLY RECOMMEND THE POH PIA ROLLS THOUGH.
SO. YOU'VE HEARD THE NEWS.
WHAT DO YOU THINK?
WELL, MAEVE SHANAHAN--
--I THINK YE'RE ALL FUCKED.
End book one.

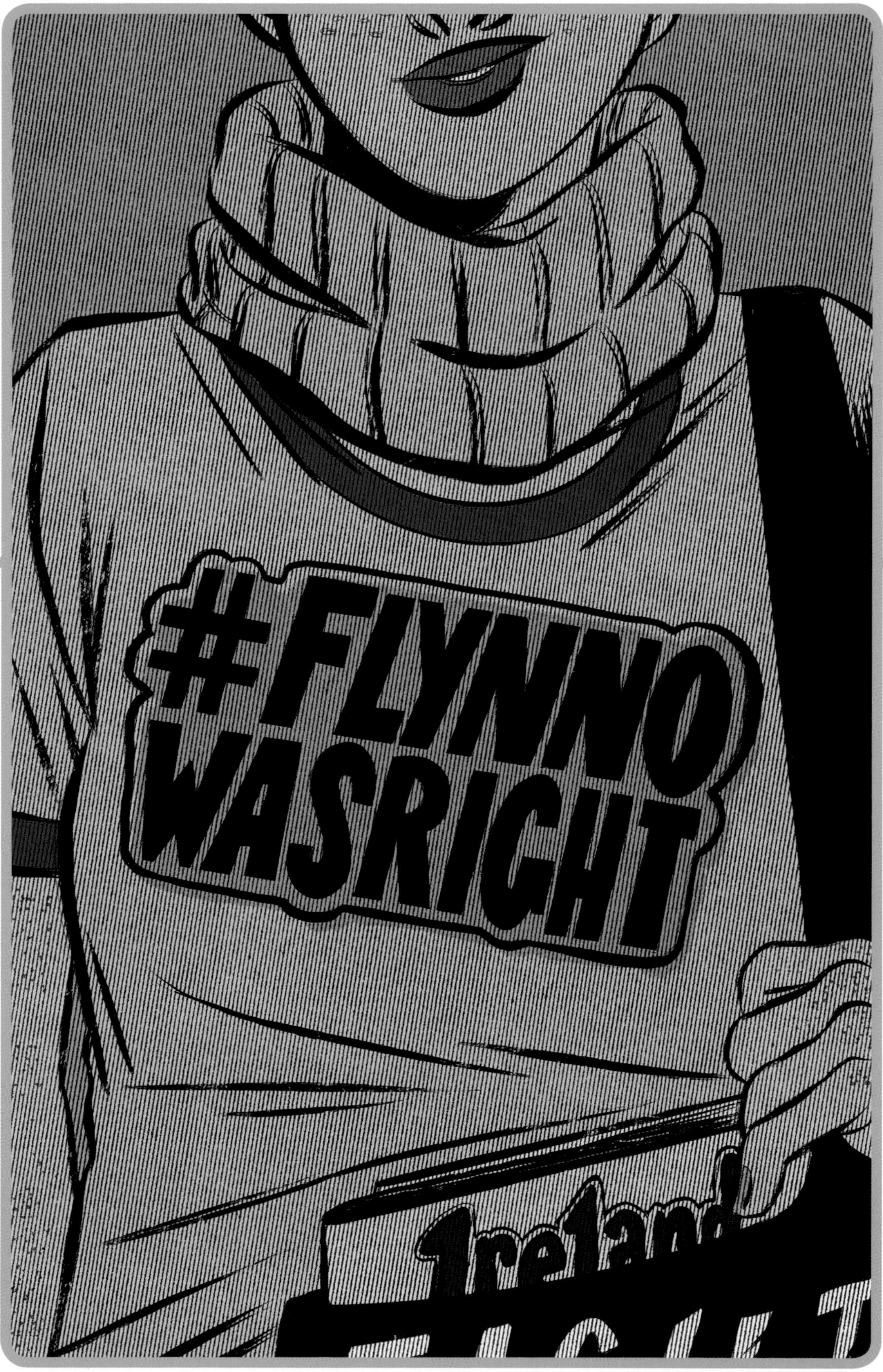
#FLYNNO
WASRIGHT

Art by
TARA O'CONNOR

Nachie Marsham, Publisher
Blake Kobashigawa, VP of Sales
Tara McCrillis, VP Publishing Operations
John Barber, Editor-in-Chief
Mark Doyle, Editorial Director, Originals
Erika Turner, Executive Editor
Scott Dunbier, Director, Special Projects
Mark Irwin, Editorial Director, Consumer Products Mgr
Joe Hughes, Director, Talent Relations
Anna Morrow, Sr. Marketing Director
Alexandra Hargett, Book & Mass Market Sales Director
Keith Davidsen, Senior Manager, PR
Topher Alford, Sr Digital Marketing Manager
Shauna Monteforte, Sr. Director of Manufacturing Operations
Jamie Miller, Sr. Operations Manager
Nathan Widick, Sr. Art Director, Head of Design
Neil Uyetake, Sr. Art Director Design & Production
Shawn Lee, Art Director Design & Production
Jack Rivera, Art Director, Marketing

Ted Adams and Robbie Robbins, IDW Founders

Originally published as SCARENTHOOD issues #1–4.

ISBN: 978-1-68405-831-0
24 23 22 21   1 2 3 4

SPECIAL THANKS: to Laura, Egg, Ab, Juggins, Pat, Wayne and Damien
for ground support; to Dave Hendrick, Declan Shalvey, Will Sliney, Stephen
Mooney, Nate Stockman, PJ Holden, Stephen Thompson, Ben Hennessy and
the entire Irish Comics Crew; to Chris Ryall, David Hedgecock and Tom B Long
for getting the greenlight, and to Shawn Lee, John Barber and David Mariotte
for getting us out the door; to Kieron Gillen, Eoin Colfer, John Allison, Gerry
Duggan, Brian Lynch, Dave Harper, James Roberts, Simon Furman. John
McCrea and Tara O'Connor for lending your eyes, ears, voices and talent;
to Tara Ferguson and John, Bruno and JP at Big Bang Comics for making sure
everyone knew about it; and to Chris O'Halloran who provided colour to the
world when The Big Boy was on my back. Thanks for keeping my head glued
on, and keeping me from the whitethorns.

Facebook: facebook.com/idwpublishing
Twitter: @idwpublishing
YouTube: youtube.com/idwpublishing
Instagram: @idwpublishing